WHITE DESERT

 AND

PORT HAZARD

· LOREN D. ESTLEMAN ·

FORGE®

A Tom Doherty Associates Book / New York

WHITE DESERT AND PORT HAZARD

White Desert copyright © 2000 by Loren D. Estleman

Port Hazard copyright © 2004 by Loren D. Estleman

A Forge Book
Published by Tom Doherty Associates
175 Fifth Avenue
New York, NY 10010

www.tor-forge.com

33614057746454

Forge® is a registered trademark of Macmillan Publishing Group, LLC.

ISBN 978-0-7653-8358-7

Our books may be purchased in bulk for promotional, educational, or business use. Please contact your local bookseller or the Macmillan Corporate and Premium Sales Department at 1-800-221-7945, extension 5442, or by e-mail at MacmillanSpecialMarkets@macmillan.com.

First Mass Market Edition: October 2016

Printed in the United States of America

0 9 8 7 6 5 4 3 2 1

Praise for the Page Murdock Novels

"Estleman is in top form here, providing a refreshingly original Western cop story filled with crackling action, snappy dialogue, and bone-chilling descriptions of frozen Canada."

—*Publishers Weekly* on
White Desert

"Wonderfully entertaining and filled with enough action and humor to satisfy the most demanding armchair buckaroos."

—*Booklist* on
White Desert

"Snappy dialogue, fast-paced action, colorful characters, and plenty of bullets, booze, and blood make this Western crime drama a wicked romp through the legendary gutters of the Barbary Coast."

—*Publishers Weekly* on
Port Hazard

"[There's] enough action in this Western novel to satisfy any reader."

—*The Dallas Morning News* on
White Desert

"A historical Western in mirror-smooth mahogany prose . . . Louis L'Amour looks down with envy."

· BOOKS BY LOREN D. ESTLEMAN ·

*Published by Tom Doherty Associates

Contents

WHITE DESERT

For Barbara Puechner,
in her memory:
It's not a tragedy
that she left us so soon.
The miracle is
that we had her as long as we did.

PART ONE

Maintain the Right

1

Forty years have passed, and I still can't look at a game of billiards without thinking that's the game that got me shot in Canada. I don't mind telling you it's spoiled me for indoor sports.

In September 1881, Judge Harlan A. Blackthorne suffered a heart attack, the first totally selfish act I had known him to commit in his long tenure on the federal bench in Helena, Montana Territory. It happened while he was presiding over a case of rape and murder on the Blackfoot reservation. He was quiet in his habits, and his seizure was no exception; the opposing sides went on pleading their cases for several minutes until the prosecutor raised a point of law, and when Blackthorne didn't rule right away, the lawyers noticed his slumped posture and gray coloring and after arguing about it for another minute sent for a doctor.

The Judge spent the next six weeks in bed, during which Chester Arthur replaced him with a carpetbagger named Kennedy, whose legal instructions resulted in more hung juries than had ever taken place in the history of the territory. (Four years later Grover Cleveland named him assistant secretary of the treasury.) In November, a reluctant Dr. Albert Schachter allowed his heart patient to resume his duties, on the condition that he abandon his practice of studying the docket on Sunday and seek lighter recreation. Blackthorne gave his word that he would.

I should have known right then that trouble was making my bed.

To pledge one's word was never a light thing among frontiersmen, who knew that straying from it invited swift and bloody retribution. The Judge, who had no such fear, valued his honor as did few gentlemen born. (He was the son of a failed farmer and self-educated.) Anyone else in his position might have driven a couple of wooden stakes ninety feet apart in some town lot and started pitching horseshoes. Harlan A. Blackthorne, deciding that billiards were the thing, sent all the way to Chicago for the most expensive table and accessories featured in the Montgomery Ward catalogue. The shipment traveled by rail to the end of the line in western Dakota, where it was loaded aboard a wagon and freighted four hundred miles overland to Helena. This took another six weeks, the last part of it during the first blizzard of January 1882; one horse died from exhaustion and Dr. Schachter treated two members of the crew for frostbite. But the table and its equipment arrived intact.

At the time the order was placed, Blackthorne was not entirely himself, or he would have known where to put the table when it came. Since he had not used federal funds to make the purchase, he was loath to take up space in the courthouse, and the only room that would have answered in his house outside town contained his wife's pump organ. This item would vacate the premises only in the company of Mrs. Blackthorne herself. At length he entered into an arrangement with Chink Sherman, manager of the Merchants Hotel: In return for allowing the table to occupy a guest room in the establishment, Sherman would have the use of the pump organ the first and third Saturday of every month to rehearse the Sacred Hearts of Jesus and Mary Choir, of which he was master. Mrs. Blackthorne, a Presbyterian and the daughter of a thirty-third-degree Freemason, was rewarded for her assent with the gift of a Jewel stove, to be shipped from Detroit sometime in the spring. Observers who amused themselves with arithmetical problems concluded that the Judge's heart attack had at this point set him back some eight hundred fifty dollars, not counting Schachter's fee.

The owner of the billiard table, however, was satisfied. The hotel was no more than a brisk, doctor-approved walk from both the courthouse and his home, refreshments were available from the Merchants' kitchen and bar, and he had a place to amuse himself when court was in recess. Not to mention the first and third Saturday of every month, when his house was invaded by tone-deaf Catholics.

It was a beautiful table, carved from Central American mahogany the color of oxblood, with mesh pockets and a green baize top as thick as the rugs in Chicago Joe's whorehouse. The slate alone weighed three hundred pounds and had required six men to carry inside. The cues were made of white ash, hand rubbed to a golden finish and straight, the balls of enameled African ivory. Nothing had been seen like it in town since Uncle Abe Cotton, one of the first prospectors to tap into the lode, fell ill of pneumonia and ordered a custom coffin all the way from San Francisco; and in fact the Judge's billiard set might have had the edge, although no one was willing to dig up Uncle Abe to make the comparison. Pierpont Morgan was said to have installed the same set in his Fifth Avenue mansion. There really was no reason, given the quality of the equipment and his frequent use of it, that Judge Blackthorne should have been the worst player west of New York and east of Hong Kong.

No man alive could get the better of the pioneer jurist in a battle of wills or wits. Reliable witnesses claimed to have heard him call Boss Tweed a crook to his face, at a time when a twitch of the Tweed eyebrow could have brought down the chief justice of the Supreme Court, and I was present in his courtroom the day he talked the defendant in a murder case out of the pistol he had snatched from the bailiff when none of the armed officers present dared risk a shot for fear of hitting the Judge. But the balls on that table were unimpressed by his reputation. He was incapable of making the simplest shot. Worse, he insisted upon attempting the most complicated banks, with results that ranged between pathetic and disastrous; a sternly worded letter from the State Department had been addressed to him after he bounced the four ball off the forehead of a visiting Russian grand duke. At that point the table had been in his possession three years, and he had been practicing almost daily. The game I'm talking about now took place three days after it arrived.

At that point he had played a couple of dozen games with deputy marshals and other employees of his court, most of whom had been hard put to lose to him. I should mention here that the American justice system never had a fairer man than when Blackthorne was on the bench. Although he hanged forty-seven men, a record for legal executions in the Northwest, a judicial review of those cases in 1901 found that the evidence presented would have held up in any proceedings in the country, and that in fact the Judge had in each case allowed the defense greater latitude than precedent required. Unfortunately, this balance did not always apply to his behavior once court was adjourned. He played favorites, stooped to nothing short of blackmail to work his will with associates and inferiors, and never forgave a humiliation, no matter how trivial. Most of all he hated to lose. He never ran out of ways to torture subordinates who forgot themselves and bested him in a game of skill.

I was the lone exception. I was a long way from his pet and would more than likely have hanged for his murder if

I didn't spend most of my time hundreds of miles from the capital, chasing fugitives and transporting prisoners; a lifetime of sudden justice hadn't done much to develop my Christian understanding, and Blackthorne was as hard to get along with as a bad case of the shingles. However, there was no misery he could arrange for me that compared with what I faced most of the time I was doing my part to enforce the law in the territories. He must have sensed that early in our acquaintance, because after a couple of halfhearted attempts to make me plead for mercy he left off trying and contented himself with black looks and shortfused retorts whenever I managed to make him appear less than omnipotent.

Which wasn't that often, except in billiards. He was the best and smartest man I ever knew, as well as the pettiest and worst tempered.

He rose in darkness and was seldom up after ten at night. This Sunday—the first since the table was delivered—was different. There were twenty inches of snow on the ground, a forty-mile-an-hour wind was whipping up twelve-foot drifts, and neither of us was in any hurry to wrap himself in his furs and go home until Montana decided to lie down for the night. His credit with Chink Sherman was good enough to swing us rooms in the hotel, but he wasn't about to do that. I had beaten him six games in succession; he was determined to win one before we packed it in. I was just as determined not to let him, tired as I was. That kind of thing can become a habit. The frontier was a forest of wooden markers bearing the names of deputy U.S. marshals who had decided to show someone mercy. None of them was going to read PAGE MURDOCK because I broke my own precedent with a stick in my hands.

Blackthorne shot first after the break. He was in his vest and shirtsleeves, rare event. Almost no one saw him that way except when he was changing out of his robes into his

Prince Albert coat, but we were both working up a sweat in the overheated room. Leaning across the table under the light of the hanging Chesterfield lamp, the Judge's hair and beard were as black as onyx and his lips were compressed into a Mona Lisa smirk of intense concentration. His teeth fit poorly, and he seldom wore them when he wasn't in court, but he was vain of his looks and didn't want to show his gums when he smiled.

"Bliss and Whitelaw are in Canada," he said, and shot. For once the ball went into the pocket.

"Wishful thinking?" I chalked my cue. His luck couldn't hold.

He shook his head. "I got a wire this morning from an Inspector Vivian with the North-West Mounted. The gang hit a settlement on the Saskatchewan over Christmas, wiped out the population, and rode away with everything that wasn't frozen to the ground. They weren't in such a hurry they forgot to set fire to the town. There's nothing left."

I watched him line up his next shot. "If they wiped out the population, who identified Bliss and Whitelaw?"

"That's what identified them." This one missed the pocket by six inches.

"Could have been Indians."

"The inspector doesn't think so. Their beef is with the railroad. Anyway, Indians haven't much use for gold."

I waited for the cue ball to roll to a stop and studied the choice. "How much gold?"

"A few hundred. The settlement was made up of panners and their wives. Nobody was scalped. There were some throats cut, and some of the women were naked, probably stripped and raped, but there were bullet holes in most of the corpses, what was left of them. Indians aren't that wasteful with their ammunition. Bliss and Whitelaw spend it like water."

"Stakes seem low." I made my choice and sank the shot.

The cue ball bounced off a cushion and clicked against the eight.

"You're forgetting they destroyed a village in the Cherokee strip for less. Tricky shot."

I ignored him and pocketed the six. The eight tried to follow but ran out of momentum at the edge. I stopped holding my breath. "Bliss and Whitelaw it is," I said. "What makes it our problem and not the Mounties'?"

"Eight banks in Wyoming and Montana, a train in Colorado, and thirty or forty dead across four territories, including mine. I'm sending a deputy up to advise the redcoats. He'll supervise the extradition when they're caught."

I missed the next shot, a simple bank. "Not me. I'm on holiday."

"Since when?"

The grandfather's clock in the lobby struck eleven. "Since eleven o'clock. You promised me a month off after I did you that favor in New Mexico Territory last year. I never took it."

He took his turn and missed. "Damn. What are you going to do with a month off in the middle of a Montana winter?"

"Eat steak, drink whiskey, and loaf. Beat you at billiards. Read *Ben Hur*. Run up my bill at Chicago Joe's. Cut a hole in the Missouri and hook bass. Take good care of the parts I'd just freeze off in Canada. The only reason anyone lives up there is Cornwallis lost." I chalked my cue more energetically than usual.

"I could order you to go."

"I could take off my badge."

"You never wear it."

"That's not the point."

He thumped the butt of his cue against the floor. "There's a friendly way of settling this."

I grinned. "What are you putting up?"

"Two months off," he said. "Starting anytime you say."

"This game, or do you want to start fresh?"

"This one will do. I believe it's your shot."

The game went back and forth twice and then I ran the table. At the end, the eight ball was in direct line with the corner pocket with the cue ball perched halfway between it and the opposite corner. A drunken Indian could have made it. I took my time and shot. The eight dropped in. The cue ball teetered on the edge and went right in after it. I threw down my stick with an oath my father used to use; he'd learned it from Jim Beckwourth.

"Scratch," Blackthorne said. "I'll wire Inspector Vivian to expect you."

2

What anyone in 1882 knew for sure about Lorenzo Bliss and Charlie Whitelaw didn't begin to stack up to the lore.

It hasn't gotten any better. Every year, it seems, someone publishes a new book about one or the other or both, and all it does is embroider upon the malarkey that appeared in every journal from the old Indian Nations to Dakota, and as far east as New York and Boston. If you took it all for gospel, you had to wonder why the authorities in four territories had so much trouble locating a pair of killers ten feet tall riding at the head of an army of a thousand men.

After four decades of dime novels, saloon ballads, "real-life" memoirs, and one jerky photoplay featuring Broncho Billy Anderson and an unbilled William S. Hart, I haven't learned anything more than I knew when I read four columns in the *Fort Smith Elevator* written by a journalist named Fairclough in August 1881. His account was based on interviews with Bliss and Whitelaw's acquaintances and eyewitnesses to the gang's depredations.

Lorenzo Bliss, the accidental issue some twenty years before of a business transaction between an Irish federal quartermaster sergeant named Bliss and a Mexican whore called Cincuenta Maria, or Fifty Times Mary, had fled Amarillo around age thirteen after taking off the head of one of his mother's customers with a shotgun. Like other desperadoes before and after him, he sought sanctuary in the Nations, but did not behave himself there, either. He had been arrested twice for smuggling whiskey and escaped both times, the first by setting fire to his jail cell in Cherokee and slipping out during the confusion; the second time he managed to work himself free of his manacles while riding in the back of a wagon driven and escorted by deputy United States marshals bound for the federal court in Fort Smith, Arkansas, and used them to cave in the head of a deputy. With the deputy's pistol he shot two more officers, killing one and crippling the other, and made his way to freedom aboard one of their horses.

One of the other prisoners in the back of the wagon was Charlie Whitelaw, whose history up to that point made Bliss's read like Tom Brown's. He was the son of civilized Christian Cherokees who had hacked his parents and his younger brother to death with a splitting maul when he was eighteen, then burned down their cabin on the Canadian River in an unsuccessful attempt to destroy the evidence. When a warrant was issued for his arrest he shot the constable who came to serve it, using his father's old cap-and-ball Navy .36, shot him again in the head when he was lying on the ground, and took off on the man's horse. There was another shooting incident at a Guthrie whorehouse when the constable's horse was spotted tied up in front and a pair of city patrolmen went in to investigate; Whitelaw, who was in an upstairs room spending the money he had stolen from a peach tin in his parents' cupboard, set fire to the mattress to create a diversion and went out the window, where he was seen by a third officer stationed in the alley. Slugs were exchanged, the policeman fell, and Whitelaw made his getaway on another stolen horse.

A posse was convened. They tracked him to an abandoned cabin on the Cimarron, surrounded it, and forced him to surrender. He spent a month in the city jail, where deputy United States marshals took him into custody and loaded him in chains aboard a wagon bound for Fort Smith. Lorenzo Bliss was one of the prisoners already on the wagon. When Bliss made his break, Whitelaw accompanied him. They had been together ever since.

It was a match made in hell. Neither man had a future or a conscience, and they both liked burning things. They quickly assembled a band of like-minded individuals—these were never in short supply in the Indian territory—and spent the next five years laying a path of blood and ashes north to Canada.

The military precision of their raids led to speculation that some of their people were guerrillas trained during the late Southern Rebellion, but this might have been only the wish-dream of journalists who had missed the best days of Frank and Jesse James and the Youngers. Certainly they were well led, or they would have broken apart in confusion during their encounters with the law. They had sprung traps in Colorado, Wyoming, and Montana, and suffered only one casualty, a Creek half-breed named Swingtree; a slug from a sharpshooter's Remington fired from the roof of the Miner's Bank in Butte took off his right arm and deposited him in the territorial prison at Deer Lodge for life. If Swingtree had been a member of the James gang, the columns would have been full of stories of the leaders' attempts to rescue their loyal minion in the face of withering enemy fire, but no such blanket got stretched for Bliss and Whitelaw. They were exciting press, but they were not heroes. Their chief claim to notoriety, at a time when it seemed you couldn't throw a dead cat between St. Louis and the Barbary Coast without hitting a daylight bandit, was the targets they chose. The Jameses and Youngers only robbed banks and trains. Bliss and Whitelaw destroyed whole towns.

What's more, they enjoyed it. Thirty or forty dead was

the official estimate of the human cost of their spree before the mess on the Saskatchewan, but when you figured in the amount they'd stolen, it came to less than three hundred dollars per corpse. Even the medical students in Chicago were offering better than that.

I began my preparations for Canada by arranging transportation. I enjoyed this just a little more than I did the idea of spending the winter north of Montana. Shoot me, I hate horses. I had bite scars on my backside that were older than some of the deputies I rode with and a broken leg going back to my cowpunching days that still gave me hell whenever the weather turned; and on the frontier it turned faster and more often than a jackrabbit. If my contribution could speed up the Great Northern's efforts to lay track across the territory and give me the chance to trade my saddle for a first-class Pullman ticket, I'd have been on my way to the Dakota line with a sledgehammer over my shoulder a long time ago.

Ernst Kindler ran the livery, but he only reported to work three days out of the week. He wasn't lazy. It hadn't taken him long to learn that he did his best business when one of his part-timers took his place. Ernst had been Judge Blackthorne's hangman until he laid down his ropes for his first love, which was tending livestock. But a lot of people were superstitious; those five years of service on the scaffold had put something in the old man's eyes—or taken it out, no one was sure which—that made them decide they could get along without a horse or a trap for another day or two until Lars Nördstrom or Cracker Tom Bartow reported for work. I was under no such constraint. I trusted Kindler's knowledge of animals as I did Blackthorne's understanding of statute, and anyway there were people who said the same thing about my eyes that they did about his. Also I liked to watch him tie knots.

I found him doing just that next to the barrel stove in

his reeking little office. It took him all of five minutes to enter his day's transactions in the ledger, giving him the rest of the twelve hours to pluck his prodigious eyebrows, read the Bible—he was not God-fearing, but during his tenure as executioner he had made it a point to attend every trial that might end in hanging, and claimed that nothing but Kings I and II could compare to the testimony he'd heard for sheer harrowing detail—and practice his sailors and squares. Today he was sitting stooped over in the burst horsehair swivel next to his cracked desk, putting the finishing touches on a Gordian masterpiece nearly as big as his head. It must have consumed ten feet of tarred hemp.

"You wouldn't even have to put that around his throat," I said in greeting. "Just hit him in the head with it, and his criminal days are over."

He looked up with that dead gaze under his thatched brow and grinned. Those customers who got along all right with his eyes tended to lose their resolve when he smiled. It wasn't that he had bad teeth; in fact, he took better care of them than most men in the higher professions, which may have been why they made you think of bleached white bones half hidden in the wiry tangle of his beard. The starched white collar he insisted upon wearing even when he cleaned out the stables contributed to the overall impression of a dressed corpse.

"Good morning, Mr. Murdock. I thought at first you was a half-growed bear standing there. They only come into town when they're starved."

I didn't resent the bear remark. I had on a bearskin I'd taken off a big black I shot in the Bitterroots in '77, with a badger cap pulled down over my ears. It was the "half-growed" I didn't care for. You can only be told you're not as big as Jim Bridger so many times before it starts to tell on your good disposition. "Why do you bother to keep in practice, if you don't intend to go back to work for the Judge?"

He sat back, turning the great twisted ball around and around in his hands. He had long, elegant fingers with callus between them; the fingers of a painter or a concert pianist. He had been an artist in his way, never having had to hang a man twice because it didn't take the first time or left one to strangle slowly. The neck had snapped each time, clean and crisp as a shot from a carbine. "You can always trust a knot if you tie it right," he said then. "Knots ain't people."

I told him I needed a horse.

"You got a horse. You owe me two weeks' board on that claybank you brought back from New Mexico."

"That's a desert horse. I need to trade it for one that's good in snow. You know you can count on me for the bill."

"No horse is good in snow. What you need is one that ain't as bad as most. I got a mustang I can let you have for the claybank and fifty bucks."

"How is it a short-legged animal like that comes so high?"

He grinned and started pulling apart the knot. "I got it and you don't."

"How much mustang is it? I need a horse with bottom."

"Oh, it's a regular mongrel. Fellow I got it from said if he had his choice he'd be buried with it, because he was never in a hole it couldn't get him out of."

"Why'd he part with it?"

"He sunk every cent he had into a shaft that turned out to be full of water. Traded me the animal for the board he owed on it and ten bucks, took himself a room at the Merchants, and blew his brains out with a Sharps pistol."

"Let's have a look."

He set the ball of rope on the desk, got up, pulled on a stiff canvas coat, and led the way to the stalls, where a bar-

rel stove identical to the one in the office glowed fiercely
with each gust of wind that knifed its way through the
chinks in the siding. The horses standing between the par-
titions stamped and blew clouds of steam in the lingering
chill, but the fumes from the fresh manure and the animal heat itself kept the temperature above freezing. We
stopped before a stall containing a scrawny-looking sorrel with a squiggly blaze on its forehead that reminded me
of a snake. It had a black mane and a red glint in its eye I
didn't like by half.

"Fellow called him Little Red," Kindler said.

"If I called it anything I'd call it Snake. But I don't name
horses and mosquitoes." I took a fistful of its mane to
steady it and peeled back its upper lip. In a lightning flash
the mustang broke my grip and snapped at my hand. I
snatched it back in time to avoid losing a finger, but the
beast took off the top of a knuckle. "Son of a bitch."

"Teeth are fine," said the old hangman.

The horse nickered and showed its gums. Its grin reminded me of Kindler's.

I dug my bandanna out of the bearskin and wrapped it
around my hand. The blood soaked through the cotton immediately. "I'll give you the claybank and ten. We'll forget about what Doc Schachter's going to soak me for the
lockjaw treatment."

"You won't get lockjaw. He's clean. Fifty's the price."

"I suppose it's gelded."

"I don't traffic in stallions. I like to keep the boards on
my stalls."

"Twenty."

"Talk around town is you're headed north," he said.
"You can't take an ordinary horse up there this time of
year unless you figure to cook and eat him when he lays
down on you. An animal that will fight you is an animal
that will save your life."

I looked at him. He was heartier than his gaunt frame and lifeless eyes suggested. He seldom shook hands with anyone because all those years working with ropes and counterweights had made his fingers as strong as cables, and he was afraid he'd forget himself and crush bone.

"You're selling hard for the price," I said. "If you're that keen on getting rid of it, you need to budge."

He looked away. That never happened; it was always the other person who lost in a staring contest. He ran a finger down a fresh yellow post holding the stall together. It hadn't been up more than a few weeks. "Bastard knocked down a partition last month and killed my best stepper."

"Not the gray."

"It was Parson Yell's favorite. He ain't been around to rent the calash since. Thirty-five, and I'll throw in what you owe me on the claybank's board."

"Done."

He turned back toward the office. "Let's splash some whiskey on that knuckle."

At the door I looked back at the mustang. It met my gaze, tossed its black mane, and grinned its hangman's grin.

3

"**S**loan McInerney, have you anything you wish to say before this court passes sentence upon you?"

"Yes, Your Excellency."

"'Your Honor' is sufficient."

"I wish to say that if I wasn't drunk I wouldn't of done it and that I have gave up the Devil Rum for good and all. It is strong drink that has brought me to this sorry pass."

"That's a fine sentiment, but if you were truly repentant, you would tell this court what you did with the money you stole from the Wells Fargo box in your charge."

"I spent it, Your Excellency. I said that at the start."

Judge Blackthorne hooked on his spectacles and thumbed through the stack of sheets on the bench before him. "At six forty-five P.M. on Thursday, November twenty-fourth, 1881, you told Marshal Pendragon that the Overland stagecoach you were driving had been waylaid by three masked men ten miles east of Helena and that you were forced at gunpoint to surrender the strongbox containing eight hundred sixty-eight dollars and thirty-three cents. At half-past three the following morning, acting upon information supplied by an unidentified party, Marshal Pendragon arrested you in a room at Chicago Joe's Dance Hall and charged you with grand theft. A search of your person and rooms failed to discover more than eleven dollars and thirteen cents in cash. Do you intend this court to believe that in less than nine hours you managed to spend the sum of eight hundred fifty-seven dollars and twenty cents on women and whiskey?"

"I bought a cigar at the Coliseum."

Blackthorne gaveled down the roar from the gallery. When the last cough had faded he folded his spectacles and rested his hands on the bench.

"Sloan McInerney, having been tried and found guilty of the crime of federal grand theft, it is the decision of this court that you will be removed from this room to the county jail, until such time as you can be transported to the territorial prison at Deer Lodge. There you will be confined and forced to work at hard labor for not less than fifteen, nor more than twenty-five years. If upon your release you take it upon yourself to recover the money you stole from wherever you have it hidden, you will be satisfied to know that you sacrificed half your life for a wage of slightly more than one dollar per week." The gavel cracked.

As the jailers were removing McInerney, I waved to catch the Judge's eye. He crooked a finger at me and withdrew to his chambers.

It was the room where he spent most of his time when he wasn't actually hearing cases, and he had furnished it with as many of the creature comforts as an honest man could on a government salary. Walnut shelves contained his extensive and well-thumbed legal library as well as a complete set of Dickens and his guiltiest pleasures, the works of Mark Twain and Bret Harte, with space for his pipes and tobacco and cigars in their sandalwood humidors. The black iron safe where he kept petty cash and the court officers' payroll supported a portable lock rack in which his cognacs and unblended whiskeys continued to age patiently between his rare indulgences. The scant wall space left by his books and the window looking out on the gallows he had decorated with a small watercolor in a large mahogany frame of a French harbor and a moth-eaten, bullet-chewed flag on a wooden stretcher to remind him of his service in the Mexican War. He read for work and recreation in a well-upholstered leather swivel behind his polished oak desk while his visitors squirmed on the straight-backed wooden chair in front.

"Fifteen to twenty-five seems stiff," I said, when he had traded his robes for his frock coat and we were seated across from each other. "You gave Jules Stoddard less than that when he stuck up the freight office for twenty-five hundred."

"Stoddard didn't work for the freight company. I haven't a drop of mercy for traitors. Are you packed for Canada?" He never spent more than thirty seconds reviewing a judgment.

"Oskar Bundt said he'd have those new grips on my Deane-Adams by tomorrow. I'll be ready to go as soon as the weather breaks."

"I hope you lose that English pistol in a drift. All the other deputies carry Colts and Remingtons and Smith and Wessons. Six-shooters. The time will come when you wish you had that extra round."

"If five won't do it I might as well haul around a Gatling. You've just got a thistle in your boot about the English."

"Port drinkers and sodomites." He clacked his store teeth, shutting off that avenue of discussion. "Inspector Vivian replied to my wire. His office is in Moose Jaw. He's reserved a room for you at the Trappers Inn there."

"I'm sure it's full up this time of year. This is the rainy season in Paris."

"You will of course leave such observations this side of the international border. I intend to press for Bliss and Whitelaw's extradition and would rather not bog down the process in a petty cultural squabble."

"If I were you I wouldn't lose any sleep over it until your best deputy manages to capture them both alive."

"My best deputy is in Fort Benton picking up a prisoner. In any case your responsibility is to advise the North-West Mounted Police and to offer your assistance in the fugitives' apprehension. You are not to behave as a one-man committee of public vigilance."

"When did Tim Rourke become your best deputy?"

"When you stopped listening to me. Did you hear what I just said?"

"I heard. Bliss and Whitelaw's scalps have nothing to fear from me. I didn't know any of their victims."

He leaned back in his chair, retrieved a cigar from the humidor on the bookshelf, and used the platinum clipper attached to his watch chain to nip off the end. "That's the reason I selected you for this mission," he said. "All the men I can count on to follow my instructions to the letter have some personal stake in this manhunt. If they're allowed to go on much longer, there won't be a lawman west of St. Louis who isn't related to or familiar with someone they've killed or robbed or set fire to." He lit the cigar with a long match and blew a thick plume at the ceiling. "I'd offer you a smoke, but I know you don't indulge."

"I'm saving myself for that eight-hundred-dollar brand at the Coliseum."

"McInerney." He frowned through the smoke. "I hope Rourke doesn't take long getting back when the weather breaks. I don't trust the county jail to hold a hard-time prisoner for long."

"If all you need is someone to take McInerney to Deer Lodge, I'm your man."

"You have business in Canada."

"I'm not going after Bliss and Whitelaw knowing just what's in the papers. There's a man in Deer Lodge who knows more about them than anyone."

"If you mean John Swingtree, he won't talk. He'll die in prison."

"He might talk if I promise him a commutation."

"I can't offer that even if I wanted to. Only Governor Potts can do that."

"I didn't say I'd keep the promise."

He drew on his cigar, watching me, then propped it in the brass artillery-shell base he used for an ashtray and slid a sheet of stationery bearing his letterhead from the stack on the desk. "You'll need a letter from me before they'll let you see him." He dipped his pen.

The next day I went to see Oskar Bundt. A glum pack of city employees was at work in the street, shoveling the heavy snow into piles alongside the boardwalks. The sky was iron colored but looked less oppressive than it had for a week. We were in for a thaw.

The gunsmith, Bundt, was Scandinavian, but he could seldom get anyone to believe it. He was Finnish on his mother's side, and the line went straight back to the squat, swarthy Huns who had fled north to escape Rome's retribution after the death of Attila. That was his story, anyway, and since no one else in Helena except perhaps Judge Blackthorne had read all of Gibbon, he never had to argue the point. His low forehead, sharp black eyes in sixty-year-old creases, and cruel Mongol mouth didn't invite conflict in any case. I found him behind the counter in his shop, gouging a two-foot curl off a block of walnut that was beginning to resemble a rifle stock in the vise attached to the workbench. The tidy room with its pistols and long guns displayed on the walls and kegs of powder stacked on the floor smelled of sawdust and varnish and the sharp stench of acid. NO SMOKING signs were everywhere; one spark and the entire local shooting community would have to go all the way to Butte to have its firearms repaired. Every tool in the shop was made of brass.

When he saw me, he put down the gouge, wiped his hands on his leather apron, and took my five-shot revolver from a drawer. I took it and inspected the new grips. He'd hand checked them and stained the wood so that it matched the brown steel of the frame. "It doesn't look as if anything was done to it," I said.

"That was the idea. Five dollars."

I paid him in gold as expected. If I'd used paper, it would have cost me eight. In addition to being the most expensive gunsmith in the territory, he was the most suspicious; whether because he thought the notes might be counterfeit or the government was going to fall and make them worthless, I was never sure. He was also the best at his craft in three territories.

He watched me load the chambers from the box of cartridges I'd brought, nodding approvingly when I filled the fifth. Neither of us had ever actually known anyone who had shot himself for failing to keep one empty under the hammer.

When I looked up, the expression on his face scared the hell out of me, until I realized he was smiling. It was a good enough specimen of a smile, nothing out of the ordinary—Ernst Kindler's graveyard grin had it beat for sheer sinister quality—but I'd never seen one on that face, and it gave me a turn. If the sun had risen out of the pit behind the Highland Meat Market where they threw away the bones and gristle, the effect would have been the same.

"I have a rifle for you," he said. "A carbine."

"I've got a carbine."

"Not like this one." He went through a door at the end of the workbench and came back carrying a lever-action carbine with a nicked stock that had been varnished and revarnished many times.

I said it looked like a Spencer repeater.

"Looks ain't is." He thumbed aside a sliding trap in the brass butt plate, exposing an opening the size of a half dollar. "That's the end of the magazine. The tube extends all the way to the receiver. Holds thirty-four rounds. You load her on Sunday and shoot all week."

I took it from him. It was as heavy as a full-size rifle. I peered at the engraving on the receiver. "Who's Evans?"

"Company in Maine."

"What's it take?"

"Forty-four centerfire. Two-twenty-grain bullet with thirty grains of powder. This is the 1877 model. They goosed up the range since they came out with it in '71." He paused. "Buffalo Bill owns one."

"That's no recommendation. Every time a company comes out with a new weapon they present one to him for the publicity. He must have more guns than Harpers Ferry." I shouldered it and drew a bead on the Winchester advertisement tacked to the back wall. "It's like hoisting a hodful of bricks."

"All those extra rounds. If they weren't there you'd be carrying them in your saddlebags. It's yours for twenty-five."

I lowered it. "Why so cheap?"

"Company went out of business last year. No replacement parts."

"If it's so good, how come nobody bought one?"

"Too heavy, I suppose. Ladies' guns are the thing now. Muff pistols and hideouts."

I swung the lever forward and back. It moved smoothly, sliding a round into the barrel with a crisp chunk. "How much to try it out?"

"Twenty-five. I don't rent weapons."

"Gold or paper?"

"Gold if you got it."

"I don't." I pulled three notes out of my poke and laid them on the counter.

He made a face at the presidents. "How much ammo can I sell you?"

"One round ought to do it." I added a penny to the stack.

4

The weather broke during the middle of January. The overcast thinned and shredded, letting the sun through, and the mercury in the thermometer on the front porch of the Nevada Dry Goods stirred itself and climbed hand over hand above freezing. There were floods and drownings—cattle and people, including both cowboys sharing a line shack on the Rocking M south of town when the Missouri jumped its banks and swept away the log structure overnight. Butchering crews hired by the ranches set to work to process as many as possible of the beef carcasses piled in the bends of rivers before they began to rot. Steaks and roasts were cheap at the Highland Meat Market and in the restaurant of the Merchants Hotel. A cured leather hide in fine condition could be bought for the price of oilcloth.

After the thaw came the rains to batter down the drifts and transform the roads and Helena's main street, already saturated by departing frost, to ropy mud. I spent this period eating cheap tenderloin, watching teams of mules and workers hauling wagons out of the soup, and waiting for the next cold snap to make the roads passable. My greatest challenge was to avoid catching the eye of Judge Blackthorne, who not counting felons hated nothing so much as the sight of a federal employee collecting taxpayers' wages with his thumbs in his belt. He was quite capable of offering my services to the county jail as a turnkey just to get me out of his sight. I didn't mind the work, but I hated the smell of such places, the stenches of disinfectant and human misery, and as I figured to get my fill of them in Deer Lodge I restricted my loafing in public to the hours when the Judge was busy in court.

After a week the mercury started back down, although the sky remained clear, and the syrup hardened into ruts and ridges that broke axles and chipped teeth. I bought a shaggy gray from Ernst Kindler for my prisoner to ride, packed my bedroll and saddle pouches with supplies and provisions, threw a spare saddle and roll on the gray, and slung the new Evans over one side of the snake-faced sorrel, balancing it with my Winchester on the other. On my way to the jail I stopped in to see Blackthorne in his chambers.

"Are you taking a pack animal?" Since the brutal trek that had brought him there from Washington City, he had traveled rarely, but he was always fiercely interested in the details of departure.

"Not for this leg," I said. "After I drop off McInerney, I'll reprovision in Deer Lodge and use the gray."

"You're traveling through the Rockies. Can you carry enough for two men on only two animals?"

"Prisoners are easier to manage if you keep them hungry."

"All the other deputies are right, Page. You're a mean bastard."

Since he only addressed me by my Christian name when he was feeling tender toward me or wanted something, I didn't take the comment to heart. He scribbled a note to the head turnkey to release Sloan McInerney to my custody and I went to the door. He called my name again. He had taken down his book on Montana territorial law—

ridiculously thick in view of how little time had passed since the first settlers had wandered in, but then, a lot of laws had been broken—and was bent over it, following the dense columns with the butt of his cigar.

"You will want to tread lightly around those Canucks," he said. "Some of them are still fighting the Revolution."

McInerney turned out to be entertaining company. A short Irishman, with powerful forearms and black mutton-chop whiskers of the type they called "buggerlugs" in the British Army, he'd been recruited under another name into the Union infantry in County Limerick, only to learn when his ship dropped anchor in New York Harbor that Lincoln was paying for volunteers. He dived overboard, swam to shore, and signed up again, using the name McInerney. His intention was to desert and open a saloon with his recruitment money, but he lost it all at cards the first night and wound up fighting in three major battles, collecting a ball in his right leg at Chancellorsville that still gave him trouble when it rained or snowed. He confided to me that he was still wanted in Virginia under his original name for an indiscretion he had committed while drunk following Lee's surrender, but he neither identified the nature of the charge nor told me the name. The incident was serious enough to drive him west, where he'd made his living as a bullwhacker, muleskinner, and finally Overland stagecoach driver, in which capacity his weakness for Mammon had placed him at Judge Blackthorne's mercy. He told these stories on horseback and across campfires with a light in his eye and a good ear for dialect that shortened the trip through the pass into the Deer Lodge Valley. He regretted nothing, including the prospect of spending the last good part of his life behind bars. For this reason I took pains to inspect his manacles often and stretch a rope from his ankle to mine when we slept, to awaken me whenever he stirred. He was too cheerful to have ruled out escape.

He made his move three days out of Helena. We'd stopped to water the horses in a runoff stream, and he squatted in a stand of scrub cedars to move his bowels. I'd been watching his hat for a couple of minutes before I realized he wasn't wearing it anymore; he'd slipped it off while I was distracted by the animals and propped it up on a branch.

I backed the horses onto the bank, hitched them to a cedar, and squeaked the Evans out of its boot. He'd left a clear trail in the snow—not because he was clumsy or stupid. I followed it for a while, letting him think he'd outsmarted me, then cut back through the trees and shot off his bootheel while he was trying to mount the snake-faced sorrel. He went down on one hip and curled himself into a ball. I went over and gave him a kick.

"You make a better impression than you thought," I said. "You didn't convince me you were empty-headed enough to make your break on foot in mountain country."

He stood up, brushed off the snow, and scowled at his ruined boot. "You're good with that trick rifle."

"I've been meaning to take a practice shot since we left town."

"You mean that's the first time you fired it?" He was staring at me with his eyebrows in his hairline. "How'd you know the sight wasn't off?"

"It is, a little. I was aiming higher." I handed him his hat. He didn't make a second try.

Deer Lodge was a ranching town, the harness shops and feed stores built of logs on perpendicular log foundations like rafts, with a main street wide enough to turn a wagon around in and the usual assortment of loafers in pinch hats and spurs holding up the porch posts in front of the saloon. The penitentiary, altogether a more substantial construction, occupied twelve acres outside the limits. Three years and fifty thousand dollars in the making, it was built entirely of native granite up to the pitch-pine roof, with bars in the windows made of iron imported from the States, wrought and set by skilled workers brought in from as far away as California. The additional cost had restricted the facility to fourteen small cells, in which at present some twenty-four men were serving out their time stacked on top of one another like ears of corn in a rick. The stink of so much humanity encased in clammy stone reached to the office of the warden, a young Irishman named McTague, whose sober dress and dour face suggested he'd come from an entirely different part of the island from his newest prisoner, whose aborted escape attempt had done nothing to dampen his affability. As I signed off on McInerney I wondered how long all that formidable construction material would hold his unquenchable spirit.

When the captain of the guard had removed McInerney, I showed Judge Blackthorne's letter to the warden. McTague read it with a frown.

"Swingtree is a recalcitrant," he said. "Last month he bit a guard during a fight in the exercise yard. He's been in the hole four weeks."

"How is the guard?"

"The stitches come out tomorrow, but I fear he's ruined for the work. I can't let you see Swingtree until he's finished his time in the hole."

"How much time did you give him?"

"Two months."

"I can't wait that long. I'm expected in Canada."

"The regulations are clear in a case like this."

I tapped the letter on his desk. "Judge Blackthorne is a

presidential appointee. He has seniority over the governor in this territory, and he certainly has authority over you."

"My instructions come from the governor. He can take it up with him." He pushed the letter toward me without expression.

After a pause I picked it up and refolded it. "I hope you're this determined when a hundred or so more convicts show up at your door from the court in Helena."

"I'm afraid I don't understand." But his eyes said he did.

"Blackthorne's an old political in-fighter. He can look at a situation from all sides and decide whether a suspended sentence or a hundred and eighty days in Deer Lodge serves the public better, or if a murderer is to hang in Helena or die of old age in the territorial prison. Which way he leans might have serious bearing on your problem with overcrowding. I understand you missed a major riot by a hair a few years ago."

A tiny vein stood out on his left temple; aside from that he might have been deliberating over whether to visit the barber today or put it off for a week. "Are you speaking for Judge Blackthorne or yourself?"

"I'm an officer of his court."

A silent moment crawled past, during which the stench from the cells entered the room like a third party. At the end of it he held out his hand. I laid the letter in it and he spread it out and scribbled beneath Blackthorne's signature: OK. T. MCTAGUE. He handed it back. "Go to the end of the hall and knock on the door. Captain Halloran will take care of the details."

"Thank you."

"I hope you're careful in your responsibilities, Deputy. It's a sad thing whenever a former law enforcement officer enters this house in chains. They are in for a bad time of it from the inmates as well as the guards."

5

Halloran, the captain of the guard, was a short, thick hunk of carved maple with his head sunk between his shoulders and the look of a prizefighter beginning to go to seed. His belly had started to loosen, cinched in with his belt, and bits of steel gray glinted where he had shaven his hair close to the temples. His faded blue eyes had all the depth of tacks holding up a wanted poster.

His lips moved behind his handlebars as he read Judge Blackthorne's letter and Warden McTague's brief addendum, then without a word he stood aside from the iron-reinforced door for me to pass through into the corridor that led to the cells. He locked it behind us with a key on a brass ring as big around as a lariat and led the way between walls of sweating granite, lit by barred windows set eight feet above the floor and fifteen feet apart. The place held the dank, earthen smell of a neglected potato bin.

At length he unlocked another iron-bound door and let me into a tiny room containing only a yellow oak table carved all over with initials and a pair of split-bottom chairs that might have come from different hemispheres for all they matched. A dim shaft of gray light fell through yet another high barred window I could have covered with my hand onto a dirt floor trod as hard as bedrock.

"I'll have your sidearm," Halloran said.

I hesitated, then unholstered the Deane-Adams and offered it to him butt first.

"Sit on this side, with your back to the door." He shook the cartridges out of the cylinder into his palm, pocketed them, and threaded the revolver's barrel under his belt. "Off to the left is best, out of the crossfire."

He went out and shut the door. A key rattled in the lock.

I was alone long enough to wonder if an old warrant that was still out on me in Dakota had found its way to the warden's office. I fell to calculating how much time had to pass before the Judge realized I hadn't made it to Canada and traced me to Deer Lodge; my head was full of arithmetic when the key rattled again and the door sighed on its hinges.

John Swingtree was smaller and more frail-looking than his reputation suggested; but then, the recent amputation of an arm might have had something to do with the latter. His head was shorn so close I could see the muscles working in his scalp, his ears stuck out. The hollows in his cheeks and the deep set of his eyes left nothing to the imagination about the configuration of his skull. The skin stretched over it was the color of terra cotta, the only visible inheritance from the Creek side of his family.

None of this meant anything in relation to what he was and what he had done and could do if given his freedom. For that I looked to the hardware that accompanied him. An iron belt encircled his waist, secured with a padlock the size of a stove lid, with a manacle attached that prevented him from bending his left elbow. The manacle on the other side was empty; the vacant sleeve of his striped tunic was folded and pinned to the shoulder. A pair of chains clipped to the belt hung to iron cuffs welded about both ankles and linked together with another length of chain that forced him to walk with a shuffle, the thick soles of his shoes rasping the floor with the chain dragging between them; the sound set my teeth on edge, like someone sliding a coffin. The arrangement put me in mind of a Bengal tiger I had seen pacing its cage in a traveling show in Denver. I'd thought at the time that I'd have been less impressed with its savagery if we'd met face to face in the woods, without all that iron standing between us. It didn't mean I wasn't grateful for the iron.

Halloran, who came in behind him, had acquired a hickory truncheon since we'd parted, two feet long, three inches thick, and polished to a steel sheen. He steered the prisoner around the table with the stick resting on Swingtree's right shoulder—it would be the most sensitive—and applied pressure as if the push were needed to seat him in the chair opposite mine. Only then did he withdraw the truncheon. He stepped out into the corridor and swung the door shut with enough force to dislodge a stream of dust from the seam where the rock wall met the pitch-pine rafters. The lock clunked. There was no sound of footsteps going away. I could feel him watching us through the square barred window in the door.

A sour smell of unwashed flesh filled the room. There were no bathtubs in the hole, just an open latrine and the sound of one's own pulse. And absolute darkness; even the weak light we were in made the man in chains blink. His coarse cotton uniform was clean, so he had probably spent the last four weeks naked as well. When they chose not to hang you, they made you be good.

"Your name is John Swingtree?" The question broke a silence as hard as the granite that surrounded us.

Another silence, just as hard, filled the break. His vocal cords were rusty.

"Not in here," he said.

A swelling around his left eye gave his face a lopsided look. Nearly a month had passed since his tussle with the guards and he still hadn't healed completely. I could only guess how many welts and bruises were concealed by the uniform.

"I'm Murdock, deputy United States marshal. I've got a badge if you care to see it."

"Why'd you lie about a thing like that?"

I searched the gaunt face for some sign of amusement. It looked like a place where smiles went to die. I asked him if he wanted to talk about Butte.

"Nice town," he said. "Up to a point."

"The point where you got shot?"

His eyes went to his empty sleeve, an involuntary movement. He snatched them back. They had begun to adjust to the light. "Them rolling-block rifles are built for buffalo. A Winchester would of did as good and I'd still have both wings."

"You were robbing the bank. I don't suppose he had time to make a better choice."

"I never robbed no place. I take care of horses. I got horse blood in my veins. My grandfather stole a thousand horses from the Comanche."

"The man with the Remington didn't know that. All he knew was someone was hollering that the bank had been robbed, and a dozen or more men were galloping away, busting caps at everyone that stood between them and the town limits. You were the one he got a bead on."

"I have a bad spirit."

As he said it, his face showed expression for the first time. He wasn't being ironic or avoiding the subject. He was addressing the issue of why that bullet had found him while all his companions had ridden free, addressing it with the resignation of a man who had been born blind or deaf or deformed. Then the expression was gone, evaporated like a drop of water in a desert.

"You and your spirit might have had a better chance if

Bliss or Whitelaw or any of the others had bothered to stop and give you a hand up. They left you there to die."

"Only I didn't."

"No thanks to them," I said. "Thanks to them the U.S. government is going to bury you inside these walls when your time comes. What's left of you."

He said nothing.

I joined him in that for the better part of a minute, which in those surroundings you timed with a calendar. During that time I discarded entirely the idea of offering him a break on his life sentence. He wouldn't have believed it even if it were true. He had retreated into a redoubt where hope of any kind was as destructive as bullets. That came from the part of him that was Creek. You could take everything away from an Indian, even his life, but you couldn't destroy him the way you could a white man, because when you stepped back to give him room to imagine anything less than the worst, he didn't take it. What had seemed natural when I discussed it with Judge Blackthorne in his chambers faded away in that dim cell.

"Bliss and Whitelaw are in Canada," I said. "They looted a village on the Saskatchewan and burned it to the ground. I'm on my way up there to give the Mounties a hand tracking them down. You know that will happen. All we have to do is follow the trail of burned buildings and corpses. You can shorten it and get in a lick for what they did to you in Butte."

"Why should I shorten it? Every less person left breathing on the outside makes rotting in here a little easier."

I sat back and folded my arms. I knew that would irritate him. His would be going numb with the elbow locked straight. "Do you think your name ever comes up when they're talking? More than likely it doesn't. They've forgotten you. Maybe not, though. Maybe thinking about you spread out in the dust with your arm stuck on by a thread makes them laugh. Did they ever laugh about the people they killed? My bet is they did. They've killed more times in five years than the Jameses and Youngers did in fifteen—and stolen a whole lot less money. They have to be getting something out of it. What do you want to bet they serve you up with all the rest when they're stretched out around a fire up north?"

"What do you want?"

He snapped out the question at the heels of my little speech. I was surprised and a little disappointed; I'd begun to build up some respect for him, and what I'd said had seemed pretty transparent even to me. But then I hadn't been left naked in a black hole for twenty-eight days with nothing but my thoughts for company.

"I've read everything the newspapers have to say about Bliss and Whitelaw," I said. "It didn't take long, and most of what I read I didn't believe. Journalists are just liars who can spell. I wouldn't go lion hunting without knowing first what they eat and where they sleep. The only one who can tell me that is another lion."

"You don't have to know how to spell to know how to lie. I could just stretch a parcel of blankets and finish out my time in the hole entertaining myself thinking about you trying to wrap yourself up in them."

"You could. You won't. You hate your old partners a deal more than you hate me."

"I only just met you," he said. "I been hating the law all my life. That's a big hate and I won't have no trouble at all fitting you in."

I unfolded my arms and rested them on the table. "Why don't you just start talking and let me worry about sorting out the lies from the gospel."

"I got to warn you, I'm pretty good." But he wasn't listening to himself. His eyes had retreated even farther back into his skull, searching the darkness there for glittering bits of the past. "I was running with these boys from Texas, not one of them worth the sweat it took to chop 'em up for compost. Fat Tom was always blowing about how tight he was with Lorenzo Bliss back in Amarillo. Johnny Dollar bet him a double eagle Bliss didn't know him from Garfield. Well, everybody but the law knowed Bliss was catching up on his whoring in Buffalo, so we drifted down there to see him call Fat Tom a liar and maybe hook up with his outfit.

"The barkeep in this rathole where we wound up pointed out Bliss drinking under a big sombrero at the back table. Fat Tom told the rest of us to stay put at the bar till he gave Lolo the office and wobbled on over. Lolo, that's what anyone called him that called him at all, though we didn't know that then; we thought Fat Tom was just being Fat Tom. The two of 'em started talking low, and I don't know what Tom said, but knowing him I reckon he was jackass enough to say something about Bliss's mother being a whore—you know, to poke his memory about how they knowed each other—because Lolo stood up with a big old bowie in his hand and just kind of gutted Fat Tom like a catfish. I remember he give the knife a twist when he pulled it back out and Tom's heart came out with it. It didn't look near big enough for a big fat man like Tom, just a mess of red gristle no bigger than a potato. Anyway somebody started hollering for the law and we all cleared out. We all happened to head in the same direction. You could say I came to run with Bliss and Whitelaw on Fat Tom's introduction."

"I thought they'd be more particular."

"Well, they was just getting started. I reckon now they ask for letters of character."

"It doesn't sound like Bliss's temper has cooled down since Amarillo. What about Whitelaw's?"

"Oh, Charlie's the thinker. He put up with his family for eighteen years before he got around to hacking them to pieces. Fat Tom might have lived another thirty minutes if it was Charlie in that saloon."

"My guess is Whitelaw does all the gang's planning."

Swingtree nodded animatedly. He was enjoying himself now. "If it was up to Lolo, he'd gun everybody in sight, then turn out their pockets for change. But don't get to thinking that means he don't run the ball when it opens. He's got the reflexes of a diamondback. Charlie'd be dead a hundred times over if it wasn't for Bliss. He is always thinking when he ought to be doing."

"Jack Sprat."

It was an absentminded comment; I didn't expect an unlettered breed to pick up on the reference. But his mother must have read to him, because he bobbed his head up and down again and his eyes had come back from the shadows, nut brown and bright.

"They are hell together," he said. "They wasn't nothing till they met, just a couple of bad hats rolling along, waiting for somebody to stomp 'em flat. Split them up and that's what will happen. Only you'll get dead trying to split them up."

Captain Halloran entered. "On your feet, 'breed. One more minute's another week in the hole past your two months."

I wanted to hit him with the table, and I might have if I thought I were going to get anything out of Swingtree that was as good as I'd gotten. (I might have anyway, for no other reason than that the Hallorans of this world could only be thus improved.) But I was in a good mood, and I let him take the prisoner out the way he'd brought him in.

The mood faded when I spotted a second guard standing in the corridor. He was half Halloran's age, barely more than a boy. The smooth brown barrels of his sawed-off shotgun made him older.

"What was that story about sitting outside the crossfire?" I asked. "Either one of those barrels would kill us both."

There was no humor behind the captain's handlebars. "We don't get a lot of time to practice our marksmanship."

6

The clerk who filled my order for bacon, beans, flour, and coffee at the general mercantile, a goat-faced Scot named Kilmartin, informed me my best route to Canada from Deer Lodge lay along the Rocky Mountain Trench, a trough of lowland between the Flathead Mountains to the west and the Swan and Galton Ranges to the east. He traced the path with a thick-nailed forefinger on a map tacked to the back wall that might have been drawn up by Lewis and Clark.

"That takes me thirty miles out of my way, with the Rockies still to be crossed," I said. "What's to stop me from cutting through that creek pass up north? After that it's all tableland."

"That's Métis country. You know Métis?"

"French Indians. I had a transaction with one in Dakota a few years back. I never did work out if he was Christ or Satan."

"That sums up the breed. Talk is they're fixing to go to war with Canada again over land. When the Mounties crack down, which they're bound to do anytime, the Métis will bolt back this side of the border to regroup. I would not want to be in their path when they do."

"I heard it was the Cree making all the trouble."

"Aye, them as well. Their aim is to stop the Canadian Pacific from laying track through buffalo country. If they

attack at the same time as the Métis, there won't be Mounties enough to go around. You're sure you don't want to
winter in Montana?"

"I'm sure I do. But I haven't put aside enough to retire
just yet. How high is the creek in that pass since the thaw?"

"I've not heard. With luck ye'll drown. Them frog Injuns like to take their time with captured lawmen."

I paid him for the provisions and the advice, loaded the
gray, and struck out for the pass that led to the tableland.

It was bone cold but dry. The sky was a sheet of bright
metal, with the Rockies' white-capped peaks bumped out
on this side as if an angry god had kicked in the sheet with
his foot on the other. I'd brought along a small pot of lampblack and smeared it beneath my eyes to cut down on the
glare. Tiny icicles pricked inside my nose, but there was
no wind, and the sun lay across my shoulders like a warm
shawl. I rode with my bearskin unbuttoned until dark,
when the chill came in with the suddenness of night in
the mountains. My fingers were numb, and my hands were
shaking uncontrollably when I finally got a fire going. Every
time I started a long trek in the northern winter, I had to
learn all over again what I'd known most of my life. *Live
and learn*, my father, the trapper, used to put it. *Die dumb.*

I got up at first light with every muscle in my body
screaming, fed the horses, fried bacon in the skillet I'd
been carrying for ten years—stolen, along with a couple
of other things, from my last ranch job in lieu of two
months' pay—poured boiling coffee down my throat, and
picked my way through the foothills along Salmon Trout
Creek, shining like quicksilver with splinters of ice glinting in the swift current. The debris along the banks told
me I'd missed a honey of a flood by a week or so, but it was
still swollen. In places only a strip of level ground three

feet wide separated the shoulder of a hill from the water and I got off and led the sorrel mustang and the shaggy gray to avoid a bath. I don't swim any better than the odd petrified stump. I reached the pass around noon, and by the time dusk rolled in I was in the tablelands with nothing between me and the Dominion of Canada but a hundred miles of Montana Territory.

I made good time my first day clear of the pass, but a fierce squall late the next morning forced me into the lee of an old buffalo wallow to wait it out. The flakes, flinty little barbs of ice, swarmed in the gusts—at one point I swore they were blasting from four directions at once—and swept away sky and earth in a white wipe. I hobbled the sorrel and the gray to prevent them from drifting before the wind, turned up the bearskin's collar, tugged down the badger hat, tied my bandanna around the lower half of my face, and sat hugging my knees with my back against the wallow's north slope, breathing stale air and putting the devil's face on the cue ball that had shot me to this remote pocket of the earth. I fought sleep, but I must have lost, at least for a few minutes, because I dreamed that a blizzard hit Helena so hard and stayed on for so long that Judge Blackthorne was forced to chop up his billiard table for firewood.

By then the squall had passed, leaving me tented with snow to my knees. I stood and shook it off. The brief storm had spread a white counterpane from horizon to horizon; even the firs and cedars were bent like old men beneath its weight. The horses, stupid, pathetic creatures, had managed despite their hobbles to move a hundred yards away from the shelter of the slope. The ice caused by their own spent breath had pulled their lips back from their teeth to form death's-head grins. It fell away in sections when I tapped it with the butt of the Deane-Adams. I fed them handfuls of oats to restore their body heat, stroking their necks and telling them in soothing tones that I was going to sell them for steaks to the first starving Indian I met. Only the mustang appeared to understand. Its eyes went hard as marbles and it snickered.

The rest of that day was an uphill push through drifts nearly as high as my stirrups. It was just a taste of the country I was headed for, where the snow fell twice as hard for days instead of minutes, and the wind struck with the force of God slamming shut the pearly gates.

I came across my first fence the afternoon of the next day. It was four strings of barbed wire without a gate in sight, but I was pretty sure I had drifted off the road. I turned in what seemed a likely direction, followed it for several miles, and was beginning to think I'd made the wrong choice when I spotted smoke from a chimney.

The chimney belonged to a small cabin built of pitch-pine logs with a steep shake roof stacked with snow. Behind it, three times as large, stood a barn with proper siding, altogether a more expensive construction; but then, it was built to shelter wheat, not just people. A plank sign leaned against the post to the left of the gate before the house. I had to take one foot out of its stirrup and kick loose the snow to read the hand-painted legend:

DONALBAIN FARM
BUYERS WELCOME
TRESPASSERS SHOT
MARAUDEURS ETRE FUSILLE

I leaned down to unlatch the gate and started through, leading the gray.

"Turn right around, ye damn toad-eating savage!"

I drew rein and slacked off on the lead. I couldn't

remember when was the last time I ate a toad, but since a
greeting like that is generally backed up with something
more substantial than invective, ignoring it did not seem
the best course.

The sun was just above the log shack and square in
my eyes. I shielded them with my forearm. There was a
shrunken solid something under the overhang of the porch,
a little darker than the shadows, vaguely man shaped; and
it was holding something at shoulder height.

"This here's a Springfield musket," said the man on the
porch. "If ye don't turn around right noo, I'll put a fifty-
eight-caliber ball straight through you and knock doon a
barn in the next county over."

Well, you have the idea. His Scots brogue was heavy
enough to sink to the bottom of a peat bog. It's as hard to
spell as it is to read, so I'll lay that part to rest.

"Hold on," I called out. "I'm a federal officer."

There was a silence long enough to make the horses
fiddle-foot to stay warm.

"Say something more!" demanded the man on the porch.

"To hell with this. It's too goddamn cold to sit here and
make a speech." I started to back the sorrel around.

"Come on ahead," he said then. "Ye don't sound like no
frog I ever heard."

Close up, he was a brown and gnarled fencepost of a
man in a faded flannel shirt and heavy woolen trousers
held up with suspenders. A black Quaker beard ringed his
seamed face and bright, birdlike eyes glittered in the
shadow of his shaggy brows. When he got a good look at
me he lowered his weapon, which wasn't a Springfield at
all but a Henry rifle with a brass receiver.

"Whoever sold you that firearm was pulling your leg,"
I said.

"I traded the musket for the Henry and a case of ammunition in '78. I made worse mistakes but not lately. If ye

wasn't what you said ye was and ye'd known the ball wouldn't reach the damn gate, I'd be deader'n Duncan." He screwed up his face, bunching it like a fist. "Ye got papers?"

"No papers." I had the badge ready. I tossed it to him. He caught it one-handed—a surprise, for I had him pegged at past fifty—looked at the engraving, and tossed it back. "It don't mean much, but I'm satisfied you ain't one of them damn bloodsucking Métis."

I didn't pursue that. "I'm bound for Canada. If you let me camp on your property tonight and cut through in the morning I'll thank you."

He scratched his chin through his whiskers. "Feed you supper for a dollar."

"I'll make my own."

"No sense us both eating alone," he said after a moment. "You can bed down your animals in the barn. Spread your blanket there. I'll fill the basin out back of the house. I got a pot of venison stew on the stove. That's my dollar's worth of good works for law and order." He uncocked the Henry.

"The sign means what it says. Buyers are welcome; the wheat or the farm, it don't matter which. I lost my taste for the life when my Marta died."

The orange glow from the coal-oil lamp on the table filled the lines in Donalbain's features, increasing his resemblance to the young man in the sepia-tinted wedding photograph that hung on the wall behind him in an oval frame. We were drinking sherry from an old green bottle, using barrel glasses with bottoms as thick as sadirons. The venison stew sat pleasantly in my stomach.

"Is that when you took up French?" I asked.

"I got it out of one of Marta's books. She was a teacher in Boston when I met her."

All of the cabin's decorations, including the rag rug and

linen shelf linings, obviously predated his wife's death. The air was a stale mulch of woodsmoke, tobacco, coffee beans, damp wool, kerosene, and rank male. Sooty cobwebs hammocked the rafters. Loneliness hung as heavily as the carcass of an old bull buffalo.

"You translated 'trespassers shot.' Why not 'buyers welcome'?"

"There ain't a Métis alive who's begged or stole enough to meet my price. And they're the only ones around who read French. I translated the one I needed."

"They told me in Deer Lodge the Métis are getting ready to declare war on Canada."

"They'll just lose their shirts like they did the last time. Then they'll come back down here begging and stealing and making life hell all over again for the honest. I've found it's easier to blow them out of their moccasins than talk to them at all." He refilled our glasses from the bottle. He'd emptied his three times since we'd started drinking, and his speech and his hand were as steady as when he'd had me under the gun. "Don't tell me the government's taking an interest in them after all this time."

"No, I'm chasing a couple of fugitives. You might have read about them: Lorenzo Bliss and Charlie Whitelaw."

"I don't take the papers. They're full of lies. Murderers, are they?"

I nodded. "They've run out of laws to break in the United States. The prevailing thought seems to be the Mounties need my help stopping them before they start on the North Pole."

"Know them well, do ye?"

"I haven't had the pleasure."

He drank, tipping the glass at a careful angle to prevent sediment from stirring from the bottom. His eyes never left me. "Ye'll not take offense when I say ye don't look like that such of a much."

"There's more to me than meets the eye. Except when it comes to billiards."

"Billiards?"

"It's a story I don't feel like telling."

"Golf's my game, or was before I left Benmore at the request of the queen's soldiers." He reached for the bottle, shook it, and thumped it back down with a scowl. "I'd not insert myself betwixt the Cree and the damned Métis and the railroad for all the wheat in Montana. They won't welcome ye, and neither will the North-West Mounted. Those redcoats have had the run of that country going on ten years. They don't answer to Ottawa nor the Colonial Office in London, though they'll no admit it. They'll take tea with ye Monday, push ye off a mountain Wednesday, and write a letter to Chester Arthur Friday with their regrets. But ye'll no have to concern yourself with any of that, because long before ye get on the hair side of them the winter up there will kill ye like spring grass."

7

I crossed into Canada a week out of Deer Lodge. Or so I thought.

There were no signs or checkposts, and the climate and scenery didn't change. But something happens to my body whenever I enter foreign country—a lifting of the hairs and a heightened sensitivity in the skin, that I learned long ago not to ignore. I had no official papers apart from Judge Blackthorne's letter introducing me to Inspector Vivian of the North-West Mounted, and I almost never wore the badge, but I'd been in possession of it for so long I felt the exact moment when I stopped being a lawman and reverted to private citizen. I had a sudden, giddy urge to keep on riding, all the way to the uncharted territories, where I could build a cabin on some river loaded with trout and beaver and never have to worry about serving another warrant. Then I remembered I'd left the wilderness to get away from trout and beaver in the first place, and stopped to ask a gang of loggers clearing timber for the Canadian Pacific for directions to Moose Jaw.

The foreman, short and thick in a woolen shirt and trousers, lace-up boots, and a red stocking cap, leaned on his ax and built a cigarette. "Shortest way is through that gap in the pines," he said. "You will want to go the long way, north to the river and follow it east."

He had a husky French accent, but there was no Indian in his puffy, black-bearded face. He wasn't Métis.

"Why would I want to do that?" I asked.

"The short way takes you through Cree country."

"Are they fighting?"

"Not yet. But I would not wish the honor of being the first white man to die."

"I'm surprised you're not posting guards."

"There is a rifle trained on you from up in that lodge-pole on the ridge."

A sparse stand of tall pine topped a rise to the west, one of them taller than the others. After a moment I made out a dark bulk high in the branches. "He must be part tree frog," I said.

"He is American, like you. He was, how you say, a sniper in your Civil War for two years." He put a match to his cigarette and cocked his head to keep the smoke out of his eyes, watching me.

"Which side?"

"I have forgotten. They are all the same."

There was a time when I would have given him an argument. But it had been seventeen years. Stone's River seemed like something that had happened to someone else.

"What makes you think I'm American?" I asked.

"Because you are going the short way."

I looked him in the eye, and he saw in mine that he was right. I thanked him for the information and started for the open space in the line of trees to the east.

Saskatchewan, which was where I judged myself roughly to be, had either enjoyed a mild winter so far or had experienced a thaw about the same time as Montana, or the snow would have been deeper; that north country tending as it did to pile snowfall upon snowfall until settlers had to dig tunnels between their houses and outbuildings. Whenever the freeze had come, it had been in effect long enough to freeze the ground as hard as iron. Wherever the wind had scraped out a bare spot, the horses' shoes rang like a blacksmith's shop during the busy season. The flakes that were falling about me were large and cottony and made no sound when they landed. I rode through ten miles of forest hearing nothing but the creak of my saddle and the horses blowing steam.

I saw no Indians the first day. That meant nothing, not that they had any reason to hide in their own country, and from a lone rider; they were so much a part of the land-scape that I would have had to concentrate hard to see them, just as it would have taken me a minute to spot a thirty-year bookkeeper in a room full of ledgers. But I had grown up in Blackfoot territory, had a pretty good eye, and was convinced that if there were any Cree close by, they weren't interested enough in one man on horseback lead-ing a pack animal to brace him, kill him, or show them-selves. When I reached a cut of swift black water I guessed was the Moose Jaw River, near dusk, I made a bit of noise breaking up pine boughs for firewood and built a nice big fire with plenty of smoke. In bear country, you make it a point not to startle the big brutes by sneaking up on them, and it's not all that different with Indians. They might make fun of you for your clumsiness and for burning too much fuel for one man, but at least they didn't consider you a threat. It was a theory, and if it explained why so many fools and tenderheels passed unscathed through ground that had claimed men wiser and more seasoned, it was worth a try.

My chance to test it came earlier than I'd hoped.

I'd broken camp shortly after first light and had secured

everything aboard the gray except the skillet, which I'd left
in the snow to cool, when I heard the measured creak of
stealthy hooves setting themselves down in the fresh fall.
I didn't think it was the loggers. They had no reason to
come this way unless they were clearing timber, and I'd
ridden beyond earshot of their saws and axes half an hour
after I talked to the foreman. There were few ranches in
that wooded country, so it wasn't line riders. Wolfers possibly, hunting pelts for bounty.

I clung to that last thought, because it gave me the sand
to turn my back on the sound as if I hadn't heard it. I strode
over to the skillet, scooped it up by its handle, and started
back toward the horses as if I were going to slip it into a
pack. When I had the animals between me and my visitors, I let go of the skillet and veered toward the snake-
faced sorrel. Fortunately the Winchester was hanging on
my side; it had a true sight, unlike the Evans, and I knew
what to expect of it in the heat of a fight. I slid it out of its
scabbard, levered a round into the chamber, and laid the
barrel across the throat of my saddle, all in one movement.

The riders kept on coming at the same pace, just as if I
were still holding the skillet instead of a carbine. At a distance of a hundred yards they didn't look much like Indians. The one nearest me had on a mackinaw and his five
companions wore bearskin and buffalo coats and one canvas jacket trimmed with fleece, the kind of variety com-
monly found among parties of white men out hunting or
searching for stray cattle. Two of them were wearing hats.
There wasn't anything about them to suggest Indian from
where I stood, except their formation.

White men could live outdoors for years and never manage the shapeless, scattered quality of a group of nomadic
tribesmen traveling together on horseback. The party
looked as if it might break up at any time, one or two or
all of the riders deciding to abandon the others on some

whim and strike out on their own. That was the point. One sign of trouble and they vanished in several directions, like smoke in the wind. Fire into a tight pack and you were bound to hit something, but if your first bullet didn't find a target in this bunch you might as well shoot at fog. I fixed my sights on the one in the mackinaw and waited while the band approached at a casual pace, trickling between and around the trees like rivulets of water.

Mackinaw seemed to know the precise moment when he drew within effective range, because he raised his right hand and held it palm forward to show there was no weapon in it. The others did the same. I raised my cheek from the stock but kept the Winchester where it was, Indians being nearly as sneaky as white men and just as good about keeping their word.

They leaned back on their hackamores forty feet short of where I was standing, just as I was thinking of chugging a round into the earth at their feet to warn them against coming too close.

There followed a silence that was supposed to frighten the hell out of me. Nobody likes to talk more than an Indian, and nobody knows better the power of a pause. High up in the straight pines where the boughs grew, a small bird fluttered between branches, loud as a steam engine starting up. Even the sorrel snorted and rippled its skin. I grew roots and waited it out.

The one in the mackinaw had some years on him. Bars of silver glinted at his temples, and thinner strands wound through the braids framing his face, which was burnt umber and canted back from an impressive nose, like the corner of a building in a lithograph on a bank calendar. A beaded ornament on a leather necklace cinched in the loose skin of his neck. From there up he was all native. The rest of him would have been at home in Denver, from his trousers of tightly woven wool to his stovepipe boots smeared with grease to make them waterproof to the platinum watch chain that described a fashionable J from the right slash pocket of his mackinaw to the placket where it buttoned at his throat. I wondered if there was a watch at the end of it, and if he ever took it out and popped open the face to check the time, like a senator with a train to catch.

He carried no weapons that I could see, but he didn't have to. I counted three Springfield carbines and two Spencers among the others, tarted up with brass tacks the way they liked them, and just for old times' sake a longbow and a quiverful of arrows. None of them was trained on me. Small comfort; what the tribes back home lacked in accuracy they made up for in speed, and I had no reason to believe a line drawn on a map had any effect on that.

A minute had crawled past, and I was getting cold standing there without moving. I gave in then. Indians liked to win, and they hadn't been doing much of that since the Little Big Horn. I raised my right hand and made the Cheyenne sign that said I wasn't looking for a fight. I hoped I got it right. It had been years since I had had anything to do with Indians other than run away from them.

There was a general letup in pressure then. One of the two men in hats chuckled and said something to the other one, who nodded. A look from the one in the mackinaw and they both settled down.

Mackinaw spoke. "You are with the railway?"

It was only five words, but he rolled his r's with the theatrical assurance of Donalbain the Montana farmer. He had learned his English from the Scots immigrants who had settled the area.

"No," I said. "I'm on my way to Moose Jaw on private business." I'd decided against identifying myself as a U.S. federal officer. I didn't know how much contact he might have had with the Sioux and Cheyenne who had migrated north after the Custer battle, carrying their tales of injustice at the hands of the authorities in America.

"You are American."

I was beginning to wonder if it was tattooed on my forehead. "I am."

"Why do you travel alone?"

"I'm not alone."

"It is a lie." There was no emotion in the statement. "This is the land of the Cree. You ride across it as if you own it. You lay the forest naked, tear the earth, and lay steel across it. The buffalo will not cross the steel and so the great herd is sliced in two, the easier to rub it out. Why do you do these things?"

"I'm not with the railroad," I said. "I'm on my way to Moose Jaw on private business, and this way was pointed out to me as the shortest."

"What is your business?"

I shook my head. "It's private."

He thought this over, or maybe not. Indians' faces as a rule might have been made of glass, exposing the workings of their brains, but this one was painted out. The dark eyes traveled over my outfit.

"You must pay to cross the land of the Cree," he said then. "You have two rifles. You will give us one."

I thought that over, not knowing if he could see what I was thinking. It was standard practice to trade something for the privilege of passage through Indian territory; I had done it on more than one occasion and never missed the item, which had bought back my life. I had no special attachment to the Evans, despite the awesome capacity of its magazine. I thought about all this, and I knew as surely as I could no longer feel my feet in the cold that if I gave up so much as a spoon from my kit I wouldn't live to see noon. It was in the air, if not in the aging brave's face.

"No."

The five others exchanged glances. Even their horses—
gaunt, grass-fed paints with shaggy winter coats—shifted
their weight restlessly from hoof to hoof and shook their
manes, blowing up clouds of steam. Only the Cree in
the mackinaw remained motionless, his gaze locked with
mine. I did something very difficult then. I lowered my
cheek to the Winchester's stock and closed one eye, drawing a bead square in the middle of Mackinaw's chest.
Dying was a little less frightening when you took along a
companion.

Forepieces rattled as the Spencers and Springfields
lifted into firing position. It occurred to me then I had a
better chance if I shifted my sights to one of the armed
warriors. I didn't. I played out the hand I'd dealt myself.
The platinum watch chain made a bright target.

I was so tense I almost squeezed the trigger when Mackinaw gathered his reins.

"Do not stop again in the land of the Cree," he said.

He turned his horse then. After a moment the others followed suit, in a ragged order that would have made an Irish
drill sergeant hurl his hat to the ground in frustration.
Sloppy or not, in a moment the band was gone, as completely and silently as breath on glass.

I blinked. After a while I took the Winchester off cock
and finished breaking camp. When I pulled out I swung
the mustang past the hoofprints in the snow where the
Indians had stopped, just to make sure I hadn't dreamt the
whole thing.

8

"**Y**ou're certain it was a watch chain? Not an ornament of native manufacture that looked similar? They're devilishly clever at imitation."

The man seated behind the desk might have been in his middle thirties or his late fifties. His hair was absolutely without color, chopped close at the temples and full on top and brushed back. His square face was deeply sunburned, nearly as red as his tunic, bringing into prominence his sandy, military-cut moustache and pale eyes in which the pupils were like black specks on blue china. URBAN VIVIAN was engraved on the heavy brass nameplate on the desk, no rank or title provided.

"It was a watch chain," I said. "German, I think. At forty feet I couldn't be sure."

"It could have been any Indian bugger in a mackinaw. They've been trading with explorers and settlers since before the Revolution; I wouldn't be surprised to find an icebox in one of their tipis, with kippers inside and a bottle of tawny port on top. But there's only one Cree who sports a platinum watch chain in the proper gentleman's manner. It had to have been Piapot himself."

His English accent was as brittle as his appearance. The war in the South had burned away most of my patriotic pride, but hearing him talk made me want to whistle "Yankee Doodle" just to see what he'd do. Instead I asked him who Piapot might be.

His flush deepened. "You Yanks really don't pay heed to anything that don't threaten your precious Union. Piapot's the chief of the entire Cree Nation, that's all. His warriors have been busy as teamsters pulling up survey stakes along the Canadian Pacific right-of-way for a month. Up till now we hoped it was just some disgruntled renegades, but if Piapot's in the area it means it's got his seal. Indians go their own way as a rule, and hang the chief if his interests ain't theirs. It's different with him. There are seasoned braves who have never known another leader. He might as well be jerking up the stakes with his own two hands."

I'd been with Vivian ten minutes, long enough for him to read Blackthorne's letter and hear my account of the palaver in the woods. His office was a one-story walk-up by way of an outside staircase next to a feed store. The room took up the building's entire second story, with only his desk and a work table and a row of upright wooden chairs to occupy it. A skin that must at one time have belonged to a fifteen-hundred-pound grizzly managed to look small in the middle of the plank floor. Apart from that the place resembled any city lawman's office in the American territories, complete with a row of rifles and shotguns glistening in a locked rack, a corkboard stacked with wanted readers three deep, and the obligatory blue-enamel pot boiling away on a potbelly stove that might have come from the estate of Ben Franklin. (It was a *tea*pot; but then Canada was mostly settled by people who would never forgive Boston its party.) The maple-leaf flag hanging from a standard in one corner provided a colorful change of pace, along with a gold-fringed blue banner tacked to the wall behind the desk, featuring a buffalo head beneath a coronet encircled by the legend NORTH-WEST MOUNTED POLICE. At the bottom appeared the motto MAINTIEN LE DROIT, which Judge Blackthorne had translated for me: Maintain the Right.

A pair of tall, narrow windows looked out on Moose Jaw: all two blocks of it, log and clapboard buildings with signs in English and French advertising stores (shops, they called them there), drinking establishments, and one hotel, the Trappers Inn. The street separating them was a hundred feet wide, scored and rutted and frozen as hard as granite. It had all the appearance of a town founded by trappers and Indian traders struggling to stay alive between the crash of the fur market and the coming of the railroad (railway, they called it there). The very fact that the North-West Mounted had decided to open an office there must have given the locals hope to go on.

"Why don't you bring in the British Army to deal with Piapot?" I asked.

"We don't handle things that way. Unlike your American cavalry, we've managed to learn from our mistakes."

"You wouldn't know that from your record in India and Africa."

He had a silver snuffbox on his desk. He used it, sneezing into a handkerchief he drew from his left sleeve. All he had to do now to make me like him less was hop on a pony and whack a wooden ball with a mallet.

"I was a regular army officer for twelve years," he said, tucking the handkerchief back into his cuff. "Worked my way up through the ranks. Fought in Abyssinia and at Roarke's Drift. Bloody buggers, both campaigns, and all we managed to win was the contempt of half the world's native peoples."

"And most of the African continent. Don't forget that."

He pointed a finger at me. There was an impressive callus on the end of it, but he might have gotten that from a pen. "Yes, and in the end you Yanks will have a continent as well, and spend the rest of the century fighting to hold on to it. Blood for dirt ain't a fair trade."

I had nothing to throw at that, so I withdrew from the field. "I can't feature Piapot letting me live. I had a bead on him, but I never knew an Indian to be afraid to die. The others would have chopped me to pieces before I got in a second round."

"Crees are hard to predict or explain. They respect a show of sand. Or he might have thought you were daft, which is bad medicine. You're a lucky bloke either way. You should have given up the rifle."

"If what you say is truc, that might have gotten me killed."

"Perhaps. Your government doesn't have the corner on treachery."

Now we were moving in circles. "What news of Bliss and Whitelaw?"

"Nothing since that bad business on the Saskatchewan at Christmas." He relaxed a little; his shoulder blades actually touched the back of his chair. "It wasn't enough for them to steal every dollar and gold filling in the settlement. They had to take target practice on the locals as well, and put a torch to everything that wouldn't bleed. I helped bury the bodies. Some of them were burned all in a heap, their flesh melted in one lump; rather than try to separate them we dug a big hole and pushed them in like rubble. They smelled like burnt pork. I sent to Regina for troops and we tracked the buggers as far north as Saskatoon when a blizzard wiped out the trail. They didn't pass through town. I wired the constable in Prince Albert to keep an eye out. I'm still waiting for an answer. That far up the lines are down as often as not."

"What's past Prince Albert?"

"Eight hundred miles of wilderness, clear up to Victoria

Island. Beyond that's the Arctic Ocean. Oh, there's a river settlement two hundred miles north of Albert, founded by former American slaves, and a stronghold up on Cree Lake full of Sioux Indians who chose not to surrender with Sitting Bull last summer, but even Bliss and Whitelaw aren't barmy enough to take on either one. They're armed camps."

"The slaves are armed?"

"*Former* slaves—and free up here since long before Lincoln. They'll shoot a white American as soon as look at him. There's not a one of them as didn't have a wife or mother or some other close kin sold down the river at one time or another. Americans have been known to disappear in that vicinity, and there's not a Mountie in the country could track them to where they're burned or buried. The locals are always polite to redcoats, invite us in for dinner and a jug, but when we ask them what became of so-and-so, they roll their eyes and shake their heads, laughing at us the whole time behind that plantation-nigger show. I hope to blazes Bliss and Whitelaw tried them on; it would save Her Majesty the cost of a trial and Washington the price of extradition. But I don't count on it."

"What's the name of the settlement?"

"Shulamite. Not that you'll need to know it, except as the name of the place you want to ride wide around. The settlers put their trust in a hag of an African shaman, and I don't set any store by such claptrap, but she'll see straight through you if you try to brass it out and claim you're anything but a wicked slave-taking white American. I suspect her hideous old face is the last thing those men who vanished ever saw."

"How many men are riding with Bliss and Whitelaw?"

He took another pinch but didn't sneeze this time. He seemed relieved not to be still discussing Shulamite and its witch queen. "The survivors of the massacre couldn't

agree on a number. As few as eight, as many as fifteen.
The witnesses were in shock, and it's usual in those circumstances to count high. Enough, anyway, to call for a
company of Mounties when we find out where they're hiding." He glanced down at Blackthorne's letter. "You
know, I sent wires to the capitals of all the American territories where these animals committed atrocities, but Helena was the only one that offered to send help. I suppose
the others think Bliss and Whitelaw are our problem now.
But this letter don't say anything about how many men are
coming behind you. I frankly don't care for the prospect
of a gang of heavily armed strangers loitering about town,
and neither will Superintendent Walsh. Such men become
bored easily."

"Tell Superintendent Walsh not to worry. I'm the entire
expedition."

"I'd feared that. Your Judge Blackthorne is disingenu-
ous. He has no interest in assisting us, merely in protecting the United States' claim on Bliss and Whitelaw and
their accomplices when they are apprehended. You're here
in the role of a spy to see that Canada doesn't hang them
first."

"Blackthorne's a low fighter," I said. "He's vain, too, and
he cheats at billiards. But it won't do to run down the authorities in the other territories because they'd just as soon
you dealt with the situation and then run down the Judge
for saying it's his responsibility too. Bad form, I think you
Brits call it."

"Only in cheap novels written by Americans." He refolded the letter, smoothing the seams with his horned
fingers as if they needed it after riding folded in a saddle
pouch for three hundred miles. He would do everything
twice, minimum; I was betting that under his tunic he wore
galluses and a belt. He said, "I can't offer you a thing beyond the quarters I arranged for you and the opportunity

to submit a request for extradition once the fugitives are
in custody. I shan't stop you if you volunteer to accompany
any party I assemble when we receive news of their where-
abouts, but I remind you that you have no official status
in Queen's country. You will obey my orders. And before
you leave this office you will surrender to me any firearms
you have on your person. They aren't permitted in town."

I shifted my weight in the hard chair, unholstered the
five shot from under my bearskin, and passed it across the
desk butt-first. "What about my rifles?"

"You can leave them with Jules Obregon at the livery
when you board your horses. He'll see they're delivered
here." He frowned approvingly at the revolver. "English
weapon. Do you not subscribe to the popular Yankee con-
ceit that only Sam Colt made men equal?"

"I won my first Deane-Adams off a stock detective in
Kansas in '76 on a jack-high straight. He bought it back
from me and then used it to try to hold me up for the rest
of the pot. I shot him with the Army Colt I was carrying at
the time and took the English gun for my trouble. He didn't
see me palm the cartridges when I sold it to him."

"You killed him?"

"Not right away, but it's difficult to shoot someone at
that range without blowing out too much to put back in."

He smoothed his moustache with a knuckle, evaluating
me with those pale eyes. "I should think the incident was
a better argument in favor of the Colt."

"Not really. A pistol without cartridges hasn't had a fair
comparison. I liked the feel of the Deane-Adams. It took
me six months to find a replacement after I lost it somewhere between Bismarck and Fargo in '78."

"Another shooting incident, no doubt."

"It's a frontier, Inspector. That's not a police whistle
hanging from that peg."

He didn't bother to turn his head to look at the cartridge

belt and what looked like the handle of a Russian .44 sticking out of the flap holster on the wall where he hung his white cork helmet. "I've drawn that weapon once in the line of duty since I was assigned here four years ago, to disarm a drunk. Moose Jaw isn't Tombstone. It's a wild land, but most British subjects respect the law even when they can't see it. If it weren't for your Indian wars and your expatriate desperadoes, I should be sitting in a comfortable office in Ottawa, sipping whiskey and soda and discussing the fights."

"Well, I'll try and take Bliss and Whitelaw off your hands at least."

"Right." He placed the revolver and the Judge's letter in the top drawer of the desk and banged it shut. "The linen in the Trappers Inn is above reproach, but if you heed my advice, you'll sleep there only and take your meals at the Prince of Wales. I recommend the fried chicken, and I'm told the cook poaches an excellent trout. As I'm one Londoner who can't abide fish, I'm unable to offer an opinion based on experience. Is there anything else I can do to make your stay more pleasant?" He wasn't gentleman enough to bother to make the invitation sound sincere, but then he'd come up through the ranks. It cost him plenty to avoid dropping his *h*'s.

"Just one thing."

I surprised him, not for the first time, nor yet again for the last during that brief meeting. He had a leather portfolio of papers on his desk and had already begun to absorb himself in them. He looked up, brows lifted. That's when I surprised him again.

I said, "Tell me where I can find the survivors of the massacre on the Saskatchewan."

9

The lobby of the Trappers Inn was less than half the size of Inspector Vivian's office and contained twice as many fixtures and furniture. A great shaggy moose head with a six-foot antler spread seemed to breathe down my neck while I registered for the clerk, three hundred pounds of solid fat with long gray hair and no discernible gender. A pair of crossed snowshoes hung on the wall next to the stairs and a smoothbore musket of Revolutionary War vintage decorated a ceiling beam, looking not so much like ornaments as things that were taken down frequently and used. So far everything I had seen about Canada made me feel that the entire country had been pressed between the pages of a novel by James Fenimore Cooper.

The room I got smelled suffocatingly of cedar and soiled wool with a single discolored window, a smoky fireplace, a chipped-enamel washstand, and a cornshuck mattress on a narrow iron bedstead. The sheets and pillowcases were white and freshly pressed, as Vivian had promised. After so many nights sleeping on the frozen ground, I thought it was the presidential suite at the Palmer House in Chicago. I built a fire from a box full of seasoned pine and cedar, pried the window up an inch to let the smoke out, helped myself to a swig from a bottle I'd bought in Deer Lodge, and slept for two hours without even trying.

I awoke at dusk, sore all over and hungry enough to order the moose head for dinner. Stripped to the waist, I washed with cold water and scraped off the top layer of stubble, then put on a clean shirt and went downstairs to ask for directions to the Prince of Wales. The clerk, who I guessed was some mix of French and Indian, but whose sex I still could not decide upon, looked at me with small black eyes like a mole's.

"Dining room's through that door. Tonight's pot roast of beef."

"Thanks. I asked about the Prince of Wales."

"You must be rich as Gladstone." But the clerk told me the way.

His Royal Highness might have stuck his nose up at it, but the restaurant was as civilized as anything I'd seen in months. The floor was sanded and scrubbed white, the walls were plastered and papered and hung with portraits of H.R.H. and his mother the Widow of Whitehall, and the tables were covered in white linen. The room was half full at that hour, the locals in mackinaws and woolen shirts and heavy knitted pullovers, some in stocking caps and brimmed hats with stains on the crowns where they gripped them between greasy thumbs and forefingers. Some of the diners were women, dressed like men for the most part, skirts of durable material and no particular color hanging to their boottops so that they looked like male-female combinations in a medicine show, divided halfway down. They would save their femininity for the short warm season.

I hung up my bearskin on a peg already layered with coats and scarves and found a corner table. A waiter with a shorn head and handlebars appeared while I was reading the menu. I asked for fried chicken and a bowl of mushroom soup.

"Anything to wash that down? We got red and white."

"Just water."

He went away with a shrug, a large man in a clean apron who walked on the balls of his feet like a prizefighter. He didn't take the menu. I pretended to interest myself in the breakfast bill of fare while my fellow diners stole glances at me. They would know who I was by now, small towns being the same on both sides of the border, and they would want to know if the American lawman was as tall as Pat Garrett or as curly-headed as James Butler Hickok. I wasn't either one; little by little their attention strayed back to their meals and stayed there.

The soup was good if slightly musty, made from mushrooms dried during autumn for keeping and soaked in water when they were prepared. I'd had better fried chicken in Virginia, but I could see how it would impress an Englishman like Vivian. At that moment the man himself entered, shook the snow off his flat-brimmed campaign hat and sheepskin coat with the fleece turned inside before hanging them up, and came straight my way without appearing to have looked around. Probably he had spotted me through the window. He would be the kind of man who never wanted to look as if he didn't know where he was headed, a man accustomed to being watched and who behaved accordingly. I hoped he wasn't going to get me killed.

"I see you took my advice," he said by way of greeting. "How do you like the chicken?"

"It's all right. At this point anything that doesn't taste like bacon suits me down to the ground."

His attempt at a smile soured. I'd intended to compliment him, but even when I try to say something polite to someone I don't like it comes out wrong. "May I sit down, or are you one of those blokes who prefers to dine alone, like a Neanderthal?"

"It's a free country," I said. "Whoops, no, it's not. But suit yourself."

He sat with his hands on his thighs and watched me finish off a leg. "We've started off poorly, I'm afraid," he said. "My grandfather was killed at New Orleans. What I've seen of most Americans who come up here hasn't done a great deal to eradicate the family antipathy."

"I'm surprised you came here."

"I haven't eaten since breakfast. Oh, you mean *Canada*." He bared his teeth. "Rank can be purchased in the British military, if you have the wherewithal. I bought mine with blood and sweat. The wealthy class is not overrun with idiots, but they have their share, and most of them seem to think they'd look good in brass buttons. One morning a colonel whose father was serving in the House of Lords asked me if I didn't agree that the Sikhs and Muslims ought to be able to sit down and work out their differences in the spirit of Christian good fellowship. I resigned my commission that afternoon. I was among the first three hundred Mounties dispatched to Fort Garry in '73."

He paused, then recited, in a clear, pleasant tenor that turned heads at the nearby tables: "'Sharp be the blade and sure the blow and short the pang to undergo.' That's what the *Toronto Mail* predicted when we rode west. Nobody gave us a Chinaman's chance against the northern tribes after the massacre in Cypress Hills. And yet here we are. That wouldn't be the case if the idiots had come out with us."

"Maybe. The Army of the Potomac had more idiots than Robert E. Lee had gray hairs, but we managed to beat him anyway."

"Fought the good fight against slavery, did you?"

"I never saw a slave in my life, and neither did a good many of the men I helped kill in that war. It wasn't about slavery. I can't tell you just what it was about now, though I was pretty sure then."

"We all were," he said; and for a moment there we were

thinking about the same thing, if not the same war. Then the waiter came and he ordered the chicken and a bottle of white concord. "That is if you'll join me, Deputy."

"Thanks. Wine sours my stomach."

"A glass, then." When the waiter left, Vivian drew an envelope from inside his tunic and placed it beside my plate.

I mopped the grease off my hands with my napkin but didn't pick up the envelope. "I haven't been in town long enough to acquire an admirer, and you're no messenger."

"Directions. You'll find the place inaccessible without them. I can't guarantee she'll talk to you even when you find her. But it's all I can do."

"She?"

"You said you wanted to interview survivors of the massacre. Most of them have been moved four hundred miles east to Fort Garry, to await relocation next spring to the homes they left behind, some of them in England and France. Only one elected to remain in the area. She's living in a tent on the site of the cabin she shared with her husband and two children. She won't leave their graves."

"Is she too heavy to scoop up and carry?"

"She has a shotgun and a great blunderbuss of a pistol that belonged to her husband, neither of which she is ever without. I cannot say whether she intends to use them on herself or whoever draws near enough to seize her. I'm reluctant to find out. I make it a point to ride out there every ten days or so and deliver provisions. She is always sitting Indian fashion outside the tent, with the shotgun across her lap and that big revolver strapped about her waist. I don't know if she ever goes inside. The only evidence that she moves at all is the provisions I left last time are always gone when I bring replacements. I leave them on a flat rock, outside shotgun range."

"How long's it been since the last time?"

"I was planning to make another delivery tomorrow. I cannot predict how she'll react if two men ride out there at the same time," he added.

I picked up the envelope then and took out the directions. He had a neat round hand, symmetrical if not elegant. His wrist would never touch the desk while he was writing. "What is it, about a day's ride?"

"Count on being gone two nights. It gets dark early in that thick forest."

"Mining settlement, wasn't it? Did they see much in the way of color?"

"Just enough to trade for supplies once or twice a month here in town. It's a hard life. Some trapper who hasn't got the word there's no more market for beaver pelts in London finds a nugget and they come pouring out here planning to get rich in a fortnight. If they have any luck at all they make wages. Have you ever met an old prospector?"

"Only in dime novels."

"Forty's the expected span. They die of pneumonia or starvation or fall off mountains or follow color too deep into Indian country, and no one knows what happened to them until some other twit stumbles over their bones. Partners kill each other over a handful of dust or just because they tire of staring at the same face all the time, or they kill themselves because it's easier than going home failures. Or they manage to survive all that, and a pack of animals on the run from America slaughters them for two or three hundred in raw ore. All to make an attractive setting for the diamond on Jim Brady's pinky finger."

"That's not why," I said, "and you've been out here long enough to know that."

"Oh, I know bloody well the importance you Yanks put on your precious liberty. You'll sacrifice everyone else's to maintain the illusion."

"You English always make good points. I'll take it up with my Irish and Scot friends and get back to you."

The waiter brought his fried chicken. When we were alone, Vivian spent some time arranging his napkin in his lap, then sipped his wine. "It seems we're destined to remain at loggerheads."

"Destiny's overrated. That's why I carry a gun."

"In that case I suggest we make an effort to put aside our cultural differences while you're here. We're not likely to agree in any case, and it will make your stay far more pleasant for both of us."

"We need to save the unpleasantness for Bliss and Whitelaw," I said.

"Right." He tore apart a wing. "I was undecided whether to share this with you, but since we're determined to get on, here it is. There are no telegraph lines between here and the northern posts, so I depend on the monthly mail packet and the occasional long rider for news from that area. Fortunately, the service processes requests for transfer on a regular basis from troopers who find the life up there too stark for their adventurous fantasies, and these individuals carry messages from their former posts. One of them stopped here yesterday from Fort Chipewyan, up on Lake Athabasca."

I watched him nibbling at the bone in his hands. He managed to do it without getting grease in his moustache.

"The fort sends out patrols in a two-hundred-mile loop around the lake," he went on. "For supplies and information the patrols stop regularly at a trading post on the Methye Portage. The day this trooper left Chipewyan, a rider came in from the patrol with word that the trading post was in ashes. They found a burned body, which may or may not belong to the trader, a Métis named Jean-Baptiste Coupe-Jarret. That's Cutthroat in English. Colorful chap, rode with Louis Riel in the uprising in '69."

"Witnesses?"

He shook his head, deposited the bone on his plate, and used his finger bowl. "Beastly place, Methye: solid cliff with the Athabasca River boiling round it like Saturday night in Picadilly. Only reason the post is there at all is to do business with Indians and voyageurs carrying their canoes around the cataracts. If anyone saw anything he's down the river and gone. Only damn fools and Mounties mind anyone's business but their own in that wild country."

"It has Bliss and Whitelaw's signature."

"It could just as well have been Cree, or those Sioux from the stronghold, or those rum Métis. The Canadian Pacific has got them all stirred up this year."

"You said Coupe-Jarret was a Métis."

"He ain't the loyalist he was a dozen years ago. There's some as say he never was, and claim he sold out Riel at Fort Garry. I do know he's one of them we've depended upon for information about what the half-breeds are up to. *Coupe de poignard*, I've heard them call him: Backstabber. If he's dead, I hope they buried him deep. Otherwise the blighters will dig him up and feed him piece by piece to their ugly dogs." He bit into a breast.

"How soon do you expect details?"

"Mail packet's due any day. If it's an uprising, Chipewyan will send to Fort Vermilion for reinforcements and notify Ottawa through here. If it's your marauders, they'll handle it themselves and report. Three hundred troopers ought to be more than enough to cane a ragtag bunch of American bandits."

In the interest of putting aside our cultural differences I held my tongue. I looked at the directions again, returned them to the envelope, and put it inside my shirt. "I'll ride out tomorrow and talk to your survivor," I said. "You didn't tell me her name."

"Weathersill. Her Christian name is Hope, if you can believe it."

"I wouldn't want to know a set of parents who would name their daughter Despair."

"Yes," he said, and remembered his wine. "Quite. Perhaps I shall have good news for you when you return. You may be back in Helena in time to celebrate George Washington's birthday. Gala event, I suppose: Fireworks and pageants and the mayor parading about in tights and a powdered wig."

"No, we generally save that for Independence Day, when we beat the tights off King George." I paid for my meal, excavated my bearskin from under the coats that had accumulated on top of it, and went out, leaving George Washington face up on the table.

10

A pair of large charred log timbers formed a rude cross at the top of a mound of freshly turned earth overlooking the roiling Saskatchewan, visible for a mile through gaps in the tall pines. It marked the mass grave where Inspector Vivian and his volunteers had buried the victims of the Christmas massacre, and if it weren't for that feature I might have been a week finding the remains of the settlement; for reasons roughly having to do with the banishment from Eden, God never places gold in the middle of a well-traveled road.

However, the inspector's directions were accurate. Late in the forenoon of the second day out of Moose Jaw I pushed the mustang and pulled the gray up a hill covered with sugary snow and looked down from the top upon the black and broken evidence of atrocity.

Snow had fallen since the event, but not enough to cover the raw wound. Piles of scorched logs lay in regular patterns, spaced evenly apart like the shacks and cabins that had preceded them, with stone chimneys rising obstinately from the rubble. Some of the logs had burned entirely but retained their original shape even though they were made completely of ash and would crumble apart at the touch, like cigars left to burn themselves out forgotten in an ashtray. On the downhill side of the river opposite the settlement, a sluice built of logs sawn in half for the purpose of washing away silt and sand from recovered ore had collapsed in a broken line, its supports knocked loose with axes or kicks from horseback. After a month the scene still smelled of soot and burned flesh. I could swear I heard the echoes of gunfire, rebel yells, and the screams of the maimed, raped, and slain. Perched on that hill I felt twenty years wash away; I was back at Stone's River, after the battle.

At the near end of the string of debris appeared a white pyramid which I took at first for a snowdrift, but it turned out to be a tent made from a wagon sheet. There was no sign of life nearby. I called out that I was a friend come with supplies, and listened to my own echo bang around among the trees and ridges for the better part of a minute. When no reply came after the second time, I transferred the Winchester from its scabbard to my lap and picked my way down the grade.

The sorrel became skittish and the gray tried to back up when we reached level ground; the stench of death was faint but unmistakable. I used my spurs and jerked the lead, but after another fifty yards the gray set its feet and would not budge. I stepped down, dallied the lead around the saddle horn, and hitched the sorrel to a low spruce, then approached the tent carrying the Winchester. There was no sign of a recent campfire outside the tent, and no smoke-hole in the canvas to accommodate one inside Indian fashion. I was cold enough in my bearskin, and I had been moving. How a person managed to stick in one place in that frozen country without a fire and avoid freezing to death was a mystery. Perhaps she had died, and been dragged away by wolves or a bear. Camping the night before, I had heard the weird baby-cry of a grizzly not far away, and had built my fire large to keep from waking up with a leg gnawed off. What Bliss and Whitelaw had started, the Canadian woods might have finished.

In front of the tent I stopped and called out again. When no one answered I pulled aside the flap, sidestepping quickly in case lead came out. It didn't. I ducked my head and went inside.

What light there was came filtered through canvas. The sun was dazzling on the snow outside, and I waited a minute for my eyes to catch up to the change. Otherwise I would have been out in thirty seconds. I was alone in the tent with a buffalo-plaid blanket someone had been using for a bed and an iron-bound trunk with the lid thrown back.

Out of curiosity I stepped over and poked through the contents with the barrel of the Winchester. The trunk was full of tangled cloth, patching and dress and curtain material selected with care by a woman determined to make a civilized life for herself and her family in the wilderness. There was calico and denim and tightly woven wool, flannel and duck canvas and one slim roll of damask, expensive to obtain and wrapped in cheap blue cotton to protect it from handling. Everything else looked as if it had been pawed through recently. Some of the material was brown at the edges—part of the trunk's lid was scorched—and there was a strong smell of stale smoke, but the trunk must have been stored somewhere the flames hadn't reached. I used the carbine's muzzle to work the top off a straw sewing basket. It contained spools of gaily colored silk and cotton thread, a sheaf of dress patterns on tissue carefully folded and tied with a pink ribbon, and a handful of shriveled black walnuts stashed by a squirrel.

Two large scraps of gingham and gauzy lace were spread out side by side on the earthen floor. A pair of shears with black enameled handles and sawtooth blades lay on the gingham, freckled slightly with rust. Bits of brownish fabric lay nearby, curled like dead centipedes. Someone had been busy trimming the smoke-stained edges.

I withdrew the Winchester from the trunk, hoping I

hadn't gotten any oil on the fabric. Out there among the wolves and Indians I felt as if I had violated the sanctity of a woman's bedroom. I slunk out—and that's when someone shot me and ruined billiards forever for Page Murdock.

PART TWO

Runners in the Woods

11

I've had forty years to sort things out and I still can't swear to how much of what I witnessed next actually happened and how much I dreamed through a haze of pain so thick it could almost be called a form of sleep.

Start with the shot.

The evidence of all that domestic activity involving the scraps of material in the tent had knocked the edge off the caution I normally carried into open territory along with my weapons and provisions. I threw the flap wide and stepped right out into the open with the Winchester dangling at the end of one arm. The sunlight was brilliant after the dimness inside. I saw a purple shadow against the sky and my hands were just receiving the signal to raise the carbine when something struck my right side with the force of a boulder and my feet went out from under me and I went down hard on my tailbone. My lungs collapsed and a lightning-bolt of pure white pain shot up the base of my spine to the top of my skull. I have a clear memory of realizing what had happened to me, of the importance of finding my legs and scrambling for some kind of cover before a second shot came, and then a red-and-black wash took away my sight and I teetered over backward into a hole I hadn't noticed before and fell into warm darkness. It was like tumbling back into the womb.

The rest is a tangle. I remember a woman with her hair

loose and blowing wild; Farmer Donalbain's weathered features ringed by his Quaker beard; an Indian with a platinum watch chain strung across his middle just the way the meat millionaires wore them in Chicago; striped and solid-color ivory balls rolling on green baize; John Swingtree's hairless skin plastered to his skull, his body in chains; the smell of uncured buckskin boiled in some solution made of pure stench; Sloan McInerney telling Judge Blackthorne he'd spent eight hundred dollars on a cigar at the Coliseum; the sound of bone utensils clanking against each other like hollow metal; a clear tenor voice chanting, "Sharp be the blade and sure the blow and short the pang to undergo"; the taste of something warm and liquid with a greasy base and dried greens floating in it. I'm pretty sure now the chant and the ivory balls and Sloan McInerney were left over from before, and I doubt either Swingtree or Donalbain had shaken loose from their respective prisons—the territorial house in Deer Lodge and the lonely wheat farm below the Canadian border—and traveled north, but I'm undecided whether I actually saw the Cree chief Piapot, particularly since he made a strong enough impression to visit me in my dreams as recently as two months ago.

The rawhide and foul stench were real enough. When I awoke for certain and pulled aside my bear coat, which someone had spread over me like a blanket, my shirt was open and the lower half of my trunk was encased in a buckskin wrap from which all the hair had been scraped and which had dried as hard as plaster. I rapped it with my knuckles, testing it, and got a crisp report as if I'd knocked on a door. It was as tight as a corset and restricted my breathing, but I wasn't in pain. I had seen Indians repair shattered buttstocks and splintered lodge poles with the same device, but this was my first experience with it in healing.

Sunlight filtered through canvas. I was lying on the buffalo-plaid blanket I had seen before, and when I turned my head the trunk full of fabric was still there, but with the lid shut. I spotted, perched on the ground beside the blanket, a white china bowl with a delicate scalloped design around its lip, marred by a black stain and a crack on one side. I smelled cooking grease and boiled greens, and something clawed at my stomach lining. I was famished. I reached over and touched the bowl. It was still warm. I twisted a little to get both hands around it.

That was a mistake.

Pain lanced my left side. I gasped, dropped the bowl, and fell back while a sheet of white fire swept over me. Someone groaned loudly in the cracked, froggy voice of an old woman. It was me.

Something tore aside the tent flap then, allowing a brass beam of pure sunlight inside and in its middle the same purple shadow I had seen just before the door slammed in my face. I saw a glint off gun metal. I put my hands on the ground and tried to slide backward, like a startled snake slithering for cover in the shadow of a rock. The pain rocketed up my side, paralyzing my right arm. It buckled and I fell over sideways, into a fresh country of pain.

I had been shot before, and taken blows, fallen off horses and trains and mountains; broken bones and been bunged up for weeks. The agony I had known those times was something I prayed to get back to from where I was now. On none of those occasions had I been hurt so badly I didn't care if someone put a bullet in my brain. I peered through the throbbing watery fog at a woman with her hair loose and blowing wild, at the great gaping muzzle of the horse pistol she had pointed at me, and didn't care which end she used on me as long as it put me back in that warm dark womb I'd had the bad sense to crawl out of in the first place.

The pain reached high tide and began to recede. My vision cleared, particle by particle, like bubbles bursting. The woman was a giant, standing over me with her shoulders hunched slightly to keep her head from brushing the top of the tent; but then I remembered I had had to stoop as well the first time I entered it, and that now I was looking up from the ground. She wore a man's canvas coat that hung loosely enough to expose the blanket lining, the cuffs turned back a couple of times, but apart from that she was dressed as a woman, in a plain brown dress whose hem hung to the insteps of her lace-up boots, its edge dirty and tattered from dragging the ground. She had a cartridge belt buckled around her waist with six inches of leather flapping free because she'd had to punch an extra hole to make it fit and an empty holster. The revolver that belonged to the holster, a huge Walker Colt designed for carriage in a scabbard attached to a saddle, was heavy enough to bend her wrist with its weight, but she didn't look as if she wanted to put it down any time soon. Her other hand was occupied with a double-barreled Stevens ten-gauge shotgun, the kind Wells Fargo messengers carried, with the muzzles pointed at the ground. I counted myself fortunate that when the time had come to shoot me she had decided to use the pistol. If it had been the shotgun there wouldn't have been enough left of me to shovel into the tent.

She had a good face, if you liked strong bones and eyes that didn't shift. The skin was sunburned from the light reflecting strong off the snow, peeling like old paint, but with a good scrubbing and some powder and rouge, it would turn the occasional male head at even so jaded a place as Delmonico's in New York. Just now it was severe and hawklike, the pale gray eyes as hard as January ice and just about as responsive. There was an animal alertness in them but no sign of human intelligence.

"I'm guessing you're Mrs. Weathersill." My voice

scarcely qualified as a croak. "My name's Murdock. I came from Moose Jaw with provisions."

Hope Weathersill—for it could have been no other—said nothing, and gave no indication that she'd understood my words. After a long time her eyes moved, flicking toward the spilled bowl next to the blanket, then back to me quickly, as if I might make an attempt of some kind while her gaze was elsewhere. After another long silence she moved, and at the end of so much stillness it was as if the Cascade Range had lifted its skirts and danced the Virginia reel. However, all she did was insert the muzzles of her shotgun inside the bowl, slide it over toward herself, and stoop to pick it up, during which her eyes and the Colt remained on me. When she had the bowl in the same hand in which she held the shotgun, she backed out of the tent. Through the open flap I saw an edge of yellow flame and heard wood crackling.

She returned without the shotgun, but still held the big revolver in one hand with the bowl steaming in the other. The bowl must have been hot to the touch, but as she holstered the Colt and shifted the bowl to that hand I saw that her palms were shiny with callus; the life out there had been hard long before the massacre, and she would have taken her turn chopping wood and driving the mules and horses to pull up stumps. Beyond that her hands, face, and dress were smudged with soot. There was soot in her hair as well, and it was tangled and snarled so badly it would have been easier to cut than comb. Only that delicate bowl and, when she knelt beside me and shipped soup into a spoon, the ornate filagreed silver of the handle between her thumb and forefinger bore witness to more civilized aspirations, clouded now by green tarnish.

Painfully I propped myself up on one elbow to accept the spoon between my lips. She made no attempt to support my head, although as a wife and mother, she would have been skilled in the details of tending to the injured and ill; as a widow with slain children, she knew that I could not attack her easily as long as I needed one arm to keep from sprawling onto my back.

The soup tasted better than I remembered from my delirium—less greasy, the greens richer and more full-bodied. Her eyes—close up, they had a yellow-amber tint, like those of a wild creature encountered unexpectedly—never left me as she worked the spoon. She might have been nursing a wounded predator, keeping it alive for reasons of her own without trust or tenderness.

"The supplies are on the gray pack horse I brought," I said between swallows. "I was riding a mustang. I hope you're taking as good care of them as you are of me."

She filled the spoon again and brought it to my lips. There was no sign that she understood.

When the bowl was empty she rose and backed out of the tent once again. Alone and still supported on my elbow, I inspected the stiff rawhide wrap. It was Indian work, I was sure. What I wasn't so sure of was whether Piapot had had a hand in it or if I had dreamt his presence. If he had, I was at a loss to explain why he should care whether I survived. The Indians I had known respected a man with sand in his belly, if that was what I had shown during our parley, but in time of conflict they were not so beguiled by it they went out of their way to restore life to a man who might bring that sand to bear against them another day. Maybe the Indians in Canada were different. Certainly the Mounties had a lower casualty record in their dealings with the northern tribes than had the American cavalry on the high plains. Given that, what influence they had with the feral thing that had been Hope Weathersill was a mystery. They revered—or feared—human madness, but the mad did not generally return the favor. The whole damn country was upside-down.

I probed my left side gently through the wrap. A sharp stab answered, but I forced myself to continue exploring until I was satisfied as to the extent of the damage. I had two or three cracked ribs anyway, but I was pretty sure there wasn't a bullet in there. Either the woman had grazed me with the big Colt or the bearskin had stopped or deflected the bullet so that I took only its impact and wasn't punctured. But the impact of a two-hundred-grain ball of lead traveling at the rate of 410 feet per second is nothing to ignore; a six-hundred-pound log rolling off the back of a lumber wagon couldn't hit harder or make a bigger bruise. The entire side was tender, and since I couldn't inhale deeply enough to fill both lungs because of how tightly I was constricted I wasn't sure that one of them hadn't collapsed.

I felt my head getting light and lay back. Now I saw there was much less room in the tent than when I had first entered it. I recognized some of the bags of flour and the huge salt pork I had brought out from town for Inspector Vivian stacked to one side. It was a heavy load for one woman to carry. The Indians had probably helped, either for a percentage of the goods or because they felt sorry for the madwoman living alone in the wilderness—or just because they were Indians and made a point of bizarre behavior. On that thought I drifted off. I dreamed I was in Helena, dealing myself a hand of patience on the rickety table next to the Detroit stove in the house I rented in town and getting up from time to time to turn the trout I had frying in my old skillet, covered in corn-flour batter and swimming in hot butter. With the part of me that was still alert I thought that if I could keep that dream going long enough I'd wake up into it from the reality I was living.

12

When I awoke again, night had fallen. I didn't know which night it was, or how many I had slept through or ignored in my delirium. The fire was still burning outside, casting rippling shadows through the canvas.

The frozen earth beneath me was as stiff as hardrock maple and made me ache in a hundred places where my body curved and it didn't. My bladder was full to the point of agony. But I was reluctant to try to get up because I knew a universe of pain was hovering just above me, waiting for me to stir from the safe haven beneath. I was forty years old, if the faded brown ink on the end pages of the Bible that had come over from Scotland with my father meant anything, and had faced more punishment than most adventurous men twice my age, but the older I got, the more it hurt, and the less prepared I was to suffer it. I was going to be a cowardly old man.

I rolled over slowly, out from under the bearskin cover, stopped to breathe, placed my palms flat against the earth, took in as much breath as I could hold, and pushed myself up onto my knees. A wave of thick gluey fog rolled in, gray and glistening. My eyesight started to go. I caught it when it was reduced to pinpoints of light and forced them open by sheer force of will and a lifetime's experience of blackouts; when you've lived through the same nightmare a score of times you learn to recognize it and exercise

some control over it. My elbows wanted to buckle, I wobbled. The wave passed on through the other side of my
skull. I remained motionless on my hands and knees until
I was sure it was all out. Then I shoved myself upright and
let the momentum carry me off my knees and onto my feet.
I did this all in one movement, like ripping off a bandage.
Getting the worst part out of the way all at once.

The worst was worse than I thought. The wave reversed
itself in a towering curl, blocking out the light. I grabbed for
the tent pole with both hands, felt the coarse bark, and
tightened my grip, imprinting the whorls and ridges on my
palms. The inside of the curl was lined with hot orange
pain. It was like getting shot all over again. I increased
my grip on the pole, tried to crush the straight pine, to
make my hands hurt worse than what was going on around
the middle of my body. The wave crested, hung frozen for
a week, then ducked its head and went on over. I hung on
to the pole and rode it out. The burning slid down from
my trunk to my pelvis and down my legs and out the ends
of my toes. I stood shaking in the aftermath.

When I thought I could support myself I took one hand
away, then the other. Some of the bark came off with them.
My fingernails were bleeding. They throbbed when I
fumbled the bone buttons of my shirt through the eyelets.
One side of my body, the side opposite the fire burning
outside the tent, was cold. I looked down at the bearskin,
lying at my feet, as far away as Helena. I didn't dare bend
down and try to pick it up. I didn't have enough left to
make that trip all over again.

I pulled aside the flap and stepped outside, hugging
myself to keep the heat in. The sky was clear of clouds, allowing outer space to come clear to the ground, black as
a bottomless well and studded with stars like ice crystals.
The air was searingly cold; breathing it in was like plung-
ing chest deep into an icy creek. A fresh fall of snow, over

now, covered the raw broken edges of the ruined settlement and gentled the steep slope to the river, chuckling away between the jagged wafers of ice that lined its banks. The place looked as it might have before civilization had stretched out its left arm and closed its fingers around it.

Hope Weathersill sat cross-legged in the snow twenty feet from the tent, on the far edge of the firelight. Her back was turned my way, but she must have heard me, because the snow squeaked like sprung planks beneath my boots. She didn't turn around or stir as I approached the fire. It had begun to burn down. I spotted a pile of limbs nearby, powdered with snow. I went over, bent my knees to keep from stooping, slid one off the pile, shook off the snow, and dragged it over to the fire, where I dropped the end into the flames. Breaking it up would have damaged me worse than the limb. I saw the other end had been chopped with an axe or a tomahawk; either the pile was left over from Vivian's last visit or the Indians were helping out.

A spluttering snort drew my attention to the horses. The sorrel mustang and the woolly gray were standing a hundred feet closer to the tent than the spot where I had hitched them. I walked that way. They were hobbled with braided rawhide thongs and someone had unsaddled them and unfolded their saddle blankets and spread them over their backs for warmth. I found the saddles themselves close by, stacked and covered with the canvas wrap from my bedroll, sifted over with snow. The bag of oats was there as well and I fed two handfuls apiece to the horses, who accepted them greedily as if they hadn't eaten in days. But whoever had relieved them of their burdens and bothered to cover the saddles would have taken care to feed them as well. I assumed the bedroll and my pouches were also underneath the cover but I didn't investigate that far because I felt myself getting weak.

The fire was going well now. I stopped next to it to warm

my hands and draw the chill out of my bones, then approached the woman, once again making plenty of noise to avoid startling her. She didn't move. Her back was so straight and she was so still sitting there in just the canvas coat with her head uncovered that I had a bad feeling even before I circled around to face her. Her eyes were open. There was frost in her eyebrows and bits of ice in her wild hair. The shotgun lay across her lap with her hands resting on it, the fingers as blue as bottle necks. I took in air, held it against the pain in my ribs, then let it out in a thick plume and bent my knees to see if there was any vapor at all coming from her nose or mouth.

The shotgun came up fast and struck me along my right jawline with a noise as if a great iron bell had rung inside my head. I lost my balance and fell backward into the snow, which wasn't as soft as it needed to be for a man who didn't take pain as well as he used to. The wave came back, all bright orange now and no longer thick or sluggish. When it subsided, dragging its flotsam of razor-sharp needles, I found myself staring up both barrels of the shotgun. The woman was standing over me once again, with the wildness in her eyes and her hair blowing about like smoke. Both hammers were back and her finger rested on the front trigger.

The only thing I was thinking was what a shame the Indians had wasted all that time wrapping my ribs, just to get shot again and for keeps.

Her expression—it was no expression at all, comes to that—didn't change. She lowered each hammer in turn, using her thumbs, then poked me in the chest with the muzzles. When I didn't react she poked me again, hard enough to awaken the pain. I got the meaning then and gripped the barrels with both hands, feeling them weld themselves to the metal in the cold. I drew up one knee and she braced herself and leaned back, hauling me to my feet with the shotgun as a lever. I hoped neither of the hammers was loose and the powder in the shells was stable, because the muzzles were pointed at my midsection the whole time.

Then I was on my feet and she snatched away the gun, taking some of the skin of my palms along with it, and returned to the hollow in the snow where she had been sitting. In another second she was back in position with the shotgun across her lap with hands resting on it and her eyes wide open, breathing so shallowly she made almost no steam. I followed the line of her gaze to the charred timber of the cross overlooking the mass grave on the ridge, where her husband and children were lying in a jumble with the rest of the massacred, joined for eternity.

I waited with her for a little, then I got cold. I went back to the fire and stood with my back to the flames to dry my clothes. When that was done I dragged another two feet of unburned limb into the fire and returned to the tent, where I picked up my dream where I had left off, my first lucky break of the trip.

When morning came around—the next one or the one after that; it's been too long and at the time the passage of hours and days held no significance—I knew I was getting better because my brain had begun to go bad from boredom. I was slept out. The soup, which never seemed to run dry, had lost all taste, and I only tolerated it because the feeding sessions broke up the day. For a time I amused myself wondering why the Weathersill woman bothered. That stopped interesting me when I decided it gave her something to do aside from sitting and staring. She had me down as the enemy, but she had spent too much of her life taking care of someone to resist the habit. She didn't give this any more thought than one of those birds that continue to care for strange hatchlings long after they were aware that the eggs had been left in their nests by a trespasser. Everything she did came from instinct, like breathing. Bliss and Whitelaw had gutted her as effectively as their torches had the buildings of the settlement.

Or perhaps not. For all I knew she spent her silent hours thinking up recipes for when the soup finally ran out or composing speeches for the Grand Army of the Republic. Assuming too much was what got lawmen shot.

When I sat up this particular morning, the pain had backed off to the extent that I welcomed it as a trouble-some friend whose visits gave structure to one's life. I stood, caught my breath when one of my cracked ribs pinched my side, but prevented myself from grasping the tent pole. I found my balance without it and even worked up courage to lift the bearskin and slide it over my shoulders cloak fashion. I had trained myself to take shallow breaths and make them satisfy. I stroked my matted beard, attempting to reckon the time I'd been there by the length of the whiskers; but if I were good at arithmetic I wouldn't have agreed to the salary I was being paid.

I went out—and blinked at the sight of a thousand bright-red tunics facing the tent in a semicircle on horse-back. It was more color than I'd seen since the leaves fell in autumn.

13

"Behold the prodigal," Inspector Vivian said. "Except his father didn't have to go looking for him."

He was seated astride a tall chestnut so dark it could have passed for a black in slight shadow, curried to a high gloss like burnished leather. He held the reins in one gauntleted hand while the other rested on his thigh. Only a career British cavalryman could have looked so uncomfortable in the saddle. He was dressed, like the others, in heavy scarlet wool, with a belt making a diagonal white slash across his torso and a white cork helmet with a spike on top and the strap buckled tight to his chin. The red-white combination put me in mind of strawberries and cream.

There weren't really a thousand of them, of course. The actual number was closer to fifty, but the effect of that crimson band separating white earth from blue sky inflated the initial estimate. I understood then the reason behind the color choice in London; no matter what the size of your own force, you couldn't look at it without feeling outnumbered.

In the middle ground between the semicircle and the tent, Hope Weathersill sat Indian fashion in her usual spot, still as a plaster Buddha. The great armed body of men didn't exist for her. She saw straight through it to the cross on the ridge.

I slid my gaze from one end of the line to the other and back to Vivian. "All for me?"

"Yes, they are debating your predicament on the floor of Parliament. Gladstone himself took up your case. We are here on his orders to escort you to Balmoral, where you will be knighted by Her Majesty. Moose Jaw Murdock, they shall call you in the *Times*. Like Chinese Gordon."

"She'll have to come here. I get seasick."

His sense of humor had reached its shallow bottom. "When you hadn't returned after five days I decided to look in on you on our way north. These men have been dispatched from Fort Walsh and placed under my command. This expedition is bound for Fort Chipewyan."

I had to pry my brain loose from where it had been stuck for days to recall our conversation in the Prince of Wales. I remembered the dead trader on the Methye Portage. "On your way to avenge John Cutthroat?"

"Not entirely. The mail packet I was expecting from Chipewyan arrived the day after you left. It contained a general recquisition for reinforcements from throughout the Dominion. The commander up there believes the same band that killed Jean-Baptiste Coupe-Jarret and burned his post are responsible for the slaughter of a Métis family living on the south shore of Lake Athabasca, directly across from the fort. With the Métis situation as it is, the government in Ottawa is granting the request for reinforcements to prevent civil war."

I felt my strength returning. It started as a tingling sensation at the base of my neck and shot through my body in a flash of heat. "Survivors?"

"One, briefly. A boy of about ten. Before he died he provided a description of the men he saw assaulting his mother after they shot him in the chest, evidently to weaken her resistance. Two of them match the readers your Judge Blackthorne sent on Lorenzo Bliss and Charles Whitelaw."

"I'll get my gear together." I started toward the canvas covering my saddles and pouches.

"You'll slow us down. What happened to you, by the way?" He might have been asking about a holiday in Scotland.

I found the Winchester carbine and Evans rifle under the cover, also the Deane-Adams with my cartridge belt neatly wrapped around the holster. Whatever medicine a crazy woman carried, it must have been plenty powerful to prevent the Indians from confiscating good weapons.

"Let's just say I got a little more out of the Weathersill woman than I came for." I buckled on the belt.

He turned his pale eyes on the woman. "I'm half surprised she didn't make an end to the job once she'd started."

"Only half?"

"I doubt even Canada could blow all the female out of her. Or out of any woman, for that matter. I suppose it was she who patched you up."

"No, I have your renegade chief to thank for that."

"Piapot? That old rotter! You must have made quite an impression on him." He gathered his reins. "When you get back to Moose Jaw, ask for Bernard Eel. He ain't a doctor, but he put in a year as a dresser at St. Bart before he lost his place; something about theft. He's the closest thing to a medical professional in this damned part of the country."

I checked the load in the Deane-Adams. "I'm not going back to Moose Jaw."

"Go where you like, so long as it ain't with us. I'm not in the habit of carrying wounded *into* battle."

"A few days ago you told me three hundred Mounties ought to be more than enough to handle Bliss and Whitelaw. One battered American lawman more or less shouldn't make any difference."

"Ottawa doesn't agree. When a general order goes out, it's to be obeyed yesterday. We're not waiting round while you get saddled. Sergeant Major?"

A pair of black moustaches with a sunburned face behind them stood in his stirrups and bawled something incomprehensible, at least to me. The line of men turned their horses north in a single graceful movement, as easily as a man swinging one arm.

I had to raise my voice above the jingling of bit-chains. "When you see you're being followed, do me a favor and don't shoot."

"It won't be a favor when you lose the trail in a great bloody blizzard," he called back. "I smell one coming."

"Where can I find a guide?"

"Moose Jaw."

If I'd been any longer outfitting the sorrel and getting the pack saddle and the supplies and provisions I needed onto the gray, the Canadian Pacific would have finished laying its tracks, and I might have ridden to Fort Chipewyan in a Pullman. I had to rest often to keep my ribs from poking out my side, and when the damn mustang puffed its belly to prevent me from tightening the cinch I had to wait until it couldn't hold its wind any more, then yank fast; kicking the animal in the gut wasn't an option in my condition. Finally I cut the hobbles, found my badger hat, and stepped into leather with the help of a pile of half-burned logs to start from. I snicked my way over to where the woman was seated. Her hands, red and chapped with black ragged nails, dangled between her spread thighs, and the only movement was her hair crawling in the gusts and the faint gray jets of smoke her breath made when I leaned out from the saddle to see it. She neither blinked nor moved her eyes from the cross on the ridge. I couldn't tell if she was aware of the Mounties' visit or if she cared. To this day I don't know whether her method of living was a form of surrender or a determination to survive; or if the enormity of the catastrophe that had befallen her had reduced her to the level of a machine, which continued to operate long after those who had depended on it no longer had a use for it. If that was the case, I wondered how long it would go on. I couldn't tell if the assistance she received from the Indians and Vivian was a kindness or a despicable evil, sentencing her to a lifetime of bleak vigilance at the grave of those she loved when it would be more merciful to let her perish. Whatever the situation, I have only to sit back with nothing occupying my thoughts to see her again as clearly as if I were still in that ruined settlement; watching, always watching.

I turned the mustang's head, jerked the pack line, and left her there.

I had no intention of going back to Moose Jaw. I'd brought enough provisions beyond those I'd left for the woman to see me through several more days on the road. If I could follow the Mounties' trail as far as the next settlement or lumber camp, where I could trade for more or at least hire a guide, I stood as good a chance of survival as came to a peace officer west of St. Louis and north of God. Game was plentiful, according to the rabbit and deer tracks and great cowlike prints left by elk that crisscrossed the trail. I wouldn't starve, although I'd miss the coffee when it ran out.

Vivian was right about snow coming. I'd grown up in mountain country, recognized that bitter-iron smell, and felt a fresh ache in my damaged ribs and in an old bullet wound I'd forgotten except when the weather was about to change sharply. I calculated I had about twenty-four hours before it came in hard enough to obliterate the trail and picked up my pace. The hide wrap was acutely uncom-

fortable in the saddle, but as it kept the cracked bones
from shaking the rest of the way apart on the trot I was
happy I had it.

I'd brought a map of western Canada I'd acquired in
Helena, full of blank spots and scratchy lines that might
have been rivers or marks made by hairs stuck to the car-
tographer's pen. Nearing dark I heard water chuckling and
decided I'd reached the north fork of the Saskatchewan
River. There was a Mountie post in that area, Battleford,
where Vivian's men would likely put in for the night, but
I could no longer see the trail. The energy I'd have to spend
looking for it was better invested crossing the river; ford-
able streams had a way of becoming torrents overnight,
adding days or weeks to a journey in the search for a place
to cross. I had just enough light to pick my way among the
rocks visible in the shallow bed, kneeing the reluctant sorrel and jerking at the lead line when the gray balked at
the icy water coursing past its fetlocks. Once on the opposite bank I dismounted quickly and built a fire with pine
needles and boughs for the horses to thaw their numb legs.
The air was bitter cold, and not cold enough; not far enough
below zero anyway to prevent snow from forming. I
smelled the air and changed my mind about my earlier estimate. The flakes would be falling by dawn.

I fed the horses, cooked bacon and beans in the skillet,
washed them down with coffee, and wrapped myself in my
furs and blanket, drawing down the badger hat until it
touched my collar and leaving no skin exposed. Sometime
during the night I heard the wind starting, whistling
through distant pines and coming my way with the speed
of a late freight racing to make up time on the downgrade.
By the time it got to the branches overhead it was howling.
I got up to feed the fire and ran right into the gray. Both
horses had moved in close, rumps to the wind. I stroked
and patted them to assure them I had things under control

and bundled myself up again to sleep the sleep of the innocent. There's no sin in lying to a horse.

I heard the first grainy flakes pelting my furs, then slid off into senselessness. When gray light woke me, the furs felt as if they weighed a hundred pounds. I raised my head and a shelf of snow avalanched down my neck, chilling me to the base of my spine. When I looked down, my body had disappeared. In its place was a white tent. I was a human snowdrift.

Pushing myself to my feet required both hands. It was like sliding out from under a cloak of lead. The stuff was still falling, if *falling* was the word; the wind hooted and the snow came in sideways, stinging my face like flung pebbles. I leaned into it, snapping my eyes open at intervals to see where I was going, then squeezing them shut, full of water, to keep the snow out. The fire had gone out long since, suffocated beneath a thick wet blanket.

The horses were huddled together for warmth. Snow clung to their coats and masks of hoarfrost encased their faces, made of their frozen breath with their eyes looking pitiably through the holes. I used the Deane-Adams to break up the ice, fed them each a handful of grain to start their blood flowing, shook the snow off my gear, and led them to the shelter of a tight stand of pines farther up the slope from the river. The snow was nearly waist high where the ground dished in. Inside the stand, where the trunks grew so close they made a sort of rick and acted as a drift fence, the earth was almost bare. I strapped on the horses' nose bags, opened a can of sardines with my knife, and sat down in a cradle formed by forked trunks to eat and wait out the worst of the storm. I couldn't build a fire for fear of loosening the snow in the treetops and creating a slide that would bury us all.

The blizzard broke shortly before noon. The last gunmetal-colored cloud slid across a hole in the trees like a window shade going up, exposing bright blue sky. The wind leveled off, then quit abruptly. The silence hurt my ears. When I stepped outside the pines, into a horseshoe of ankle-high snow left by the passage of wind around the dense stand, surrounded by towering drifts, the geography had changed completely from the night before. From one horizon to the other stretched a dazzling clean sheet of white. Even the trees were mere shadows beneath heavy clumps that bent them nearly to the ground, as if the wind together with the flinty abrasive grains had planed the landscape clear of everything vertical except the mountains, which stood impossibly high and aloof to heaven and earth. Sunlight walloped off the brutal white, blinding me like a photographer's magnesium flash. I was looking out at a white desert.

The trail I had been following was gone, utterly and forever. I went back, blacked my eyes from the can of lampblack, mounted the mustang, and led the gray out of the trees. The little sorrel had to raise its legs to its belly to gain leverage against the drifts. I rode it down the slope to the river and turned west. If there was a guide to be found who could lead me to Fort Chipewyan, I would find him near water. Failing that, I stood a better chance of having my remains discovered on the bank come the thaw than if I ventured across the vast blankness to the north. I couldn't have Judge Blackthorne thinking I'd welshed on our bet and deserted.

14

"**F**ils de la catin!"

The words, delivered in a loud, phlegmy baritone, carried a long way. I heard them, and those that followed, twenty minutes before I saw the cabin, a low dugout affair, built along the lines of a railroad car, with its roof heaped with snow. French was not my long suit, but I had heard enough of it during my travels in a frontier made up of expatriates from around the world to figure out, with the help of the vicious flood of language that came after, that someone or something was being called a son of a bitch.

As I drew near I made out the figure of a man standing atop what appeared to be a stack of corrugated-iron sheets at the end of the cabin, sunk up to his knees in snow and using a shovel to scoop the heavy white stuff off the surface and onto the ground eight feet below. The underarm movement was what I first noticed, because the heavy capote the man was wearing was the exact blue of the sky behind him. The hood was flung back to expose a fall of curly black hair to his shoulders and the glint of a piratical gold hoop in the lobe of his left ear. His diatribe, punctuated with grunts and short exhalations that issued from his mouth in bright silver jets, continued unabated as I came to the edge of the shadow the cabin threw in the late afternoon sun; I couldn't tell if he even knew I was there.

I was close enough then to realize he wasn't standing on iron sheets. My nose told me they were green buffalo hides, stiff with frozen gore. The mercury would have to go down a lot more to stop them from stinking.

"*Merde!*"

This last remark was accompanied by a flash of bright metal as the shovel skidded out of his hands, executed a somersault in the air, and knifed down blade first straight at me. I yanked the reins left, the sorrel leapt sideways, stumbling. Instinctively I leaned right to keep it from falling over left. This put me back in the path of the flying shovel, which glanced off my shoulder, ripping a long gash in the bearskin, and chunked solidly into the snow with the handle twanging. The pain arced around to my left side, just in time to connect with the one coming from my ribs. My whole body went into shock, but I managed to jerk the Evans rifle from its scabbard and point it at the man standing atop the hides.

"*Non!*" He spread his arms, showing his open palms. There was English mixed in with the flood of French that followed, but it came too fast for me to make it out. His tone said he was explaining or apologizing or both.

I didn't shoot him. He wasn't armed, and with the pain coursing through my body the effort of squeezing the trigger sounded like no fun. I let the hammer down gently.

"You are not injured, *monsieur*, no?" He lowered his arms.

"I am injured, yes," I said. "Climb down off those stinking skins."

He had the agility of a monkey. A narrow lodgepole stripped of its bark stood at each corner of the stack of hides and he gripped one in both hands and slid down slick as grease. I saw then that the poles had been erected to support a flat roof made of shakes to shelter the hides and that it had collapsed under the weight of the snow. He had been standing on what remained of the roof, shoveling it clear.

The little man—his chin came just above my knee where I sat aboard the mustang—saw that I was surveying the snow damage. "I am not so fine as a builder, monsieur. I am the hell of a fine hunter of the buffalo."

"I can see that." I scabbarded the Evans and probed at my shoulder through the tear in the bearskin. It was tender, but no blood came away with my hand. The blade hadn't broken the skin. "You're Métis?"

"Métis, *oui*." He lowered his eyelids. They were heavy to begin with, and along with the pencil-thin moustache that followed precisely the line of his delicately curved upper lip gave him the look of the lecherous villain in a melodrama on stage. His dusky features were more pretty than handsome. "You are Mounted Police, no?"

"I'm American. You're alone here?"

"My friends are near."

That was a lie. There wasn't another manmade structure in sight, and there was only one set of tracks between the cabin and the hide stack.

"I'm not a bandit," I said. "I'm a deputy United States marshal trailing a gang of desperadoes from Montana. Do you know the way to Fort Chipewyan?"

"I know the way. Also I know the way is long. You seek a guide, yes?"

His lids opened on the last part, light showing in his dark eyes. Buffalo butchering paid well, but it was brutal work and unless the operation was outfitted well enough to ferry the hides to civilization on a constant basis, paydays came many months apart. In guide work you got paid just to ride; and as everyone in Mexico and Canada was aware, Americans were all robber barons and rich as Vanderbilt.

I saw no reason to set him straight, but produced a leather sack containing the money I'd drawn from Judge Blackthorne for expenses. The heavy gold coins shifted and clanked when I bounced it on my palm. I tossed it at him without warning. He fumbled, then slapped it against his chest in both hands. While he was doing that I unholstered the Deane-Adams and rolled back the hammer.

"Take out a double eagle and throw the rest back. You get another one when we get to Chipewyan. Don't try to help yourself while I'm sleeping. I keep one eye open and my finger on the trigger."

He hesitated, hefting the sack. Then he shook his head and threw it back without taking a coin. I caught it one-handed—barely—and studied him closely. He was dressed colorfully after the fashion of the Métis; the capote open to expose a calico shirt and yellow buckskin leggings with a scarlet military sash knotted about his waist, fringed moccasins to his knees, but he was by no means prosperous or he wouldn't be living in a dugout with greased paper in the windows for glass and wrestling the hides off buffalo.

"I cannot, monsieur. It is ten days to Chipewyan, longer in this deep snow, and that much again to return. My wife and boy will starve." He looked ineffably sad, double eagles being scarce everywhere, and rare as jackalopes in that wild country. Then the lower half of his face broke into a gold-toothed smile. "They will not starve if they go with me."

"This is a manhunt, not a family picnic. We'll be traveling slow enough as it is."

"Fleurette rides as well as any man, and Claude can run like a rabbit and catch game with his bare hands. They will not slow us down."

"I'll keep looking. Where is the nearest settlement?"

"You'll not see another soul for two hundred miles. I am, you see, the court of last resort." The gold teeth shone.

"I don't see any horses."

"Down by the river there is a hollow in the bank with the overhang for a roof. I could not have built a better barn."

"What do they call you?"

"Philippe Louis-Napoleon Charlemagne Voltaire Murat du la Rochelle." He snapped his head forward in a bow, the hoop in his ear catching the light. "You may address me as Philippe."

"I think I'd better. Page Murdock." I leathered the pistol, drummed my fingers on my thigh, then braced myself for the pain and dismounted into the knee-deep snow. "Let's go meet the wife and child."

The inside of the cabin was surprisingly pleasant. We stepped down onto a glazed earthen floor and stood in the light from a fireplace built of river stones worn as smooth and round as forged cannonballs. The log walls were chinked expertly and hung with steelpoint engravings slit from periodicals and mounted in handmade frames. There were three split-bottom chairs, an oilcloth-covered table, a narrow bed built into one corner beneath a crucifix on the wall, and in the opposite corner a stand supporting a carved figure of the Virgin Mary with a squat tallow candle flickering in front of it.

A small woman in a plain gray dress stood on the hearth, stirring a pot suspended by chains over the flames. Her black hair was cut boyishly short, but when she turned to see who had come in, her face was as dark as any Indian's, darker than Philippe's. She had small sharp features and eyes that tilted toward her nose. Plainly she was the mother of the boy of about ten who sat on one of the chairs tying a shoe: short black hair, dusky skin, small pointed nose, and those eyes, almost Oriental and as shiny as polished obsidian. He wore a plain homespun shirt and trousers with nothing Indian about them. He showed no fear at the appearance of a stranger in his home, only quiet curiosity.

Philippe handled the introductions as if he were reading from a book of etiquette, presenting me to Fleurette and young Claude to me and repeating all our names. Fleurette, abandoning her cooking, surprised me by sinking into a quick curtsy. Claude kept his seat, studying me, until his father barked at him in French, whereupon he hopped to his feet and bowed from the waist.

"I ask you to pardon the behavior of my son, who seems determined to remain a savage." Philippe directed this at the boy with an edge in his voice.

There was nothing to say to that, so I unbuttoned my coat. It was close in the cabin. Claude raced up to take the bearskin and stood on tiptoe to hang it on a peg by the door. I hung the badger hat on the same peg and ran my fingers through my hair. I felt disheveled in the presence of so much domesticity. But for the logs and the plain furnishings and the buffalo robe on the floor, which probably served as the youngster's bed, I might have been standing in a parlor in Chicago. The place had that feel.

"You will eat with us." It was a thing settled, the way Philippe said it. "I hope you have no objection to squirrel."

"Thank you. I've eaten wolf and was glad I had it."

He laughed, loud and booming for a small man. "Someday I shall meet an American adventurer who has *not* eaten wolf. I begin to think you serve it at Easter. *Non, mais, non!* The head of the table." He pulled out a chair from the other side.

The table was square, and I could see no difference, but I came around and waited beside that chair while Fleurette brought the pot to the table and seated herself, her husband hastening over to hold her chair. He took the third.

I sat, and realized all the chairs were taken. "What about Claude?"

"When there is a guest he dines later. That is a rule of this house." As he spoke he stared at Claude. The boy turned away, stood on tiptoe again to slide a book from the fireplace mantel, and sat on the edge of the bed to read. When he opened the book I saw the title: *Wuthering Heights*.

Philippe saw where I was looking. "I traded a good robe in Battleford for a valise full of books last year. Claude is learning to read. He will not be illiterate like his mother and father."

"No one's teaching him?"

"An American missionary taught him to read and write his name. He can pick out the letters. The rest will fall into place with time."

"If his name is as long as his father's, he's got most of the alphabet already."

Philippe lifted the pot and ladled a steaming heap of meat, thick gravy, and what might have been chunks of wild onion onto my tin plate. When I smelled it, I realized I hadn't eaten since sardines for breakfast. He served his wife and himself, then lowered his head and spoke quietly in French. He and his wife crossed themselves and we dug in. The squirrel was as tender as aged beef and the pungent onions tamed the gaminess. Given more genteel ingredients, Fleurette could have been head chef in any hotel in St. Louis; except as a half-breed she'd have been barred at the door.

"You will pardon me while I explain our plans to my wife," Philippe said. "She is ignorant and does not understand English."

I told him to go ahead. Carefully he put down his spoon, a wise move because he gestured with both hands when he talked. It was not all French. Although I'd heard Sioux and Cheyenne and even a little Apache down in New Mexico, I wasn't familiar with most of the tribal dialects, but the throat action is similar among Indians everywhere and I assumed he was speaking Cree part of the time, or a mix of Cree and some French dialect no self-respecting Parisian would acknowledge as stemming from his language. Her responses—some of them seemed to be questions— were more Indian than French, but she had a low silken voice that sounded pleasant even when she was plainly upset by what her husband was saying. I didn't need to speak the language to know she was in favor of staying put. I heard Claude's name frequently; she didn't like the idea of exposing her son to what fate held in store for travelers in the Canadian wilderness.

Claude, I saw, was only pretending to read *Wuthering Heights*. Whatever her charms as a novelist, Emily Brönte's windblown moors didn't stack up to a frontier manhunt in a boy's imagination.

Abruptly, with a Gallic grunt and an outward slashing motion of his hands, Philippe put an end to the discussion. He turned to me with a deep flush showing beneath his dusky pigment. "It is all arranged, *monsieur le depute*. Madame du la Rochelle and young Master Claude will be enchanted to accompany us upon our great trek north."

He flinched when Madame du la Rochelle shot to her feet, but held my gaze as she snatched away our plates and utensils, marched to the wooden tub set beside the fireplace, and dumped them inside with a clatter. I had the thought then she wasn't entirely ignorant of English.

15

Women are impossible to feature. Being the man responsible for the prospect of Fleurette and her son traveling some four hundred miles through the dead of winter from the comfort and safety of their home, I expected little in the way of welcome. Instead I was forced to conduct a fierce argument through Philippe to persuade her to let me sleep that night in my own blankets rather than surrender the bed she shared with her husband. That was the Indian side of her nature coming through, as much as the female; tribal law since before Columbus dictated that not even a mortal enemy will be denied the full hospitality of the lodge when night fell.

I awoke at first light to the smell of baking. Fleurette had biscuits baking in a Dutch oven, with coffee boiling in a blackened pot. Philippe was sitting on the edge of the bed, scratching his scalp through his spill of tightly curled hair and yawning, with his hairless legs showing between the hem of his nightshirt and the rolled tops of heavy gray woolen socks like lumbermen wore. He stood and stretched, his joints popping like small-arms fire, then stripped off the nightshirt with no concern for his nudity or who saw it. He had the muscles of an athlete, egg-shaped and fluid, and an ugly pale oblong scar just below his right shoulder blade where a bullet had been removed years before, creating as always worse damage coming out than it had going in. I made a note to ask him about it as soon as my voice woke up; discretion went out the window when it came to the past of someone you were planning to pack along through raw country.

He dressed in the same calico shirt, leggings, and moccasins he'd had on the day before, shrugged into his ankle-length capote, and headed outdoors, presumably to visit the little slant-roofed outhouse behind the cabin. On the way to the door he nudged his son awake with a toe in the ribs. Claude, still dressed, rolled out of the buffalo robe on the floor and got woozily to his feet. He was no better outfitted for morning than I. I approved of him for that. Most of the world's wickedness is done by men who go to bed with the birds and wake up sharp as fangs.

When I put on my bearskin, I saw that the gash in the shoulder was repaired, the stitches so small and tight, I had to spread the hairs to locate them. I summoned all the French I had to tell Madame du la Rochelle *merci*.

"C'est bien a votre service, monsieur." She spoke in her smooth contralto while lifting the lid to inspect her biscuits. There was no rancor in her tone. The storm had passed. Living out there, she would be accustomed to resolution.

Steam rose from a chipped enamel basin set up on a chopping block outside the door, where Philippe had hung his capote on the protruding end of a log rafter, rolled up his sleeves, and begun washing his face and hands. I used the outhouse, replenished the water in the basin from a tall kettle standing in a melted hole in the snow, washed up, and while Claude was taking his turn in the outhouse I fed the horses and used my bowie to carve half a pound off the bacon I'd packed on the gray. This gift was met with a bright smile from Fleurette, whose bad teeth subtracted from her good looks, and very soon the smell of frying filled the little dugout. The biscuits were light, absorbing the tasty bacon grease like sponges, and the coffee was thick and strong, the way the French preferred it. I didn't, but it finished waking me up. I asked Philippe about the wound in his back.

"A remembrance of war, *monsieur le depute*. A Canada Firster shot me from the roof of the storehouse in Winnipeg during the Great Rebellion of '69." He crunched bacon.

"Canada Firster?"

"White Protestant whiskey swindlers from Ontario. When they were through getting the Cree drunk and cheating them of the land, they decided to form their own political party. Canada First, nobody second, including Indians, half-breeds, and Roman Catholics." He crossed himself. "We fought them. We lost. *Ce que c'est, que c'est.* What is, is."

"I hear there's another rebellion brewing."

"I have heard the same thing for twelve years. It may brew, but it must brew without Philippe. What fights I fight I fight for my family." He helped himself to a gulp of piping-hot coffee that would have scalded my throat.

I changed the subject. "What kind of country are we heading toward?"

"The worst, *monsieur le depute*. Blizzards, ice storms, vertical cliffs, hostiles, bandits, wolves, bear, puma, buffalo, moose. It is a mistake not to take the last two seriously. They are savage when surprised or when separated from their young. My wife's brother was crippled by a bull moose in Alberta three years ago." He lowered his voice on the last part, either forgetting or not trusting his statement that Fleurette knew no English. The woman herself, leaning over to wipe Claude's chin with her checked napkin, gave no sign that she understood.

I wiped my own mouth and pushed away my plate. "Let's get started."

The head of the house showed his gold teeth. "You are a man who thirsts for adventure, no?"

"Adventure thirsts for me. If I had my way I'd open a bank and die in my bed at the end of a safe and very dull life. But I'm no hand at arithmetic." I thanked Madame du la Rochelle for another fine meal and rose.

A nomadic Indian might have found fault with the length of time it took the Métis family to gather its gear, secure the homestead, and move out, but any single white man who had observed such an arrangement take place in civilization would have been greatly impressed. From the time Fleurette cleared the plates from the table until we were in the saddle, less than twenty minutes had slid away. This included the following exchange, when Philippe returned from the river leading an enormous dun draft-horse, twenty-two hands at the inside, with a milky eye and white all around its muzzle. It bore a wooden saddle like even no Indian mount had borne since Pizarro shipped home, with three brightly colored blankets beneath it to prevent the clumsy construction from rubbing bloody sores in the beast's hide.

"If you're planning on delivering a shipment of beer to Chipewyan," I said, "you're a little light on barrels."

Philippe grinned from the depths of his hood and stroked the great horse's neck. "King Henry is descended from the mighty steeds of Pepin's stable. He is built to carry eight hundred pounds of armor at full gallop."

"That will come in handy, if the war of the Roses comes back. What about that torture trap of a saddle?"

"I carved it myself from the best white pine. No other will fit his back."

As he spoke, he impressed me by hauling himself five feet from the ground into the wooden seat and pulled his wife one-handed into the space between him and the packs he had fixed behind the cantle. Fleurette hiked her skirts and rode astride, something no respectable white woman would consider; once aboard she looked as natural and dignified as any banker's wife at a charity social. She wore a gingham bonnet and a coarse woolen cloak that left her arms free to encircle her husband's waist.

"What will Claude ride?" I asked. The boy had on a pilot's cap with a shiny black sealskin visor, lace-up boots, and a capote like his father's that looked as if it had been cut down from an old garment to fit him.

Philippe curled his lip at the question. "I said the boy can run."

"All the way to Fort Chipewyan?"

"Even the horses cannot run that far. You Americans are always in a hurry."

We made thirty miles the first day, a feat I would scarcely have credited when we set out; but high winds had planed the snow flat across the tableland, and whenever I looked back, Claude was always the same distance behind, stepping inside the horses' hoofprints to avoid wallowing in the snow. His face was red—but from cold, not exertion. He was built wiry like his father and had a man's idea of how to pace himself. A single drop of Indian blood is strong enough to turn a bucket of white paint bright scarlet.

The second day we made even better progress. Yesterday's sun had melted some of the snow, and when the temperature plunged at night, it froze a crust strong enough to support even the gray and its packs, creating a pavement as hard and smooth as macadam. The weight of the big dun was too much for it, but the horse's hooves were as large as dinner plates and churned through the broken pieces of crust as if it were meringue. Claude broke into an occasional sprint across the sturdy surface, outdistancing us at times so that his father had to call him back to keep him from blundering into a grizzly or worse. Fleurette rode without complaint, speaking only when addressed by Philippe. Her general silence might have been interpreted as a protest, but I decided that she reserved the energy that might have gone into speaking for the journey. She had gone on record against the expedition, been vetoed, and left it at that. In unity lay survival.

Nights we pitched camp, built a fire, and watched Fleurette perform miracles with beans, bacon, and flour in my old skillet while Philippe hauled out a wooden flute no longer than a Sharps cartridge and played tunes going back to the first *coureurs de bois,* trappers and traders who blazed the original Canadian trails a century and more before.

"Runners-in-the-woods," he translated the term between tunes. "Pirates, *monsieur le depute,* trespassing upon territory claimed by the Hudson's Bay Company and the Indians with whom the company traded. Death awaited them from the natives, from whose children's mouths the *coureurs* stole food whenever they pulled in their traps; death awaited them from the company when they blundered into traders. However, one can die but once. They had nothing to lose, and so they went where no white man had gone before. But for them, the whole of Canada would be an empty white smear on the map, populated by dragons and savages with two heads. Ironic, is it not, that I, who am descended from these visionary brigands, should find myself guiding an expedition to bring to justice a band of rogues not unlike them?" He tapped the flute against the sole of one moccasin to clear it of spittle.

"Only if the *coureurs* were in the habit of murdering women and children and burning settlements to the ground for sport," I said.

"A valid point. Those were the tactics of the Hudson's Bay Company."

Claude, seated cross-legged by the fire, looked up briefly

from *Wuthering Heights*, then returned to his reading. He had walked and run seventy miles in two days and looked as if he had just finished playing outdoors.

I drank coffee. I was becoming accustomed to the thick strong brew, which seemed to draw the pain from my damaged ribs like whiskey. "When do we reach the next settlement?"

"Three days, if this weather holds." Philippe ran a brown finger along the rim of his delicate moustache. "I would go around it, monsieur."

I remembered what Inspector Vivian had told me in his office in Moose Jaw of the territory beyond the north fork of the Saskatchewan. "Shulamite?"

He nodded. He seemed impressed by my information but too polite to inquire after its source. "It is, perhaps, the first community founded entirely by former slaves since Moses wandered the desert. Needless to say they are not friendly to white Americans."

"This white American fought for the Union."

"Ah, but they know their history. That war was not fought to end slavery, but to establish the authority of Washington City."

"If Bliss and Whitelaw passed near there, would they know it?"

"The wilderness is not a desert, monsieur. It is filled with the noise of life. When strangers pass through it, they create disturbances in the noise, like a stick dragged across the current of a swift stream. That is the natural reality. Beyond that, the woman to whom Shulamite looks for leadership is said to possess second sight. It would not surprise me to learn that she knows of us three already." He studied me from beneath his heavy lids. "It is possible you do not believe in this?"

"The older I get the less I know what I believe. But if

this woman has news of Bliss and Whitelaw, I need to talk to her."

"I would be of no assistance in this. Many of their grandfathers were sold to the slave traders by others of their own tribe. The color of one's skin is no guarantee of safe passage."

"If you'll lay out the route, I'll be on my way and send you home. You have a family to protect."

"They will spare us, I think. I would not be a good guide if I did not warn you of the danger to yourself."

"Thank you. I need to talk to the woman."

"In that case, perhaps you would consider giving me that second double eagle now."

I surprised him by producing the leather sack and handing him one of the gold cartwheels. He balanced it upon his palm as if weighing it. Then he gave it to Fleurette, who bit it, studied the result in the firelight, and consigned it to a pocket in the lining of her cloak. Then she returned to her cooking. Philippe lifted his tin cup.

"*Mes compliments,*" he said. "It is a rare wise man who accepts his own mortality."

"One can die but once," I said.

16

"**M**onsieur le depute, I cannot impress upon you too strongly the need for absolute silence."

Philippe's whisper was warm in my ear. I nodded. He lowered his cupped hands then and leaned back into his wooden saddle, wincing when it creaked slightly. He had said nothing to Fleurette riding behind him or Claude standing up to his calves in snow by King Henry's woolly left flank. The boy's labored breath—he had been running—clouded thickly around his head. Both kept silent.

A brush fire had scalped five or six hundred acres of trees sometime within the past year. Crossing that bald country, we had topped a rise overlooking a stream where the forest resumed abruptly. At the base of the hill, standing hock deep in icy water, an enormous shaggy moose raised its head and looked our way, twitching nostrils as big as hen's eggs. Its heavy coat, deep red-brown streaked with black, stretched taut over raw, unfinished muscles that put me in mind of exposed machinery. A ragged beard like a buffalo bull's hung from its chin, shallow beneath the long curved snout and streaming water, and its shovel-shaped antlers spread six feet. The beast would have dressed out at twelve hundred pounds easily—if one could picture its ever placing itself in that position.

Its black eyes, small and almond shaped in nests of wrinkles like an old Indian's, were fixed on the mounted strangers staring at it; but it must have trusted its nose before its eyesight, because after two or three minutes—or hours, take your pick—the great head swung back around and it waded on across the stream slowly and gracefully, mounted the opposite bank with an elegant hop, shook itself with a grunt that reverberated among the trees on that side, and slid in among them without ever looking back. The impression remained that it was aware of us the whole time but didn't estimate us highly enough for hurry.

Thirty more seconds crawled past, then Philippe let out his breath. "A near thing," he said. "The moose, he does not like surprise."

The ground shook suddenly, heavily enough to vibrate up to the seats of our saddles. The great bull crashed out of the brush, pounded down the bank, and smashed into the water, charging straight at us. It raised its head just once, opening its pink mouth with a bawling roar, then lowered its muzzle, nodding as it ran, the huge antlers tipped fully our way like the icebreaker on a snow train. My mustang nickered shrilly and tried to back up, hunching its shoulders to buck when I pulled the reins tight. Out of the corner of my eye I saw the big dun lift its head and look alert for the first time.

Philippe's weapon was a single-shot Springfield carbine he wore slung behind his shoulder. He unlimbered it, but not before I slid the Evans from its scabbard and, squeezing the mustang with my knees, nestled my cheek against the stock and drew a bouncing bead on the broad space between the moose's eyes. The head kept bobbing and I missed the first shot. The Springfield boomed just after; the moose stumbled, found its footing on the near bank, and continued its charge up the slope with a stream of blood glittering between the bunched muscles of its chest.

That was it for the Springfield. The mustang screamed and twisted away from the onrushing beast. I turned in the saddle, drew a fresh bead, and fired, racking and firing again and again without pausing to see where the slugs were going. I fired a dozen times, the smoke of my own fire obscuring the target, but I squeezed three more into the haze. I heard a grunt like a boulder falling onto soft earth. When the smoke thinned, the moose was on its knees ten feet in front of us, struggling to rise, its antlers tilting right and left with the effort. I took aim again, but by this time Philippe had reloaded. The Springfield boomed, the great head swung around and up with a snap, and dashed to the ground. The shoulders bunched twice as if the will to stand up had outlived the animal itself; then the body sagged on over. One rear leg kicked twice, bent to kick again, and settled into the snow.

The echo of our shots walloped around among the trees for a long time, then growled away like far thunder and died with a hiss.

"*Mon dieu!*" breathed Philippe.

I couldn't think of anything to improve on that.

The moose's musky odor reached us, a swampy stench of heavy sweat and tremendous heat. It did nothing to calm the mustang, and I bailed out, leaning back against the reins when I hit the ground. I fought it for twenty feet until my foot found a burned-over stump under the snow, and I took a hitch around it, knotting it tightly beneath a knob where the grain twisted. Then I retraced my steps to where King Henry stood calm as Sunday with nobody on his back and his reins on the ground. All three du la Rochelles had gathered around the fallen hulk, where Philippe knelt with a butchering knife, carving a chunk out of its coarse-haired rump.

"By Mary, but I wish we were near home," he said. "We would eat for a month."

I said, "You wouldn't have any teeth left at the end of it."

"But you have not tried moose. The meat melts like lard

upon your tongue. Afterward the strength of the beast passes into you."

"What made him charge like that? He was safe on his way."

"Who can say? He was an old bull, many times the victor. See those scars upon his shoulders? They are made by the antlers of other bulls who envy his station. One does not survive such a battle unless he who left them perishes. 'This river, and everything you see,' he says perhaps, 'is mine. I shall not share it.' *Un bâtard magnifique,* this fellow. A magnificent bastard." He patted its side. It sounded like someone slapping a drum. "It is a heroic thing to live and die upon one's own terms."

Fleurette said something in which I caught the word *imbecile*. During the quarrel that followed I thought again that she took in far more than she let on.

I noticed Claude then, on his knees in the snow beside the huge carcass, stroking the long stiff hairs that covered its neck. I had yet to hear the boy speak in any language, and wondered if he was mute.

At length, having harvested some steaks and gone inside for the great quivering liver, Philippe packed them securely behind his pine cantle and we crossed the stream, upwind of the moose to mollify the little snake-faced sorrel. The gray, which had stopped below the rise, had neither seen nor smelled anything to upset it, and had held its ground when I let go of the line to wrestle with the mustang. I'd begun to wish I'd traded for another saddle horse when I bought the gray.

After we'd ridden a mile, Philippe asked me how many times I'd fired at the moose.

"Fifteen."

He thought about that for another twenty or thirty yards. "Hadn't you better reload? There is more than one moose in Canada—and many grizzly."

"I still have eighteen in the magazine."

That kept him silent for a quarter mile.

"This is truly a magical weapon, monsieur," he said then. "What is it called?"

"Evans repeater. They quit making it a couple of years back."

"I should not wonder. A shopkeeper would die of loneliness waiting for a customer to return for more ammunition." He touched his moustache. "I have a cured buffalo robe of unusually fine quality I have been saving. It would bring as much as two hundred dollars in Ottawa. Would you consider trading your Evans repeater for this robe?"

"The gun isn't worth two hundred. When a part wears out you can't replace it."

"I am not without ingenuity in these matters. Will you trade?"

"I may look you up when this is over."

He uncorked his golden grin. "I cannot guarantee this offer will hold, *monsieur le depute*. When this is over there may not be as much need for a rifle that shoots thirty-three times without reloading. The market is, how you say, not stable."

"Thirty-four," I said. "I discharged a round at an escaping prisoner in Montana."

"The robe, monsieur."

"I'd consider it a favor if you stopped calling me monsieur. Deputy Murdock will do, or Murdock if you're in a hurry. The other makes me want to order frog legs in St. Louis."

"I did not intend to commit offense. I await your decision, Deputy Murdock."

"I'll have to see the robe."

"It is in a cedar chest in my cabin."

"In that case I may look you up when this is over."

"You do not trust me, Deputy Murdock?"

I shook my head. "Too many gold teeth."

"*Fils de la catin.*" He spoke beneath his breath.

"I understand a little French," I said.

"I felt certain you did, Deputy Murdock." He put his heels to the big dun and cantered out ahead. Claude sprinted to keep up on foot.

The sun was two hands above the horizon and still yellow when Philippe drew rein and said we would camp.

"Getting tired?" I asked. "We've got another half hour of daylight."

"That would put us too close, *monsieur le*"—he corrected himself—"Deputy Murdock." He swung down and gave Fleurette his hand to help her out of the saddle.

"Too close to what?"

"Shulamite. Those settlers have lived here for a generation; they can smell strangers an hour away. We do not want to come upon them without sufficient light to defend ourselves."

"The night's as dark for them as it is for us."

"I will not argue. You have hired me to guide you. If you will not accept this guidance, I will return to you your double eagles and leave you to your fate. Perhaps the wolves will have left me a portion of that moose."

"You ought to write ten-cent dreadfuls, Philippe. Your talent's wasted in this rough country." But I stepped out of leather and went back to unpack the gray.

We built a small fire to avoid attracting undue notice, and Fleurette cooked the moose, which was as good as Philippe had said. After supper, he produced his wooden flute and stretched one leg to jostle his son, who was dozing over his book, with the toe of his moccasin. "'Ma Petit Marie,' Claude, eh?"

Instantly the boy was awake, his sunburned face bright

with anticipation. He listened to his father tootling the opening bars of some bright tune I had never heard, lips moving slightly as if he were counting the beats, then opened his mouth and sang, in a pure, clean soprano:

> *Au printemps,*
> *l'été, l'automne,*
> *et passer par tous l'hiver,*
> *je promene la ruelle*
> *avec ma petit Marie.*

When the song was finished, Philippe barked a short laugh of Gallic pride, leaned forward, and, taking Claude by his ears, pulled him close and kissed him on both cheeks. When he let go with a push, the boy nearly fell over on his back. His father turned his bright dark eyes on me.

"A *protégé,* is he not? If we but lived in Paris, he would be the toast of a continent."

"*Et pas Métis,*" put in his wife.

"*Oui.*" Philippe nodded, the brightness fading. "And were we not Métis."

"I'd made up my mind the boy couldn't speak," I said.

"There is no need for speech when one can sing like the angels."

"Angels you all be, iffen you don't keep still."

This was a new voice, harsh and deep, and belonged to a scarecrow figure that had materialized against a night sky made pale by starshine reflected from the snow. The figure itself was dead black, as if it were gathered from the darkness the sky had surrendered. For punctuation, an angular elbow straightened and bent with a jerk, accompanied by the crisp metallic crackle of a shell jacking into the chamber of a lever-action carbine.

17

We remained quiet. Not even Fleurette made so much as a gasp. We kept our places around the fire and watched as another figure, this one shorter and broader, joined the first, and then a third came into the group, all armed with rifles and carbines. At length an arc of orange light crept above the bulge where they stood, and rose like a miniature dawn swinging from a bail in the hand of a fourth party who appeared to carry no weapons. The lantern painted glistening stripes along the long guns' oiled barrels and made ovals of the facial features beneath the floppy brims of the newcomers' hats. I was not much surprised to find they were black faces, male and grim as open graves.

"This the bunch, Brother Enoch?" asked the man with the lantern. His voice was a gentle rumble, oddly soothing.

Enoch, evidently the scarecrow who had appeared first, stirred himself. But the question was answered by a fifth man who slid out of the shadows on the other side of our camp; a man nearly as large as all the others put together, who made no noise at all when he walked. He carried a full-length Sharps big-bore rifle that looked like a boy's squirrel gun in his huge hands.

"There's only three horses," he said. His voice was light for his size.

The man with the lantern nodded. "I'll have your weapons. Take them out slowly and throw them into the light."

I unholstered the Deane-Adams between thumb and forefinger and flipped it onto the ground near his feet. Philippe slid the Springfield carbine from beneath his blankets and tossed it after. I had my Winchester leaning against my saddle, which I was using for a backrest, and the Evans lying alongside. I added them to the pile.

"The woman and the boy are unarmed, monsieur," Philippe said.

The lantern came up a little, spreading its light over Philippe's face. "You Métis?" The rumbling tones smoothed out another notch.

"*Oui.* Yes. The woman is my wife and the boy is my son."

Now the lantern swept slowly across the others and stopped. I squinted against the glare.

"Who's this, your brother?" Now there was nothing soothing about the man's speech.

I'd been working on a number of answers to just that question since the moment I'd made my decision to stop at Shulamite, but I discarded them all in favor of the truth, which required less effort to maintain. "The name is Murdock," I said. "I'm a deputy United States marshal in pursuit of a gang of fugitives wanted in Montana Territory."

Enoch took in his breath with a little rattle, like a snake's. I got the impression then he was consumptive. That would explain his thinness. In the lantern light the skin of his face barely covered the bone. "I knowed he was some kind of law. They all gots that mean look."

"Any of these fugitives happen to be black?" asked the man with the lantern.

"Not that I know of. One of the leaders is half Mexican. The other's Cherokee."

"That sounds mighty like a description of Lorenzo Bliss and Charlie Whitelaw."

"You've seen them?" I asked.

The man with the lantern shook his head. "Read about them. Brother Enoch goes to Fort Chipewyan once a month for needs and possibles. He brings back the Ottawa newspapers when the Mounties are through with them. Does it surprise you to learn a black man can read?" There was no hostility in his tone. The words carried all that was necessary.

"Some of the places I've lived I was surprised to meet a white man who could. We all have the same opportunities."

He laughed then, loudly, deeply, and entirely without amusement. Then he stopped. His face more than the others' was a mass of ovals, turned this way and that to represent nose, cheeks, forehead, and chin, as if it were assembled from identical machine parts, with each part moving independently of the rest. When he spoke and laughed, only his mouth moved. When he registered curiosity or surprise, his forehead shifted upward like a type-writer carriage. "It's a good thing you didn't lie about where you came from, Marshal. Only a white American could say what you just said without spitting."

"I didn't mean to offend."

That brought about the shift of the forehead mentioned above. He could tell I hadn't said it just because he held my life in his hands. "My name is Hebron," he said. "I am the elected leader of the free African community of Shulamite, of which these four gentlemen comprise the Committee of Public Vigilance. I am telling you this so you don't take the idea you've been unlawfully abducted. You are all under arrest and will come with us."

"What's the charge?" I asked.

His mouth formed a smile, again without amusement. "In your case, trespassing while white. These others are your aides and abetters."

"Will there be a trial?"

"Possess your soul in patience, Marshal. All things will be known in the fullness of God's time."

I'd attended church often enough to take that to mean he didn't know the answer to the question.

The men formed a circle around us with their rifles and carbines at hip level while we saddled up and I untied the packs from the tree where I'd hoisted them out of the reach of bears and wolves and secured them on the gray. Hebron insisted that Claude ride behind me on the mustang so they could keep an eye on him. Ropes were produced and Philippe's hands and mine were tied to our saddle horns. The big man, whose name was Brother Babel, brought the men's horses—older mounts mostly, some as old as King Henry, but well fed and groomed to a high shine—and without awaiting instructions the riders split into escort formation, three in back and two in front, the leaders taking charge of our reins while one of the men at the rear led the gray. Four of them rode bareback, but I noticed that Hebron straddled a McClellan. That—and the way he rode, back straight and elbows in—suggested cavalry experience. That explained the formation, which came right out of the section on prisoners in the manual of arms; I'd used pages torn from it to light fires during the winter of 1863.

I don't know why—never having seen one outside of a framed lithograph hanging on a wall in Judge Blackthorne's private study—but whenever I'd thought about Shulamite I'd pictured a walled city, with or without a moat to repel invaders. But there was nothing medieval or even forbidding about the scatter of log buildings that greeted us as we followed the long gentle slope to the S-shaped river at its base, the buildings black against the snow,

with lighted windows hanging among them like pinecones. It might have been any settlement of trappers or
miners, carved from the evergreen forests that surrounded it, with a large meeting hall standing more or less
in its center and a watchtower affair built like a derrick
with a roofed platform for spotting Indians and fires.

Hebron drew rein fifty yards short of the riverbank, raising one hand for the others to do the same. Enoch, seated
to his right, lifted his carbine from across his lap—I saw
now it was a Spencer—pointed it skyward, and fired. The
echo of the report was still snarling in the distance when
a puff of smoke answered from the high platform, followed
closely by the crack of a rifle. Hebron's hand came down
then and we crossed the river. The water was just fetlock
high, but there were ice shards glittering in the current and
I had to kick the sorrel twice before it would step off the
bank. I knew by the sound of its snort as it made contact
with the water that I would pay later. King Henry, the big
dun of chivalric stock, crossed without protest.

The buildings were laid out in two ragged rows alongside a rude street, bare of snow and ringing like iron beneath the shoes of the horses. I saw heads silhouetted in
the windows, but no one came out, as might normally be
expected in a remote settlement when strangers entered.
The man in the tower, outlined against the square of sky
between the roof and the platform, turned as we rode past,
the barrel of his rifle following us like the head of a coiled
snake. I felt uncommonly white. I had experienced that
same sensation years before, when I had entered a hostile
Cheyenne village as the captive of the chief; but even on
that occasion, the warriors and their women had stepped
outside their lodges to stare at me, and packs of nonde-
script yellow dogs had come trotting alongside to yip and
snap at my heels. Of all the places I had visited, of my own
free will and otherwise, Shulamite alone met me with only

silence. I thought that if someone would take a shot at me I'd welcome the variety.

At length we stopped before the big meeting hall, if that's what it was, and Hebron handed Enoch King Henry's lead and stepped down and tied his slat-sided chestnut to the hitching rail in front. A shallow flight of steps made from half-sawn logs led to a porch that ran the length of the building, but unlike similar porches on ranch houses across the American West this one contained no rockers or gliders or anything else to indicate that the porch was used for anything other than to keep rain and snow off whoever crossed to the door. Hebron knocked at the door, waited, then went inside.

My fingers were numb, either from the cold or from the tightness of the ropes binding my wrists. I asked Enoch if I could step down while we were waiting. He didn't answer or even turn his head to show he'd heard. He coughed a little—the phlegmy, hollow-lunged cough of the consumptive—but it wasn't intended as a response. He hadn't spoken since Hebron had made his appearance.

In a little while the door opened again and Hebron stepped out. In the light coming from the window on either side he was a middle-built man of about my age, with a black goatee trimmed close to his chin, a broad mouth, and sad eyes—or eyes anyway that didn't appear to expect much beyond more of what they'd already seen. He wore, in addition to the floppy farmer's hat that seemed to be a uniform among his group, a sheepskin coat with the fleece turned in, heavy woolen trousers stuffed into the tops of high lace-up boots like lumbermen wore, a flannel shirt, and a broad belt with a U.S. Army buckle, which backed up my supposition about his cavalry training. All of these items had seen their share of wear—scuffed, faded, torn, and patched—but they were clean and well kept, the belt and boots shining with oil and the brass buckle polished. Whatever the nature of his service was, it had taken.

He had been wearing leather gauntlets, which he had taken off inside. He seemed to realize he was still holding them and stuffed them into his belt. Then he pointed at me. "The others can wait. She wants to see you."

"Who does?" I asked.

He showed surprise for the first time, edged with contempt for my ignorance.

"Queen Fidelity," he said. "Who else would *she* be?"

18

Enoch dismounted and used a narrow-bladed knife of Indian manufacture to slice through the ropes on my wrists. I worked my fingers and when the pins and needles went away gripped the horn and swung down to the ground. Hebron, who still showed no weapons, stepped aside from the door, motioning me to enter ahead of him. I climbed the steps and obeyed.

The interior of the lodge—it was too big to call a cabin—was darker than outdoors, lit only by scattered candles and a hurricane lamp suspended from the rafters by a rope smeared with glistening tar. As my eyes adjusted I made out the oblong shapes of long trestle tables arranged in rows on either side of the door with a wide aisle leading between them to the back. The room was apparently a combination meeting place and dining hall; the odor of roasted meat and old grease was too strong to have come from just the tallow candles.

At the end of the aisle, the head of a moose at least as large as the one Philippe and I had shot, but whose antlers spanned a good eight feet, decorated the wall above a door cut from the boards that surrounded it. The reflected glow of the room's tiny flames in the glass eyes, and the crawling play of shadows, made the head seem as if it were still alive. Knowing that it wasn't didn't do a thing to prevent my stomach from tying itself into a clammy knot.

I followed Hebron to the end of the aisle, where he tapped softly on the door. There was a muffled response from the other side. He took off his hat, exposing a receding hairline of tight curls with silver glittering in them, and jerked his chin. I understood and removed my badger headpiece. The great room was unheated; dank cold touched my scalp. He pulled open the door and once again stood aside for me to go through first. I did so, and was blinded by the light.

I had been to St. Louis, where the finer homes, hotels, and saloons were lit by gas, bright as day where the proprietors were not overly concerned with the cost. None of these establishments was brighter than this room. Candles of every shape and size—some tall, thin, and aristocratic, others short and squat as toads, still others carved into human silhouettes—burned on trays and in jars on pedestals and shelves and along a narrow raised platform against the far wall, dripping wax onto the black cloth that covered the last, filling the place with light and the smell of hot wax; no tallow here. The smoke rose and roiled around among the rafters, which like those in the great hall were fifteen feet above the floor, with no ceiling to contain the heat. Even so the room was warm enough from just the candles to make me unbutton the bearskin I was wearing. The walls were undecorated, bare logs with a window on either side covered by more black cloth. The room was less than half the size of the other, which made it plenty spacious, but the atmosphere was as oppressive as if I were standing in an airtight closet. It made my skin crawl and made me drowsy at the same time. It was well past midnight, but the effect would be the same at high noon. In here the sun would rise and fall without notice or importance.

The least impressive thing about the room was the old woman who sat in a spindle-backed rocker in front of the platform, a shrunken Negress with a cap of white hair wrapped in a worn and ragged shawl, a thick steamer rug draped over her knees and hanging down to cover her feet. Her face was as brown and wrinkled as a shriveled apple and showed no life beyond a pair of rimless spectacles whose thick lenses seemed to gather the light from the candles. When she moved her head slightly, the flash raked my eyes as if someone had swept a bull's-eye lantern across them. Apart from that she might have been carved from the same wax as the candles, and beginning to melt from the heat.

A stretch of silence went by, during which I heard a thousand wicks burning. When she opened her mouth to speak, I saw the pink of her gums. She had no teeth.

"What is your name?"

"Murdock."

She shook her head, semaphores flashing off her spectacles. "What is your *Christian* name?"

She pronounced the *h* in *Christian* and flicked her tongue off the floor of her mouth on the *r*. She had not learned English in America or Canada.

"Page."

She repeated the name silently, her lips touching on the *p*. Her hands moved then, sliding a small book bound in tattered black cloth from beneath the rug that covered her lap. It might have been a pocket Bible. Tissue-thin pages slithered between fingers as wrinkled as ill-fitting gloves. She moved her lips as she read. Finally she looked up, adjusting her glasses.

"A name of French derivation. I assume you know what it means."

It wasn't a Bible. "My father told me my grandfather was through using it."

"It means 'attendant on a noble.' Which noble do you attend?"

"That would be Judge Blackthorne." When she went on staring at me without response I said, "Harlan Blackthorne."

Pages slithered.

"Prussian. 'From the land of warriors.' This is appropriate?"

"Oh, yes, ma'am."

"My name is Queen Fidelity. You will address me by my full name at all times."

"What does it mean?"

"'Faithfulness.' I assure you it is appropriate." She put the book—and her hands—back under cover. "Brother Hebron, see that the three people who accompanied Page Murdock are made comfortable."

Hebron said, "I'll tell Brother Enoch."

"See to it yourself. I wish to have a private audience with Page Murdock."

"That's not a good idea."

A cross of white light leapt off the spectacles. "Your opinion of my ideas is of no interest to me. Move them into Chapter Six."

"That's my cabin!"

"I said I wish them to be comfortable."

The silence that followed was twice as long as the first. No two buffalo bulls ever butted heads with more determination. Hebron blinked first. The door closed softly behind him.

"The people of Shulamite are former slaves and the sons and daughters of slaves," she said when we were alone. "It is a small community now. Most of the original settlers returned to America after emancipation. Those who voted to remain did so because they would not reconcile with a nation that would allow this monstrous evil to exist for two hundred and forty years. They are at war with the United States."

"They're short on manpower if they mean to make any kind of fight."

"It is a defensive war. They do not invade. They slay invaders."

"I fought for the Union."

"You fought for the Union. You did not fight to end slavery."

"It's the same thing."

She touched her spectacles. I was a difficult student. "All the other civilized nations volunteered to abandon the practice of taking and keeping slaves without having to shed blood over the issue. It took a war to show you the evil, and even then you fought only because you were attacked."

"You don't know that about me."

"Nor do they." She spread her hands, showing the pale palms. "For four years the enemy wore gray. Now they must go by skin alone."

"You consider that fair?"

"They did not set the precedent. You did."

It was like arguing with that warrior Judge Blackthorne.

"What about my friends?"

"Your friends are Métis. The free African community of Shulamite is not at war with the native peoples of the Dominion of Canada. They will be free to go in the morning. Tonight they are guests."

"And me?"

"Your fate is in the hands of Brother Hebron and the Committee of Public Vigilance. I never interfere with them unless I am invited."

"Aren't you their leader?"

"Brother Hebron is their leader, with the assistance of the committee. I advise the residents of Shulamite upon spiritual matters only. I am *mambo* here."

"Mambo?"

"Priest, healer, exorcist, sayer of the sooth. I also organize public entertainments and train the choir. We have a soprano who shows promise for the spring planting services if his testicles do not drop before then."

She sounded exactly like the Reverend Royden Milsap of the First Presbyterian Church in Helena.

"You're a preacher," I said.

"I am *mambo.*"

"Christian?"

She shook her head. *"Voudoun."*

My ignorance must have showed on my face, because she opened her mouth in a toothless pink grin I can still see when I close my eyes.

"Voodoo," she said.

19

"**B**rother Hebron will take you to your quarters."

It was a dismissal—and a disappointment. In view of her late announcement of her religious denomination, her own disappearance in a puff of green smoke would have been more appropriate.

I left Queen Fidelity alone with her book of names and found Hebron waiting for me in the gloom of the great hall. His mood went with the atmosphere. He didn't take to having been turned out like some kind of servant, particularly with me as a witness. He made no remark as he escorted me back down the front steps and, accompanied by the members of the Committee of Public Vigilance, across a stretch of snow-covered field as flat as a parade ground to a tiny building constructed of the same pine logs as all the rest, with a slant roof and no windows. The moon had risen and the entire settlement was lit as brightly as at noon.

The door was secured with a plain block of wood that turned on a nail. Enoch turned it straight up and down and the door fell open on leather hinges. Hebron relieved one of the others of the lantern he had been carrying earlier and waited for me to go in first.

The inside smelled dankly of decaying wood. When Hebron entered with the lantern I saw that it was a storage building for rakes and hoes and a wicked-looking scythe like the one Death carried in fanciful illustrations in the copies of the *New York Herald* that arrived at Judge Blackthorne's chambers once a month in bales. Bushel baskets nested inside one another in one corner, and jars of nails and square bottles of horse liniment lined a shelf built across the back wall. Even without the clutter there would have been barely enough room for Hebron and me both to stand inside. Brother Babel would have poked out a log with an elbow the first time he had an itch to scratch.

"Lean back against that wall and fold your arms across your chest."

I did as directed, using the only wall that wasn't supporting some piece of long-handled equipment. He hung the lantern on a nail, gathered a double armload of tools, and thrust them through the door at Enoch, who turned his head toward Babel, the biggest man in the group—in *any* group—who stepped forward to take them.

That exchange told me most of what I needed to know about Brother Enoch. A second-in-command who passed the menial work on to others wasn't planning to remain second-in-command forever. I wondered if having figured that out was going to do me any good.

Hebron looked at the bushel baskets and the jars and liniment, decided apparently that they were harmless in my possession, and gave me the presidential stare.

"You'll sleep here tonight. I wouldn't advise anything bold and reckless, like trying to kick your way through the door. You and the door will both be shot full of holes at the first blow. I won't lose any sleep over you, but making and hanging a new door takes time and it's already a twenty-four-hour-a-day job bringing a settlement this size through the winter." He stuck a foot outdoors.

"Can I trouble you for my bedroll?" The floor was bare earth and frozen hard as stone.

He considered the question. He was a thinking leader. I'd heard that was what had cost Jefferson Davis the Confederacy.

"I'll see what I can do. This ain't the Palmer House."

That was the first chink that had opened in his carefully constructed English. He saw that I noticed and if a black man can flush I swear that's what happened. "Mind what I said about those guards."

Once again I caught him on the fly. "What will they do to me that won't be done tomorrow anyway?"

"You don't know that. Neither do we. We'll decide tonight. In any case I never knew a man who wouldn't put it off until later if he could."

He left, taking the lantern with him. The door thumped shut and the block of wood squeaked into place. I was alone in the darkest place I had ever been.

I stood my fur collar up against the dank cold and explored my options.

I groped for one of the square bottles and pulled the cork with my teeth. The sharp fumes stung my nostrils and made my eyes water. I dug out the little oilcloth bundle I kept in a pocket, removed a match, struck it against the rough bark on a log, and touched it to the bottle's thick rim. A blue flame flickered.

I blew it out, stuck the cork back in, and returned the liniment to the shelf. If I splashed the contents over the wall at the back of the building and set the logs afire, the flames just might have burned through before dawn, by which time I'd have choked to death from the smoke. Even if I survived and got past the guards, I'd have to make my way to a horse, and since I had no firearms or provisions, the Canadian wilderness would only finish what the flames and the guard would have started. I pocketed the matches and sat down on the skirts of my coat with my back against the wall and my knees drawn up to my chest for warmth.

The building wasn't big enough for me to stretch out even if I'd wanted to.

When the door came open it startled me from a doze. I didn't know how long I'd been out. Hebron was back with the lantern and my bedroll.

"Don't get up." He hung up the one, tossed the other on the ground, and upended one of the stout bushel baskets to serve as a stool. When he sat down and pushed his hat back with a knuckle, he appeared more relaxed than he had since we'd met. He looked at me with the machinery of his thoughts working behind his face. Then he unbuttoned a pocket on his flannel shirt and drew out a leadfoil pack of ready-made cigarettes and a box of matches.

He held out the pack. I shook my head. "I never got the habit."

He speared one between his lips and set fire to it. He counted the cigarettes remaining in the pack before he put it away.

"I've had good reasons to wish I'd done the same," he said. "No matter how careful I am about it I always run out a week or so before one of us makes the monthly trip to Fort Chipewyan for supplies. Some winters the month between runs ninety days. Then there's the cost."

"I never heard anyone who uses tobacco complain about the price."

"That's three cents a pack that could be spent on candy for the children. Life up here is hard for the small ones. It's like burning up the one thing they might have to look forward to."

"Cheaper to buy the makings and roll your own."

He let the cigarette droop and held out his hands. The palms were shiny with callus and the knuckles were swollen as big as walnuts. I understood then why he didn't carry a gun; he'd have had to file off the guard to get one of those fingers close to the trigger.

"Rolling your own requires dexterity. I took rheumatism cutting cane in Mississippi for fifteen years. Some days I can't bend my hands around a pick handle."

I didn't say anything to that. The lantern was putting out heat, but the air inside the building felt as cold as it had at the start. He was being too friendly. Anyone can manage to work up affection for the soon-to-be extinct. Sometime while I was asleep a decision had been reached.

"How long have you been behind a badge?" he asked me then.

"Coming on six years."

"I guess a man has to be able to take care of himself to hang on so long in that line. Deputies especially; they get all the muddy work. I know a little about that. I was a sergeant with the Tenth Cavalry."

"I figured something on that order. I rode cavalry during the war."

"I was infantry then. Thirty-sixth Colored. I was among the first to sign on with the Tenth when they were putting it together."

"That was after the war. Then you didn't come up here as a slave."

He flicked a scrap of glowing ash at the ground, then returned the cigarette to its groove in his lower lip. "No, I didn't."

Seeing the barricade across that road, I asked him if the Committee of Public Vigilance had settled my case.

"We're going to put you in with Brother Babel. You know which one Babel is?"

I nodded. "Pike's Peak with a hat."

"The last time he changed hands as a slave, he sold for a thousand dollars. That's five times what a prime specimen of healthy buck brought on the Virginia market. It was a bargain. The first time he tried to ride a mule it bucked him. He got up, shook the dust off his pants, picked up the mule, and threw it. That's not a story. I saw him do it."

"I'm supposed to fight him with what?"

"Your hands." He spat out smoke. "It was Brother Enoch's idea."

"I was pretty sure I wasn't popular with him."

"Nothing personal. There was nothing personal about taking slaves either."

"Where'd he get this idea?"

"He was just a boy when Sherman burned the plantation where he worked with his mother. His father went down the river to auction before Enoch was old enough to remember what he looked like. Whenever two bucks got into a fight, the overseer broke it up and told them to work out their differences in the barn. He invited his friends and took bets, just like at a cockfight. Usually one of the brawlers took a beating and gave up. Occasionally one died. When that happened, the overseer had to pay the owner of the plantation for the loss of a good field hand, but he usually made enough laying bets to make a profit even then."

"Then the free African community of Shulamite is just a plantation with the colors reversed."

"What did you expect, some kind of noble experiment? Everything we learned about governing we learned from the white man."

I said nothing. He smoked the cigarette short enough to singe his fingers, then dropped it and pressed it out with the toe of his boot. "I didn't vote in favor of it, if that means anything. I wanted to shoot you and be done with it. I've got no stomach for drawing things out."

"What did Queen Fidelity say?"

"She never takes a hand in these things unless she's invited."

"How did you wind up with a voodoo witch for a priest?"

"All the Negro ministers we knew preached the white man's gospel. Voodoo belongs to us. I can't say I care much for it. The ceremonies give me a headache and are a waste of good chickens besides. When I cut one up, it's to eat. But then I wasn't much of a Christian, either. Turning the other cheek is what got us over here to begin with."

"Whose decision was it to name you all after cities in the Bible?"

"Not all. Some of us hung on to the names we used in the States. The women especially. Those who decided to change chose the Old Testament. It got Jesus out of the picture and the names were easier to pronounce than African. Queen Fidelity's the only one here who ever even saw that place. She left Capetown, where the competition was too thick to make a living, and got run out of Philadelphia and Baltimore by witch burners. She came up here from the American territories ten or twelve years ago. You need women to make religion take and there weren't enough of them down there." He dug out the cigarette pack, but just to play with; the cigarettes stayed inside. "She spends most of her time casting spells to help the crops."

"Do any good?"

"Most of the Shulamites seem to be of that opinion. I suspect we'd have the same number of droughts and blights and bumpers with or without her dead chickens, and have that many more eggs to eat without. A lot of our people came straight up here on the Underground without learning anything of the world on the way, so it makes as much sense to them as the miracle at Cana. My thought is anyone who could make wine out of water ought to have figured out a way to come down off that cross."

"I've been wondering where you took your schooling."

He showed his teeth in an idiot's grin.

"Ain't all us nigras as dumb as rocks, boss. I had me the benefit of a master who taught the classics at Jefferson be-

fore he retired to the genteel ways of the gentleman farmer.
I reckon I was his pet. He showed me how to read the
Bible in English and then Caesar in Latin. It got me out of
the canebrakes, so I didn't put up no holler. I dipped me a
toe in Homer, too, but he was all Greek to me. Hee-hee."

His imitation of a whiny coon set my teeth on edge.
"You don't have to do that. I'd have asked the same of any
white man this side of Chicago who talked like Matthew
Arnold. Most of them can't manage *Frank Leslie's Illustrated Newspaper.*"

"I beg your pardon. We aren't equal no matter what
John Brown said. When someone says something *you*
don't take to, you've got the privilege of thinking he just
doesn't like you. I've got to figure in being black as well."

"I wish I could say for sure your being black didn't have
anything to do with what I said."

"You're honest, and that's a fact." He took out a cigarette this time and lit it. "Who'd you ride with in the war?"

"Rosecrans."

"Army of the Cumberland. I heard he was good. Lincoln almost put him in charge of the whole shebang."

"It would've been a mistake. He was a stubborn Kraut,
and he read too much history. He'd have thrown away the
best we had defending Little Roundtop with a copy of Napoleon's *Maxims* in one hand."

He smoked for a moment in silence. "I fought the Cheyenne in Nebraska."

"I fought them in Dakota. They were worth fighting."

"I deserted."

I let that one drop all the way to the ground. "I guess
you had your reasons."

"I thought so at the time. After Custer and the Seventh
wiped out Black Kettle at the Washita I couldn't see cel-
ebrating my freedom by making slaves of some people I
didn't have any complaint with. That's how I wound up

here. I'll warrant there's a firing squad waiting for me at Fort Kearney."

"In that case you were right to keep running once you started. The army used up all its sharpshooters in the war. What's left would shoot you in all the places that didn't count and some lieutenant would have to walk up and put a ball in your head with his side arm."

"I wouldn't mind too much if the lieutenant was Henry Flipper. He's a Negro, first one to graduate West Point. I never knew him, though; he came after I left. I read about it in the *Toronto Mail*. Could be he's whiter than some whites. They tell me that can happen when you live among them." He got rid of some ash. "But even if it was him and he was black through and through, I wouldn't take to being shot for a coward. The cowardly thing would have been to stick and keep on doing what I'd been. Most of the brave things that are done get done because someone was more afraid not to do them."

"That may be your problem," I said. "Too much education."

"There isn't a day goes by I don't cuss out that damn schoolteacher."

The lantern began to flicker. It was running low. He stood up, turned down the wick, and took the lantern off its nail. He looked down at me from the doorway.

"Not that it will do you any good," he said. "There's a stronghold on Cree Lake up north where some of Sitting Bull's Sioux live. They didn't turn themselves in with the old man and they're pledged to fight to the death to avoid going back to America. We trade with them sometimes. Brother Zoan speaks a little Sioux and is friendly with their leader, Wolf Shirt. He's been known to offer hospitality to desperadoes from below the border."

All the cold went out of me then. "Did your Brother Zoan see Lorenzo Bliss and Charlie Whitelaw there?"

"He hasn't been there in a month, but when a door opens for a man on the run, it doesn't take him long to find it. I'd look for your fugitives there before I went anywhere else."

"Wolf Shirt would have to be worse than Geronimo to harbor a bunch like that."

"Whitelaw being Cherokee would help. It's a Sioux trait to look down on every tribe that isn't Sioux, but they don't hate the others the way they hate Americans. Americans at war with America are another story. That's why Wolf Shirt trades with us. The fact that Bliss and Whitelaw are wanted would only sweeten the pot. Indians will do just about anything to inconvenience the big chief in Washington."

"Do the Mounties know this?"

"If they don't, they will. Canada has no beef against the Sioux for what happened to Custer, but after what this gang did on the Saskatchewan, the Mounties would track them through hell and fight the devil on his own ground."

"That's the first good thing I've heard you say about a bunch of white men."

"*Canadian* white men. Canada never took slaves."

"Thank you for the information. I'll follow up on it just as soon as I finish with Brother Babel."

He looked down at me from the doorway, sucking on his cigarette.

"Babel has long arms," he said then. "As long as your legs. Some men try to stay outside their reach. That's a mistake when you don't have room to run. You want to get inside them if you plan to do any damage."

"You betting on me?"

He dropped the butt and squashed it out, shaking his head. "If anyone in Shulamite had money to bet with I wouldn't put mine on you, and there aren't any takers on Babel. He'll kill you, all right. I'd just like to see someone in your situation get a better chance than those chickens."

20

I actually slept the rest of the night. I'm an old man now, and wakefulness has never been among my maladies. It might have been then, if I'd had any hope of surviving a fight with Brother Babel. When you know how a thing is going to come out and that nothing you do will change it, you can stop thinking and rest. I wrapped myself in my blanket, tugged the badger hat down over my ears, put my head down on my knees—and the next thing I knew there was sunlight sifting through the places where the chinking had fallen out from between the logs and the noises outside of a settlement coming to life.

The door opened and Brother Enoch stood just outside it with his Spencer across his thighs while a man whose name I didn't know, but who had been present among the members of the Committee of Public Vigilance when our camp was broken, set a tin cup of steaming coffee and a plate heaped with scrambled eggs on the ground inside my reach. That meant at least one of Queen Fidelity's chickens hadn't yet gone to the altar.

Smelling the eggs, I realized I was famished. I shoveled them in using the wooden cooking spoon provided and drove the chill out of my bones with the hot coffee, either one of which would have passed muster in San Francisco; as indefensible as slavery was, it had taught some talented people a good trade.

"Let's don't keep Brother Babel waiting," said Enoch when I set aside the plate and cup. "He ain't as patient as he looks."

He and the other man flanked me to the meeting hall. The sky, clear yesterday, had turned the color of tarnished silver and rolled down almost to the ground. A dull pain in my cracked ribs, nearly healed now, told me we were in for a change in the weather. The air smelled and tasted of iron.

They had shoved and stacked the trestle tables against the walls in the great dining room and uncovered the windows, but the gray sunlight was inadequate, and so pitch-smeared torches burned in brackets and a wagon-wheel fixture with lanterns attached hung from the center rafter, casting pools of shadow at the feet of the assembled citizens of Shulamite. There were right around a hundred of them, the men in overalls and flannel, the women in print dresses and gingham, all homespun. The collected years of enforced servitude had taught them all the skills necessary for a community to survive amid the desolation of unsettled territory. No cry went up when I entered with my escort, and no cheer either when Babel came in a few minutes later, attended by another member of the committee; the spectators remained silent in their wide circle, their faces as solemn as the jury they were. This was no sporting event but an execution.

I looked for Philippe, Fleurette, and Claude, wondering if they had left as Queen Fidelity had promised. I spotted them finally near the south wall, the woman and the boy standing atop one of the tables to see above the heads of the crowd. Philippe nodded slightly when our eyes met. His expression was grave.

No one stood along the west wall. There below the stuffed moose head hung a black cloth the size of a bed-sheet, with a chalk drawing on it of a cross with a skull and crossbones suspended beneath the axis, surrounded by symbols that meant nothing to me. It might have been painted by a moderately talented child. In front of the cloth sat Queen Fidelity in her rocker. The effect of those stacked heads—moose, skull, old hag—was comical and ghastly at the same time. She looked exactly as she had the night before, in spectacles, ratty shawl, and steamer rug. A fixture of the building, she might have been picked up, chair and all, in the adjoining room and set down on that spot without stirring.

She could have been mistaken for an ebony carving for all the life she showed as I was led to the center of the plank floor and stopped with a prod of Enoch's Spencer. Babel joined me a moment later, and we stood four feet apart without speaking. He had on loose woolen trousers held up by braces and a faded striped shirt made from enough material for two garments of ordinary size. His bare feet were as big as skillets and gripped the floor as if they had been bolted in place. My head came to his breastbone. I could have hidden behind his bulk on the back of the little mustang. His big face was blank; given the atmosphere of black magic, I might have thought he was in some kind of trance if I hadn't attended my share of prizefights and seen that same lack of expression on the faces of the combatants. There were no thoughts in that great inverted kettle of a head beyond those connected with my annihilation.

Most of the details of the ceremony that preceded the fight were lost to me, busy as I was attempting to attain that same mental state in regard to Babel. When Queen Fidelity arose finally, with the assistance of a woman on each side wrapped in an identical white sheet secured at the shoulders with pins, she was barely taller than she had been sitting. Behind the chair, nearly touching the cloth, stood the black-covered platform I had seen in the other room, moved there and set up with a collection of clay vessels arranged at precise intervals in a straight line. She lifted the largest of the jugs and, raising it above her head, offered it to the four directions, the way I had seen Indian shamans do with a medicine pipe. As she did so she recited something in a singsong language that I identified belatedly as English, sprinkled with foreign terms such as *loa, rada,* and *petro.* Lowering the jug, she turned and poured some of its contents into each of three smaller jars on the platform, muttering something that I thought at the time sounded like Father, Son, and Holy Ghost, though I don't credit it now. After setting down the big jug she took a handful of sand or coarsely ground flour from another vessel, then turned and stepped in front of her chair and let it sift out the bottom of her fist to the floor in a rotating motion, so that the pattern roughly resembled the shape of the skull painted on the black cloth behind the platform. Then she stood aside while the two women in sheets came forward—or rather backward, as they advanced with their backs turned away from the wall—until they stood on either side of the crude skull on the floor.

The planks beneath my feet began to vibrate. The spectators stamped their feet in a precise three-beat rhythm— blam blam *blam,* blam blam *blam*—like fists beating a drum, only amplified by the number of beaters and with the inescapably eerie effect of a hundred people acting in unison without a signal and without one foot missing the beat. It made my scalp move.

While this was going on, the women in white gyrated to the rhythm, twisting their torsos and snaking their arms about their head, but without moving their feet, which were bare and like Babel's fixed to the floor. The dance itself looked joyful, but whenever I glimpsed their faces, they were glued into the motionless empty grin of the skull on the cloth and the skull on the floor. The room began to

fill with the heat of overactive bodies and the thick musk
of sweat. I began to feel woozy, and wondered if the breakfast I'd eaten had contained some kind of drug. I was pretty
sure it didn't, and that the ceremony was not meant to upset me before the fight. It all had the feeling of something
that had been done many times before, that no longer
needed rehearsal. For all I knew, they did it before every
event, even the ordinary ones, like Christians saying grace
before eating.

Some, I noticed, did not take part in the stamping. These
included Brother Hebron and the members of the Committee of Public Vigilance, who stood in one corner with
their arms folded and their eyes on Brother Babel and me.
I couldn't tell whether they disapproved of the ceremony
or were indifferent to it, or if they were just waiting for
the fun to start. Enoch especially looked eager, tapping
one foot out of rhythm with the stamping and unfolding
his arms to flick at his face from time to time in a nervous
tic. Despite what Hebron had said he looked like a man
who had a bet down on the outcome.

I have no idea how long the dancing and the stamping
went on. It couldn't have been as long as it seemed. When
it stopped, all at once so that the silence boxed my ears,
the two women were wet and gleaming and their sheets
were plastered to their flesh, showing their nipples, navels,
and pubic mounds as clearly as if they were naked. Their
heavy breathing was the only sound in a room that rang
with silence like the inside of a great bell.

I didn't let them distract me. I had eyes only for Babel,
who sank into a crouch the instant the stamping stopped.
That was my signal; I charged him, intending to catch him
off balance. But a stone wall is always balanced, and he
didn't budge an inch as I hit him with all my weight behind my right shoulder. His long arms closed around me
in a bear hug that would have ended the fight there and

then if I didn't bend my knees and duck out from under, driving my bootheel into his bare instep as I backpedaled.

That part of the foot is one of the four or five most painful places you can hit a man, but he showed no reaction. Instead, he lunged and backhanded me with a long sweep of his right arm. His knuckles struck the right side of my head like a tree limb; a blue-white light burst inside my skull, and I went down on one knee. He was still coming and I hung on to enough sense to throw myself to the side and roll and come up outside his tremendous reach.

He had fast reflexes for a man his size; for a man of any size. He pivoted just as I let go with a right that I had brought up with me from the floor, shifting his chin so that my knuckles raked his jaw without making square contact. I was still dizzy from the blow to the head, and off balance. He stepped aside, something struck me in the small of my back, and I sprawled headlong to the floor.

I had reason then to thank Hope Weathersill, the madwoman on the Saskatchewan. The buckskin Chief Piapot's Cree had wrapped around my trunk to heal the ribs the woman's bullet had broken had dried as hard as boilerplate. Babel's kick to my back might have cracked my spine if I hadn't still been wearing it When I scrambled to my feet and turned to meet him again, he was hopping around in a limping circle, trying to walk off the pain of a broken toe. I butted him in the sternum, hard enough to sprain my neck and knock the wind out of a man of normal proportions and take him off his feet. Babel, however, just backed up a step. But it was enough for me to throw both arms around him and snap my head up hard under his chin, colliding with a crack I felt all the way to the ground.

Once again I backpedaled before he could close his arms around me. He blinked, shook his head, spat out a tooth, and went into a fighter's crouch, rocking on the balls of his feet with his big, half-closed fists out in front of him. He knew something of the science of boxing, which made him as dangerous as any man or beast this side of a bull elephant. I feinted with my right, then ducked left, his own left whistling past my ear. I jabbed with my left, but he blocked it with his right and followed through with a blow that caught me in the chest and paralyzed me to the waist. I scissored my knee up into his crotch, but his was higher than most men's, and the pain wasn't enough to slow down his momentum. His looping left fist had by this time completed its circle and caught me behind the neck. My knees buckled, but the blood returned to my head before I finished falling. I dove between his knees, got my shoulder up into his crotch, and lifted with all my strength. Log bridges don't lift, stone viaducts don't give. He was rooted there. One of his hands closed around my belt in back and he pulled me out from between his legs and lifted me off my feet and threw me away. I had a sensation of flying, of the whites of eyes as the spectators in my path recognized the danger and got out of my way, and then I piled up against the base of a trestle table stacked against the wall.

This was no ordinary fight in as many ways as I could count. There should have been cheering and shouting, but the great hall might have been empty for all anyone raised his or her voice for Babel or against me. In that gulf of silence I found enough of my wind to stand and turn again just as the big man bore down on me in his closed crouch.

Instinct told me to get out of his way. Brother Hebron's voice in my head was louder. *Babel has long arms. . . . You want to get inside them if you plan to do any damage.*

This time I didn't feint. I stuck my right in his face, and as he moved to block it and swoop his own right around, I ducked underneath inside the circle of his arms and hit him with a combination, left-right-left, treating his head like a light bag. That was when he closed his arms around me and squeezed. I heard the ribs Hope Weathersill had broken giving way again just before my lamp went out.

PART THREE

The Stronghold

21

"It is never a good idea, Deputy Marshal Murdock, to take advice from one's enemy."

It seemed when I opened my eyes that this conversation had been going on for a while. I was looking up at the rafters of the great dining hall, and certain numb spots in my back told me I was stretched out atop one of the trestle tables. Something cool and damp touched my face; I turned my head just in time to see Fleurette take away the wet cloth and wring it out over a chipped enamel basin balanced on the edge of the table. I knew without turning my head that Phillippe stood on the other side.

I said, "Someone's been talking in his sleep." Taking in air to speak brought needles of pain to my injured side.

"We French are not able tacticians," he said. "It must not be forgotten that Napoleon was Italian. Still, it is no great revelation to determine that the logical direction to take in a fight with a man twice one's size is away from him."

"I'm not prone to argue."

Fleurette laughed at that, proving that she did know some English. She had a light, musical titter.

"Where's Claude?" I asked.

"I sent him for our horses. We are free to go as soon as you are ready to ride."

Fleurette said something, and the two conversed in

French for a minute. He put an end to it with a harsh "*Non!*"
To me: "You can ride, Deputy Marshal Murdock, yes?"

"I can if it's away from here. Are you sure I'm included?
I lost the fight."

"You should have asked for an explanation of the rules
of combat in Shulamite. It is not necessary that you win,
merely that you survive. Evidently that is no small feat
where Brother Babel is concerned."

"I had a little help."

"So I see." He knocked a knuckle against the buckskin
wrap, and I realized my shirt was spread open to expose
it. "One would think you knew what was in store."

"One would be wrong. God must love a fool or there
wouldn't be so many of us my age."

"It was not just the hide. Queen Fidelity commanded
Babel to stop when you were senseless. I gathered from
the excitement that it is very rare for her to take a hand in
such matters. You must have made a favorable impression
upon her."

"I think she liked my name."

"A formidable woman. It is a shame that she must go to
hell."

Fleurette crossed herself, then reapplied the damp cloth
to my face. She had a sure and gentle touch. The various
rebellions and buffalo hunts in which her man had taken
part had made her an expert in tending to the sick and injured.

"How far is Cree Lake from here?" I asked.

"Two days in good weather," Philippe said after a moment. "The Sioux stronghold is there. Many of them rode
with Crazy Horse in the Little Big Horn fight. You will
find the free African community of Shulamite a place of
great warmth and hospitality once you approach the
stronghold."

"Hebron says that's where I'll find Bliss and Whitelaw."

"Hebron said you would be wise to step inside the arms of Babel."

"He didn't have any reason to lie to me about Bliss and Whitelaw if he expected Babel to kill me. They're there, all right. You have your family to look after, so if you'll direct me to the lake I'll say good-bye. You've earned that second double eagle and a share of the reward as well."

"My family and I have nothing to fear from our brothers the Sioux. We will go with you. An American can lose himself in that country for a month."

I made a note to stop at Donalbain's farm on my way home and set the old Scot straight about the Métis.

Against Fleurette's protests in rapid French, I sat up and buttoned my shirt. The pain in my ribs was as bad as it had been the first time they were broken, but I had survived it before, and anyway I was sore all over from the beating I had taken, so I just rolled it into the inventory. With Philippe's assistance I got into my bearskin and we went out. The little snake-faced mustang, the gray, and King Henry were packed and waiting for us at the base of the steps. Brother Babel was holding them.

The big man had his boots on now, along with a heavy canvas coat and his floppy hat. There was a purple swelling along the side of his jaw where my fist had raked it, but aside from that he didn't look any the worse the wear for our fight, any more than a tree whose bark I'd nicked with my initials. When I appeared he showed a wealth of teeth—minus one—as crooked as neglected tombstones in what I took to be a grin of recognition from one combatant to another, although twenty-four hours earlier I might have seen it as a savage challenge. If the scar tissue on his face was any indication, I gathered that it was a rare thing when one of his opponents lived for him to grin at.

The members of the Committee of Public Vigilance were standing nearby. The look on Brother Enoch's gaunt face was no greeting. Gripping his Spencer tightly, he turned to say something to Brother Hebron, who shook his head and stepped forward. He didn't offer his hand.

"I didn't mean to give you bad advice," he said. "It was one thing no one ever tried and I was curious to see what would happen."

"No charge for settling the question," I said.

"Queen Fidelity is resting. She claims to be a hundred and ten, and she looks it, so I'm guessing she needs what she gets. She asked me to give you something." He took a small leather pouch from his coat pocket and held it out.

I accepted it after a moment. It was tied with a cord and something made a whispery sound inside when I shifted it on my palm. It was barely heavier than air. I started to undo the cord.

"Don't open it. She says you'll waste the magic. It's just old bones. She said they belonged to an eagle her grandfather captured with his bare hands. Apparently you impressed her. She says he was a powerful chief."

"Everybody's grandfather was." But I left the knot alone. "Voodoo?"

"She says it's older than that. The magic belongs to the ancient gods, who died before the white man came. She says it will see you home safe."

"What do *you* say?"

"I say bones are bones and there's nothing saying those couldn't have come from last week's chicken. This is the magic I trust." He drew my Deane-Adams from his belt and held it out butt first. "Your long guns are on your horses."

I inspected the loads in the cylinder and holstered the revolver. "I guess this makes me the first white man to leave Shulamite alive."

"That's just a story the Mounties tell to scare the little Mounties. They wouldn't let this settlement stand five minutes if we went around killing every pale-skinned American we saw."

"What made me a special case?"

"Every now and then I have to throw one to the committee. It was just your bad luck to have come along at the end of a long dry spell."

I lowered my voice. "You want to watch your topknot around Enoch. He's hungry."

"That's why I made him number two man. If I learned anything in the army it's to keep your enemies close."

"Indians don't sneak up on that easy."

"I wasn't talking about Indians." He wasn't smiling.

Philippe gave me a boost into the saddle and I rode out in front with my right side on fire. I didn't look back, and I never saw Shulamite or Brother Hebron again, although I heard a year later he came to a short end when one of his own fellow settlers shot him by accident while they were out hunting meat for the winter. There is close, and there is too close, when you do your measuring by the length of a Spencer's barrel.

22

An hour out of Shulamite, the snow I'd been smelling all day came pouring out of the low clouds like bits of candy from a piñata.

The flakes were big to start, floating like paper and melting with sizzling sounds where they landed on coat sleeves and the backs of gloves. They hung up on our eyelashes and left wet trails behind when they slithered down our faces. As the sun descended and the wind picked up, they became smaller and harder, bits of jagged granite rattling against our standing collars and welting our skin. The wind lifted the snow where it fell and threw it at us in buckets. Philippe gave Claude a hand up behind Fleurette and steered King Henry in close to the mustang to shout into my ear, but the wind snatched away his words at a distance of six inches. He jabbed a finger at a patch of shadow a hundred yards ahead. I nodded energetically and we made for the shadow.

It belonged to a stand of virgin pine, the straight trunks so close together we had to go in single file, Philippe's big dun leading the way. We rode for miles through that dense wood, the wind howling outside as around a stockade, before we found a clearing big enough to make camp. While gathering wood in the thickening dark, I stumbled over something and discovered it was the stone foundation of a cabin, the logs having long since burned or rotted away.

"*Coureur de bois,*" said Philippe, once we had built a fire big enough to warm our hands. "One of the first, I should imagine. He must have been the only white man for a thousand miles. Perhaps he died of loneliness."

Fleurette said something.

Her husband nodded. "*Oui, ma petit.* More likely he was eaten by a bear. You see what I mean, Deputy Marshal Murdock, about a man alone?"

"You said an American."

"I intended no offense. You carved North America from the wilderness, killed the Indians and the buffalo and felled the trees to make room for your civilization. Here in Canada we did not conquer the wilderness, merely made our peace with it. But a truce with a bear is only valid until he hungers again."

" 'Grandmother's land,' the Indians call it," I said. "After Victoria. But it's no place for old ladies."

"My grandmother was a Cree, a fierce, white-haired woman who buried two husbands and once beat a puma to death with a piece of firewood. She would feed and shelter you if you loved her, but she never forgot a wrong, and she never slept. You must never think Canada is asleep, or that she has forgiven you your transgressions. Our *coureur* may have expired peacefully in his bed. It is more likely that he fell down a ravine and broke his neck. It would have been a ravine he had descended a thousand times without slipping and thought as safe as a pasture."

"Tell me about the stronghold."

"It is well named. Ten thousand years ago, the big ice that scooped out Cree Lake pushed a million tons of rock into a tower on its eastern shore. It sits like a lion upon its haunches and can only be scaled from the north, where one side of it was beaten into rubble by storms that would have destroyed our *coureur*'s cabin a hundred times a hundred. That side will be guarded heavily. We will not climb it without the permission of those who live on the crest."

"Tell me about them."

"They are Sioux from America. They came here with Sitting Bull after the Custer fight, as you know, and retreated to the stronghold when Sitting Bull agreed to return. They are led by a man called Wolf Shirt. His sister married Crazy Horse, who Wolf Shirt advised not to give himself up to General Crook. It was wise counsel, as history proved."

"I doubt he's reasonable on the subject of white Americans."

"After Crazy Horse was murdered, his wife starved herself to death at the Red Cloud Agency. Peace with white Americans deprived him of his friend and his sister. He has reason to be unreasonable."

"Well, we sure are popular up here."

Philippe blew through his flute to clear it of lint from his pocket. "*I* like you, Deputy Marshal Murdock. However, I do not run with the herd. The one time I did I got shot."

"Brother Hebron said Wolf Shirt harbors fugitives to make himself a nuisance."

"He was right. The Sioux know they cannot win this war, but they can make winning less pleasant for the victors." He moved his shoulders in a Gallic shrug. "It is a small thing, but it is all your army has left them."

"The Sioux must want something they'll take in trade for Bliss and Whitelaw."

"The Black Hills of Dakota, free of white settlers. And sixty million buffalo." He played the flute.

The storm blew for a week, after which the sun came out and we waited another week for the drifts to melt before

we could resume our journey. We finished the bacon and
the last of the moose. Claude earned his keep by running
down snowshoe hares and bringing them into the clearing
at arm's length, kicking and screaming at the ends of their
powerful hind legs, for Fleurette to bash in their skulls with
a chunk of firewood and then skin and clean and cook them
on a spit made from pine branches. For variety I went
goose-hunting with the Winchester, and nearly wound up
meat myself when what I thought at first was a big musk-
rat hut sticking up out of a frozen pond raised itself to its
full height, streaming water, and I found myself staring
face to face at eight and a half feet of grizzly. It was covered with silver-tipped hairs like hoarfrost. Its head, with
the hair parted in the middle the way bartenders wore it,
was as big as a pig, with the little black eyes glittering
alongside the great snout, so like the butt end of a charred
log.

Bears are nearsighted, but they can detect movement at
a greater distance than most humans can. I froze. If I was
lucky it would take me for a tree. It grunted, the noise as
loud as gravel shifting at the bottom of a sluice, and raised
its snout, the nostrils working. I hoped I was downwind.
A .44 Winchester will stop a bear, they say, but the bear
doesn't always realize it. Not in time to do the shooter any
good. At thirty yards only ten leaps kept us apart. I wasn't
sure if I could get off twelve rounds in that time, or whether
twelve rounds would do the trick.

I willed myself into a pile of rock. A magpie could have
landed on me and plucked out an eye and I wouldn't have
budged. An eye is a fair trade for not being eaten. The patch
and the story would keep me in free drinks for the rest of
my life.

The grizzly wasn't any more sure of me than I was. If it
thought I was another bear in my coat, it might challenge
me for the fishing hole, or go off and look for some less

populated spot. It made a test roar: a ripping, rending sound like someone tearing corrugated iron with a wrecking bar. It made every hair on my body stand out, but I didn't move. When it lowered itself I thought it was getting ready to charge. Instead it slapped at the water with a paw the size of a kitchen table, splashing water out over the edges of the jagged hole and onto the ice. Still I didn't react. The bear grunted again and sat back on its haunches, sinking into its rolls of fat and fur in an attitude of frustrated contemplation. It did everything but scratch its head.

It sat there a long time, although nowhere nearly as long as it seemed. I second-thought my plan. If I could shoot it where it sat; but I couldn't will myself to raise the carbine and trigger an attack. I could make a run for it, climb a tree. This time ignorance held me. I couldn't remember if it was a black bear or a grizzly that could climb trees like water rushing up a straw.

And I wondered why in hell this brute wasn't hibernating with all the rest of the bears.

All of which helped to pass the time while the grizzly got tired of waiting. It raised itself again, cuffed the air with a set of claws like railroad spikes, roared again, then shifted its fifteen hundred pounds or so of fur and fat and muscle and short temper onto its forefeet and turned around and mounted the bank on the other side of the pond. It shook itself, water radiating everywhere in lances, and looked back at me over its shoulder one last time, just in case I'd moved or grown a moustache or done something else to make myself look edible. Then it swiveled its head back around and moved off into the trees, making no more noise than a drawer sliding shut.

I held my position, and my breath, for another minute. I didn't want to repeat the episode of the returning moose. Then I heard a crashing back in the underbrush, the bear picking up speed as it went in search of less complicated prey. I let the barrel of the Winchester droop finally. My shoulders ached and the muscles in my jaw felt as if I'd been chewing rawhide for an hour. My clothes beneath the bearskin were drenched. I couldn't have been wetter if I'd swum across the pond. The chill set in then and I turned back toward camp. I completely ignored a goose that exploded from the ground ten feet in front of me and flew in a long rainbow loop down to the hole in the ice the bear had made. I had lost my taste for meat.

I found Philippe clawing the tangles out of King Henry's shaggy coat with a curry comb and told him about the bear.

"You disappoint me, Deputy Marshal Murdock. A bear steak is worth ten rabbits for stamina on a hard trail. The heart will take you as far as Siberia."

"It was more a question of how far that bear could travel on a Murdock steak."

"You are armed."

"So was he."

"You are sure it was a grizzly?"

"It was big and hairy and a swipe of one of its paws would have sent my head into camp ahead of the rest of me. I didn't ask for further identification."

"Up here the black bear grow nearly as big. Some of the older ones are tipped with silver, as well. One way to make certain is to anger him and then climb a tree. If he climbs up after you, he's a black. The grizzly will merely wait with the patience of Saint Anne for you to come down and be eaten."

"I wasn't that curious."

"You disappoint me," he said again. "I was told all you American frontiersmen shit bear and keep puma for pets."

"That was Jim Bridger. He died last year of a goiter."

"You should have brought the marvelous Evans rifle.

Even if you did not kill him the weight of the lead would have slowed him down so you could walk up to him and cut off a steak for your friend Philippe."

"I went out after geese. I didn't think I'd need eighteen rounds to bring down a gander. Do you want to talk about that bear all day?"

"I did not introduce the subject." He slapped the big dun on the neck and got a purring snort in reply. Then he slipped the comb into the kit at his feet and stretched the kinks out of his small frame. Currying was strenuous work; he'd chucked his coat and rolled up his sleeves to expose muscles in his arms as big as train couplings. "How were the drifts?"

"Down," I said.

"Good. We will leave for the stronghold at first light."

The sun was well up when we cleared the woods at last and squinched up our eyes against a plain of white as bright as a salt flat. The trees stood out like embroidery on a sheet, and the sky was bottle-blue and just as clear. A bald eagle had it all to itself, flapping its wings dreamily between up-drafts, where it rode the air like a kite. I thought of the eagle bones in the leather pouch in my pocket and hoped they were genuine. It wasn't country for chickens.

"*Monsieur le depute!*" Philippe's whisper was a harsh rasp, accompanied by his upraised hand.

I heard nothing but the wind in the pines behind us; but the ears of the Métis were as sharp as a deer's. I drew rein.

Fleurette removed her arms from around her husband and craned her neck, pointing her sharp features to the sky as if to smell the air. Young Claude, who had been walking behind King Henry to avoid wallowing in snow to his waist, leaned out to see past the big dun, fixing his bright eyes on what appeared to be an empty space of ground some three hundred yards from where we were waiting. I felt blind and deaf.

The landscape was deceptive. It was not as flat as it seemed under its blanket of snow, which masked long deep depressions gouged by glaciers, like the troughs between waves at sea. As we waited amid clouds of steam from our horses, I heard the first silvery tinkles and flatulent leathery creaks that Philippe had been hearing for minutes, and the others had heard before me. The sounds chilled me to the marrow. In a magnesium flash I was transported back to Murfreesboro, where I had waited with a small patrol in a stand of hickory, covering our mounts' muzzles with our hands to keep them from wickering while Braxton Bragg's Confederate cavalry passed by within pistol range.

The nearest trough shallowed out where Claude was watching. I caught a glint of sunlight off burnished steel, then the brown head and neck of a horse whose coat gleamed like a well-polished boot, and then in a burst like a flock of cardinals, the bright red tunics and brass buttons and spiked white cork helmets of the North-West Mounted Police drawing a brilliant slash four abreast and a quarter of a mile long against the stark white countryside. The Mounties had come to the stronghold.

23

"**C**ompanyyyyyyyyyyyyyyyy . . . *Ulp!*"

The master sergeant who bawled the order had been in the military twenty years, minimum; a figure arrived at by assigning a year to each *y* in *company* and adding three for the total incomprehensibility of his pronunciation of *Halt*. When their commands could no longer be understood by anyone they were forced into retirement.

It was the same sergeant with black handlebars I'd seen on the Saskatchewan. He relayed the order as reluctantly as he'd put away his side arm when Inspector Urban Vivian identified me as an ally and not an enemy come to ambush four hundred Mounties with a force of two men, a woman, and a boy. The command was repeated a couple of times farther back, and with a racket of creaking saddles, jingling bit chains, snorting horses, and rattling rifle stocks, the column came to a stop. A warm vapor of perspiration and spent breath drifted forward and settled over Philippe, Fleurette, Claude, and me like a mist of rain. Then there was eardrum-battering silence.

Vivian broke it. Weeks of riding with the sun slamming off the snow had burned his face as dark as the chestnut he rode and bleached his hair and brush moustache as white as his helmet and belt. His pale eyes stood out like newly minted coins.

"I gave you up for bear bait long ago," he said.

He didn't know how close he'd come to guessing right, but I didn't give him the point. "In Montana we use bears to catch buffalo. I've been taking in the scenery."

"Who is that with you?"

I introduced the du la Rochelles. Vivian surprised me by unstrapping and removing his helmet to nod at Fleurette. His hair, darker on top, had grown out at the temples. He put the helmet back on to address Philippe. "I know you, I think. We have you down as an insurgent."

"Your information is out of date, *monsieur l'inspecteur*. I fight no one these days."

"What brings you this far north?"

I said, "I hired him as my guide."

"He must not be very good. I've been to Chipewyan and back, and this is as far as you've got."

"We liked Shulamite too much to leave. Then a blizzard hit."

One eye twitched. It was as much surprise as he would show in front of his command. "I don't believe you. Shulamite? You're a liar."

"I'd throw down my glove, but I need it." I let my gaze wander down the line of horsemen. "Every time I see you, you've got a bigger army. Another week or two of Bliss and Whitelaw on the loose and you'll strip the queen of her palace guard."

"That Métis family they butchered up north had a house guest the night they visited. The guest was a priest. If we don't get them first the Métis will do it for us, and burn down every square mile they pass through on the way. This isn't your fight any longer, Murdock. Canada has the greater claim."

I took another look at the column. It was as good a light-horse cavalry as the continent had, if you didn't count the Comanche and northern Cheyenne. In nearly ten years fighting renegades and settling disputes, the North-West Mounted had lost just four men, as opposed to Custer's two hundred during one day's fighting in southern Montana. If I ever wanted to turn over a manhunt to someone else, I wouldn't find a better candidate.

"I'll go home if you'll put it in writing that Judge Blackthorne's court gets Bliss and Whitelaw when you're through trying them."

"I can give you my word to that, as an officer and a gentleman."

"I believe you, Inspector, but if you take a bullet to the head, your word won't be worth one cent more than your brains. I'll need it on paper."

He flushed beneath the sunburn. "Damn it, man, I haven't writing materials to hand."

"Then I'll just ride along with you."

"I can't offer you safe passage. You might think about that before you drag along a woman and a boy. We are on our way to parley with a band of Sioux."

"Wolf Shirt. I got that much from Brother Hebron."

Vivian recognized the names. His nose was running in the cold; he flicked a drop off the end with a white-gloved finger. No one before had ever made so elegant a gesture of it. "Perhaps you were telling the truth about Shulamite. I ask your pardon."

That surprised and irritated me. Most of the fun I'd had in Canada so far, after the weather and renegade slaves and madwomen, was hating Inspector Vivian. "I've been called worse than a liar, and earned some of it," I said. "What's your plan? From what I've heard about Wolf Shirt, he won't give up Bliss and Whitelaw for a sack of beads."

"That's how you Americans handle it. That's how he and his people came to be up here in the first place." Having thus reestablished our animosity, he said, "I intend to appeal to his common sense. Up until now the Sioux have enjoyed the hospitality of the authorities in Canada and sanctuary against prosecution for their differences with the United States of America. If he insists upon harboring fugitives from Canadian law, he sacrifices everything. We have warrants for the arrest of Bliss, Whitelaw, and their companions, and we shall serve them if it means war with the entire Sioux Nation."

"Now you're beginning to sound like Phil Sheridan."

He turned to the man with the black handlebars. "Sergeant Major. Walk-march-trot."

"Wukmutchtut!" bawled the other.

The column started forward. I turned the mustang's head and gave the lead line a flip to clear the path. Philippe backed King Henry out of the way.

"Indians are muleheaded," I called out above the noise. "They can't count, or they won't. They'll go to war with the rest of the world rather than back off from a position."

"Then they have something in common with Great Britain," he called back over his shoulder.

Philippe and I watched the Mounties pass with our arms folded on our pommels. "What scares me is he thinks that's a good thing," I said.

"It is the same with buffalo," said the Métis. "That's why there are so few left."

We watched the scarlet column trot past, their mounts' hooves churning clouds of powdery snow. Rattling at the rear was a sight that never failed to chill my blood: A pair of men driving a reinforced wagon with the brass bunched barrels of a Gatling gun mounted on a tripod poking out the end of a canvas tarpaulin.

Philippe took in his breath sharply. "A machine for killing," he said. "It is a great time in which we live."

Fleurette, looking confused, leaned forward and said something to her husband, who responded briefly in French. She sat back, crossed herself, then looked around for Claude, who had slid down from behind her. When she spotted him she called his name shrilly. Startled, he scampered over and was caught in a maternal headlock.

I got out my leather pouch and placed two double eagles in Philippe's palm. "The extra is for Shulamite," I said. "I'm pretty sure Brother Enoch was in favor of killing all three of you for riding with me. You didn't have to wait around to watch the fight after the committee said you could go."

He didn't close his hand. "The job is not finished, Deputy Marshal Murdock."

"I hired you to guide me. If I can't follow four hundred Mounties and their eggbeater on wheels from here, I'm no kind of a manhunter. Go home and shoot buffalo."

Fleurette asked another question. When Philippe translated what I'd said, she shook her head, let go of Claude, scooped the gold coins out of her husband's hand, and thrust them toward me.

"She says you hired me to take you to Fort Chipewyan," he said. "Since that is no longer necessary, we will accompany you the rest of the way to the stronghold."

"She didn't say anything."

He showed me his gold teeth. "We have been married a long time, Deputy Marshal Murdock. We do not always have to speak to say what we are thinking."

I took back the eagles. There is no arguing with a woman in any language.

24

French blood leads to exaggeration, and I was prepared to find the Sioux stronghold at Cree Lake a good deal less formidable than Philippe had described it. A half-day short of the lake, however, I saw the broken granite peak of the formation sticking up above the towering white pines that separated us, as straight and tall and imposing as any of the multistory buildings that were going up in Chicago for the greater glory of the meat barons whose slaughterhouses butchered western beef for New York and London and Paris and a hundred other cities whose residents had never seen a cow any other way but cut up and packaged for sale: *Skyscrapers*, they called them; but the name had never seemed so appropriate as when one applied it to the present feature. When Wolf Shirt and his followers first set eyes upon it, they would have given thanks to the Wise One Above for his sacred gift to Custer's conquerors. I had to think there was something to that, or the Last Stand would have taken place somewhere more defensible than that pimple of a hill on the Little Big Horn.

The Mounties reformed into column of twos to slice through the girdle of forest that surrounded the lake, sending a cloud of gray squirrels scampering to the tops of the pines to chatter at them from the safe distance of a hundred feet. The du la Rochelles and I got the worst of that;

they came down to perch on the branches just above our heads and harangue our tiny group with jabbers and bombardments of pinecones. Claude, riding behind his mother, shocked them into temporary silence when he stood up on the back of the saddle, snatched one off a bough by its tail, and hurled it to the ground, all in one motion. Helena had a baseball team that could have used him at first base.

A rifle cracked when we were still in the woods. No shots followed it, and I concluded that the report was a warning signal fired by a lookout atop the rocks to alert the others to the presence of Mounties. A few minutes later we were clear of the trees and in full view of the lake, broad and flat and painfully blue with white all around, dotted with green scrub and with the red uniforms spreading out to form a straight line between the shore and the forest like a bloody finger drawn across the bottom of a sketch done in colored chalk. Directly across the lake stood the stronghold, a vertical gray cliff thrust like a spear into the level ground, waiting for its gigantic owner to pull it back out and shake loose the trees and shrubbery that clung like moss to the irregularities on its face. It looked twice as tall as it was because nothing separated the base from its reflection on the surface of the water.

The machinery of the cavalry formation was still in motion, the horsemen riding into position to right and left of the center where the inspector and his sergeant major sat as still as the rock itself, the topkick now with his saber unsheathed and resting on his right shoulder after the fashion of a standard. The men in charge of the wagon had drawn it up behind them, and now one was unhitching the team while his partner mounted the bed to remove the tarp from the Gatling. I knew the maneuver that would follow, if reason failed; whether the Indians knew it as well and acted upon that knowledge would make the difference between just a lot of impressive noise and a slaughter.

I handed Philippe the packhorse's lead, told him and the others to stay where they were, and cantered up to join Vivian. He looked at me out of the corner of one pale eye without turning his head. "Sergeant Major, divest this civilian of his rifles."

"Suh!" said the other, gripped his pommel to swing down. I clapped the muzzle of the Deane-Adams to the bridge of his nose. The front sight barely cleared the lip of his helmet. His eyes crossed comically.

Something triple-clicked in my left ear. I didn't turn my head Vivian's way.

"Murdock," he said.

I said, "I don't want to go to war with Canada, but if I'm going to die anyway I'd just as soon be written about as the man who started it."

A light wind combed the surface of the lake. The inspector let down his hammer gently and holstered his side arm.

"Cancel that order," he said.

I pointed the Deane-Adams skyward and seated the hammer. The sergeant settled back into his saddle and breathed

Vivian said, "The last time I allowed a civilian to retain his weapons during a parley, he winged a tree-cutter over a boundary dispute. Another lumberman shot back and my French interpreter lost a leg."

"I haven't been a civilian since First Manassas." I leathered the five-shot. "I'll promise not to pot an Indian or a desperado if you'll put the canvas back on that chattergun. I've got sensitive ears."

His face was unreadable beneath the helmet. With the visor covering his brow and the strap buckled at the point of his chin he showed all the individuality of a lead soldier. Finally his gaze shifted toward the sergeant.

"Tell those men to recover the Gatling."

While that was being done I asked Vivian his plan.

"Wolf Shirt affects an ignorance of English, though I suspect he could hold his own in conversation with an Oxford don. However, Indians are muleheaded, as you say, and humoring them takes less time than argument. Corporal Barrymore here is an adept at sign language." He tilted his head an eighth of an inch toward a mass of freckles and sparse red side whiskers mounted at his left. "He will interpret while I determine whether Bliss and Whitelaw and their companions are with the Sioux. If that's the case I have every hope he'll agree with the very good reasons I'll propose for giving them up."

"What makes you think he'll even agree to talk to you?"

"I have four hundred men and he has sixty."

"And a rock," I said. "Don't forget the rock. He can take target practice on your four hundred redcoats all day while you kick up stone dust."

"I doubt he has the ammunition to withstand a long siege. When he runs out we'll go in and arrest him and hang him in Ottawa if he's killed one trooper or one hundred."

"Now you're talking like an American."

He said nothing, although the muscles of his jaw stood out like doorknobs.

The sergeant major returned then. Vivian tugged a square yard of white handkerchief out of his left sleeve and passed it across the neck of my horse for the other man to take. The sergeant tied it to the end of his saber and trotted up to the edge of the lake with the hilt propped on one thigh, the wind snapping the banner.

A ball of gray smoke appeared in a cleft in the tower of rock near the crest and tore apart in the wind. I heard the crack just as something plopped into the water two feet in front of the sergeant's horse. It wasn't a frog. Man and mount remained motionless, an impressive feat on both counts.

"A warning, I should think," the inspector said.

I said, "Maybe not. I never saw an Indian who was as good with a rifle as he was with a bow."

There were no more shots from the summit, but neither was there anything else for what seemed an hour. Then something white showed in the cleft. It waggled back and forth.

"Right. Sergeant Major, Corporal Barrymore, come with me. Lieutenant Ponsoby, you're in charge. If we're not back by sundown, open fire. Use the Gatling."

"Yes, sir!" This from a youth with a hooked nose and an undershot jaw like a monkey wrench. When his teeth went, the one would touch the other. He'd be a general by then, if one of his own men didn't shoot him first.

I spurred the mustang into line behind the others. Vivian glared back once over his shoulder but said nothing. Evidently he'd decided that humoring me took less time than arguing.

Philippe's information about the configuration of the rock proved correct. The north face bore little resemblance to the south, having collapsed into a pile of broken shards, boulders the size of the courthouse in Helena, and round stones no larger than a man's fist. It had all happened long enough ago for scrub pine and thistles to have grown from the soil deposited in the cracks. The way was not fit for horses, and so we tethered ours and began scaling on foot, the sergeant leading the way with the flag of truce.

It was warm climbing. The wind had sculpted a horseshoe-shaped concavity in the snow east of the lake, and the sun coming off that white dish had made the rocks hot to the touch; at high noon a man could have fried bacon on one of them. Grasping stones and twisted tree trunks for leverage, I kept an eye on the cracks for rattlesnakes. I had no idea if they grew them this far north, but it was an old habit in that kind of landscape. I was sweating and wanted to ditch the bearskin; the wind whistling up near the crest warned me to hold onto it. The mountain country back home was scattered with the bones of trappers and Indian traders who had abandoned their winter gear to avoid heat stroke and frozen to death a few hours later.

Twenty yards from the top the route became almost vertical. The sergeant tore loose his white handkerchief and scabbarded his saber to free both hands for climbing. Corporal Barrymore, following him, put his foot on a ledge of rock that turned out to be rotten and saved himself from falling by grabbing a handful of dense moss. Meanwhile Vivian and I flattened out against the cliff while a bucketful of rubble, twigs, and coarse earth bounced off our hats and shoulders and went down inside our collars. Then we resumed climbing with the grit rubbing our joints.

When we stood on the crest at last I was rewarded for hanging onto the bearskin. The wind was stiff and steel-cold and made my face numb. I had removed my gloves for climbing. Now I got them out of a pocket and wriggled into them. My fingers were already stiffening. The Mounties retrieved their white gauntlets from their belts and put them on.

I caught a glimpse of the lake below and the red tunics of the North-West Mounted, strung out like bright ribbons on white linen.

"Well, Charlie, look what we have here. Three red kings and a black jack. I'd call it a misdeal."

The man who spoke was short and thick and held a rifle braced against his right hip. He was standing against bright sky, which made his face a purple blur. His companion, with a spire of rock behind him, was easier to make out: slender, almost frail looking, with a round face that appeared to have been nailed to the wrong body. His skin was the color of raw iron ore, against which the whites of his eyes stood out and his long canine teeth when he smiled, as he did now. I recognized him from wire descriptions as Charlie Whitelaw, the Cherokee killer from the Indian Nations. That made his friend with the rifle Lorenzo Bliss.

25

I reckoned I was the black jack, because of the bearskin. It gave me leave to open.

"You boys should have kept traveling. You're hemmed in tight up here."

Bliss took two steps my way and swung the rifle, laying the barrel alongside my left temple. I stumbled, but I'd been anticipating something along those lines and was moving in the same direction when the blow came. I kept my feet while the black tide went out.

He was as fast with a rifle as he was said to be with a knife. Vivian's hand was still going down for his side arm when the long gun came back around and Bliss levered a shell into the chamber. As he did so a perfectly good unfired cartridge spat out of the ejector and rolled to a stop in a crevice at his feet. That told me two things about him: 1. He was wasteful; 2. He had a weakness for making dramatic gestures. I banked the information for whatever good it might do me.

"Finish what you started," he told the inspector. "I been wanting to find out if you can see blood on them pretty red blouses."

Vivian spread his arms away from his sides.

Whitelaw said, "If you're going to throw away good ammo, toss me that gun."

I could see Bliss's face now that he was standing closer.

It was all Irish except for the eyes. He had a pug nose and a long upper lip with an oddly delicate dimple, visible through his sparse, sun-bleached moustaches, that would make him appear boyish even in old age—a waste, considering his chances of getting that far. His eyes were black and Spanish. They were the humorless eyes of his prostitute mother looking out through the holes in a comic mask.

Without hesitating he threw the rifle to Whitelaw, who caught it and pulled down on us before we could react. It was a Henry, the full-length .44 with a brass receiver and a folding sight. In the same movement, Bliss scooped a huge bowie knife from the scabbard on his belt and turned it to catch the light on its oiled blade. I wondered if it was the same one he'd used to cut out a man's heart in a saloon in Wyoming.

Whitelaw said, "Take their weapons."

With a show of reluctance, Bliss scabbarded the knife and stepped forward to relieve us of our side arms and the sergeant of his saber. He tossed them onto a patch of soft earth hammocked in a hollow at the base of a boulder. When he paused to sneer at my English revolver, I got a strong whiff of sweat and fermented grain. The whiskey seemed to be leaking directly out of his pores, as if his body were saturated with it and could hold no more. For all that he was steady on his feet and there was no slurring in his speech. Men who drink constantly build up an immunity to drunkenness right up until their livers explode.

"Skinny little pistol for a man," he said. "I bet you squat to make water."

"I bet you'd watch."

His grin, split catlike by the deep dimple in his upper lip, fled. He fisted the Deane-Adams and I braced myself for another blow. But Whitelaw barked at him and he spat on the pistol instead and threw it onto the pile, hard enough to nick the metal.

That took the edge off. He stared at me from a distance of two feet, the grin working its way back. He brought up his right hand, slid his index finger across the underside of my jaw in a slow cutting motion, pursed his lips at me, and stepped away.

I stopped worrying then. John Swingtree had told me back in the penitentiary at Deer Lodge that Charlie Whitelaw did all the thinking for the pair, and it had taken me two minutes in their company to confirm that. Bliss was the one to keep an eye on—there was no connection between his brain and his hands, and even he couldn't predict what he'd do or when he'd do it—but Whitelaw was the one to outsmart. He'd have everything figured three moves ahead.

They are hell together, Swingtree had said. *They wasn't nothing till they met, just a couple of bad hats rolling along, waiting for somebody to stomp 'em flat. Split them up and that's what will happen. . . .*

He also said I'd get myself killed trying to split them up. But you can't believe everything a half-breed tells you, and a convict into the bargain.

"My name is Urban Vivian. I'm an inspector with the North-West Mounted Police. I've come to speak with Wolf Shirt, the Sioux chief. Where is he?"

Whitelaw smiled at the Englishman, showing his canines. "I'll introduce you." He stepped sideways and made a motion with the rifle.

A well-trod path led through a cleft in the rocks into a circular enclosure surrounded by granite, as if an enormous spoon had scooped a piece out of the top of the rock. It was a couple of acres, big enough to erect some lodges and build a community fire, which still crackled inside a circle of stones. There were no lodges, however; a number of distinctive hoop-shaped depressions in the dust showed where some had stood until recently, but there was no other sign of habitation. When we stepped into the area, Bliss and Whitelaw following, we shared it with a dozen white men in overcoats and an Indian woman seated cross-legged on the ground beside something stretched out on a buffalo robe. The woman was wailing softly, a sound that until that moment I had taken for the wind moaning through openings in the rock.

The men were loaded down heavily with cartridge belts, belly guns, and rifles, but I didn't need any of that to conclude that this was the gang that had raped its way across four territories and the Dominion of Canada over a period of eighteen months. Men who had been traveling and living together for a long time tended to look alike, after the fashion of stones rolled along a riverbed or more precisely a pack of mongrels; worn by constant movement and shared instinct to the same shape, color, and texture, gaunt and brown and sandy-looking, slit-eyed and jerk-jointed, with whatever humanity they might have started out with strung out in the bends and snags and cataracts upstream. Two of them were Negroes, and another was twice as old as the average, with a bad eye and dull white moustaches like dirty linen, but for that they might have all belonged to the same unnatural litter. They watched us with the steady naked intensity of scavengers standing around a shared carcass.

The woman on the ground looked sixty. She could as easily have been forty; it was a brutal life, for all the eastern writers made of its simple nobility. Her hair was unfettered and streaked with broad bands of leaden gray, her doeskin dress torn away from one shoulder, exposing nearly all of one breast. She sat with her palms turned upward on her knees. I took the three diagonal red stripes she wore on each forearm as some kind of tribal marking until I noticed that she was bleeding from them and had been for a long time. Most of the blood had dried brown

on her arms, staining her dress and the rock upon which
she sat the same rusty color. The keening noise she made
was very soft, not because she was trying to be quiet, but
because she had been doing it for at least as long as she had
been bleeding, and she was exhausted and hoarse. She was
mourning.

The buffalo robe she sat beside had been spread carefully, its wrinkles smoothed out from the center toward the
edges. Upon it lay the body of an Indian man of about fifty.
His iron-gray hair was braided, the braids socketed in cyl-
inders made of otterskin decorated with porcupine quills
dyed red and blue. He wore a headdress of white eagle
feathers tipped with black and sewn into a beaded band.
An intricate breastplate made of small bones, as flexible
as chain mail, covered an outfit of soft white skins, the
sleeves and leggings trimmed with long fringe. His winter
moccasins, decorated with beading and quillwork, extended to his knees. His hands were folded on his chest, and
a longbow and lance made of ironwood and an elaborate
quiver filled with arrows lay alongside him; he would need
them to sustain himself in the well-stocked hunting fields
that awaited him beyond this life.

The face beneath the headdress wore a permanent
scowl. The skin was cracked all over like dried mud and
the deep lines that framed the corners of the wide mouth
might have been scored with a knife. The flesh had already
begun to shrink in the intense sunlight.

Corporal Barrymore crossed himself. The sergeant
turned his head and spat over his left shoulder. They would
belong to different denominations.

Vivian looked down at the corpse without expression.
"Wolf Shirt?"

"That's what his woman said." Whitelaw's canines
clenched his lower lip like fangs. "We didn't kill him. He
died all on his own before we got here."

"Where are the others?" I asked.

"Cleared out. The chief was the only thing keeping them from going back south and turning theirselves in to the army."

"Injuns are dumb as cowflop," Bliss said.

Whitelaw said, "I'm Indian."

"You wasn't brought up in a leather house with your ass hanging out of a washrag."

"Ballocks." The sergeant wiped the spittle from his moustache with the back of a hand. "They wouldn't run off and leave their chiefs squaw out here in the open without provisions."

"They would if no one volunteered to take her in," I said. "Not many do. It's hard enough looking after one's own woman and children with the buffalo gone."

"Savages," said the corporal.

I shook my head. "Just different. Forgotten people starve to death in alleys back East every day."

"They should of held out," said Bliss. "Life on a rock beats getting hung in Dakota."

Whitelaw's laugh was a dry cough. "We ought to know."

"Their old people probably want to be buried back home," I said. "Wolf Shirt's death helped them make the decision. Some of their young have never seen the places they tell stories about. If the stories die too it's as if they never lived." I looked at the outlaws. "What I'd like to know is how you got the woman to tell you anything. They don't stop to talk when they're mourning their dead."

Bliss made that grin that gave out short of his eyes. "It wasn't her first choice. Charlie signed to her I'd cut off her man's business and throw it off the rock if she didn't answer some questions. Injuns got a thing against facing their maker without all the parts he sent them down with in the first place."

"You should have moved on," Vivian said. "Now you're trapped."

Bliss said, "We *was* trapped. Now we got us a Pullman ticket out."

"We're going to play those three red kings, misdeal or no," Whitelaw said. "You redbirds have got this far without losing too many feathers. I'm thinking your men will clear us a path if they don't want to lose three in one shot."

"A path to where?" I asked. "You're wanted in two countries now.

The Cherokee turned his round face my direction. "Talk some more."

"And say what? I'd read the Bible if I had one and I thought it would take."

"You're American," he said. "What you doing so far off your range?"

"Chasing you."

"Law?"

"I'm a deputy U.S. marshal."

"Well, we can't use you. Stick him, Lolo. Cut his heart out."

Bliss was moving almost before Whitelaw spoke. He had his bowie in his right hand as he lunged and I turned right to narrow the target, but it was just a feint. He border-shifted the knife to his left and drove in low and hard to come up under my ribcage, and I wasn't fast enough in this world or the next to protect myself.

He was as strong as a bull; I felt the blow to my teeth and my cracked ribs pulled apart and snapped back together, pinching me so that for an instant I thought it was the knife going in. But the buckskin wrap that still encased my torso was as hard as oak. I saw the surprise in his face when the blade struck it. Before he could recover I turned inside him, got both hands on the arm holding the knife, brought up my knee, and broke his arm across my raised thigh as if it were a piece of firewood. The knife dropped from his nerveless hand and I shoved him back and bent to scoop it up. Barbs of granite stung my hand and the knife sped away. I didn't even hear the report of the Henry in Whitelaw's hands. When I straightened, rubbing the back of my hand, smoke was still twisting out the end of the barrel.

"Rock breaks scissors," he said.

The rest of the gang had their weapons out and trained on me. I worked my fingers to make sure the tendons were still in operation but didn't move apart from that. The back of my hand was flecked with blood as if I'd tangled up with barbed wire.

Bliss was half bent over, holding his broken arm against his side. The pain hadn't started yet. "Son of a bitch is wearing some kind of armor!"

"You must of missed and hit his belt buckle," Whitelaw said.

"Horseshit! Make him open his damn shirt."

"I reckon you better open it. Lolo's hard to simmer down once he gets a prickly pear up his ass."

I'd unbuttoned the bearskin for the climb up the rock. Now I unfastened my shirt and spread it apart. The belt of rawhide looked like a dirty plaster cast. It was looser than it had been when it was fresh. I could have shucked it off over my head if my arms didn't get in the way.

"Jesus!" Bliss was shrill. "There's the dent the bowie made. I made deeper cuts in trees."

"That regulation wear for lawmen in Montana these days?" Whitelaw asked.

"My own invention. I thought it might keep me warm." I was gambling on a member of one of the Five Civilized Tribes knowing nothing of Cree medicine. My ribs were still healing from the fight with Brother Babel and I saw nothing good in letting this bunch in on any weaknesses.

The smell of blood has the same effect on scavengers everywhere.

Vivian stepped in to my rescue. "You'd better get help for your friend's arm. I heard it break in at least two places."

Whitelaw said, "Well, now, maybe you'd care to fix up a splint. Seeing as how the only wood on this here rock is what's burning in that fire."

"You could file the barrel off that rifle, Luther's got them tools off that blacksmith we kilt in Sheridan." Bliss's voice was getting shallow. The shock was wearing off and the pain was starting.

"I ain't going to saw the barrel off this Henry."

"Roy! You said you trusted your Colt before that Springfield."

"Not past fi'ty feet." The old man spread his moustaches to show six teeth spread out in bunches. He filled his hollow chest as if he were breathing in the other man's pain.

"Laban! Redfoot! You niggers can't hit the obvious side of a buffalo with them long guns."

The two Negroes, a big one with a scatter of black beard and a small one in a river pilot's cap, shook their heads. They were both grinning broadly.

"You goddamn cunts! Sons of bitches! Cornholers! *Hijos de las putas!*" The rest was Spanish outside my range. It was evidently a far more versatile language for the purpose he had in mind. He was holding his left arm so tight the knuckles of his right hand stood out like white porcelain drawer knobs.

"I do like to listen to Lolo cuss. Just about everything else about him gets on my nerves." Whitelaw covered his canines and poked his rifle at Vivian. "You got some talking to do. Climb up on that tall rock and show your men that pretty red uniform."

"Go to blazes!"

The Cherokee braced the Henry against his hip. Vivian folded his arms across his chest. His expression was the same as the one he had showed me in Moose Jaw when we were discussing the relative merits and deficiencies of the British Empire and the United States of America.

After thirty seconds, Whitelaw breathed in and out quickly, an exasperated sigh, and relaxed his grip on the rifle. Then he swiveled and shot young Barrymore in the chest.

The freckle-faced corporal sat down on the rock and fell over sideways with his legs still spread out in front of him. His white helmet tilted to one side and blood slid out of his mouth into a pool on the rock. It was much darker than his tunic, almost black.

Whitelaw jacked in a fresh shell and pointed the Henry at the sergeant.

"Your party's getting smaller, Inspector. You want to go down with Custer?"

After a moment Vivian uncrossed his arms and started climbing.

26

The inspector braced himself in the same cleft in the rock where the warning shot had been fired into the lake earlier. When it was certain that the Mounties stationed along the shore had recognized the uniform, Whitelaw fed Vivian the words and he bawled them out. He repeated them to make sure nothing was lost, then came down. His face was stiff and flushed beneath the sunburn. It was cold up there and the wind shrilled through the cleft.

"Think it took?" Whitelaw asked him.

"They're taught to obey orders."

You could see the Cherokee thinking. He jerked his chin toward the corporal's corpse. "Strip off that uniform."

"Do it yourself," Vivian said.

"Yours'd fit me just as good." Whitelaw raised the rifle.

Once again the inspector crossed his arms. Whitelaw said shit and motioned with his weapon. "Laban, strip off that uniform."

The big Negro set his feet. "I ain't touching no dead corpse."

"You touched plenty that had a poke in their pockets."

"I didn't take off their damn clo'es."

Redfoot, the small Negro in the pilot's cap, came forward. "I'll do it. I worked for a undertaker one whole summer in McAlester."

Whitelaw blocked his path with the Henry's barrel. "I told Laban to do it."

"I ain't your nigger."

Whitelaw stepped back and aimed low. "I'll blow off your kneecap and you and Lolo can help each other down the rock. You can watch your leg rot down on the flat."

Redfoot said, "Come on, Laban. You can give me a hand with his boots."

Laban stuck it out as long as he could, then moved in to help. Outlaws on the run had a horror of untreated wounds. They'd made their peace with the hangman's rope, but not with gangrene.

I said, "I thought you boys got along better than this. What's kept you glued together?"

"We're O.K. as long as we keep moving. Goddamn it, Lolo, quit your blubbering. You sound worse than the woman."

Bliss was sitting on the ground now with his arm cradled in his lap. His face was the color of unbleached muslin and clammy looking. "Go to hell, you cornholing son of a red squaw bitch." His voice was without tone.

"Yeller, whittle a pair of splints off that lance."

A thick-built party in a buffalo coat and a sail-brimmed hat with a feather in the band left the group and produced a skinning knife from a soft leather sheath on his belt. His beard was bright yellow against the burned brown of his skin. The Indian woman left off wailing as he approached Wolf Shirt's corpse. She was watching him out the corner of one eye. When he bent down to pick up the lance, she launched herself to her feet and fell upon him from behind, twining her legs around his waist and clawing his face with both hands.

She was silent now, saving her energy for breathing and tearing skin. Yeller was making all the noise. He howled and cursed and spun around, trying to throw her off, while

Whitelaw and the others—all except Bliss—laughed and shouted encouragement to the woman: "Claw out his eyes!" "Bite his ear!" "Throw him down and squat on his face!" Finally he remembered he was holding a knife. He slashed at her left arm, and he must have cut a tendon because she let go of her grip and she was too weak from loss of blood to hold on with the other. He flung her off and she fell on her back and before she could get up, he bent over her and slashed right and left with long hacking movements of his arm, like a farmer cutting wheat. A lariat of blood unfurled in the air and splattered the toe of my right boot. I stepped forward, but Whitelaw was between us in a stride with the Henry raised and I stopped. My hands hurt. I was making fists so tight my nails cut into my palms.

It was over in three or four seconds. Yeller straightened, breathing heavily and dripping blood from the deep scratches on his face. The woman lay without moving.

"Now cut those splints," Whitelaw said.

Ironwood doesn't cut easily. Yeller worked for an hour at the handle of the lance, cursing under his breath and drawing a sleeve across his face from time to time to clear his eyes of sweat and blood, while Bliss moaned and cursed and rocked back and forth over his shattered arm and Whitelaw tried on the uniform that Laban and Redfoot had removed from Corporal Barrymore. The others played cards with a tattered deck on a saddle blanket spread on the ground, betting gold watches, paper money, and silver forks they'd plundered across the north country. Roy, the old man with the bad eye—it looked like a gob of yellow spittle quivering between his corrugated lids—sat out to guard the prisoners with his Springfield carbine across his lap. We prisoners sat on the ground and conversed in low whispers.

"I promoted Barrymore from the ranks," Vivian said. "I planned to recommend him for officer's training in Ottawa."

The young man lay on his back in his white longhandles, clean except for the stain around the blue hole in his chest. One of his heavy ribbed woolen socks had come off when his boots were removed. His foot was clean and white, like a woman's hands.

The sergeant ground his teeth on his moustaches. "They're a pack of dogs. Hanging's too kind for their like. We ought to bring back drawing and quartering."

I said, "I'll sign the petition. Right now I wouldn't give us until midnight to finish drawing it up before they kill us. They'll wait for dark to move out. That's their best chance to confuse your men with that Mountie uniform. After that they'll put us away to make time."

"Where are their horses?" asked the sergeant.

"This looks like box canyon country," I said. "They'll have them corraled in one and under guard. They'll head there first thing."

Vivian was still thinking about Barrymore. "My fault. Stubborn old regular army officer. That's what's costing us India."

"He's dead," I said. "We're not. If we can get to our horses on the way down we might be able to make the break."

"My fault." Vivian was looking at the ground.

He wasn't going to be any help.

Whitelaw tried tugging on one of the corporal's boots, then gave up and stamped his feet into his old worn stovepipes. The black cavalry trousers with the white stripe up one side were a good fit and the tunic answered, although it was a little long in the sleeves and snug across the chest, where the buttons strained. The helmet was too small but he adjusted the chinstrap and it looked as if it would stay put if he didn't move too hastily. He could have fooled a good eye at some distance and in the dark. If the Mounties shot anyone it wouldn't be him.

Bliss must have been reading my mind. "I need a red suit too. That muckety inspector's getup looks like it might fit."

"You'd never get the coat on over that arm," Whitelaw said. "I ain't just out to save my hide. They sent three of their men up here. If only two come back down they might open fire out of pure orneriness."

"Horseshit. You're a yellow injun."

Whitelaw made one of his long strides and kicked his arm. Bliss made a high-pitched shriek, then rolled over, pinning the arm to his side, and vomited. A sharp stench of half-digested whiskey soured the air. Whitelaw made his dry cough of a laugh and went over to join the card game.

"Thieves' honor." The inspector seemed to have stopped thinking about Barrymore.

"Outlaw fever," I said. "When wolves run together long enough, they start going at each other."

"Drawing and quartering," said the sergeant.

Vivian said, "They'll expect us to go for our horses. They'll send a man ahead to cut them loose."

I said, "Hold them, maybe. Whitelaw will want them close in case anything goes wrong between here and where they're hiding their own mounts. If it comes down to shooting he'll save himself first. Bliss was right about that business of keeping the count. He's betting on that uniform to save his life."

Vivian shook his head. "It's a wonder they stayed together this long."

"They were born to ride partners. No one else but the devil would have them."

"Ghastly country you have, that turns out beasts such as them."

This time I didn't rise to the inspector's lure. If I did, we wouldn't be getting on any better than Whitelaw and Bliss.

Yeller finished the splints finally and cut a dozen long fringes from Wolf Shirt's sleeve to tie them in place on Bliss's arm. Before that he placed his foot against the injured man's chest and jerked back on the arm with both hands to set the bone. If the Mounties down on the flat didn't hear the scream, they must have been paying attention to something else. Bliss passed out after that.

Whitelaw measured the height of the sun with his hands and told Yeller to wrap the chief in the buffalo robe before he began to stink. "Throw the woman and that redbird corporal in with him."

"Tell one of the niggers to do it. Redfoot can paint them pink and stick a lily in their paws." He was sitting on a rock with his greasy hat balanced on its crown in his lap and the sweatband turned inside out to dry, dabbing at his scratches with a filthy blue bandanna wetted down from his canteen. Wispy blonde strands crawled about his naked scalp in the breeze. It was a pale cap above the line where his sunburn left off, white as a grub.

The Henry's stock swung and collided with Yeller's head. He fell off the rock and came up holding his skinning knife. The blade was clotted with gore. He hadn't bothered to clean it before putting it away.

The Cherokee followed him up with the barrel of the rifle. His sharp canines slid out. "You want to run this outfit?" he asked.

Yeller looked at the muzzle but didn't let go of the knife. The whites of his eyes swam with blood.

"I'll make it easy." Whitelaw lowered the rifle from his hip. He sank into a crouch, laid the weapon on the ground, and stood back up. He moved slowly and his eyes never left the other man's. "You want to run this outfit? Tell me what you're fixing to do when you get off this rock."

A gray tongue slid along Yeller's lips and went back inside like a toad. He bounced the knife in his hand, improving his grip. "Make a run for it."

"If you run they'll fire up that chattergun and cut you into smaller pieces than you did the woman. You can do better than that. Think with your head, not your feet."

"After I stick you I'll put on that there uniform. They won't shoot one of their own."

"That might work. What about the others, Lolo and Roy and Laban and the rest? There ain't uniforms enough to go around. You need a plan to make them follow you down the rock that won't spare you and kill them. Otherwise you'll never make it down alive."

"You ain't told us *your* plan."

"I never tell you anything you don't need to know. That's got us this far, all of you know that. You're brand new. You got to show them they can trust you to take them through. Come up with anything yet?"

There they were, Whitelaw smiling, showing his sharp teeth with his hands empty, and Yeller holding the knife he'd killed with once that day, looking as if he were the one under the threat. Remington could have painted the picture down to the last detail, caught the glint in the Cherokee's eye and made the beads of sweat glitter on the bald man's head, and nobody would have bought it or risk having to explain the picture to everyone who saw it.

"Well, how do I know you even got a plan?" Yeller wanted to know.

"Because God gave me brains, and all He gave you is

that little knife. I was you, I'd take better care of it. Your good looks won't get you off this rock."

The others had lost interest in their game. Only Roy, who kept his good eye on us with his carbine across his thighs, wasn't watching. The men's faces were alive with interest, but none of them seemed eager to take a hand or choose sides. They didn't want to wind up on the wrong one. Bliss was either still out or listening quietly. It was anyone's bet which one he'd root for.

"Any luck?" Whitelaw asked. "I don't want to make you nervous, but there's only an hour of daylight left."

"Shit." The bald man with the yellow beard wiped off both sides of the blade on his pants, jammed the knife into its sheath, and turned to look after the corpses.

The air lifted then. The men picked up their cards and resumed making bets. Whitelaw picked up the Henry. He'd stopped smiling.

"Leave off that," he told Yeller. "Laban, Redfoot, wrap up them carcasses. You was right, Yeller. It ain't work for a white man."

Yeller turned back and stared at him a long time before he scooped up his hat and slapped the dust off it and jammed it onto his head with both hands. His face was absolutely empty of intelligence. Mine was too, or I was a better poker player than I thought.

27

The sun slid into a slot in the granite pinnacle on the west side of the stronghold, throwing long fingers of shadow across the two men struggling to drag the bodies of the Indian woman and the Mountie corporal onto the buffalo robe. When they stooped to lift one side of the robe, Lorenzo Bliss stirred himself for the first time in an hour.

"Hang on." Throwing his splinted left arm straight out for balance, he put his right hand on the ground and pushed himself to his knees and then his feet. He found his bowie knife where it had fallen and knelt over the bodies. After a minute he wiped the knife on the robe, sheathed it, and rose, holding a long iron-gray banner in his right hand. I looked down, saw the raw red patch on the front of Wolf Shirt's skull, and directed my gaze to the scuffed toe of my left boot until my stomach walloped to a halt.

"I always wanted a chief's scalp." He held the thing by one end and snapped it several times like a whip to shake off the loose gore. "You know how to tan one of these things, Charlie?"

"Cherokee don't take scalps." Whitelaw buckled on Barrymore's belt.

"I reckon if I soak it in brine and dry it in the sun, it'll keep. I'll get it wove into a belt or something later." He pulled off the kerchief he had tied around his neck and tried wrapping the bloody end in it one-handed, but he was clumsy. Whitelaw took the scalp from him, wound it a few times around one hand, then took the kerchief and tied it into a neat bundle and stuck it into the side pocket of Bliss's canvas coat. "Don't forget and leave it in there if you don't want to stink like a goat."

"Or an injun." Bliss grinned.

"Better an injun than a greaser mick bastard."

They were friends again now.

Bliss sent Yeller to collect the hip guns he'd taken off us. When he returned carrying one in each hand with two more stuck in his belt, Bliss relieved him of my Deane-Adams and came over to where I was sitting on the ground. He cocked the revolver, stuck the barrel under my chin, and lifted it. I saw my reflection in his black eyes.

"What do they call you in Montana?" he asked.

"Murdock."

"Hell, I never heard of you." He raked the sight across the underside of my chin, took the pistol off cock, and shoved the barrel under his belt. "You want it, take it," he said.

I yanked it out and thrust it into his groin in the same motion. I felt his reaction right through it. He'd expected me to think about it first.

Something hard and cold touched my left temple, still tender from the blow earlier: the muzzle of Roy's Springfield.

"You shoot, you die," he said.

I spun the Deane-Adams, offering the handle to Bliss. I managed to loosen my grip before he could tear my hand with the sight the way he had my chin.

"Lolo, if you was any dumber you couldn't bore an asshole in a wood duck," Whitelaw said. "He ain't one of them tin panners on the Saskatchewan."

"Blast him, Roy," Bliss said.

"Back off, Roy. Them Mounties will think we're shooting our prisoners."

Roy backed off.

Bliss leaned his face close to mine. Beads of sweat showed in the delicate cleft in his upper lip. "When I get you down on the ground, I'll gut you like a frog."

I said nothing. He walked away.

"You should have pulled the trigger." The sergeant's voice was a hissing snarl.

Vivian said, "If he had, you'd be sitting with his brains in your lap."

I didn't take part in the discussion. Roy's carbine wasn't the reason I hadn't fired. I never drew a weapon just to make a point. In the natural order of things I'd have emptied the chamber under the hammer as soon as I felt resistance on the other end, before the old man had a chance to throw down on me. If it had been Whitelaw instead of Bliss, or any of the others, I wouldn't have hesitated. One of the things I'd learned from war is that wounding a man causes more trouble for the enemy than killing him outright; if they cared about their own, an injured man took two more out of combat to carry him to safety, and a delay of a few minutes can make the difference in the way a battle comes out. Bliss's arm was already crippled. That meant he'd need help getting down off the rock and making his escape with the others. Dead, he'd be left where he fell to feed whatever did the work of buzzards in Canada, and the rest would be free to flee at their own pace.

Of course, I was counting plenty on Vivian's Mounties being in a position to take advantage of the slowdown—and on Whitelaw and the rest of the gang thinking enough of Lolo to mess with the burden.

In a little while the sun had gathered up the last of its heat and stolen below the edge of the rock. The last yellow flames of the campfire were licking at the crumbs of unburned wood that remained and warmed little but themselves. The first steel clamp of Arctic cold closed around my ears and neck. I turned up the bearskin's collar and buttoned it to my throat. It chafed the flesh beneath my chin where Bliss had raked it with the Deane-Adams' front sight.

The chill made Bliss's arm throb. He paced about to increase his circulation, working the fingers that stuck out as red as radishes between the splints and calling Whitelaw in English and Spanish a whore's son for ever suggesting they leave the Nations for this frozen shitpile in the middle of no place. The fact that Bliss's own mother was a whore didn't seem to enter into the logic of the moment. The Cherokee paid him no attention. He was busy drilling the others on what he expected of them when he gave the order to pull out. Corporal Barrymore's uniform had begun to have its effect upon his tone and bearing—and on the way Laban and Redfoot and Roy and Yeller and the rest nodded assent. In all that murdering crew there was not one word said in interruption. Brass and bright colors were much easier to make sport of at a distance than close up and when your immediate future depended upon who was wearing it. Beneath that lay the understanding that Whitelaw and Bliss had taken them this far, with hundreds of peace officers in two countries wearing out horseflesh and telegraph wires to capture them and stretch their necks. These men would have laughed to read the superhuman stuff that was written about the pair in the eastern dreadfuls, but they would not have discounted it as impossible.

It was nearly dark now in that high hollow circle of weathered and broken stones, but there was still plenty of light on the flat. We were waiting for the darkness to reach the ground. A lantern was lit so Roy could keep an eye on us prisoners, but the wick was turned low to preserve the gang's night vision. The coal-oil fumes mingled with the lingering sulphur stink of spent powder and the stench of butchering, and might have made me retch if I had anything in my stomach. I realized then how many hours had passed since I'd eaten. My stomach rumbled.

The top layer of purple turned dirty-brown over the western territories, then disappeared beneath the black. There was no moon, but the snow provided its own illumination, with the lake a tattered black oval in the white. A pie-faced youth the others called Stote, with a downy froth of whiskers and nails gnawed down to bleeding stumps, produced a grubby almanack, moved his lips over it in the light from the lantern, and announced they had an hour before the rise of the quarter moon. Whitelaw's instructions kicked in then. Vivian, the sergeant, and I were told to stand up and herded through the cleft to the ledge where Bliss and Whitelaw had first thrown down on us. There, armed with the lantern and his Springfield, Roy held us at bay while the two Negroes went over the edge and Yeller tied a rope from his kit around Bliss's chest under his arms. Then Stote and a man with yellow-brown eyes like a wolf's helped Bliss over the edge and lowered him, grunting advice and curses, to where Laban and Redfoot waited to receive him where the descent relaxed into a gentle grade. The process must have been agonizing for Bliss, but he bore it in silence, probably with teeth clenched; any complaint would have carried down to the lake and given the Mounties too much time to think. I caught a glimpse of him on the way down, dangling with his splinted arm stuck out to the side like a damaged wing, and remembered the too many men I had seen hanged. And I wondered if he was in too much pain to ask himself if this was what he had to look forward to.

When he was safely down and untied, Stote and the wolf-eyed man made the end of the rope fast to a rock for the rest to clamber down. Yeller, who had rescued Wolf Shirt's longbow from the buffalo robe, passed it down for Bliss to use as an alpenstock to steady himself during the walk down, then used the rope to lower himself hand over hand. The others, all except Roy and Whitelaw, followed him; then Whitelaw fixed the Henry over his shoulder by its sling and made the descent somewhat clumsily; a century of the white man's brand of civilization had leeched away most of the survival skills of his Cherokee ancestors.

Then it was our turn. Roy stood back with his carbine while the sergeant climbed down and then Vivian. The bearskin dragged heavily when I was hanging by just my hands, and I wished I'd thought to toss it down ahead of me; but then I found a foothold on the cliff and the rest wasn't much more difficult than climbing down a ladder. I jumped the last three feet and grabbed the twisted trunk of a small jackpine to find my balance on the slope.

Roy had no sling on his carbine and so passed it down by its barrel for Yeller to take hold of the stock. I saw then where someone had carved a series of shallow nicks in the walnut near the buttplate. Just five notches seemed low, given the gang's run; but then he might have lost interest since he'd cut the last one.

He was older than any of the others and probably had rheumatism, which the cold would only have aggravated. It took him the best part of five minutes just to climb over the edge, where he rested with one knee braced against it before trusting his weight to the rope. Silhouetted against the slightly lighter sky, he appeared to be shaking. Whitelaw had to bark his name before he decided to push off and hang by his hands, and then his grip wasn't up to it. He made a croaking little gasp and dropped ten feet. One leg turned under when he hit. I heard the bone snap clean as the rest of him flopped into a heap at Whitelaw's feet.

"My leg's busted! Oh, Mother of God!" His voice cracked.

"Try getting up," Whitelaw said. "Maybe you just banged it good."

Laban stuck out his hand. Roy grasped it and tried to stand. He howled and fell back. Yeller, who had carried the lantern down, held it while the big man leaned over Roy. Laban straightened. "Bone's sticking right out through his pants."

"Jesus God!" Roy groaned. "Oh, Jesus."

Yeller said, "We can't carry him."

"He knows where we're headed," Whitelaw said. "No shots."

Yeller handed the lantern to Laban and got out his skinning knife. Roy was hurting too much to see what was coming until just before Yeller cut his throat. His cry ended in a gurgle.

"Old Roy." Stote stroked his nascent beard. "I'll miss his lies about riding with Frank and Jesse."

Bliss said, "Don't you boys go getting no ideas about me. I can move just as fast with both arms busted."

"Hell, Lolo." Yeller wiped off his knife on Roy's shirt and returned it to its sheath. "You ride with *both* arms stuck out like that, you'll just take off and fly like a big old kite."

"Just don't you boys go getting no ideas about me."

Whitelaw picked up Roy's Springfield from where Yeller had left it leaning against a rock and handed it to the wolf-eyed man. "Keep an eye on Murdock and the red-birds. Hands high, the three of you." He gave Stote the Henry and lifted his own hands. He was playing the part of a prisoner; the only difference was he had one of the confiscated side arms in his belt holster with the flap undone.

With Whitelaw leading we picked our way down the

rockfall. It was treacherous going in the dark without the use of our hands. The sergeant, walking in front of me and behind Vivian, put his foot wrong once and would have fallen against the inspector and knocked him down if I hadn't caught him by the shoulders. For my trouble I got a poke in the kidneys from the carbine in the hands of the wolf-eyed man, who thought I'd tried to make a break.

The closer we got to the ground, the better we could see. The surface of the snow gathered the high dim dusting of starlight and threw it back magnified, like the crystal in a chandelier, slicing the shadows off crisp at the edges and washing everything else in icy white. Even distant details seemed more sharply defined than in daytime, as if I were looking at them through a pinhole in a sheet of foolscap. When we got to within a hundred yards of where the horses were tethered, stamping and shaking their manes for warmth in the silvery smoke of their spent breath, I could make out the snake-shaped blaze on the mustang's forehead. The chestnut coats of the animals belonging to the North-West Mounted gleamed like silk hats.

The mustang spotted us first. Hungry and cold, it raised its head and cut loose with a shrill, querulous neigh.

That was when the night blew apart with orange and blue muzzle-flashes and the *tchocketa-tchocketa-tchock* of the Gatling coughing up its lungful of lead.

28

Charlie Whitelaw went down hard, rolling the rest of the way down the grade and coming out on the level, flat on his stomach, where he lay unmoving while the bullets buzzed over him. I couldn't tell if he was hit or had acted from reflex because I was down myself by that time, knocked flat by the weight of the Mountie sergeant. I didn't know where he was struck or how badly. I shoved him off me and crawled over to where Inspector Vivian lay hugging the pile of rocks that curved down from where the stronghold had begun its collapse one or ten thousand years before. His whole body jerked when I gripped his shoulder; he wasn't dead.

"Is this how you obey orders up here?" I asked him. "Whitelaw made you call down to hold their fire."

I saw one pale eye and the flesh of a bitten-off British smile.

"I could have given them the rest of the month off from up there and they'd not have budged. Ottawa issued a standing order when the police were commissioned, and no one's disobeyed it yet: No bargains. No negotiations. No hostages."

"Not even their own?"

"Especially not their own. No part of the force is more important than the force. The force is not more important than the law. How is the sergeant?"

"Dead or wounded. I can't tell."

"Stupid blighter. No etiquette at all. I never commanded a better man." He made a noise of discomfort.

"Are you hit?"

"Right in the old breadbasket. Good job I haven't had a bite since breakfast. Not that even Saint bloody Bartholomew could do a thing for me out here."

I felt empty. I didn't know why. I didn't like the man.

The deep barking cough of the Gatling had continued, the blue flashes tinged with orange sparking clockwise in a circle and sweeping left and right as the gun turned on its swivel. Ragged small-arms fire opened up, throwing up little arcs of snow from the ground behind a figure running in a crouch across the flat toward the horses, one arm stuck awkwardly out to the side.

Vivian spotted him at the same time I did. "That rotter Bliss! After him, man! Hurry!"

The Gatling had swung right to chop at a number of gang members fleeing in that direction. I pushed myself up and ran, pausing when I reached level ground only to look down at Whitelaw. The back of his coat was stained dark, with blood bubbling out of a hole in the center of the patch. He'd been shot through a lung. When I resumed running the Gatling swiveled back around; I felt the vibration made by the heavy slugs striking the ground behind me. A clump of snow and mud struck my pantslegs. I picked up my pace. If I slipped and fell they'd have to shovel me into the ground.

Bliss had got hold of one of the Mountie horses and hauled himself one-handed into the saddle. He lunged straight at me to run me down. I sidestepped left, putting him and the animal between me and the big gun, and snatched at the bridle. Stinging heat lashed the right side of my face; he'd quirted me with the ends of the reins. I fell backwards, my legs sliding in front of the chestnut's hooves. It reared and a bullet from the Gatling buzzed under its belly and tore the badger hat off my head. The horse leapt over me, scrabbled for its balance in the snow, and took off at the gallop.

I threw myself into a roll, came up alongside the mustang, and got hold of its reins as it was straining to rear against the tether. I fumbled for the loop, slipped it, and got a foot into the stirrup just as it took off. I groped for the saddle horn and hung on in a crouch Comanche-style, using the horse for a shield. Something thudded into the mustang's side, it grunted and stumbled as if the wind had been knocked out of it, but caught its balance and found its pace; a slug must have struck the saddle.

The Gatling continued to chatter, with lighter rounds cracking and popping in between, but by then we were moving too fast to make a good target in the ghostly light conditions. I got my other leg over the horse's back and bent low for speed. Bliss's chestnut had left a clear trail in the snow, with here and there a spot the size of a silver dollar that looked black on the white surface. One or both had been hit, although I couldn't tell how badly.

Mountie animals were bred for speed, but cow ponies are accustomed to cutting through scrub and cactus and are tough to beat on the flat. I knew I was gaining on him when something cracked overhead and I realized it was a ball from my own Deane-Adams. It didn't slow me down. The odds of hitting anything with a belt gun from horseback are too small to figure, and with his left arm out of action Bliss couldn't neglect the reins long enough to take aim. I hunched lower and raked the mustang's flanks with my spurs. The sound of gunfire faded behind us like something belonging to someone else's battle.

We kept it up for what felt like hours. Most likely it was no more than ten minutes before we entered some rolling country north of the lake, and I slacked off a little in case he'd decided to dismount and set up an ambush from a crease between hills. As I swung down, a bullet split the air where my head had been a second earlier, followed by the report.

I saw the fading phosphorescence of the muzzle flare, squeaked the Evans from the scabbard on my side of the horse, and snapped off a shot in that direction to keep him busy while I got into position for a better shot. I sank to one knee in the snow, wrapped the reins loosely around my boot to discourage the mustang from bolting, and drew a bead just above a dark oblong that lay across Bliss's trail some four hundred feet ahead. I guessed what it was without wasting time looking any harder; either the chestnut had been wounded and had given out finally, or Bliss had killed it to make a breastwork.

I was still lining up the sights when flame spurted again. He was using the rifle that had come with the horse, but he was unfamiliar with it or he was a lot less handy with a long gun than he was with his bowie because I never found out where the bullet went. I fired at the spot, jacked in a fresh round, and followed it up.

There was a long silence then. I unwound the reins from my ankle, looped them around each of the mustang's forelegs in a makeshift hobble, and moved away from it in a duckwalk. Just then a volley broke out from near the carcass up the trail—he was racking them in as fast as he could squeeze the trigger—and I threw myself flat on my belly to wait it out.

When it stopped I came up again, just in time to see something dark moving quickly against the snow beyond the carcass. Bliss was making a run. I took careful aim, leading the moving thing slightly with the barrel, but he changed courses abruptly just as I squeezed off, and I wasted the next shot jerking to adjust. I lost him then.

I let a minute go by I couldn't afford, in case he was

playing possum and waiting for me to show myself. Then I went back to the mustang and slipped its hobble.

I led the horse to the spot where the chestnut had gone down. It lay on its side with its tongue out and its eyes grown satiny soft, a great gout of blood glittering on its exposed side. The bullet had passed through both its lungs and exited there, and being a horse the animal hadn't thought to fall down until it was strangling in its own blood.

My Deane-Adams lay in the snow near where Bliss had knelt to use the Mountie rifle. I brushed it off, checked the load, replaced the spent shells with cartridges from my belt, and reunited it with its holster. Then I got back aboard the mustang and kneed it into the path of footprints in the snow. I kept it to a walk to avoid galloping into another ambush.

The moon and I came over the next hill at the same time. Now the white landscape was as bright as the desert by daylight. The trail of footprints made a straight black line over the hill beyond. Beyond *that* was black sky stained by uneven light: the glow of a large campfire.

Most fugitives in Bliss's position, pursued and finding themselves approaching other men, would have changed their course in the direction of friendly darkness. From the beginning, Lorenzo Bliss and Charlie Whitelaw had not behaved like any other pair of outlaws. Hunted, they had never stopped hunting. Fire meant people. People were game, a source of supplies and weapons and fresh horses, soft and secure in their numbers and easily disposed of by a man on the prod. The trail divided the hill in a straight line toward the light.

Nearing the top of that hill I stepped down and led the mustang. I added a hundred yards to my journey circling around to the west to keep the moon from silhouetting me from behind.

"You will lay the rifle at your feet."

The owner of the voice had followed my plan as carefully as I had. He stood facing me on the downslope of the hill, just as if he were blocking an existing road instead of a mound of undisturbed snow.

I didn't recognize the voice at first. Too much had happened since I had heard it last. But the mackinaw the man wore looked familiar, the white man's garment making a strong contrast with the braided silver of his long hair and the dusky face that looked as if it had been hacked out of red sandstone. And I had seen the watch chain before, glittering now like a thread of molten silver in the moonlight.

"We've met before," I said. "I didn't know your name then. You are Piapot, chief of the great Cree Nation."

Some Indians were mollified when a white man remembered to address them with the respect they took for granted when it was one of their own speaking. This one just told me again to lay my rifle at my feet. His tone was without threat or anger, but indicated clearly that he would not repeat himself a third time. I obeyed, moving slowly. He stood with his hands loose at his sides without a weapon showing, but there were others standing behind him, vague shadows against the flicker of the fire burning at the base of the hill. I'd been under the gun too many times not to recognize the feeling.

"You are the man who would not give us one of your rifles."

That impressed more than it frightened. The incident had taken place weeks ago and four hundred miles to the south. He had to have seen many white men in the time between, and we all look alike to many Indians. I didn't even consider denying it. "Yes," I said, and took a chance. "And you are the man whose medicine healed me after I was shot on the Saskatchewan."

He was silent long enough for me to wonder if I'd been mistaken about that after all.

"The medicine was not mine," he said. "Small Man is our shaman. It is against your law to kill another white skin, though it does not stop you from doing it. Your death would have brought harm to the crazy woman who shot you, and she is good medicine to the Cree. Therefore you did not die."

"I brought food to the crazy woman. She thought I was there to harm her. She made me well. I am not angry."

"You said before you had business." He buzzed the word with which he was only half familiar. "Is that the reason you have come all this way?"

"Yes. I'm a deputy United States marshal from the territory of Montana. I am hunting the men who killed the crazy woman's family and friends and made her crazy. I mean to bring them home to hang."

"You were chasing the man whose arm is broken."

"Yes. His trail led me here."

"You cannot have him. He will answer to the Cree."

"Answer for what? All his crimes are against the whites."

Piapot put a hand in one of the mackinaw's side pockets and drew something out of it. As he stretched it between his hands my stomach did a slow turn and landed with a thud.

"He had this on him. It is not the scalp of a white man or woman.

"It isn't," I said. "He cut it off the body of Wolf Shirt, a Sioux chief."

A brief pause was all he gave up to show surprise. "The man whose arm is broken killed Wolf Shirt?"

"No. He died of disease. The man with the broken arm is named Bliss. He took the scalp as a souvenir."

"I do not know this word."

"A trophy. He said he always wanted a Sioux scalp. He cut it off Wolf Shirt where he was laid out for burial."

"I do not understand why a man would want to claim a scalp from a man he did not kill. I will never understand why white men do what they do. Yet our friends the Sioux tell us the whites in America wish the red men to live as they."

"I stop trying to think the way men like Bliss think once I find out where they are," I said. "If you spend too much time in your enemy's skull you become the enemy."

He folded the scalp. No honor guard ever folded Old Glory with more reverence. "It is the—business—of a chief's woman to stay with him until he is buried. What was Wolf Shirt's woman doing when the man Bliss stole his scalp?"

I told him what Yeller had done when the woman tried to stop him from stealing the dead chief's lance to make Bliss's splints. He was as silent as the hills while I told him that Yeller was either dead or in Mountie custody. I hoped I was right.

"Bliss will answer to the Cree," Piapot said again.

Just then I heard a high-pitched curse from somewhere on the other side of the fire. The mix of Spanish and English ended in a ragged whimper I can still hear all these years later.

The chief spoke as if he had not heard it. "I see you still have two rifles. Will you now give us one?"

"No."

One of the men standing behind him seemed to know that English word very well. He said something to the chief with an edge that went up my spine like a rusty blade.

Piapot didn't appear to be listening. He folded the scalp once more, taking more time with it than simple respect alone commanded. Gently he returned it to his pocket.

"This is twice you have entered the land of the Cree and refused to pay tribute."

"I'd stop coming if I could figure out where Canada left off and the land of the Cree began. It seems to be spreading."

"It is not. In my youth it stretched from the Great Sea of Ice to the stinging sands where only the gila and the Apache live. When the snow came we rode down to where it is always warm and when the great heat came we rode up to where the pines grow through the clouds. In all that time we saw nothing of the white man. Now there is only one way we can ride so that we do not see him: North, where the white man will not live. There perhaps we can hunt and fight our old enemies and make love to our women and not hear white men gnawing down the trees like beaver to build the railway to bring more white men. When that happens, there will be nowhere left to go but out on the Great Sea of Ice."

He turned his back on me then and walked down the hill. The others lingered for a moment after he passed them, then followed. I was alone.

After a moment I picked up the Evans and returned it to its scabbard. When I put my foot in the stirrup, something fell out of my pocket. It was the leather pouch containing the bones of an African eagle, a charm to see me home safe. I scooped it up and put it back in my pocket. I still have it.

29

The firing had stopped by the time I got back to the lake, although smoke was still billowing, eye-stinging clouds laden with sulphur and mingling with steam from men and horses. To avoid getting shot I whistled loudly—"My Country, 'Tis of Thee" was the tune I chose, but if they decided to take it for "God Save the Queen," so much the better—riding with my bearskin spread open with the six-pointed star pinned to my shirt for the first time since I was almost shot out from behind it in '76. Even then, I learned later, a Mountie sharpshooter had been sighting in on me with a Martini-Henry when Philippe du la Rochelle put a hand on his arm and bought a gash in his scalp from the butt of Lieutenant Ponsoby's side arm for his trouble. It was only then that someone had spotted the badge.

I was ordered to dismount anyway, disarmed, and compelled to tell my story to the lieutenant before I was taken to a tent where Inspector Urban Vivian lay on a bedroll with his shirt off, and a Mountie wearing a bloody apron in place of his tunic was tying off his bandages. A trooper was pounding home the last stake into the frozen ground when Vivian glared at me in the light of a hissing lantern. His face was the color of water beneath his sunburn, his eyes unnaturally large and swimming. I knew the look of a corpse in the making, but I gave him the details anyway, knowing I'd have to do it all over again for whoever took his place. He was too weak to ask questions, but I could feel his irritation at my unsatisfactory report. The lieutenant made it clear that I was confined to camp until such time as my story could be passed on to Ottawa and instructions came back.

Vivian died just before dawn. He had served with distinction in Abyssinia and at Roarke's Drift, holding out in the latter place with a handful of British regulars against the same 40,000 Zulu warriors who had destroyed the Queen's army only a few days before at Isandhlwana. His body was packed with salt and shipped back to England for burial with full military honors, the first in a family of candlemakers and cloth merchants to receive them.

Corporal Gale Barrymore, whose mother had died during the ocean voyage to the New World and whose father lived on a government pension in Ottawa, was laid to rest in that city.

I understand the names of the Mounties who were killed at the stronghold are engraved among others on a brass plaque mounted on a marble wall in the capitol building in Ottawa. I don't know if the official record states that Inspector Urban Vivian was slain by his own men, but I approve of the honor. He led thirteen enemies of the Crown straight into police fire, knowing that it meant his own death. I admired him. I just couldn't get along with him.

The sergeant major's name was Rice. Although the bullet that smashed his pelvis gave him a permanent limp, he was promoted to inspector in 1891 for his part in a forty-seven-day manhunt resulting in the arrest and conviction of a Canadian Army deserter named Oberlin for the ambush-murder of three wealthy excursionists on the Yukon Trail. A year later he was considered for the office of superintendent, but rejected for his extreme views on the subject of criminal punishment, notably the suggestion to

revive the medieval practice of drawing and quartering. He
retired soon after.

Four members of the Bliss-Whitelaw Gang were killed
in the opening fire at Cree Lake, including young Stote,
the Negro Redfoot, and the wolf-eyed man, a quarter-
breed Ute named Dick Nighthunter. The fourth was not
Yeller, born Gunther Braun in Pennsylvania; he was captured along with Laban and three others, tried in Ottawa,
and hanged for the murder of a Métis family of four and a
Roman Catholic priest named Capet on Lake Athabasca.
The big Negro and one other were condemned, as well.
The remaining pair were sentenced to a lifetime at hard
labor in the penitentiary at Quebec.

Two more who had been with Bliss and Whitelaw at the
stronghold slipped away during the fight; their footprints
were traced to a half-moon-shaped cleft hollowed out by
glaciers a mile east of the lake, where a number of horses
had been picketed. The man who had been watching the
animals was never found, but a month later a farmer named
Donalbain shot to death two men he caught stealing horses
from his barn below the border in Montana. Pinkerton
detectives came out from Fort Benton to take pictures of
the corpses and make Bertillon measurements, then sent
the results to the home office in Chicago, where the two
were identified from penitentiary records as Virgil Hearn
and John Thomson, both of whom had served time in the
territories for armed robbery. Thomson's brother Ned was
the fourth man killed by the Mounties at the stronghold,
and so that loose end was considered tied down for good
and all.

I never saw Philippe or his family after we parted company at the Mountie camp. I found the little Métis sitting
on King Henry's wooden saddle on the ground near a
little campfire, not far from where the prisoners were being held under guard, complaining in mixed French and

English that Fleurette was tying the bandage too tight around his scalp wound. He wouldn't say how it happened, and Fleurette hadn't the English for it, but Claude broke his silence for the second time since we'd started out, providing a full and lucid account of how his father had managed to keep my name off a brass plaque in Ottawa; or more likely a wooden cross in Helena. (His choice of words and phrases puzzled me until years later, when I read *Wuthering Heights* for the first time.) Philippe barked at him. The boy stuck out his lip. Then his father said something just as gruff, but not as harsh, tweaked Claude's already scarlet cheek hard enough to hurt, and sent him off with a smack on the rump to look for his book and a spot by the fire.

"That was taking a chance," I said. "Once the killing starts, it's hard to stop, no matter what kind of training you've had."

He showed his gold teeth. "I have earned those double eagles, yes?"

I fished them out of the sack. When he reached for them, I dropped them into his palm and laid the Evans rifle across his lap with my other hand.

He looked up. "You will come home with us and I will give you the buffalo robe."

"I won't need it. After Canada, winter in Montana will feel like springtime in Missouri."

"That was not our bargain." He pocketed the coins and held out the rifle for me to take. I didn't.

Fleurette said something quietly. After a moment he said, *"Bon,"* and returned the rifle to his lap. *"Merci, monsieur le depute.* Deputy Marshal Murdock."

"Page will do. It's easier to say." I went back into my pocket. "Good luck finding ammunition. These are as many shells as I could gather up." I tipped the handful of brass empties into his hand. He gripped mine before letting go.

"The Métis are not without ingenuity in these things," he said. "You will return for the trial, no?"

I glanced toward the tent where the man who had dressed Vivian's wound was working on Whitelaw. "My part ends here. Anyway, I doubt he'll live long enough to see a courtroom."

"He will recover. A man with so much poison in him does not die like other men."

They had eaten, but there was some rabbit left and Fleurette insisted on warming it over the fire even though I was hungry enough to eat it cold, or for that matter with the fur on. We said good night and I cleared a space nearby for my bedroll and went to sleep immediately. When I awoke at dawn, the family had pulled out for home.

Three years later, the Métis rebel leader Louis Riel Jr. returned from exile to lead a second insurrection against British rule in Canada. The civil war came to a head in May 1885 in the village of Batoche, where two hundred Métis held out for four days against nearly a thousand militiamen and Canadian regulars before they were overrun. During the standoff, Métis sharpshooters supplemented their waning ammunition with pebbles, nails, and metal buttons against some seventy-thousand Gatling rounds and hammering blows from seven-pounders. I did not hear if Philippe Louis-Napoleon Charlemagne Voltaire Murat du la Rochelle and his marvelous Evans rifle were among the sharpshooters, or if he was one of those tried in Regina for treason and sentenced to life at hard labor, but I remembered what he had told me about Métis ingenuity. Riel himself was convicted in Regina of treason and incitement to rebellion and hanged.

At about the same time, eight members of the Cree

Nation were hanged in Regina for their part in an attack on the Mountie stockade at Battleford in conjunction with Métis rebels. Chief Piapot was not among them, having died of natural causes the year before near the Arctic Circle, the place the Cree called the Great Sea of Ice. Construction on the Canadian Pacific Railway resumed and sped to completion.

The free African community of Shulamite barely survived the century. In the nineties the generation that had grown up since slavery went to the cities to look for work. Their children joined the Canadian colored regiments during the World War, and when they returned they did not go back to the settlement except only briefly, to visit elderly relatives who spoke of nothing but life on the plantation and the adventure of the Underground Railroad. By then developers had bought and torn down the cabins and the great lodge, replaced them with proper houses, and renamed the place in favor of something less contentious. Its current residents have never heard of Brother Hebron or Queen Fidelity. The leading church is Southern Baptist.

Nothing was heard of Lorenzo Bliss after the night of the Mountie assault on the Sioux stronghold at Cree Lake, although the legend grew up that he had somehow escaped Indian justice to rob Canadian trains with Bill Miner's gang in 1906. They say Jesse James and Billy the Kid were never killed either. I suppose somewhere there's a private club where these latter-day Lazaruses gather to drink and play cards and compare stories of life on the scout.

Charlie Whitelaw, the renegade Cherokee who with Lorenzo Bliss led a band of murderers on a bloody rampage from the Nations to the wilderness of Canada, beat all the odds and recovered from his injuries. After six months he was declared medically fit to stand trial, but the proceedings were delayed for another year while the U.S. State Department and the Canadian Ministry of Justice fought over who got first crack at him. Finally, in response to a letter from President Arthur, Sir John Macdonald, the prime minister, agreed to remand the prisoner over to the American authorities once a verdict had been reached in Ottawa. He was quickly found guilty on twenty-three counts of armed robbery, rape, arson, and murder, and sentenced to death, whereupon he was transported under guard to Helena. There Judge Blackthorne ordered him to hang following his conviction on thirty-eight counts of capital crime in territories belonging to the United States.

As it turned out, though, he didn't hang even once.

In June 1883, while awaiting execution in the Montana territorial penitentiary at Deer Lodge, Whitelaw strangled to death a guard who passed too near his cell and used the guard's key to unlock the door. He got almost to the end of the cellblock before Halloran, the captain of the guard, stuck a sawed-off ten-gauge shotgun between the bars of the block door and blew him to pieces at a range of three feet. What was left of him was shoveled into the ground in the prison courtyard without so much as a plain wooden cross to mark the spot. He was twenty-four years old.

They say you always remember where you were when you heard such news: I suppose I'm the exception. All I know for sure is I wasn't in a room that contained a billiard table.

PORT
HAZARD

For Louise A. Estleman:
September 13, 1918–June 30, 2002.
A swell prim, and now with God.

PART ONE

The Double Eagle

1

I was killing a conductor on the Northern Pacific between Butte and Garrison when my orders changed.

He wasn't a real conductor. They all have bad feet, to begin with, and the three-inch Texas heels poking out of his serge cuffs caught my eye just before he tried to punch my ticket with an Arkansas toothpick the size of a sickle. I was half out of my seat and used the momentum to grasp his wrist, deflect the blade, and butt him under the chin, crushing the crown of a good pinch hat and making him bite through his tongue. He bled out both corners of his mouth. I drew my Deane-Adams awkwardly with my left hand, jammed it into his crotch, and fired.

He fell on top of me, there not being any other place to fall in a sleeping compartment. I had several pounds on him and I'm not a big man, but deadweight is deadweight. I was still climbing out from under when someone knocked at the door. In the throbbing echo of the .45's report, he might have been tapping on a door at the other end of the train.

I was plastered with blood from collar to knees when I opened the door. The Negro porter paled beneath his deep brown pigment at the sight of the blood and the revolver in my hand, but he had an old scar on his cheek that looked combat-related, a saber cut, and in any case, they're trained by Pullman not to panic easily. He held out a Western Union envelope.

"Wireless for Deputy Murdock," he said.

I holstered the Deane-Adams, tore open the flap, and read while he took in the heap on the floor:

RETURN TO HELENA AT ONCE STOP YOUR LIFE IS IN DANGER

BLACKTHORNE

"That man ain't a conductor on this train," said the porter.

"I guessed that when he tried to hack me open. Is there a detective aboard?"

"No, sir. We ain't been robbed on this run all year."

"When do we get to Garrison?"

He had a little trouble thumbing open the lid on his turnip watch. "Eighteen minutes."

"The town marshal's name is Krueger. He knows me. Send someone to tell him I'll need help with this extra baggage."

"I needs to tell the conductor."

"If that's his uniform, you might have trouble getting an answer."

He dipped a knee and turned the dead man half over on his side. Then he stood.

"Yes, sir. Mr. Fenady was missing that there third button this morning. You reckon this fellow kilt him?"

"He didn't strike me as the bargaining kind. What's that?" I pointed to something on the floor that glinted.

He bent and picked it up. "It must of dropped out of his pocket when I turned him over." He handed it to me.

It was a double eagle, solid gold, the size of a cartwheel dollar. It threw back light in insolent sheets, and the edges of the eagle's wings were sharp enough to cut a finger. "See if there are any more."

If I expected the porter to balk at the prospect of rifling a dead man's pockets, I was disappointed. He knelt again, and in less than a minute he rose, shaking his head. He was used to searching drunken passengers for their tickets to find out where they belonged.

I felt the coin, reading SAN FRANCISCO, CALIFORNIA, with the ball of my thumb. "Is your Mr. Fenady the kind to carry around uncirculated double eagles?"

"No, sir, he sure ain't. That, or he lied about not having the cash to replace that lost button."

I pocketed the coin. He watched without expression. I said, "You want a receipt?"

"No, sir." He turned to go.

I put a hand on his arm, stopping him. It was hard under the uniform sleeve, roped with muscle from carrying trunks and hoisting fat women aboard parlor cars.

"Thirty-sixth Infantry?" I asked.

"No, sir. Tenth Cavalry. Buffalo soldiers. I was too young to serve in the War of Emancipation."

"That doesn't look like a tomahawk scar."

He grinned joylessly. "Wasn't always the red man we was fighting, sir."

"What's your name?"

"Edward Anderson Beecher."

"Did you ever consider serving the law, Beecher?"

"What's the pension?"

"No pension. Congress covers the cost of your burial."

"Thank you, sir. I reckon I'll go on taking my chances with Mr. J. J. Hill."

"That's the problem. The good ones are too smart to serve for the money."

He said nothing, saying plenty.

"Don't forget to tell Marshal Krueger about the double eagle," I said.

That took a moment to filter through. This time when he grinned, the sun came out. "Yes, sir."

"Did you think I intended to keep it a secret?"

"It ain't my place to think, sir."

"I'm a killer, not a thief."

"Yes, sir."

"Stop calling me sir. I quit the army in sixty-five."

"Yes, boss."

After he left, I took the coin back out and weighed it on my palm. Its face value was twenty dollars. That bothered me more than the attack. I'd thought my life was worth a little more.

2

They found the conductor, Tim Fenady, a twenty-year man with a wife and four minor children, in the baggage car wearing only his long-handles and lace-ups, with a single stab wound between his shoulder blades that matched a rip in the uniform the man I killed was wearing. They couldn't tell me the hired killer's name in Garrison. When his own clothes were found, the pockets were empty, which meant that either he was a professional or there had been one more crook aboard the train. By the time they dumped him into a hole in potter's field—burial cost two dollars out of my pocket, a policy of the U.S. District Court, Territory of Montana—I was riding an express back to Helena, sitting up in a chair car. Apparently I'd lost my compartment privileges by not dying.

That season, Judge Harlan A. Blackthorne was smoking his cigars and studying his cases in a room at the Merchants Hotel, his chambers at the courthouse having been gutted by one of Helena's frequent fires. His desk had been rescued, albeit charred on one corner, and the room's bed had been removed to make room for it. When I reported there directly from the station, the clerk in the lobby told me the Judge was in court, but that Marshal Spilsbury was expecting me.

Spilsbury was a Montana native, the son of a Scots farmer, and a decent man who had no liking for me. This wasn't entirely his fault. At the time of his appointment, he'd vowed to rid the federal service of killers, and placed me third on the list for termination. He'd found out quickly that Blackthorne didn't share his views. A bit less quickly— letters of complaint to the White House in 1883 carried an average turnaround time of three weeks—he'd learned that a United States marshal's position in that territory was redundant as long as Blackthorne ran the court. To Spilsbury's credit, he made no more attempts to circumvent recognized authority, and in fact listened attentively when the Judge, with uncharacteristic patience, pointed out to him that if all the killers in the district court system were let go, the deputies who remained would be of insufficient number to deal with the throngs of homicidal parties who would suddenly have returned to the civilian population.

"Your Honor, these are jackals we're discussing," he'd argued.

"Very true," Blackthorne had said. "However, they are *our* jackals."

I found the marshal studying his pocket Bible in a straightback chair, the only place to sit in the room apart from the great overstuffed horsehair that stood behind the desk, another aromatic survivor of the courthouse fire. There was no indication that he'd even entertained the notion of changing seats in the Judge's absence. He was a lay reader with the Presbyterian church, and although he could quote the gospel chapter and verse, he never did. His restraint carried the respect of the most blasphemous among the deputy marshals, who theorized that he was settling the account for the sins of some father on some haunted moor three generations back.

He raised his long narrow face from Revelations to greet me. He wore all black from neck to heels except for his white collar and the plain six-pointed star pinned to his broadcloth vest. He'd been in mourning three years for a wife dead of diphtheria in populous St. Louis, which may have explained his decision to decamp to a region less settled, and there was about him a quality of gentle brooding that caused men several years his senior, me included, to address him as an elder.

"I hope your journey back was more pleasant than the one out," he said.

"The one out wasn't so bad, if you don't count the stretch between Butte and Garrison." I didn't shake his hand. He didn't offer it. He wasn't being rude, just unhypocritical. You couldn't hate him for that.

"I suppose you had no other choice but to kill the man."

"I might have. I wasn't thinking about choices at the time."

He glanced down, saw nothing on that page to comfort him, and closed the Bible. He poked it into his watch pocket. Then he drew a fold of stiff paper from inside his coat and held it out. "Is this the fellow who assaulted you?"

I took the paper and unfolded it. It was a wanted reader issued by the Department of Justice in Washington, D.C. I read the description and handed it back.

"Tobias Mimms," I said. "It could have been. When you're on the scout, you're sure to lose a little weight. 'Wanted in Missouri.' Who isn't? He's too young to be a former guerrilla, but back there they serve that up with the beans and fatback. Murder, conspiracy to commit murder, and aggravated assault, which would have been a murder interrupted. Paid killer?"

"It doesn't say. But then there is no specific charge for that." He put away the reader. "I understand you found a gold piece on his person?"

I fished out the double eagle and put it in his hand. He studied both sides as carefully as he read Scripture. "This was minted very recently. Gold stamping needn't pass through many hands before it begins to lose definition. Have you ever been to San Francisco?"

"No, sir."

He looked at me for any sign of irony in the address. "Mimms has. He was seen there last month. Agents from the Pinkerton office there obtained a federal warrant and mounted a raid on the disorderly house where he was staying, but he'd disappeared. Ten days ago he resurfaced in Montana." He returned his attention to the coin. "You were on your way to Bannack to identify a prisoner. Is there anyone who can perform that duty in your place?"

"Treadway was the deputy he made the break from, but he's on furlough. His wife is expecting."

"Yes. Well, unless she's expecting something other than a child, I am of the opinion she can spare him. Nothing in his history says he trained as a midwife."

I nodded. That made one more reason for Treadway not to buy me a whiskey on my birthday.

"There are other ways for a coin to make its way here from California," I said. "It didn't have to be in Mimms's pocket. We don't know for sure it was Mimms on the train."

"The day you left for Bannack, I received a wire from Sheriff Matthias in Granite County. Do you know him?"

"Only by reputation. He has a peg leg and his own private army of deputies to do his footwork."

"Evidently an efficient system. One of them overheard a drunken conversation in a saloon in Phillipsburg, something about a number of law dogs fit for muzzling. Your name came up."

"My guess is it comes up often in that kind of conversation."

"The sheriff thought this one worthy of repeating. The fellow doing the talking is a notorious Copperhead. He was sentenced to hang for treason in seventy-two, but was pardoned by President Grant. He announced his retirement shortly afterward, but Matthias holds the opinion a case could be made for another trial based on his activities since."

"There are plenty of people who won't let go of the war. They're about as much of a threat as these blowhards who still say the earth's flat."

"It's a comforting analogy, but specious. Have you ever heard of the Sons of the Confederacy?"

I shook my head.

"They're a loosely knit organization, founded in Richmond in sixty-six, on the first anniversary of the surrender at Appomattox. The charter members were Confederate veterans, dedicated to electing Southern sympathizers to high office and effecting by peaceful means what four years of bloodshed could not—namely, the secession of states and territories whose leaders share their vision."

"It seems to me the same thing was tried in sixty-one."

"Hear me out. Today the group contains a significant number of noncombatants, many of whom were too young to serve; some, in fact, who were not born when the war ended. These youngsters are easily influenced, with emotions untempered in the crucible of cruel experience. Former spies like this fellow in Phillipsburg talk a good fight and fill their heads with poison. They could or would not take up arms, and so are content with persuading others to take them up in their stead. They have created a rift in the ranks between those who counsel lawful action and those who would spill blood yet again. In the last three years, the Sons of the Confederacy have accounted for twenty-seven murders, including the assassination of a Massachusetts senator and the ambush slayings of three peace officers attempting to arrest members upon various charges. Their aim is to spread panic and distrust in the

Union and set the stage for a second war on behalf of states' rights."

"I don't know what it has to do with Mimms and me. I don't make it a practice to arrest rebels. Not for being rebels."

"That would be a salient point, if Tobias Mimms were not the fellow the Copperhead told to muzzle you."

I found a growth of whiskers my razor had missed and scratched it. I can't get a decent shave aboard a moving train. "If they're that dangerous, why hasn't Chet Arthur sent troops into Richmond?"

"Virginia represents the peaceful element. The firebrands have taken up residence on the Barbary Coast."

The smoke began to clear.

"You're proposing sending me to San Francisco to weed out the bad apples?"

"You're mixing metaphors, Deputy, in addition to being a damn fool. I'm sending you there to widen the rift."

This was a new voice, or rather a new one in that conversation; harsher and more sardonic. Judge Blackthorne had entered, and now he took his place behind the desk with an air as if he were calling the court to order.

3

Small men often have a way of filling a room, mainly out of spite. Harlan Blackthorne obliterated rooms; not by compensation or by denying his lack of stature, but by sheer force of the conviction that most of the men he met were unnecessarily large. Those of normal height felt unwieldy in his orbit, while tall men were made to consider themselves freaks. He was a dandy who had his suits cut too youthfully for him, and there was a lot of speculation among the deputy marshals, with considerable money to back it up, that he dyed his glossy sable hair and beard. Strangers who didn't know who he was smiled behind their hands when he strutted into a room. Two minutes into conversation with him, the smiles withered and blew away. He had more enemies in Washington than Jefferson Davis and held absolute authority over a region as large as Middle Europe.

An empty glass and a pitcher of water awaited him on the desk. Without ceremony, he filled the glass from the pitcher, removed his false teeth, and submerged them in the glass, where they grinned at Spilsbury and me throughout the interview. He only wore them behind the bench, not that either his speech or his dignity suffered in their absence. If anything, without them his rare smile gave him the tight-lipped, diabolic look of a Satanic Mona Lisa.

"The schism that exists between the law-abiding new

Confederates and their violent brethren is their problem, not ours," he continued, not bothering to greet either of us. "In fact, it offers the rest of us our first opportunity to destroy the organization, or at the very least, render it superfluous. In five years it will pose no more threat to these United States than the Knights of Columbus."

Whenever the Judge made reference to "these United States," it sounded as if he had them right there in his watch pocket. He'd fought for them in Mexico, served their military as an advisor during the Civil War, losing his teeth in battle and his digestion in politics, and seemed to consider these sacrifices some kind of down payment on proprietorship. He had opposed Southern Reconstruction in favor of punishment, and behaved in general toward the eleven former seceding states as if they'd deserted him personally. Alarmed, the moderates in his party had conspired to arrange his appointment to a territorial post as far from Capitol Hill as was available. There he continued to make his opinions known by sentencing former rebels who were convicted in his court far more severely than those who had never declared war upon the Union. Of those who appealed, only two got as far as the Supreme Court, which had reversed one sentence and upheld the other by a narrow margin. The common belief in Montana, that there was no appeal between Blackthorne and Jehovah, remained unshaken.

"What makes me the one to insert the wedge?" I asked. "I'm just a target, and a cheap one at that. Twenty dollars and train fare."

Blackthorne snapped his fingers at Spilsbury, who leaned forward and passed the double eagle across the desk. The Judge glanced at it and smacked it down on his blotter as if he'd flipped it. "This is a symbol, not remuneration. It pleases them to commission murder for the

Confederacy with the token of a Yankee goldpiece. Mimms offered his services gratis."

Now I was being discounted. The longer I stayed in that room, the less my life was worth. "How did I come to be on their list to begin with? It's been almost twenty years since I took my licks for the Union."

Spilsbury spoke for the first time since Blackthorne had entered.

"You're rather a notorious character. Evidently there are scores of schoolboys who ought to be reading Matthew Arnold who are instead persuaded by the example of a number of ten-cent shockers that you roped and skinned the elephant. That's a tempting mark for a cause looking for space in the public columns."

"I didn't write the dime novels. I barely met the man who writes them before I ran him out of Helena. There isn't a word of truth in any of them."

"Whoever said 'a lie cannot live' never saw one dressed in yellow pasteboard with a lurid title," the marshal said. "These fellows are not known for their discernment."

"Gentlemen, you're both wrong, as well as in contempt for speaking out of turn. The court is in recess, not adjournment. It goes where I go." Having swung this gavel, the Judge favored me with his Luciferian smirk. "You are exalted, Deputy. Marshal Spilsbury doesn't feel called upon often to pay you a compliment. However, he overestimates your importance. These are not unruly schoolchildren, hungering for adult attention. They never strike without reason.

"It's true you're the most infamous officer of this court," he said. "However, it's my court, and your extermination was intended as a message for me. My opinions of this treasonous trash are widely known. If they can kill my most ferocious dog, the reasoning follows that they can kill me. It's first-form Machiavelli at best, but rather impressive for a band of inbred plug-chewers and pickle-stickers."

I found this intelligence more of an irritation than a testimonial. In one choice phrase I'd gone from dime-novel hero to slaughterhouse mutt. What made it more irritating still was the conviction that he was probably right. For all their prominence in the telegraph columns and bookstalls, gun men were pawns, shuttled about by Judges, senators, and owners of railroads. Those were the only three groups whose members were difficult to replace.

I said, "How am I supposed to pull off this parting of the Red Sea? I'm not even first form."

"That's a point in your favor. Disregarding Emancipation, the principal result of four years of war was to scatter spies across the continent. Southern sympathizers are no longer to be found solely in the South. You'll find them piloting a ferry in Kansas City, bookkeeping in Philadelphia, pumping a blacksmith's forge in Texas. They're in Congress and medicine and law enforcement. An army dispatched to destroy the Sons of the Confederacy would be observed and reported upon throughout its march. By the time it reached the enemy stronghold, the enemy would have vanished, slithered down its network of holes, to reassemble elsewhere later and force us to commence gathering intelligence all over again. One man, or a small group, might slip past these Copperheads unnoticed, or if noticed, might be dismissed as no threat. How you manage the parting itself is your affair. Your experience in sowing discord in this court may show you the way."

"Where do I start? San Francisco's a big place."

Blackthorne directed his gaze to the marshal, who produced a memorandum book from the same pocket that contained the wanted circular on Tobias Mimms. He forked a pair of spectacles with egg-shaped lenses onto the thick bridge of his nose. He hadn't needed glasses to read his Bible, but then he knew most of its passages by heart.

" 'Daniel Webster Wheelock,' " he read. "Have you ever heard this name?"

"Two thirds of it," I said.

"It seems his parents had lofty hopes for him in the profession of law. If so, their disappointment was abysmal. Half of every penny that vanishes into the bagnios and deadfalls on the San Francisco waterfront finds its home in Wheelock's purse. In return, he keeps the peace, such as it is. Those who breach it either pass from sight or end up snagging some fisherman's net in the harbor. There is a name for such fellows."

"Back East, they're called captains of industry."

He went on reading as if I hadn't spoken. "He's sixty, a clubfoot, with a classical education obtained at Harvard University; a Boston native with an ancestral connection to the first pilgrims. Rather a curious background for a Tammany hack. However, he's the man to see if you want to do any sort of business in Barbary, legitimate or otherwise."

"Am I to call him out or shoot him from ambush?"

"Neither, if you can avoid it," put in Blackthorne. "Killing Wheelock would only stir up the hive and scatter its contents further. In any case, there's no evidence he's connected with the Copperheads. They're under his protection, along with every other active citizen out there, lest the top blow off and Washington declare martial law to contain the damage. Wheelock has the most to lose in that situation. As a peacemaker, he's more conscientious than the army and the Church of Rome. You need to befriend him if you're to find out who's behind the Sons."

"How I do that is my affair, too, I suppose."

"The marshal's notebook will provide pointers. He's made rather a study of The Honorable D. W. Wheelock."

" 'Honorable'?"

"He's a city alderman, as well as a captain in the fire brigade," Spilsbury said, thumbing through his pages. "He also holds—"

The Judge's teeth bumped against the side of the water glass, cutting him off. Blackthorne was fishing them out. "I've heard all this before. At present, I have a murderer to try. The marshal can give you everything you need." He worried the teeth into place and stood. "Don't forget, Murdock, you're still a target. Take along a deputy to stand at your back."

"I'll take Staderman."

"Staderman's laid up with a broken pelvis. That big roan of his put its foot wrong last week and rolled over on him. He should have shot the clumsy beast years ago. He has a soft spot where horses are concerned."

"His only fault."

"I thought you hated each other."

"I didn't choose him for company. What about Partridge?"

"He's testifying next week. Kearney's available."

"Kearney can't hit Montana with a shotgun."

"That's the lot, Deputy. Thirty-six men, one hundred forty-six thousand square miles. If you know a civilian you can trust, whom you can persuade to risk his life for posse pay, have at it."

"I can think of one," I said. "One I think I can trust. The rest of it may take some work."

4

The difficult part about tracing Edward Anderson Beecher was he worked for the railroad. The easy part was he worked for the railroad.

A fellow who earns his living carrying luggage, making up berths, and delivering messages to passengers aboard the Northern Pacific could make his home in Portland or St. Paul, Boise or Salt Lake City. All I had was a name and description, and an area of search as big as the Indian Ocean. All I needed was the name.

Chicago knew where every piece of rolling stock was sided and where every employee was keeping himself. When I told Judge Blackthorne who I wanted to stand behind me on the trip to San Francisco, he wired the name and a one-sentence request East and got a reply within six hours. The porter with the friendly saber scar was working a ceremonial excursion organized to commemorate the completion of the railroad line and was expected in Gold Creek Saturday, along with a herd of generals, bankers, congressmen, newspaper reporters, and Ulysses S. Grant, former president of the United States.

There were four trains in the excursion, pausing at every whistle-stop for speeches, libations, and gifts of wild-flowers tied with ribbon and delivered by pretty little girls in white dresses to dyspeptic old goats in stiff collars. Three had already passed through Helena. I was told I'd missed several displays of fine elocution and the spectacle of a senator's fat secretary being hauled aboard a rolling caboose by his britches after he slept through the departing whistle with one of the young creatures at Chicago Joe's. Beecher, according to the wire, had boarded the first train west of town. He must have turned back from Garrison just ahead of me to accept the assignment. The fourth and last train was due in one hour and I was expected to be on it.

I got to the station with my valise just as the locomotive shrieked to a leaky stop, hung all over with flags and garlands and gents in beetle hats leaning out the windows, firing pistols at the clouds and waving at the throngs and the firehouse band, for whom the enchantment of "O, Susanna" sounded as if it had begun to wear thin. The first team, including Grant and the railroad brass and Washington's best speechmakers, had been aboard the first train, and by the time it came to stock this one, all that was left were the wardheelers and second cousins; people not considered important enough to ride up front but too dangerous to leave behind. I swung aboard a day coach against the stream of alighting passengers, found a seat near the back, and let down the window to thin out the atmosphere of twice-smoked cigars and Old Gideon.

In due course, the electioneering blathered to a finish, reinforcements were brought aboard in the form of crates of champagne and the odd giggling girl in bright satin. The train lurched ahead, pulling away from the tinny strains of "Garryowen," and buried the end of Custer's dirge under the razz of its whistle. An old campaigner in a sour-smelling suit with tobacco juice in his beard went to sleep with his head on my shoulder. I wasn't sure whether he was too important to shoot, and by the time we rolled into Butte, my left arm was numb. We overnighted there, for no good reason except to let the excursionists nurse their headaches and to sample some more of the local fauna. All the hotel rooms were taken, so I got back on board and gave a porter a dollar to make up a berth and wake me an hour before the train was scheduled to embark. He did that, and for another dollar brought me biscuits and gravy from the Silver Bow Club, leaving the tray outside the water closet as I was shaving. I asked him if he knew Beecher and where I might find him in Gold Creek.

He frowned. He was a handsome lad of eighteen or so, with aristocratic features and skin as black as a stove. "I can't say as I've heard the name, sir, but a lot of the coloreds keep theirselves at Danny Moon's Emporium on the Benetsee."

"Do they serve white men?"

"I wouldn't know, sir. I keep temperance myself."

"How long before the yahoos start boarding?"

He looked at his watch. The entire transcontinental system would fly to pieces without its pocket winders. "Fifteen minutes, if we're leaving on time. We're sure to hear from Mr. Hill if we don't."

I gave him another dollar. "Would an abstemious gentleman such as yourself object to learning whether there's a quart of good whiskey left in town and bringing it to me?"

He took off his cap, poked the coin under the sweatband next to the others, and put the cap back on. "Mr. Drummond at the Silver Bow Club keeps some Hermitage in stock for patrons of good character."

I sighed and wiped off the last of the shaving soap. "What do you charge for a reference?"

The porter stiffened. The cap came off and he fished the silver dollars out of the band and held them out. "I ain't a grafter. You'll find plenty of them in town."

"Sorry, friend. Most people I meet, when they find out I work for Washington, start thinking they can get a little of their own back. It destroys your faith in good fellowship. I'll get the bottle myself."

After a moment he returned the coins to his cap and his cap to his head. "I'll get it, sir. These bankers and politicians will try your patience. One of them slapped me when I wouldn't fetch him a woman."

"Did you slap him back?"

"Mr. Hill wouldn't approve of that. The gentleman wouldn't approve of what he ate for supper that night, either." He touched his cap and went off on his quest.

Gold Creek was in a fever. It had never lived up to its name, the nuggets coughed up by Benetsee Creek never having compared to the strikes in Bannack, Alder Gulch, and Last Chance, and for twenty years had stood only on the loose foundation of the hopes of those residents who had gambled everything on their claims and had nowhere else to go and nothing to get them there if they had. The coming of the Northern Pacific had rekindled some of that early optimism. Fresh clapboard, glistening with new paint, had been nailed up over the log walls of the assayer's office and the general merchandise, and the horse apples swept out of sight for the first time in a decade. The street, in fact, was faintly greenish, paved as it was with the uncollected droppings of a generation. The population was five hundred, but only if you counted the flies.

Today the transient numbers were considerably higher. People had come from all around to get drunk and slap the back of the victor of Appomattox, to round up votes, fleece the sheep at the gaming tables, and lift the occasional poke in the press of flesh. There wasn't a room to be had in any of the hotels, as I found out when I went looking for a roof. Most of the private homes had temporary boarders, and tents had sprung up like mushrooms all over the foothills. The whole place looked like the night before Gettysburg.

Stepping down from the train I squeezed past a gang of Eastern Republicans handing out leaflets opposing protective tariffs and shoved aside a rodent in a striped jersey who tried to wrestle my valise out of my hand. This put me off balance, and I jostled a portly, gray-bearded gent in a suit that smelled of mothballs. I put out a hand to steady us both and muttered an apology. Someone barked at me and I turned my head that way just in time to be blinded when a heap of magnesium powder went up in a white flame. I had my Deane-Adams in my hand before I realized my photograph had been taken. Years later an acquaintance asked me how I'd come to know General Grant, and when I said we never met, he told me he'd seen a picture of me in a book with my hand on the shoulder of the eighteenth president of the United States. That made me feel bad, because if I'd known I was that close I'd have told him it was my privilege to have fought with Rosecrans at Murfreesboro. I never got another chance. Grant died two years later, penniless, a victim of his business associations.

The third hotel I tried was full up like the others, but the clerk agreed to let me leave my valise there for a consideration. My expense book threatened to create a shortage of dollar coins in Denver. I asked where I might find Danny Moon's Emporium. The clerk, a horse-faced Scandinavian, too young for his drinker's rosy nose, looked me up and down from hat to heels, then mumbled something about following the creek south until it got dark. It wasn't noon yet, but I took his meaning.

It was built of logs without benefit of clapboard, with a long front porch supported on more logs, like a raft. Boards suspended from the roof with letters burned into them advertised whiskey, lunch, and cold beer. I stopped to let a bull-necked, bald-headed Negro in dungarees and a wool flannel shirt soaked through with sweat carry a streaming bucket of beer bottles up the front steps from the creek, then followed him inside, moving aside an oilcloth flap that covered the doorway. That old familiar mulch of tobacco, burned and chewed, sour mash, stale beer, and staler bodies greeted me in the darkened interior. I let my eyes adjust to the pewtery light struggling in through panes thick with grime, then made my way to the bar, towing a path of silence through the whirr of conversation. Mine was the only white face in the establishment, and I had on the only white shirt. My entrance had interrupted a game of dominoes atop a table made from a packing crate and an argument at the bar, which was made from a door laid across a pair of whiskey barrels.

The bartender turned out to be the man I'd seen carrying in beer from the creek. He paused in the midst of unstopping one of the bottles to look at me from under a brow like a rock outcrop. I groped a nickel out of my pocket and laid it on a door panel. "I'll have one of those beers, if they're not all spoken for."

A gray tongue like a toadbelly came out and slid the length of the bartender's lower lip. "You lost, mister. You gots to follow the creek north till it gets light."

That seemed to be the joke of the town. I said, "It's a long dry walk."

The customer to my right reached over and pinched the sleeve of my travel coat between thumb and forefinger. He had on overalls with a big safety pin keeping one strap in place over a pair of red flannels gone mostly gray. "That silk?" he asked.

"Not for thirty a month and four cents a mile. What about that beer?" I was still looking at the bartender.

His eyes moved from side to side, couldn't find a quorum. He slammed a thick glass onto the bar and filled it from the bottle, not bothering to tilt the glass to cut the clouds. I thanked him and took a drink. It was homemade stuff, bitter, with hops floating in it, but I felt the cold of it drying the sweat on the back of my neck. I asked the bartender how he kept people from stealing the bottles out of the creek.

"Water moccasins."

"I didn't think we had water moccasins in Montana."

"Benetsee's got everything in it. Except gold." He opened a mouth with no teeth in it and let out air in a death rattle of a laugh.

"Maybe you just spread the story around to protect your beer."

The mouth clapped shut, then opened a quarter-inch. "Maybe I is a liar in your eyes."

"No, sir. Just a good businessman."

A full little silence followed, like a fire gulping air. A drop of sweat wandered down my spine, stinging like molten lead. I had five cartridges in my revolver and thirty-two pairs of eyes on me, if the dusty mirror strung from a nail behind the bar wasn't missing anyone in the shadows. Then someone laughed, a shrill, bubbling cackle, with no irony in it. A hand smacked the bar, hard enough to create a tidal wave in my glass.

"He's snared you, Danny." This was a voice I recognized. "I'm so scared of snakes in general I never once thought you was bluffing about them water moccasins. What you need now's a wolf trap. Man's got to be thirstier'n Christ on the cross to trade his fingers for a sip of that piss you stir up in back."

Another silence, shorter than the first. Then someone else laughed. That started a rockslide. The room shook with guffaws. I extracted a fistful of coins from my pocket and laid them on the bar in a heap.

"Pour each of these fellows a beer," I said. "If there's anything left, you can put it toward that wolf trap."

Danny joined the others this time, showing his pink gums. "I'm thinking bear. You don't know these boys when they's parched." He scooped the coins into a box with Pallas Athena on the lid and started pouring.

I picked up my glass and moved to the end of the bar, where a gap had opened in the rush to take advantage of my generosity. Edward Anderson Beecher leaned there on his forearms with one hand wrapped around his glass, a cigarette building a long ash between the first two fingers. He had on his porter's outfit, the cap tilted forward and touching the bridge of his nose—a violation of the Northern Pacific uniform code. The scar on his cheek looked like a curl of packing cord caught in fresh tar. He was smiling into his beer, his lips pressed tight.

I said, "Prefer to buy your own?"

"Don't take it as an insult. Two beers and I'm a bad risk. If it gets back to Mr. J. J. Hill I even showed up in a place like this in my working clothes, I'll be back shoveling horseshit."

"You railroad men all talk about Hill like you've met face to face."

"Could have. One white man in a beard looks pretty much like all the rest."

I drank, spat out a hop. I hoped it was a hop. "Thanks for the shove. That could have gone another way."

"I come here to drink, not see my friends kilt. I seen how handy you are with that iron."

"You make friends quick. Or is Gold Creek home?"

He dragged in smoke, the ash quivering but not falling, blew twin gray streams out his nostrils. Shook his head. "I know all the places at all the stops, is all. Spokane's home. I ain't been lately. Last time I was I had a wife."

There was nothing there for me. At forty-two, I was one of the oldest deputies in Blackthorne's string, but the younger ones had given up trying to tell me about their dogs and women. Sooner or later, all confidences were regretted; resentment set in, and always when you needed the disgruntled party to deal you out of a bad hand.

Then there was the chance of getting to like one of them. Given my choice, I'd bury a stranger.

"How was the ride out?" I said.

"Better than some. That General Grant sure can put away the rye."

"Lincoln asked him what brand he drank so he could send a case to all his generals."

"I heard that. You reckon it's true?"

"Likely not. I understand Honest Abe wasn't born in a log cabin, either."

"I was born between cotton rows myself. Maybe I ought to throw my hat in the ring."

"I'd set my sights lower to start."

"I started out a slave. What's lower than that?"

I wasn't going to get a better invitation. I fished the deputy's star out of my shirt pocket and laid it on the bar between us.

5

He shifted his tight-lipped smile from his glass to the star, then put two fingers on it and slid it back toward me, as if he were anteing up.

"We had this conversation before," he said. "I'm a porter, not a deputy."

"I'm not offering that. I don't have the authority to deputize anyone. That was just for show." I returned the star to my shirt pocket. "It's posse work; fifty cents a day and four cents a mile."

"Last time you said I got free burial."

"You still do. Of course, if you kill anyone, his burial comes out of your pay."

"That's backwards. Cheaper to get kilt than stay alive."

"Isn't it always?"

He parted with his cigarette ash finally, in a peach tin set on the bar for that purpose. He took one last pull and tipped the stub in after it. "Who you hunting?"

"It's not a who. It's a what." I turned my back on the man to my left, tall and thin with an Adam's apple that measured his swallows of beer like the stroke of a steam piston. He was eavesdropping without making any effort to hide it. "Is there a quiet place to drink? I've got a bottle of Hermitage in my valise at the hotel."

"You found a room?"

"Just for the valise. Looks like I'm sleeping at the train station tonight."

"You want to use the floor. It's softer than them benches." He emptied his glass and pushed away from the bar. He didn't invite me, but I followed him out.

When I turned in to the hotel for the whiskey, he told me to get my valise. I came out carrying it and accompanied him to the station, but we didn't go into the building. I followed him to a siding, where he gripped the rail on the back of a caboose and swung himself onto the platform without using the steps. I used them. Inside was a potbelly stove with a cold coffeepot on top, a pair of cots made up neatly, military fashion, three folding chairs, a water crock with dipper, a table holding up a checkerboard, and a brass cuspidor the size of an umbrella stand with N.P.R.R. embossed around the rim. The car smelled of hickory and tobacco juice and cigars and felt like the parlor of a private club. Which it was: the most exclusive in the egalitarian United States, open only to members of the railroad fraternity. Here the conductors retired to put up their sore feet, and the porters and brakemen gathered to play cards and checkers and read newspapers and complain about unreasonable passengers.

There was a checker game in progress on the table, although the players were absent. To avoid disturbing the pieces, Beecher removed a pair of tin cups from a built-in cupboard and set them on the stove to fill from the bottle I took out of my valise.

"What's Mr. Hill say about drinking on railroad property?" I asked.

"What you expect. I'm supposed to have a room, but Chicago kind of forgets how to count where the colored employees are concerned."

"You sleep here?"

"Just till one of them checker players shows up and boots me out. But I figure they got better games to play in town. You can take the other cot. If anybody asks we'll tell 'em you're on railroad business." He picked up one of the cups and sat down on a chair.

I got mine and took another chair. "I thought you were a bad risk after two beers."

"That's why I stopped at one. This stuff drinks like milk." He poured down half his cup in one draught. "This *what* you're after, that ain't a who; it got anything to do with that fellow you kilt?"

I nodded, and told him about the Sons of the Confederacy.

"I never made it to Frisco," he said. "I know some who did. They say Dan Wheelock's the man to see there if you got a misery. I can't feature doing that. I likes to keep my miseries close to home. I'm not good as a spy. Can't even bluff at poker."

"I'll do the spying. I just need somebody to stand behind me on the trip out."

"I ain't your man. I don't even own a pistol."

"Got anything against them?"

"Only that they don't hit what I aims at. I ain't so bad with a rifle, but it's been years."

"Any shooting you're likely to do will be at close range. I know some pistols where marksmanship doesn't count so much." I took my first sip, a dainty one. Good liquor affected me quicker than the watered-down slop you found in most saloons.

"Why pick me? Ain't you got no friends?"

"A friend can be as bad as an enemy when it comes to staying alive. I liked the way you carried yourself on the train. Also it occurred to me you wouldn't approve of the Sons of the Confederacy any more than the man I work for does."

He shook his head and drank. "I don't fight old wars. Anyway, I got a job. It pays a pension and I can't remember the last time anybody got kilt doing it."

"I can't match that."

"All right, then." He got up, topped off his cup, and plunked himself back down. "You like your job?"

"Some parts. Getting killed isn't one. How about you?"

"It's as high as I can go, mister. I disremember your name."

"Page Murdock."

"Scotchman?"

"My father was. He came here when there wasn't anything between Canada and Denver but a lot of Blackfeet and Snake. I was raised by him and a quarter-breed Snake who may or may not have been the bastard granddaughter of Meriwether Lewis, who may or may not have been my mother. Now you know more about me than I do about you."

"I doubt it. That I does. I don't know who my grandfather was. When I was little, I liked to think he was a chief in Africa. He was likely a slave like all the rest."

"You're a little more than that. The Tenth Cavalry didn't step off the boardwalk for anyone."

"I stepped off plenty since." This time he drained the cup in one gulp.

"Ever miss it?"

"Some parts."

I drank a little more. The stuff was already softening the sharp edges. I choked back a yawn. I didn't sleep well on trains. They were always taking on and dropping off cars, and making all the noise of Shiloh as they went about it. I might have dozed off. I stirred when he stood to refill his cup, and again when he lit the wick on a lantern hanging from a hook on the wall. The ends of the caboose were dark.

". . . scalped a man once," I heard him saying at one lucid point. "A boy, really. Shames me now to think on it. He was a Cheyenne brave, maybe fourteen, scrawny but a scrapper. Raped his share of white women, I expect. Still."

"Not one of the parts you miss."

"I was young and full of piss and corn liquor. Custer weren't cold yet, so I considered it personal. It weren't as if that long-haired hard-ass wouldn't of had me flayed if I kicked one of his damn greyhounds for stealing my rations."

"That happen?"

"Not to me. You hear stories when you're on sentry duty. It could of, though, if I ever got closer to him than three hundred miles of prairie. I don't like dogs or officers. Straw bosses in brass buttons."

"What parts did you like?"

He tapped his fingers on the side of his cup. It was a rolling rattle, like a military tattoo. "Parade."

"Parade?"

"Yeah. Most times you're bored, or your feet hurt, or some white officer's giving you misery on account of your galluses is showing. Everybody's bellyaching about something. On parade you ain't got time to think about all that. You're too busy keeping your chin up and your back straight and your horse from shying, and so's the man next you and the man next him, all the way from the head of the column to the rear. All that counts is keeping the line straight. So long's you do that your color don't matter."

"Parade's one of the things I left the army to get away from."

"*Your* color don't matter whatever you do. I'm talking about being part of something bigger than you."

"If you miss it so much, why'd you quit?"

"Last fight I was in, we raided a Arapaho village. It was on Buffalo Creek, down in Wyoming Territory. Don't bother looking it up, it weren't the Rosebud. When the main column took out after them that got away, I was left behind with some others to burn the lodges and shoot the ponies. Them ponies never done nothing to me. When my enlistment run out I run out with it."

"You like horses?"

He shook his head. "Sons of bitches bite. I reckon I would, too, somebody tried to throw a saddle over me. I wouldn't shoot one because of it."

"You might have to, if you're outnumbered and you need something to hide behind."

"I done that, only not at Buffalo Creek. We was the ones doing the outnumbering."

I remembered my whiskey and drank. It had grown warm from the heat of my hand gripping the cup; I hadn't been so insensible I'd dropped it. "Well, I can't offer anything like parade. I don't care if your chin's in your lap, so long as you keep me alive."

"I'm thinking that's a twenty-four-hour hitch."

"And no time off on Sunday. The Barbary Coast isn't the First Baptist Church."

"Even Mr. Hill knows a man's got to sleep."

"Your job will be waiting when you get back. The man I work for will write him a letter."

"If he ain't J. P. Morgan I don't know how it'd help. Mr. Hill wouldn't change the way he runs his road for anybody less."

"You've never read one of Judge Blackthorne's letters."

He smiled, again without showing his teeth. I was beginning to realize it wasn't connected with anything like amusement on his part. "You ride for Hangin' Harlan?"

"He prefers 'Your Honor.' "

The floor shifted slightly. Someone had mounted the platform outside the door. Beecher said, "Somebody's done come back to finish out that game of checkers. I reckon I can't offer you that other cot after all."

The caboose shifted again, this time closer to the opposite end.

"Douse the light," I said.

He got up without hesitating, raised the chimney on the lantern, and blew out the flame. In the sudden black I stood and drew the Deane-Adams.

The door at the rear swung open and banged against the wall. I fired at the silhouette I saw in the gray rectangle of doorway and swung the other direction, far too slowly, because that door had opened just behind the first, and just as violently. The man on that end fired. My shot was a split second slower, but his missed because Beecher had swept the chair he'd been sitting in off the floor and hurled it the length of the car, striking the second man and throwing off his aim. My bullet snatched him out of the doorway. I pivoted again, but that one was empty also, except for a heap on the platform. The inside of the car stank of brimstone. It had lost its club atmosphere all at once.

Beecher relit the lantern and strode over to cover the second entrance, armed only with the light, which he held out from his body. I kept the revolver in my hand and went the other way.

"This one's still breathing," Beecher called out.

"Get his gun."

The man on the rear platform sat with his back against the railing and one leg pinned under him. He had on a canvas coat, too heavy for the mild early-autumn night, but long enough to cover a firearm, which came away from his hand with no effort when I bent to take it. There was no need to feel for a pulse. In the light from the station, there was a glistening cavern where his left eye belonged. I'd still been coming up from the chair when the door flew open, and had fired high. I couldn't tell if he was young or old. A face in that condition doesn't offer much to go by.

I knelt in front of him and went through his clothes. I felt something and pulled it out.

Beecher called out again. "Three chances what I found in this one's pocket."

"One's all I need." I was looking at the gold coin glinting on my palm.

6

The man I'd killed at the back of the caboose was named Charles Worth, if the letter in his pocket signed, "Your loving sister, Wilhelmina," didn't belong to someone else. I'd never heard of him or his sister. The letter was mostly about the fine weather in Baltimore, but it told me more about him than I found out about his partner, whose punctured lung filled with blood and drowned him before the doctor could get inside. He looked to be in his early thirties and had nothing on his person to identify him; even the labels in his ready-made clothes had been ripped out.

The doctor, a young man himself but with the broken look of a professional who had come west hoping to make his fortune off the anemic wives of wealthy miners only to find himself pulling bullets out of prospectors shot in drunken duels, came out of his examining room wiping his hands with a towel. He scowled at the faces pressed against the windows of his office—bearded and clean-shaven, scrubbed and filthy, locals and visitors—and drew down the shades. The core group had followed us there from the train station. The rest had been growing up around it for twenty minutes.

"He didn't say anything," the doctor said. "You don't when your throat's full of blood and mucus. My work would be a great deal less messy if you fellows would aim for the heart."

I said, "Mine would be, too, if they'd give me time. Did you know the man?"

"I never saw him before, and I know all the residents here at least by sight. He probably drifted in with this new mob. This is my fourth shooting in two days."

"It's them politicians." Beecher was studying a diagram of the human circulatory system on a chart tacked to the wall.

The doctor noticed. "You can take that with you, if you like. It's one of God's miracles. Maybe next time you'll think twice before you blow a hole through it."

"Talk to Mr. Murdock. I ain't shot nobody since the army."

"I was thinking about my own circulatory system when I shot him," I said. "What about the other one?" I gave the doctor the letter I'd found folded in Worth's shirt pocket. A little blood had trickled onto it from the hole in his head, mixing with the yellow-brown ink.

He glanced at it, handed it back. "I knew Charlie. I never worked on him, but he kept me busy, wiring shattered jaws and patching up holes. He liked to pick fights with Yankees. You'd think he served with Robert E. Lee himself, except he was only twelve years old when the war ended."

"Local recruit." I put away the letter. "His friend didn't lose any time looking him up. He must have come in on the same train as me, maybe all the way from Helena."

"If I were you, I'd take the next train out. You, too," he told Beecher. "Charlie had friends."

"Yankee baiters, too?" I asked.

"I doubt they had a creed. In every place, there's an element that falls in behind the man with the loudest manners. They run with the pack because no one else will have them."

"Being part of something that's bigger than them-selves?" I was looking at Beecher.

"Ain't the same thing." He'd turned away from the chart.

The doctor rubbed his bloodshot eyes. "I agree with your man. Any group they join is as small as its least-significant member. That's what makes them dangerous."

Beecher said, "I ain't his man."

We went from there to the city marshal's office, which was laid out more like a parlor in a private home than a place of business. A fussy rug lay on the half-sawn logs of the floor, tables covered with lacy shawls held up bulbous lamps with fringes on the shades, homely samplers and pictures from Greek myth hung in gilt-encrusted frames on the walls, which had been slathered with plaster and papered to disguise the logs beneath. The marshal, a basset-faced forty with an advancing forehead and Louis-Napoleon whiskers lacquered into lethal points, sat behind a table with curved legs he used for a desk, examining my deputy's badge for flaws and tugging an enormous watch out of the pocket of his floral vest every few minutes to track the progress of the hands across its face.

"There'll be an inquest," he said. "You'll both have to give evidence."

I said, "We can give you statements right now. I need to be on my way to San Francisco tomorrow."

"No good. You can't ask questions of a written statement in open court."

"Wire Judge Blackthorne. An attack on a deputy U.S. marshal is federal business. It's only your jurisdiction if you want to oppose him."

"I don't expect to go to hell for it. He isn't God."

"Put that in your wire. He might even pay you a personal visit."

"What about the colored man? He federal business?"

Beecher was seated in an upholstered rocker next to an

open window, through which the noise of crickets sounded like thousands of violins having their strings plucked. I guessed he'd chosen the spot for the fresh air. The smell of fust in the room was strong enough to stand a shoe up in. "I is with the Northern Pacific, boss. I belongs to the right-of-way."

"Beecher's a civilian employed by Blackthorne's court," I said. "He's U.S. property same as me."

"Gold Creek isn't Tombstone or Deadwood. We're an incorporated city, with a charter and two churches. The local chapter of the Grand Army of the Republic meets in the basement of the Unitarian. When two men are killed, the incident is investigated and adjudicated. This is a civilized community."

I said, "According to the doctor, killing is daily business. Do you seriously intend to claim two more when Helena is offering to take them off your hands?"

"My appointment's up for review at the end of this year. I don't want to be accused of stuffing something behind the stove." He didn't appear to be listening to himself. Washing his hands of the thing appealed to him, but there was a gilt-edged Bible in plain sight on his desk. No Christian wants to be compared with Pilate.

"Blame it on de gub'ment, boss," Beecher said. "Everybody else does."

The marshal pulled on his whiskers. His neck creased like a concertina. "I don't recall asking you for counsel, boy. I can't see any time I would."

Beecher shrugged and inhaled air from outside.

However, the argument was through, and it was his suggestion that finished it. The marshal wasn't going to let things look that way, so I changed the subject, to give him time to form the conclusion independently.

"Did you get to meet General Grant?"

The creases disappeared. He held up a set of red and

swollen knuckles. "Right here's the hand that shook the hand. When I told him I served with the quartermaster corps, he thanked me for the boots that took him all the way from Fort Henry to Appomattox."

"He could probably use a new pair. I hear the business world hasn't been kind to him."

"Me neither, comes to that. I ran a mercantile in Albany, best in town. I closed it up and came out here to sell picks and shovels, and I sold plenty, all on credit. I figure to be a rich man just as soon as all those markers come in. Meanwhile, I break up fights and shoot rats and stray dogs to put meat on my table."

"What's a rat taste like?" Beecher asked.

I bulled ahead before the marshal could pull his chin back in. "Everyone I talk to came out here to make money off miners. Didn't anyone come for the gold?"

"They're still out digging."

The weapons we'd taken off the men at the caboose lay on the marshal's blotter. Worth's was a short-barreled Colt. The stranger had fired a wicked-looking revolver at me, equipped with a second barrel whose bore was larger than the one on top. I pointed at it.

"I'll be taking the Le Mat with me," I said.

"That's evidence."

"Blackthorne would just send someone to collect it. I'll save him the trouble."

"What about the Colt?"

"I don't need the Colt."

"What do you want with a Confederate piece?"

"They didn't lose the war because their weapons weren't good. They just didn't have enough men to carry them. I'll give you a receipt."

He shoved it across the table at me. "Anything else I can do for you, seeing as how all's I got pressing on my time is a town full of drunken Easterners?"

I checked the load. There were four live .42 cartridges in the cylinder, someone having taken the trouble to convert it from cap-and-ball, and a 20-gauge shell in the shotgun tube. He'd fired one cartridge and kept an empty chamber under the hammer. I was grateful he'd chosen not to use the buckshot on me. "You can direct me to a gunsmith's."

"How many weapons does a man need?"

"No more than he has hands, but guns aren't much use without ammunition."

"You want Joe Hankerd at the Rocky Mountain General Merchandise, only he's closed now. I don't know if he carries anything for a rebel gun."

"Both sides used the same calibers."

We got directions. It took five minutes of door-kicking to bring down a red-faced runt in handlebars and a night-shirt, and two more to get him to lower his sawed-off double-barrels and let us in. He charged me twice the going rate for two boxes of shells, one for each of the Le Mat's firing features, and locked up loudly behind us.

"Frontier's famous for its hospitality," Beecher said.

"That's just from sunup to sundown."

We were still towing a percentage of the local population, but they thinned out as we left the saloons behind and continued walking toward the mountains. The only light ahead of us belonged to the lanterns and campfires of the mine sites in the distance. Our breath frosted a little in the crisp air of coming autumn. Beecher asked where we were headed.

"Away from the crowd."

We lost the last straggler to a hotel whose latecomers were camped out on the floor of the lobby. Shielding the movement with my body, I handed Beecher the Le Mat and the two boxes of ammunition. "Keep them out of sight. A Negro with a gun can draw a lot of hell most places."

"I told you I'm no good with a pistol." He held the items in both hands like a balance scale.

I took back the revolver, adjusted the nose on the hammer, and returned it. "That fires the shotgun round. Scatterguns were designed with you in mind."

"I ain't said I'm throwing in with you."

"You threw in when you threw that chair. By this time tomorrow, every depot lizard from here to the Pacific will know about the colored porter who helped kill two men in Gold Creek. You're branded either way."

He touched the scar on his cheek with the Le Mat's muzzle. "I reckon I am."

"I didn't mean that."

"I know. But a nigger with a scar has a hard time blending in with the black crowd."

"Getting out of that uniform will help. Got any civilian clothes?"

"In my duffel. In the caboose."

"We'll collect it in the morning. It'll just be another caboose by then. A couple of killings won't draw attention long with Grant in town."

"*That's* what's been stinging me. I couldn't think. If these new Johnny Rebs want to make a stir, why choose you? Grant's the bigger target."

"That's the reason. Too many people around him. These boys aren't interested in making themselves martyrs for the cause. Getting away's as important to them as hitting what they aim at."

His teeth caught the light from a window. It was the first time he'd shown them. "If that's the case, they didn't think it through where you're concerned."

I didn't smile back. "My odds just got a little shorter. Meanwhile, we've got eight hundred miles to cover before San Francisco."

"You ain't asked me why I threw that chair."

"I didn't figure you gave it any thought. That cavalry training dies hard."

"I ain't no trick dog."

I blew air. "Are we going to have this conversation all the way to California? Because if we are, I'd just as soon we rode in separate cars."

"We probably will anyway."

"That's between you and Mr. Hill. Do we leave this conversation here or not?"

"I reckon," he said after a moment. "I don't see any sport in it."

"I didn't get around to thanking you for throwing that chair."

"No need. I didn't give it any thought." He stuck the revolver under his belt and the boxes in his pockets. "Where we sleeping tonight?"

"Take your pick." I swept a hand along the weak lights wavering in the foothills.

"Them miners'll likely shoot us as claim-jumpers."

"They might, if their claims were worth the filing fees. That's the thing about frontier hospitality. The poorer a man is, the more he's got of it."

I started off in the direction of the fires. Beecher caught up, his pockets rattling like a peddler's wagon. We weren't sneaking up on any prospectors that night.

7

The first train had pulled out with General Grant aboard by the time we got to the station the next morning. There were no seats on the second, so I bought a ticket on the third—Beecher showed his employee's pass—and we ate breakfast at a place called the Miner's Rest while waiting for departure. The proprietor sent us around to the kitchen, whether because of Beecher's color or the clothes I'd slept in up in the hills, I didn't know. In his corduroy coat, cotton twill shirt and trousers, flat-heeled boots, and slouch hat, my companion looked the more respectable member of our party.

The conductor, a stranger to Beecher, directed us to separate coaches, assigning the Negro to a twenty-year-old chair car well back of the Pullmans containing the dignitaries, most of whom required a porter's assistance to climb the steps from the station platform through a haze of whiskey and stale perfume. I recognized some of them from the train I'd come in on; promoted from fourth to third to fill vacancies left by those who'd taken the express back East.

I started to say I'd take the chair car, too, but in response to an infinitesimal shake of Beecher's head I asked for a pencil and paper, and when they were brought by a porter I scribbled a message and gave him a dollar to send a wire. Beecher and I separated. I lowered a window against the

stink of cigars and digested barley, swung down the
footrest, and got to work catching up on the sleep I'd lost
lying on the iron earth under a borrowed blanket in the
hills. Ten years more and I'd need a featherbed. Just plain
surviving is fatal in the end.

Shortly after the train started moving, a fat fellow with
a bad sunburn plunked himself down next to me, introduced himself as a reporter with a New York newspaper,
and asked if I'd heard anything about a double shooting
in Gold Creek. I said I hadn't.

"Someone said there was a renegade nigger involved,"
he said.

"I wouldn't know."

"Late night last night. I slept right through it, didn't
catch wind of it till the train was pulling out. Any Indian
trouble along the line?" He sounded eager.

"Not anymore. They're all on reservations."

"What about train robbers? I understand they're thick
as fleas in Montana."

I said I didn't think the fleas in Montana were thicker
than anywhere else, but he didn't take the hint. When he
started in on grizzlies I changed seats.

In Deer Lodge, the porter I'd asked to send my wire
shook me awake and handed me a Western Union envelope. I read the telegram and made my way back through
the snoring payload to the ancient chair car, where I found
Beecher jammed in between a mulatto in a valet's livery
and a Chinese with a wooden cage on his lap containing
a sitting hen. The car was so hot the flies were asleep in
midair. I told Beecher to join me up front. He started to
shake his head again, then thought better of it, got up, took
down his duffel from the tarnished brass carrier, and followed me.

Five minutes after we sat down in the Pullman, the conductor appeared. He had a drinker's face, shot through

with broken capillaries, and cardamom on his breath. Why anyone west of Chicago was in any business other than drumming whiskey was a puzzle.

"I'm sorry, sir," he said. "I guess I didn't make myself clear in Gold Creek. The other, er, gentleman—"

I stuck the telegram under his nose. It read:

DEPUTY MURDOCK
BE ADVISED EDWARD ANDERSON BEECHER
NEGRO OFFICIALLY ASSIGNED DUTIES DEPUTY U S
MARSHAL EFFECTIVE THIS DATE STOP ENTITLED
SAME CONSIDERATION AUTHORITY ALL OTHER
DEPUTIES

                         CHESTER A ARTHUR
                         PRESIDENT
                         UNITED STATES OF AMERICA

He sawed the flimsy back and forth, caught the focus, and paled a little behind the magenta.

"How do I know this is real?" Pricklets of sweat stood out like boiler rivets on his upper lip. He fanned himself with the paper, without any visible effect. "Anyone can send a wire and call himself the King of Prussia."

I showed him my deputy's star. "Wire him back. He ought to be sitting down to dinner with General Sherman about now."

For all I knew he was having his toenails painted by a harlot sent by the New York Port Authority, but the conductor knew even less than I did. He handed back the telegram and left the car, wobbling on his sore feet.

Beecher asked to see the telegram. I gave it to him. He read it and looked up. "Arthur really send this?"

"It's doubtful, but you can ask Judge Blackthorne next time you get to Helena. If he's in a generous mood he might even give you a straight answer."

"What did you tell him?"

"You're the only thing keeping me alive."

"He set this much store by all the help?"

"A good carpenter takes care of his tools."

He read the flimsy again. Then he returned it. "My luck, it'll be this same train I work when I get back. I'll be emptying spittoons come the new century."

"I wouldn't brood on it. If we make San Francisco, chances are we'll both end up on the bottom of the bay."

"That being the situation, I believe I'll ask one of these here colored boys to bring me a cigar."

"Open a window if you do. I'd as soon sit next to a chicken." I put the telegram in a safe pocket. I had an idea I'd be drawing it as often as the Deane-Adams.

PART TWO

The Hoodlums

8

Three days and as many train changes later, we rolled into San Francisco aboard the Southern Pacific through a swirling mulch as brown as brandy and nearly as thick, a combination of fog from the harbor and coal smoke from a thousand chimneys. The globes of the fabled gas lamps, their posts obscured, lay like fishermen's floats on its surface, glowing dirty orange. On the depot platform the porters wheeled trunks and portmanteaux with lanterns balanced atop the stacks toward waiting hotel carriages; the lanterns illuminated little but themselves, but they gave passengers something to follow and avoid stepping off the edge and breaking a limb. Telegraph Hill was an island in a dun sea, pierced here and there by the odd church spire and the tall masts in the harbor.

Beecher and I were looking for a porter to direct us to a hotel that didn't care which colors it mixed under its roof when a dandy materialized out of the mist in front of us. He was thirty or younger, with longish flaxen hair curling out from under a Mexican sombrero, wearing an olive-colored frock coat over an embroidered vest that looked as if it had been cut out of the carpet in the lobby of an opera house. His trousers were fawn-colored and stuffed into knee-high boots and he was carrying a walking stick too short to lean on, made for swinging when he walked. It was all good material but needed cleaning; and had for some time, from the smell of him. The stick, however, had been polished recently, gleaming in what light there was like the tongue of an exotic reptile.

"Carry your bags, cap'n?" He pointed at my valise with his stick. He was holding it by the handle, a heavy-looking blob of silver shaped into the head of some animal.

"I've just got the one," I said.

"Half a hog for my trouble? I'm past two days without gruel."

"What's half a hog?"

"A nickel, cap'n. First time in Frisco?" He showed me a gold tooth, which would have made a better impression if the one next to it weren't black.

"Is there a tax on that?"

He giggled, and twisted the handle off the stick.

He did it one-handed, with a neat, practiced flick of his wrist, but he'd have done better to use both hands, because it called attention to itself. The rest of the stick fell away from eighteen inches of bright metal narrowing to a point. I got my valise in front of it just as he underhanded it at the center of my rib cage. It sheared through the leather like a lance through a blister. Before he could pull it back out and try again, I gave the valise a twist, snapping the shaft clean in two.

He had good reflexes. Six inches of jagged metal still stuck out of the handle, and without hesitating, he drew back to jab it at my face. I swung up the valise, but the contents shifted, throwing off the angle, and in that instant I saw myself walking through the rest of my life sideways with my empty eye socket turned to the shadow. Then something cracked, a sharp, shocking explosion like a chunk of hickory splitting in a stove. The dandy's sombrero fell off and he followed it down to the platform. In his place stood a sad-faced stranger with black bartender's handlebars under a leather helmet. He had a blue uniform buttoned to his chin and an oak stick in one hand, attached to his wrist by a leather thong. His expression as he examined the results of his action looked as if he'd bashed in the head of a kitten.

However, young skulls are hard to break. The dandy pushed himself into a sitting position and blinked up through the blood in his eyes. "You can't pinch me! I'm a Hoodlum!"

The man in uniform appeared to consider this. Then he leaned down and tapped the young man behind the right ear. The arm the dandy was supporting himself on went out flat and he fell onto his back. His eyes rolled over white and a thread of drool slid out of one corner of his mouth. Apart from that, nothing moved.

I remembered Beecher then and looked his way just as he pulled out his shirttail and dropped it over the butt of the Le Mat stuck under his belt. A bit more practice and he'd have it in his hand the next time a foot and a half of sword let out my intestines. He was more reliable with a chair.

"This one ain't much older than my sister's boy," the policeman muttered. His Irish was as thick as stout. "They're getting too small to keep. Ah, me." He stuck his stick under one arm, produced a pair of manacles from a loop on his belt, and bent to work.

"I'm obliged, Officer," I said when he straightened.

He had a bulge in one cheek, which he emptied into a brown mess on the platform near where the dandy lay on his stomach now, with his hands linked behind his back. "You gents need to check those weapons first stop you make. You have run out of wilderness when you're in San Francisco."

Our pistols were out of sight, but there is no overestimating a policeman's eye. I told him my name, which meant nothing to him, and showed him my star, which meant very little more.

"What about your man?"

Beecher said, "I ain't—"

I snapped open the telegram with Arthur's signature for the policeman to read. He grunted, shifted his plug from one cheek to the other, pursed his lips to spit, thought better of it, and mopped his mouth with the back of a broken-knuckled hand. "I voted for Hancock. Come to clean up Barbary?"

"You seem to be doing a fair job of that all by yourself." I put away the flimsy.

"This?" He toed the inert man in the ribs. "This pup wandered out of his yard. Past Pacific Street I'd of wanted the militia. Just because these Hoodlums own the waterfront don't mean they hold title to the rest."

Beecher asked what a Hoodlum was. The policeman appraised him, worked up a fresh head of juice, and defiled the crown of the young man's sombrero lying on the platform.

"Dips and thieves what like to dress up like toffs," he said. "That poetist fellow Oscar Wilde hared through here last year, piping up beauty for its own sake and decked out in purple velvet, which is milk and sugar to these lads. Come sunup next day, you couldn't find a bolt of brocade that wasn't spoke for, nor an unslashed pocket to pay for it. It's how they know each other. Going in after 'em's the same as putting your fist through a paper nest of hornets. This far inland all you got to do is step on 'em."

"Are you sure he's a Hoodlum?" I asked.

"He ain't Wilde. I know, because the wife dragged me down to Platt's Hall to see him. I never wasted fifty cents worse in all my born days."

"Would you mind checking his pockets?"

"What for, iron knuckles? He didn't need 'em as long as he had that trick stick."

"I'm looking for a double eagle."

He barked a short laugh. "Twenty crackers in his pocket, and he tries to nick you for a five-cent piece?"

"It could have been an excuse to get close."

The policeman spat, sighed, knelt, and performed the chore. The young man moaned when he was jostled, but didn't wake up. He might have had a fractured skull. The policeman rose with his bounty displayed on his palm. "Two coppers and a busted watch. Fellow he nipped it from probably fell on it. If he ever had a double Ned, it's spent. Not on soap." He pocketed the items and mopped his palm on his trousers.

"These coins aren't for spending. He's just a thief, like you said."

"Wheelock's Wards, we call 'em here."

I perked up at that. "Daniel Webster Wheelock?"

"If there's more than one, it's a bigger country than they told me when I shipped over. These lads are Cap'n Dan's eyes and ears outside the Bella Union. Employing unfortunates, he calls it. I wouldn't know. The only unfortunate thing I see about these lads is they're as many as ants. I wouldn't drop my drawers in a Donegan on Kearney without a squad to stand behind me."

I remembered Wheelock was a fire captain as well as a city alderman. I only half understood the rest. I thanked him again for stepping in and hoisted my valise. The broken sword-end came loose of the rent in the leather and clattered to the platform.

"Thank Mr. Callahan," he said, slapping his palm with his stick. "It's the only English these lads savvy. Where you gents billeted? Magistrate might need you to swear out a complaint, on account of the fog."

"The fog?"

"If he's a Wheelock man, he might say I couldn't see what I saw. That's what makes these boyos so chesty when Callahan comes to call."

"No billet yet," I said. "All suggestions are welcome."

He thought for a moment. "The Slop Chest on Davis is the crib for you. It ain't so bad as it sounds; Nan Feeny inherited it from her husband, the Commodore, who was soft on sailors and named it after a captain's tackle. Twelve cents the day, eighty the week if you pony up front. Either of you gents smoke tobacco?"

Beecher said he did.

"You'll want to run the tip down the mattress seams. Discourages the active citizens."

" 'Active citizens'?" we said together.

The policeman spat and shook his head. "That's any with at least four legs more than you. Come morning, you'll think you was cut up by the tongs. You frontier folk might know your Injun palaver, but if you don't learn the local office, you'll finish up feeding fish in the bay."

The Hoodlum was coming around, moaning something about taking the jolly off, or something equally enlightening. The policeman reached down and hauled him to his feet by his shackles. This brought a howl that made me feel as if my own arms were being torn from their sockets, which the policeman silenced by punching the young man in the ribs with his stick. As he was being pulled toward the end of the platform, the Hoodlum said, "My roofer," which was the first thing he'd said that I could translate without help. The policeman bent, scooped up the tobacco-stained sombrero by its crown, and jammed it down over the prisoner's ears. Then he led him off into the fog.

Beecher said, "I didn't follow but one word that man said in ten."

"Maybe Nan Feeny has a dictionary." I tucked in the torn flap of my valise and started off in the path of the policeman and his captive.

The first cabman I told to take us to the Slop Chest ordered us out of his carriage. Since he was holding his whip we didn't argue. I told the next one in line before we got in, and we didn't get in. The third driver, who was the most polite, pretended he was too busy getting his cigar burning to hear me. When I spoke to the next one down I held up the late Charlie Worth's double eagle, turning it until it caught the light from the corner gas lamp. It brought no smile.

"That's too much." He was a lean fifty in an old-fashioned stovepipe hat and neckstock, with the sandy complexion of someone who spent most of his time sitting out in the elements.

I said, "I thought if I showed it, you wouldn't think I was luring you out there to nip you."

I must have got the vernacular wrong, or maybe amused contempt was the only other expression he had. He pointed his chin at Beecher. "He with you?"

I said he was. I'd already dismissed this driver and was thinking ahead toward the last carriage in the line. I wondered how long the walk was to Davis and what kind of hell the fog contained on the way.

"Twenty-five cents. I don't split fares."

We got in.

Either the haze was lifting or my eyes were becoming accustomed to the stingy light that managed to penetrate it. We watched ornate gingerbread buildings sliding past, a stout, homely little brick box whose sign identified it as the United States Mint, which belatedly I realized was where the coin in my pocket had come from, and to where it had returned by way of circumstances unsuspected by the men who operated the stampers. Shortly after that, the gimcrackery faded out and even brick became scarce, replaced by buildings made of clapboard and scrapwood bearing unmistakable stains from exposure to the sea; ships that had sailed their last missions, broken up for what profit could be obtained from their corpses. A dozen or so blocks of that, and then the carriage came to a stop.

"Slop Chest," the driver said.

"Holy Jesus," Beecher said.

"Home," I said; and loosened the Deane-Adams in its holster before getting out.

9

The Slop Chest— this on the basis of the driver's declaration, since there was no sign to identify it—looked at first as if it had floated in on a devastating flood, and settled on its present foundation when the waters receded. It was built to resemble an oversize flatboat, with a cabin on the deck and part of the railing removed for visitors to enter by way of three warped steps and a door that might have been cut out of the side with a bucksaw for all the attention that had been paid to plumbs and levels, and hung with leather hinges. What appeared at first to have been a hit-or-miss whitewashing of the boards turned out on examination to be a couple of decades' worth of sea salt, washed up on deck during storms and allowed to dry into a crust as hard as limestone; seasons of rain had washed some of it onto the strip of bare earth that separated the structure from the boardwalk, forever preventing the growth of so much as a single blade of grass. A dilapidated rocking chair and glider occupied the deck—I suppose it could be called a front porch—and these, together with nearly every square inch of the floor, were covered with bodies flung about in loose-rag positions that suggested either a massacre or a bacchanal of ancient Greek proportions. These men were clad in peacoats, striped jerseys, and baggy canvas trousers, sailors' garb. Their snores were loud enough to rock the old boat on its moorings.

"Looks like the Little Big Horn," said Beecher.

"Or Hampton Roads," I said. "Who's minding the ships in the harbor?"

"Twenty-five cents," said the driver.

I paid him. He stuck the coin between his teeth and gave the reins a flip. I stepped back just in time to save my toes.

Beecher slung his duffel over his left shoulder, unbuttoned his shirt to clear the path to the Le Mat under his belt, and we climbed the steps.

The interior was a saloon, better appointed than the outside would indicate. There were a couple of gaming tables covered in green baize, an iron chandelier suspended from the ceiling, beneath which a mound of pale wax from the dripping candles had begun to grow into a stalagmite on the floor, and a carved mahogany bar with a pink marble top. Behind it, above the bottles aligned on a back bar nearly as ornate, hung a canvas in a gilt frame as wide as a fainting-couch, upon which sprawled at full length a hideously fat woman amateurishly executed in thick paint. It was the lewdest thing I'd seen outside of the upstairs room of a brothel, and wouldn't have existed half an hour in any public establishment on the frontier before the decency squads poured in with their axes and wooden truncheons.

Beecher stared at the painting. "Man must of used up every drop of pink in town."

The room wasn't as crowded as I'd expected on the evidence of the front porch. A blue-chinned tinhorn in a frayed cutaway and dirty top hat was dealing himself a hand of Patience at one of the tables and three men, two of them dressed as sailors, the third in a faded wool shirt and filthy overalls worn nearly through at the knees—a miner's kit—leaned on the bar, nursing glasses of beer and conversing not at all. The hour was too early for celebration and too close to midday for the gainfully employed.

It was a depressing time to drink. Gloom hung overhead like the chandelier, dripping dejection into a sullen mound.

There was no sunshine to be had from the bartender, an old salt who at one time might have been cheerfully fat, but whom life had rendered down until the gray skin hung in sheets from his cheekbones and bare forearms, blue as old china with aging tattoos of indeterminate character. His bald head was as white as polished bone above the line where a hat protected it from the sun when he went outside; the first indication I'd seen that the city was not perpetually wrapped in smutty fog. I bought two beers, which he poured from a tap covered with green mold, and asked if Nan Feeny was on the premises.

"Who for, you or your man? She don't favor pumpernickel."

Beecher clapped the Le Mat on the bartop, which at close range was far from pristine. The marble was mottled all about with odd saucer-shaped depressions with cracks radiating out from the centers. I couldn't decide what could have caused them. "Next one calls me his man won't be one much longer," he told the bartender.

The old sailor looked at the pistol as if it were a fresh spill. "Hodge."

He barely raised his voice. I was still puzzling out where this latest new word belonged in the regional lexicon when a section of the back bar swung away from the wall and a dwarf entered the room through the opening.

He impressed me as a dwarf. From his beltline to his bowler-topped head he was normal size, built thick as a prizefighter through the chest and shoulders, his biceps straining the sleeves of his yellow-and-black-striped sailor's jersey. From the waist down, he was no larger than a six-year-old boy, and one stricken with rickets into the bargain. He paused this side of the opening, then came forward, swaying from side to side on shriveled bowlegs draped in black broadcloth. His feet kept going when he reached the bar, pumping him up until he was facing Beecher at eye-level. I went up on the balls of my feet and spotted the three-foot ladder nailed inside the bar. His face was unlined, late twenties at the oldest, with a closely trimmed black beard covering the lower half, grown probably to prevent strangers from mistaking him for a child.

An explosion shook the bar, slopping beer over the rims of the glasses perched on it and draining a trickle of plaster from the ceiling. Beecher and I jumped; the other patrons at the bar didn't stir, except to lean on one elbow to watch a show they'd seen before. I looked down and saw a fresh depression in the marble. It was occupied by a black-enameled iron sphere half again the size of a billiard ball, attached by six inches of chain to a ring poking out of the little man's right sleeve. There was no hand there. With a practiced gesture he'd swung the ball in a short arc ending in a loud bang when it struck the bar, just short of crushing Beecher's hand where it rested next to the Le Mat.

"No firearms in the Slop Chest, mate." He had a broad cockney accent, but his voice was low and silken, unlike the bray of a small man with something to prove. He didn't need it as long as he had that ball and chain. "Either check 'em here or leave 'em home."

The bartender scowled at the new dent. "Damn it, Hodge, I told you before I'm responsible for this bar. Nan said she'd dock me next time."

"I'll stake the whole bloody whack. A bar oughtn't be marble to start. It stains like cotton drawers. What's it to be, mate?" He kept his eyes on Beecher. "Lay up the snapper or take one in the brain-box?" He twirled his wrist. The ball made a shallow orbit and landed where it had started. Slivers of marble jumped up and skittered across the bar.

"Jesus, Hodge!" the bartender complained.

Very slowly, Beecher slid his hand forward and nudged the revolver's handle inside the little man's reach. Hodge scooped it up with his good right hand and thrust it toward the bartender, who took it and placed it on a high back shelf lined with backstraps of every make and model. There were more confiscated weapons there than patrons in the saloon; evidence that the place indeed took on boarders. Hodge's gaze slid my way. "What's your story, mate? Try me on?"

Using two fingers I drew the star from my shirt pocket and laid it on the bar. He barely glanced at it.

"Tin's cheap," he said. "What else you got?"

I took out the telegram and spread it on the bar. The edges were tattering. I was considering having it framed and hanging it around my neck. Beecher probably wouldn't volunteer for that.

"What's it say, Billy?"

The bartender read aloud, stumbling over "officially" and "consideration." It might have been signed by the man who emptied the spittoons for all the impression Arthur's name seemed to make on either of them.

"Paper's cheaper." Hodge looked patient.

I slid the Deane-Adams out of its holster and held it toward him butt-first.

"On the bar. I heard about the border roll in Brisbane."

I laid it down, retrieved the star and the telegram, and pocketed them. He picked up the revolver, thumbed aside the loading gate, and rotated the cylinder to inspect the chambers, all one-handed. "English piece. Limeys transported me old man's old man for picking an earl's pocket, but I ain't one to stroke a grudge. What's a Yank want with a barking-iron made in Blighty?"

"I don't care for Colts. The five-shot's lighter and packs the same fire power."

"What happens when you face six men?"

"I run."

He grinned in his beard. His teeth looked too white and even to have grown inside his mouth. I asked him if he lost his hand in Australia.

"Coming over. Worked my way across. Mainsail bust loose while I was striking it and took me rammer with it. Had me a regular hook till I rolled over on it in me doss and near crushed the old cobblers. Got a smithy on Battle Row to run me up this rig. I count me rise in the world from that day. You don't need to be as tall as Jack's hat when you got four pounds of Michigan iron slang off your fam."

"How do you sleep?" Beecher asked.

"Like a rum angel, cock's-crow to day's arse."

I said, "Sorry we got you out of bed. We need a couple of rooms. A policeman at the train station told us to ask for Nan Feeny."

His porcelains gleamed. "Best be mum about that with Nan. She wouldn't appreciate a fly-cop giving her the oak."

"Does anyone in this town speak American?" I asked.

"Nan's your mollisher. She was a governess in Boston till they caught her up to her petticoats in the master of the house. He's still rhino fat up there on Beacon Hill, but the booly-dogs stunned her right out of her regulars and she took it on the rods. She's fly to the patter when it suits."

Now he was just showing off. "You're the bouncer here?"

"Keeper of the keys, and Nan Feeny's knees. Axel Hodge is the chant, and Black-Spy take the cove says it ain't. You're this bloke Murdock?"

"Page Murdock."

"Horseshit," said Billy the bartender. He was the most articulate man in the place.

Hodge's face was an opaque sheet. "Well, you may be

flush gage out in country, but here you're just herring. Frisco's a bufe what eats anything."

I'd had my colorful fill of Axel Hodge. I nudged Beecher's foot with my boot, alerting him, then took hold of the iron ball where it rested on the bar and jerked it across and over the lip of the marble on my side. Hodge's arm came with it. His chin hit the bar with a snap that was going to send him back to his dentist for adjustments. Billy reacted, reaching under his side of the bar for whatever weapon waited there, but before he could straighten up, Beecher wrenched the Deane-Adams out of Hodge's startled grip, rolled back the hammer with a gesture that told me he'd been practicing with the Le Mat while I wasn't looking, and took aim at the spot where the old sailor's eyebrows met above the bridge of his nose.

The other patrons took their elbows off the bar and slid out of ricochet range, but not so far away they wouldn't be able to witness what happened next. This was something new at the Slop Chest, worth repeating when they were back at sea and the tall tales had spun themselves out.

Hodge tried to pull away, but I leaned my hip against the iron ball, pinning it against the mahogany on my side. He couldn't get leverage with his short legs.

"I was told folks are friendly in California," I said. "If this is how you treat all your customers, I'm not surprised they'd rather draw flies on the front porch than come in and wet their whiskers."

The air stirred. Weatherbeaten boards moaned and shifted, leather scraped wood, a dozen voices howled in protest. In a small advertising mirror tilted on one of the shelves behind the bar, I saw sunburned, unshaven faces plastered against the windows and jammed together between the doorjambs leading to the front porch. I thought at first the sleeping sailors had been roused at last by the commotion inside. Then the bodies in the doorway separated as if someone had pried them apart with a pinch-bar and ten yards of taffeta and silk petticoat rustled in through the space, wrapped around six feet of female.

Movement rippled through the crowd, and caps and hats came off heads that had been breeding lice in darkness for weeks. That was impressive.

"What's the row, Hodge?" the woman said. "I could hear you punching holes in my bar all the way from Pacific."

"Cly your daddles, Nan. It's all plummy." With his chin nailed to the bartop, the rest of Hodge's hard-hatted head had to move up and down to get the words out.

Nan Feeny—what I could see of her while dividing my concentration among Hodge, Billy, and the woman's reflection in the mirror—had a handsome head on a long neck with a choker, topped by an elaborate pile of hair—startlingly white, against a face that was still too young to need as much paint as had been applied to it.

"Plummy as a bag of nails," she observed, and unslung a pepperbox pistol from the reticule she carried.

"Red lady," muttered the tinhorn seated at the table, laying the queen of diamonds on the king of clubs.

10

"Just the one, and you're lucky to have it. Them pegos wasn't sleeping on the deck for the fresh air. Twenty-five cents a day." Nan Feeny opened the door and stepped aside.

"We were told twelve." I waited for my eyes to adjust. The room, one of several opening off a short hall behind the barroom, was a windowless den no larger than a ship's berth, with two narrow bunks built one atop the other into the wall, which I thought was carrying the nautical theme too far.

"Twelve apiece, and a penny tax."

"Who collects the tax?" Beecher took his turn looking at the accommodations. There wasn't room for two men to stand inside.

"Little squint-eyed ponce stinks of lilacs, and you don't want to turn him away without his copper. I was burned out once. That's the price of pride in Barbary."

We'd settled our differences in the saloon. Beecher had checked his revolver and I'd given Hodge back his arm, and when she'd put up the pepperbox we'd straightened out the reason for our visit. Face to face, or almost—the proprietress had two inches on me in my high-heeled boots—she had bad skin, hence the paint, and strong bones that wouldn't give up her age short of another decade. However, she was still two young for her white hair, which didn't look like a wig. She wore it in a chignon that added several unnecessary inches to her height.

I asked her how much for a week, which surprised her. Her natural eyebrows went up almost as high as the ones she'd brushed on.

"Cartwheel dollar. I don't take paper. There's more queer cole hereabouts than treasury. If it's coniakers you're after, I'd best quote you the rate for a year." She had a granite brogue with no green pastures in it.

I'd shown her the star and the telegram. "We're not interested in counterfeiters, if that's what you're asking. Tell me if this means anything." I handed her the double eagle.

She studied the coin on both sides. I thought for a moment she was going to bite it, but teeth were scarcer than gold in that neighborhood. She gave it back, and it was my turn to be surprised. I thought I'd have to wrestle her for it. "I ain't even seen one of them in lead. If you take Nan's advice you'll keep it in your kick. There's tobbies'd settle you for spud and lurch your pork in the brine."

Any way I worked that out didn't sound attractive.

Beecher said, "This one was stamped right here in San Francisco."

Nan studied him before answering. I couldn't tell where she stood on the subject of conversing with Negroes.

"Strictly speaking you left Frisco behind when you crossed Pacific Street. There's some as would say you passed right on through America and out the other side."

I said, "You're telling us you'd know if someone was walking around with one of these in his pocket."

"There's nary a thing Nan don't know what goes on between here and blue water."

"What about the Sons of the Confederacy?"

She twisted a lip. "I'd swap a week's peck to see one of them Nob Hill noddles try on Barbary. There'd be rebel red from Murder Point to North Beach."

"I was told they're thick here."

"I ain't saying you can't spot 'em, all got up in lace goods and lifting their roofers to the mollies as like to give their active citizens some sun. Past dark they don't show their nebs outside the Bella Union. Sons of the Confederacy, my aunt's smicket. They couldn't make war on Queen Dick."

"They've done a fair job of making war on peace officers," I said. "Is that the same Bella Union where Daniel Webster Wheelock hangs his hat?"

"There ain't but one." She took my measure from under her eyelids, one of which drooped a little like a broken windowshade. The powder she used by the pot hadn't quite eradicated an old scar that ran diagonally across its top. "What's your business with Cap'n Dan?"

"I heard he's the man to see in Barbary."

"That's no packet, though you'll not see him without he gives it his benison. He posted the cole to the Commodore to start the Slop Chest. He's also the cove what sent the squint-eyed ponce and the slubber de gullions what set fire to the place."

The stubborn fog had found its way into the hallway through the gaps between the boards. I held up the double eagle. "I like to listen to your Irish. Where can we go to hear more out of the draft?"

Her private quarters was three times the size of the room where Beecher and I had left our bags, which didn't make it spacious. There was a barrel stove for heating and cooking, a pair of mismatched chairs, one with a broken-cane seat, a cornshuck mattress on an iron frame, and a portrait of Nan's late husband, the Commodore, who had been twice her present age when it was painted and looked like just the kind of old walrus who would undertake to support a woman not yet born when he sprouted his first gray hair. The cut of the men's clothes in the doorless wardrobe—a number of sailors' jerseys and a full-dress suit—bore out Axel Hodge's boast that he was the keeper of Nan Feeny's knees. A seam in one wall showed where the back bar opened into the saloon. The room might have belonged to the master of the ship, if the Slop Chest had been a ship instead of a facsimile thrown together from the corpses of genuine vessels. The carpenter in charge was incapable of building anything that would float in a gentle pond.

Sitting up on the bed with her high-laced ankles crossed and peach brandy in a cordial glass in her hand—Beecher and I declined an invitation to join her in the sticky-sweet beverage—our hostess lowered her guard sufficiently to modify her language and, more revealingly, offer her colored guest a cigar from the Commodore's private stock, which she kept fresh by storing the boxes in a cupboard with fresh bread. He accepted it and made himself as comfortable as possible on the chair with the broken seat, puffing up gray clouds that found their way out through the spaces in the siding. Because the place was as private as a cornrick, we kept our voices low and Nan got up frequently to rewind the crank on a phonograph with a morning-glory horn the size of Joaquin's head. "Beautiful Dreamer" drifted out of the opening, interpreted by a tenor with bad sinuses.

Nan, for all her stature and presumed experience with strong drink, became candid under the influence of the peach brandy. We learned that the Commodore, whose given name was Cornelius, had not spent a day at sea, but had profited in Chinatown through the opium smuggled in by way of the pockets of common seamen so far as to have developed an affection for the briny breed. The policeman who had recommended the place had been mistaken about how it got its name. The Sailor's Rest, as the combination saloon and rooming house had originally been christened, had been rebaptized shortly before the Commodore's death, and without his consent, when the leader of a press gang who was variously known as Shanghai Mike, Mike the Crimp, and St. Michael the Persuader (after the effective methods by which he recruited reluctant hands for sea duty) smashed a bottle of green rum over the skull of an opponent in a game of *Rouge et Noir* and proclaimed that he had thus "launched" a new vessel he called the *Slop Chest*. No one dared oppose his fancy until his corpse was found in a Chinatown alley with its face caved in, ostensibly by a tong hatchetman, but by then a couple of generations of patrons had come to know the establishment by no other name. It stuck, although in respect to her deceased husband Nan had stubbornly refused to take down the much-defaced sign the Commodore had commissioned. After the first structure was burned to the ground for nonpayment of the penny tax and replaced by the current building, there was no need to hang any sign at all, since the patrons themselves had contributed most of the construction work in return for free grog.

I noticed she still referred to the place as The Rest, and never without lifting her glass to the Commodore's bilious likeness. He had taken her off the line at a place called the House of Blazes to make her his wife, and whatever the old man may have wanted in the way of romantic attraction, he had made a lady of her ("swell mollisher" was the phrase she used), and she observed the ceremony of buying a round for the house every year on the anniversary of his birth. The fact that he'd been a solemn teetotaler all his life failed to strike her as ironic. Nan was a woman of contrasts, as well as handy with the portable Gatling she carried in her reticule. She got up once and turned back a corner of the threadbare Oriental rug to show the stain where she'd shot an old acquaintance who'd failed to grasp the significance of her retirement from the horizontal trade.

"Kill him?" I asked.

"He took his own sweet time, but infection done for him in the end."

"Where was Hodge?"

"Tobing lushies in Brisbane would be my guess. Axel wandered in here a year ago Independence Day, dragging that slag and thimble off his flapper, cute as cows and kisses. You wanted to palm him like a pennyweight. The Commodore was gone to Grim ten years and then some, rest him. Axel ain't a patch on his articles, but an old ewe like me can't be too particular. Any old dwarf in a storm, I say.

"That scrub I put to bed with a shovel was a square citizen," she went on, refilling her dainty glass from the decanter. Some of the contents slopped over, seasoning further the blot on the floorboards at her feet. "I'd of scragged for it sure as blunt if Cap'n Dan himself didn't stand in with me at the inquest. That hedged the sink he played me on the other, where I'm concerned."

I actually understood most of that. It was like border Spanish; it made sense if you didn't think too hard or try to speak it yourself. I couldn't tell where Beecher stood. He was enjoying his cigar.

"Why do you think Wheelock spoke up for you?" I asked.

"Who knows what goes through a nob's knolly? I put on this neckweed every day so as not to disremember how near I come to mounting the ladder." She touched the ribbon at her throat. "I don't mind saying it takes the sting out when the ponce comes for his copper."

"Does he ever come around?"

"The ponce? First and fifteenth, regular as a yack."

"Wheelock."

"What for? The knock-me-down at the Bella Union don't burn holes in the glass and he don't have to break Tommy with sea-crabs. Which don't make him no jack cove in my thinking. God rest him, I never seen what the Commodore did in them fish." She toasted the portrait and drank.

"Do your customers know what you think of them?"

"I ain't said pharse in here what I'd say out front. They think it's top-ropes after eight months on pannam and bad swig. Ask the first duffer you see if Nan don't amuse."

I followed only part of that. I wondered if she made it up as she went along.

"Most politicians make it a point to get out and shake hands with the hoi polloi," I said. "What makes Wheelock so shy?"

"Most politicians ain't blessed with Hoodlums. Come ballot day they'll mark your *X* for you. You don't even need to ask." She gave the phonograph a thoughtful crank. "If guessing was my game, I'd say it's on account of his bully crab, what the squares call a club foot. He don't flash it about."

I asked if an appointment could be arranged.

She laughed. She was back in bed with her brandy. Two-score years later and I can't hear "Beautiful Dreamer" without picturing every grubby detail of that room.

"Stifle a Hoodlum," she said. "They've a place in his panter, and he might be peery enough to want to cut his eyes on you before he sends his tobbies to ease you over."

Beecher looked at me through the smoke of his cigar. "I forgot what's stifle."

"Put him to bed with a shovel," I said.

Nan laughed again. "You're a fly one, that you are. I'll wear weeds when you take scold's-cure. See if I don't."

11

For the next three days I did what Judge Blackthorne would consider nothing, or as close to it as one could come in a lively place like the Barbary Coast.

Both our berths were as uncomfortable as they appeared; after our first night, Beecher and I traded places just to make sure. The ticks were as bad as advertised, although after our inaugural experience with them my companion burned two packs of ready-made cigarettes, exterminating the ones he could find hiding in the seams by daylight. Smacking the survivors and scratching their bites gave us the benefit of taking our minds off the slats gouging holes in our hides. It all gave me a more friendly opinion of Shanghai Mike and his decision to rechristen the place: This was no Sailor's Rest.

The morning after that first night, while Beecher was using the community washbasin behind the building, I found a place down the street that served biscuits and gravy that would have passed muster anywhere I'd been, a pleasant surprise, and a cup of coffee that was not. I paid too much for the meal and went back to the saloon, where I sat down to a fast, losing game of blackjack with the resident gambler. When he excused himself to use the outhouse, Beecher sat down in his chair.

He was irritable, and with good reason. In his world, Pullman porter was as high as a man could climb, and the

Slop Chest could only remind him how short the fall was to stony bottom. Then again he might have been just tired and hungry. I told him about the place where I'd eaten breakfast, but he appeared to be just waiting for me to stop talking so he could start.

"What we doing today?" he asked.

"We're doing it."

"What about tomorrow?"

"Same thing."

He scratched at a bite on his wrist. He looked as haggard as I felt. "Ask you something?"

"Why stop now?"

"How long you been on this job?"

"About eight years."

He examined the bite, a tiny, white-rimmed volcano erupting from dark skin. "Ask you something else?"

"I'm still here."

"How you know when it's done?"

I didn't answer. He didn't have to know what I was waiting for until it was here. His cavalry experience would not have prepared him for it or its necessity. I trusted him with my life, but not the truth; not yet.

The fog, at least, was less persistent than the vermin. It was always there in the morning, although not as thick and choking as it had been on the afternoon of our arrival, but it burned off by midday. However, the presence of the sun did little to brighten Davis Street and its tributaries. The ramshackle saloons, bagnios, and rooming houses didn't cast shadows so much as drain the sunlight of its energy, and the streets were puddled with slops tossed out through their open doors and upstairs windows the night before. The flies that overhung them in dense clouds barely stirred to make room for the hooves and wheels that churned through the offal, buzzing impatiently until they passed.

Deprived of forgiving gaslight, the harlots who prowled the boardwalks—where there were boardwalks—demonstrated only too clearly that they found it convenient to paint one face on top of another without removing the previous application, often to a depth of as much as a quarter-inch. The pimps, gamblers, and cutpurses were hardly an improvement. Smallpox, knives, and coshes had left their marks on man and woman alike. On my first stroll around the block, I passed a half-dozen pedestrians, all of whom didn't total a complete specimen of human being among them. A good man with modeling wax, glass eyes, and timber legs could have made his retirement in six months in that neighborhood, if someone didn't bash him over the head and turn out his pockets at the end of the first day.

The maze of sagging, paint-peeling buildings created an impression of incredible age, yet the oldest of them was barely thirty, and most were much newer, their predecessors having burned to the ground in the five great fires that had shorn through the city in the space of eighteen months. Carelessness and arson had failed to eradicate the kind of physical and spiritual corruption that in most cases was centuries in the making. The boomtown years had encouraged construction to the point where two vehicles could not pass in some blocks without risking locked hubs and the inevitable altercation that ensued. The tight quarters bred confrontation and vice, which in turn bred more confrontation, and there seemed not a square yard of earth that hadn't been baptized in the blood of generations of innocents; which in the local dog-Latin was defined as corpses, mortals removed to a plane beyond guilt. Years later, visiting the East End of London, I was struck by that same perception of ancient evil, but there the process had been going on for four hundred years. By the late summer of 1883, I'd spent a year of wary days in cowtowns, miners' camps, and end-of-track helldorados, nearly lost my brains to a stray bullet while taking an honest bath on the other side of a wall belonging to an assayer's office when a client caught him with his thumb on the scale, but had never seen a place to compare with shanty San Francisco for unvarnished wickedry. The place wallowed in it.

I was encouraged by the law of percentages to believe there were decent people living within hailing distance of the Slop Chest: locksmiths and laundresses, bookkeepers and barbers, wet nurses and wheelwrights, glaziers and governesses; the usual mix of honest laborers struggling to pay the greengrocer from week to week. The difference here was they kept their trades behind closed doors like embezzlers, locked themselves in with their families at night, and scurried by first light and last dusk between hearth and forge, slinging frightened glances over their shoulders as if they were transporting stolen goods. Day was night in Barbary. Killers and pickpockets ran free while the law-abiding paced their cells.

Different day, same conversation:

"What we doing today?"

"We're doing it."

"What about tomorrow?"

"Same thing."

Inside Nan Feeny's place of business, the faces of the clientele kept changing. One set of sailors stopped in for a beer or twelve, gambled, fought, were thrown out by Axel Hodge or staggered off to their rooms, shipped out on the morning tide, and were replaced by another set. Mates, boatswains, swabs, cookies, ships' carpenters, and the odd captain—the aristocrat of that society, distinguished from the others by his tobacco pipe of unblemished clay and no missing buttons—tramped in and out. By the third morning, Beecher and I were the senior residents. The only constants were Nan, Billy the bartender, Hodge, the proliferating damage to the bar's marble top, and the tin-horn in the soiled topper and shabby cutaway, who slept under some other roof after he'd skinned his last sea-crab of the evening.

He called himself Pinholster. I didn't ask, and he didn't volunteer, whether he was born with the name or if any other went with it. Frontier etiquette had taught me better than to pursue the point. When he got tired of fleecing me, he confided that he'd served aboard the U.S.S. *Minnesota* during the late unpleasantness, which was the reason he gave for keeping his game at the Slop Chest when he could have tripled his fortunes at any of the better places on Pacific Street or Kearney. He said he had an affection for sailors—"a place in his panter," as Nan would have put it—and in any case an old widower such as he didn't need much to keep himself, just a dram and a plate of hot food and a soft place to stretch out while his nervous stomach processed it.

I figured he wasn't quite forty, but there were streaks of gray in his chestnut beard and his face had the tobacco-cured look of a lifetime spent shut up in saloons and fandango parlors. The beard needed trimming, his hat a good brushing, and there was no way left to turn his collar or cuffs that hadn't been tried, but as to the things that applied directly to his vocation—his hands—they were smooth and white and the nails pared and buffed. He could cut a deck one-handed without showing off, and so far as I could tell he dealt from the top and never palmed a pasteboard. However, he might just have been minding his manners when playing with me. Rumors infested Nan Feeny's little enterprise like ticks and I wouldn't have bet a dollar to a dead dog there was a beggar or a spiv between there and the harbor who didn't know two deputy U.S. marshals were in residence.

"Here's a show," Pinholster said without looking up from the deck he was shuffling.

I thought he was getting ready to demonstrate a card trick, but just then a hand touched my shoulder. I reached for a revolver that wasn't on my hip. I hadn't heard so much as a footfall.

"Chinee papah, mistuh man?"

A young Chinese stood next to the table. In his pillbox hat, black smock, and shapeless trousers he was scarcely larger than Hodge, but his limbs were all in proportion and the square lines of his jaw said he was no boy. He wore the queue of his class and held out a folded newspaper covered with Chinese characters. I was about to tell him I didn't read the language when a loud report and a rattle of shattered marble told me the bar had lost a little more of its value.

" 'Ey!" Hodge's accent was up on its haunches. "Wun Long Dong! Speel to your crib, chop-chop!"

"Stubble your red rag, Jack Sprat!" snarled the Chinese.

Hodge hopped down from his ladder and came around the end of the bar, twirling the iron ball over his head on the end of its chain. The intruder padded out.

"Two, three times a month that same celestial comes in here peddling his papers," Pinholster said. "Sometimes he makes a sale or two before Billy or Hodge hares him out."

"I didn't know Nan served Chinese customers."

"She doesn't. The Hoodlums wouldn't stand for it. You may not think there are rules of behavior in Barbary, but you're mistaken. Chinatown for Chinamen, the waterfront for the Sydney Ducks, and so forth. Just because you can't see the lines doesn't mean you won't bleed if you cross one."

"If that's true, who buys his papers?"

"It isn't the papers. It's what's inside." He cut out the ace of spades and held it up. "Black dreams."

"Opium? The Commodore built this place selling dope to the Chinese."

He flicked a crumb off his moustache that had been there all morning.

"You might have noticed Nan's her own creature. In any event, that was all before Captain Dan. He settled the last tong war by negotiating a licensing agreement between Chinatown and the Hoodlums. The jack dandies don't peddle dope and the celestials stow their wids outside Chinatown. That means—"

"Don't raise hell."

"You learn fast," he said. "You ought to apply that brainbox to cards. Part of not raising hell is keeping their hop inside their own jurisdiction. This fellow that Hodge just prodded out's a spunk looking for black powder, and he'll find it if the tongs catch wind. Wheelock doesn't maintain the peace because the sneak-thieves and swablers are afraid of him or his Hoodlums. They're afraid of each other, and they all turn to him because he's one of them."

"One of who?"

"Whoever he's with at the time."

I said, "No wonder the police can't enforce order. They aren't politicians."

"He's got the gabs, all right, but they're no good without teeth. If he thinks Nan's violating the agreement, she'll think that fire she had was love's own sweet song."

"The Hoodlums."

"They're what answers for a police force in Barbary." He dealt himself a hand of poker: four bullets and the king of clubs.

"Where does Wheelock stand with the Sons of the Confederacy?"

He lifted his brows. That was one piece of intelligence that hadn't filtered through the walls of Nan Feeny's room.

"About where he stands with the Benevolent and Protective Order of Elks, which is not at all. The baby rebels aren't a force here. If they're what brought you all this way you wasted the price of a train ticket."

"That's what Nan said. My information is this is their headquarters."

"Not knowing who gave it to you, I wouldn't call him a liar. The Salvation Army's on every street corner, but I've been here a spell and I've yet to see a soul saved. If numbers counted, we'd have a Chinaman for mayor."

I asked to see the deck. He made a face of mild disappointment and said it wasn't marked, but he slid it my way across the baize. I picked it up, shuffled, and dealt a heart flush.

Pinholster smiled for the first time. "You didn't learn that chasing mail robbers in the territories."

"I owned a faro concession and part of a saloon in New Mexico for a little while. You can get good at anything if you do it often enough. Quicker still if you don't like starving."

"You've been losing for a reason," he said. "I think I can guess what it is."

I scooped up the cards, cut the deck one-handed, and slid it back toward him. "It won't take long. You've already told me everything I needed to know except one thing."

I was drinking a beer at the bar when Beecher came in from the street and checked his revolver with Billy; in the Slop Chest, the municipal ban on firearms only went as far as the door. Beecher was unsteady on his feet and his eyes were hot. He'd found another place that served beer to Negroes.

"What we doing today?" he said.

I waited until Billy moved down the bar to fill a sailor's glass.

"What's the date?"

That gave Beecher pause. "Fourteenth."

"Fifteenth. We got here on the twelfth and we've been here three days."

"What's the difference?"

"The difference is today's the day Wheelock's tax collector comes to call."

" 'Squint-eyed ponce what smells of lilacs.' " His impression of Nan's brogue was faulty.

"I got a more complete description from the tinhorn. Also a time and place. That corner table's as good as a window on Barbary."

"What'd it cost?"

"Only my reputation as a cardplayer."

He steadied himself on the bar. He was on the verge of asking a question he didn't want to know the answer to. Then he changed directions. "Just what *is* a ponce?"

"We'll ask him when we see him."

12

We smelled the Hoodlum before we saw him.

This was no small miracle, given the variety of stenches that had laid claim to the venue. The alley between the Slop Chest and the warehouse next door—home to an illegal and unadvertised game of Chuck-a-Luck that Pinholster swore had been going on without interruption, through fire and famine and fanatic reform, since 1851—was so narrow a man could put out his hands and touch both opposing walls at the same time. Beecher and I resisted the temptation. Mold and green slime coated the warehouse brick and a wriggling heap of rats covered whatever had been flung out the side door of Nan Feeny's establishment.

Somewhere in the direction of the respectable part of the city a tower clock gonged out the hour of eleven. The last chime reverberated on the damp air like a coin wobbling to rest on a plank bar. The spill from a corner gas lamp illuminated the far end of the alley, but fell short of the bricked-in doorway where we waited, a rectangular recess six inches deep in the warehouse wall. The shadows were as thick as poured tar and a light ground fog—light for San Francisco—tickled our ankles. We took turns breathing in the close atmosphere of that medieval corridor.

The lilac smell when it came was unexpected, and oddly

more repugnant than the stink of slops and garbage; it didn't belong, and like a drop of honey on the tongue when lemon was expected, it struck me as unpleasant, nauseating. It was followed by a low, inaccurate whistling, some tinpenny tune that had swept across the frontier faster than the transcontinental, and had already been forgotten in Montana, and then an amphora-shaped shadow, slung across the Slop Chest wall by the distant gas lamp. The shadow grew smaller and more distinct as its owner came around the corner of the warehouse. Something kicked a loose stone rattling across the hardpack and a wrenlike figure followed it into the alley.

There the foul odors met him and he paused to draw something from his right sleeve and press it to the lower part of his face. A fresh puff of lilacs reached us. Beecher stirred, blew air out his nose. I touched his arm and he grew silent. We watched the newcomer return his scented handkerchief to his sleeve and continue walking. He wasn't whistling now. We could hear him breathing through his mouth.

He was my height, but lighter by at least forty pounds, buttoned snugly into a black frock coat with the kind of peaked sleeves that thrust up above the shoulders where they're stitched to the yoke and make the wearer appear as if he's hunching himself against a stiff wind. The lower three buttons were unfastened to expose a velvet vest that looked ruby red even by outdoor gaslight, and he wore calfskin boots to the knees of his pale trousers and a narrow-brimmed black hat with a low flat crown. The clothes differed in some details from those worn by the Hoodlum who'd accosted us on the train platform, but the effect was identical. They were the regimentals of a strict society. I knew then that the whispers about Wheelock were true; only a man of singular influence and de-

termination could compel a ragtag gang of hugger-muggers
and slash-throats to leave their roomy pickpockets' overcoats and anonymous black watchcaps at home and parade the streets in uniform. It went against centuries of
conditioning, of lying low and playing things close to the
vest. "You can't arrest/revile/annoy me," the clothes said.
"I'm a Hoodlum!"

He stopped before the side door of the Slop Chest and
rapped out a jaunty knock; part of the tune he'd been whistling. The door sprang inward and Nan Feeny's white
head showed against the light from inside. She wore volu-
minous skirts, and a white shirtwaist buttoned to her
throat, surmounted by the vigilant ribbon.

"'allo, Nan," said the Hoodlum. "Where's that skycer
what shares your crib? Go to blow his conk and bash in his
neb?"

His cockney was even broader than Hodge's. It had come
straight from London and lost nothing during the voyage.

"He's tending bar tonight. Billy's got Venus' Curse."
She thrust out a sack. Coins shifted inside.

The Hoodlum didn't take it. "Don't lope just yet. Let's
inside and break a leg." He laid a hand on her hip.

Nan raised the pepperbox pistol from her pocket.

He withdrew his hand. "I ain't so spooney as you think.
You wasn't always no iron doublet."

"Who says I am? You're Molly's goods. Take your pony
and scour back to Queen Street."

He snatched the sack from her, hefted it. "The game's
flush this trip. You ain't been flying hop, by any chance?
Cap'n Dan wouldn't like that by half."

"I don't even let celestials in the place. It's been a rum
week, is all. I've got aces over sevens."

"Full house is the word. You got tappers in your crib.
Two U.S. coves. Been squeaking?"

"Go hoist a huff, you kept jack." She stepped back and banged the door shut.

"Old cow." The Hoodlum bounced the sack of coins a couple of times on his palm, then slipped it into a side pocket and turned away, whistling.

Beecher's clothing rustled. I touched his arm again, settling him. When the Hoodlum was halfway up the alley, I drew the Deane-Adams and stepped out of the doorway. Beecher slid the Le Mat out from under his shirt and joined me.

We were within ten feet of the Hoodlum when he stopped and reached across his body. We thumbed back our hammers. The crisp double-click racketed off the walls.

The Hoodlum turned, holding his scented handkerchief. When he saw us, he dropped it and reached for a pocket. I fired a round over his head. Both hands shot upward, palms empty.

There was an awkward pause. I'd never robbed anyone before; I wasn't sure about the order of events. During this space, no windows or doors opened, no one came running to investigate the report. A night in Barbary without at least one unexplained gunshot would have been worth half a column in the *San Francisco Call*.

The Hoodlum's face was narrow and pinched, old pox scars visible in the gaslight reflected off the Slop Chest's salt-stained wall. Small clumps of stubble sprouted like Indian paintbrush between the craters. He blinked incessantly—not, I was sure, from fear. Nan had called him squint-eyed.

"You blokes can't stick me up," he said. "I'm—"

I said, "I know what you are. Molly's goods."

His face went dead. It was a young face. A woman with narrow options might have considered it handsome, despite the scars and his predisposition against razors. I was pretty sure I knew what a ponce was now. Someone had bought him his red vest and it wasn't Daniel Webster Wheelock.

"Throw the sack at my feet," I said.

He blinked more rapidly. "Cap'n Dan—"

I snapped a slug into the dirt between his feet. He jumped straight up and down like a startled rabbit. Looked down at his boots to count his toes.

"The sack."

He lowered his hands. One went into his pocket. I made a motion with the five-shot.

"If anything comes out of there besides a sack of coins, you can ask Axel Hodge who fitted him with his ball and chain."

He drew the sack out slowly and gave it an underhand flip. It clanked when it hit the earth.

"Empty all your pockets."

Again he hesitated.

"Pepper his legs with buckshot."

Beecher lowered his aim a notch.

"No!" The Hoodlum turned out all his pockets and threw the contents after the sack: a squat-barreled pistol, brass knuckles, a weighted sock, three clasp knives in assorted sizes.

I asked him if he was expecting trouble.

"Just looking after me regulars. Times are dusty."

"Stay away from the waterfront," I said. "If you fall in they'll need a crane to pull you back out. What's your chant?"

"My what?"

"Your name. Your monoger. What do people call you when they're not mad at you?"

"Tom Tulip."

I took aim at his red vest.

"It's me name!"

"Well, Tom, tell your friends there's a new tax in Barbary. Penny a head for every Hoodlum who shows his face outside the Bella Union."

"You ain't the tickrum to collect it! When Cap'n Dan gets drift of this, you'll be whiffling out the hole in the back of your nob!"

"He'll want names. Mine's Murdock. This is Beecher."

"And who in Black Spy's skipper is Murdock and Beecher, if you please?"

I slipped the deputy's star out of my pocket and flung it at him. He caught it against his chest in both hands, turned it toward the light.

"Tell Wheelock to take good care of it," I said. "I'm responsible for it."

"U.S. coves." He leaned forward and spat on the ground.

"Bang on, Tom. Tell him to send the swag to the Slop Chest. We're cribbed up there this week."

"He'll send the whole bleeding Bella Union! The frogs'll fish your black ointment out of the briny."

"Put out this spunk," I told Beecher.

He tilted the Le Mat a few degrees and emptied the shotgun barrel over Tom Tulip's head. In those tight quarters it sounded like a powder keg blowing its top. The Hoodlum spun on his heel and took flight, coattails fluttering. We heard his pounding feet long after the echo of the blast faded.

Beecher changed hands to blow on his fingers. He was chuckling. "I believe I missed my right calling. How much you calculate we got?"

I stepped forward, picked up the sack, and gave it a couple of shakes. "Dollar and a half and change. If we're going to make a living at this, we'd better hold off till Tom finishes his rounds."

"Drop the swag."

This was a new voice. I looked up to see Nan Feeny standing in front of the open side door with her pepperbox trained on my chest. I dropped the sack.

"I offered to topper 'em both in their dosses the first night," Hodge said.

"Shut your mummer and let me think."

The little man stood swinging his iron ball rhythmically back and forth and watching Nan pace the floor of her room. His eyes beneath the brim of his bowler were as expressionless as a shark's.

Beecher and I were the only ones sitting. Tom Tulip's pocket arsenal occupied the bed, along with my Deane-Adams, Beecher's Le Mat, and the sack of pennies, which had surely established a record for depth of feeling for so small a sum. Hodge had done the disarming and carrying. We had our legs crossed.

"The swag and Tom's trinkets blow back to Cap'n Dan, that's settled," she said. "If they don't he'll hush us all and burn the place for spite. *How's* the thing what's got me smoky. If we come a-crawling with the skep in hand, he'll hoist the tariff, and who's to stubble him? We're scraping close to shinerags as things stand."

Hodge said, "Send it to him in an eternity-box with these two inside. That ought to show him we're plumb."

"I ain't turned up the toes of so much as a slingtail hen in forty years of grief, and I ain't about to set precedent. What was that game about? You both gone cranky?" She'd stopped pacing to stand in front of us.

I said, "I got the idea from no one but you, right here in this room. 'Stifle a Hoodlum,' you said; but I'm not that bloodthirsty."

"I was just pecking words. I never thought you'd try it on, I'll smack the bishop's calfskin I didn't. Anywise, you'd of done better to twist his nub and give him an earth-bath than buzz him and leave him leg to peach to Cap'n Dan. We'll be up to our arses in Hoodlums come morning."

"Take the air, Nan," Hodge said. "Sluice your gob down at Haggerty's. When you come back, it'll all be rub." He smacked his widow-maker against his open palm.

She said nothing. Her face was impossible to read. I wondered if I could get to the weapons on the bed before Hodge caught up to me and swung his ball, and if Beecher had the reflexes to slow him down. Then there was Nan and the eight loaded chambers in her pocket. I was thinking about all this when someone knocked. The sound came from the direction of the side door to the alley.

Nan looked at Hodge.

"Could be a fish looking to flop," he said.

She shook her head. "Tide's out."

The knocking came again, louder. Someone was kicking the door.

Nan picked up Tom Tulip's bulldog pistol and gave it to Hodge. "If it's more than one, empty it. Then leg it for the front door. I'll be scarce by then."

"What about these two?"

She took out the pepperbox. He nodded and withdrew.

Beecher started to say something. Nan eared back the hammer. He fell silent.

The knocking ceased. A powder-charged silence followed. Voices rumbled. Another silence, longer than the first. None of us was breathing.

A floorboard yelped outside the room. Nan swung her pistol that way. Hodge came in. He had the bulldog stuck under his belt and an envelope in his hand.

"Just a cove with a stiff."

Nan took the pistol off cock and put it in her pocket. She snatched the envelope. The address side was blank. She frowned at the signet on the crimson seal, cracked the wax, and fumbled with the flap. She frowned again and tipped something out onto her palm. It was a deputy's star.

Hodge snorted. "Crikey! The old town's full to the facer with tin. Who's minding the store?"

I said the star was mine. He told me to shut my mummer.

Nan unfolded a square of paper, read what was written on it, and held it out toward me. I got up from my chair and took it.

The letter was written in neat copperplate on heavy linen bond with gold edges.

P. Murdock, Deputy United States Marshal
The Sailor's Rest

Dear Deputy Murdock:

I am in receipt of your communication.

Your presence is requested in my quarters at the Bella Union Melodeon tomorrow at 11:00 A.M.

Until then, I am

> Yours very truly,
> Daniel Webster
> Wheelock, Alderman,
> City of San Francisco

13

BELLA UNION MELODEON
NIGHTLY
A CONSTANTLY VARIED ENTERTAINMENT
Replete with FUN and FROLIC
Abounding in SONG and DANCE
Unique for GRACE and BEAUTY
And Perfect in Its Object of Affording
LAUGHTER FOR MILLIONS!
A Host of the Best
DRAMATIC, TERPSICHOREAN AND MUSICAL
TALENT WILL APPEAR
Emphatically the
MELODEON OF THE PEOPLE
Unapproachable and Beyond Competition.

The dodger was printed on the kind of paper that could not have associated with The Honorable D. W. Wheelock's personal stationery. Its coarse fibers were tinted an unappetizing shade of apricot and the edges of the dull black letterpress characters had bled, making them muzzy and hard to read. The character who had thrust it into my hand was of a piece with the stock: short and round, buttoned into a loud checkered vest, a morning coat two sizes too small, and loose trousers belted just under his armpits, with yellow gaiters on his black brogans and a deerstalker cap. He patrolled the boardwalk in front of the theater, accosting passersby with a nasal bray touting the wonders to be found inside and shoving the sheets into their midsections; forced to defend themselves, they grabbed at their bellies and wound up holding a dodger. No one got past him without one while Beecher and I were watching, and the traffic was heavy.

The Bella Union was three stories of frame construction—painted, not whitewashed—on the northeast corner of Portsmouth Square at the foot of Telegraph Hill, with shutters on the windows designed to repel invaders and vigilantes. Its name was painted in neat block letters across the false front, and the structure itself appeared as solid as a bank or a county courthouse. Natives referred to it as "The Ancient," which in a city that burned over every few seasons applied to anything more than ten years old. Neither fire nor scandal nor the cicada-like cycle of Community Cleansing could eradicate it. It kept coming back like a nest of yellow jackets.

We entered a cavernous saloon, whose gaming tables and long bar were already crowded at late morning, drinking under a glittering canopy of upended flutes, snifters, and cordials and waiting their turns at faro, *vingt-et-un,* and a seven-foot-tall Wheel of Fortune, the biggest I'd seen outside Virginia City. The place was a dazzle of gaslight and highly polished surfaces, which made a gaudy setting for the dingy sailors' jerseys, miners' overalls, and dusty town coats that filled it. The bouncer, whose hair slickum and tailored coat did no more than necessary to disguise the fact he was a pugilist, gave us no expression at all from behind his blisters of scar tissue when we asked where Mr. Wheelock might be found until I gave him my name. Someone had prepared him. He ducked his head and directed us to a stairwell half hidden behind a box containing a mechanical man who told fortunes.

On the way past the box, Beecher glared at the painted figure inside. It looked like Judge Blackthorne in a turban. "Reckon he's real?"

"Cost you a nickel to find out," I said.

"I didn't come here to get robbed."

"Try to blend in anyway."

The walls of the stairwell had been freshly painted; not a rare thing to find in a combustible city, but scarce enough in slap-bang Barbary. A floral carpet covered the steps, through which we could feel the buzz of brass from the band tuning up in the theater behind the saloon. That was The Ancient's bread and butter: the little stage where buffoons recited jokes from *Captain Billy's Whiz-Bang* and pretty *danseuses* in tights and short ruffled skirts performed cartwheels to *Parisien* cabaret tunes penned in New York tenement houses, and the curtained booths where breathy Southern belles with granite eyes inveigled inebriated customers to buy champagne and claret. Where the transaction went from there was strictly between the belles and the customers and the little man in the immaculate black cutaway who collected the take at the end of the evening. You could leave your money at the tables all over town, but when it came to staggering home with your pockets hanging out and an idiotic smile pasted to your face, the Bella Union was the spot—along with the Verandah, the El Dorado, the Empire, the Mazourka, the Arcade, the Fontine House, the Alhambra, and the Rendezvous. There was an unending supply of gulls and of sharpers to pluck them.

Beecher, climbing the stairs behind me, must have read my thoughts. "You been here before?"

"Couple of hundred times, from here to St. Louis."

"Me, too. Through the back door."

The stairwell opened onto a corridor with more floral carpeting, ending in a door marked PRIVATE. My knock was answered immediately by a young beanpole in a morning coat and high starched collar, balding in front. Gold-rimmed spectacles pinched his nose, with a ribbon attaching them to his lapel. A pair of watery blue eyes went from my face to Beecher's, registered annoyance there, and returned to me. "Yes?"

"Page Murdock and Edward Anderson Beecher to see Daniel Webster Wheelock."

"Nero."

I was wondering what response to make to this when a man approached the beanpole from behind. He was two inches taller, which made him six inches taller than I was, and his shoulders stuck out several inches on both sides of the other man. He was blacker than Beecher and better dressed than any of us, in a rose-colored Prince Albert cut to his frame and a ruffled white shirt. His face had the thick bone development of a born fighter, but no scars. That made him either very good or very discouraging to a potential opponent.

"I am Roland Quinn, Mr. Wheelock's personal secretary," the beanpole said. "He made no mention of a Mr. Beecher."

"He made no mention of a Mr. Quinn, but here we all are."

He touched the nosepiece of his spectacles. "Nero is Mr. Wheelock's personal bodyguard. He will look after your weapons."

"Nero?" Beecher wore his thin smile.

"My father taught himself to read from Gibbon." The big man's voice was a silky rumble.

I unholstered the Deane-Adams and spun it butt out.

"Not out here." Quinn glanced irritatedly past my shoulder, then stepped aside, holding the door. Nero moved the other direction with a gliding maneuver, as if he were mounted on oiled casters.

We stepped inside and gave him our revolvers. His hickory-colored eyes swept us from head to toe and returned to our hats. We removed them and gave him a look inside the crowns. He nodded, laid our pistols next to some others on the shelf of a massive rack with an oval mirror set in its center, then took our hats and hung them on pegs beside a couple of straw skimmers, several bowlers, and a silk topper. His gliding gait took him from there to a door at the back of the room, where he turned his back to it and became part of the architecture, hands at his sides with his thumbs parallel with the seams of his trousers.

Quinn shut the door and tipped a hand toward a row of shield-back chairs facing a Chippendale writing table.

"Mr. Wheelock is running late this morning. He'll be available presently."

It was a reception room, scattered with chairs and setees and decorated with grim-looking landscapes in heavy gilded frames. Several of the seats were occupied, by as wide a variety of humanity as could be found anywhere outside a train station: gents in morning coats and sidewhiskers, Hoodlums in their trademark motley, a decomposing old salt in his sodden woolens, tying and untying knots in a length of tar-stained hemp with his duffel at his feet, two painted tarts in laddered stockings, and a handsome woman just on the shady side of forty, seated knees together in a modest floor-length dress of costly manufacture with her reticule in her lap and her hair pinned up flawlessly under a becoming hat. What her story might be kept me occupied for much of the long wait.

A Regulator wall clock knocked out the time between chimes, patiently and in spite of one of the sidewhiskered gents, who kept dragging out his pocket winder and confirming the hour. After twenty minutes, he got up, collected his topper and stick from the rack, and pranced out, blowing out his moustaches and muttering something about how folk from the wrong side of the tracks needed taking down a peg. Quinn, seated at the writing table, went on scribbling with a horsehair pen and never glanced up. One of the tarts waited until the door shut, then said something in a low voice to her companion, who cut loose with a short nasal bray and resumed contemplating the tin ceiling. Two Hoodlums came in to take his place. When, five minutes later, the gent returned, he found all the seats taken, and resigned himself to stand next to the hat rack. No other defections were attempted during the time Beecher and I were there.

A third Hoodlum, decked out in a long navy coat with gold frogs over tan trousers, came in and shook hands with one of the pair who'd preceded him. This one wore high-peaked shoulders like Tom Tulip, with a dirty white scarf wound around his neck that only brought out the pits in his pasty complexion. I eavesdropped on their conversation, and wrote down what I remembered of it later on the greasy square of paper that came wrapped around the smoked herring I had for supper. I still have the sheet, in case anyone wants to study the exchange and translate it for later generations:

— Dance at me death if it ain't old Pox. I heard you was polishing iron.
— No, Freddie, that was a whisker. Picaroons what said they was crushers tried to put me up to me armpits, but I seen it was a lay and speeled to me crib.
— You always was a cove on the sharp.
— Well, I ain't puppy. How's Bob your pal?
— I ain't seen her in a stretch. We split out.
— Black-Spy, you say. I thought you was plummy.
— As did I. She stagged me to the tappers. Stunned me clean out of me regulars, she did, and I served her out.

—I'd of staked me intimate she was square as Mary.

—You'd be hicksam if you did. I tell you she's Madam Rhan.

—You must of felt yourself a proper put.

—Stow your wid, Pox. You wouldn't know a punk if she pulled your kick right under your handle.

—Don't take snuff, Scot. If she split on you, why ain't you in the shop?

—I had an old shoe. I was headed for jade sure as Grim, but Cap'n Dan dawbed the beak and bought me the iron doublet.

—Smack the calfskin?

—Twig me flappers. Am I in darbies?

—What's Cap'n Dan's lay?

—That's what's brought me round. If it's tobbing he wants, I'm his rabbit.

—Tobbing's cheap. He'll want more than that for his screaves.

—Old Toast keeps his cues under his top-cheat, that's dead game.

—I'll cap in on that, Freddie, old nug. Flimp me for a finiff if I don't.

I don't know if I got it down exactly as I heard it, and I'm certain—"dead game," as Pox and Freddie would say—that the spelling's wrong (assuming it was a written language at all), but it isn't likely it would read like Fields and Webber if I'd managed to record it verbatim. Most of the other people in the room took no pains to conceal the fact they were listening in, but those who understood what they heard probably wouldn't have betrayed anything incriminating to the authorities. There in Daniel Webster Wheelock's reception room was the one place in San Francisco where the criminal code was superfluous. They could have plotted to kidnap the president in plain English and not a word of it would have gone as far as the ground floor. As for me, for all I knew the two were debating the fishing off the Jones Street pier.

It's a dead language now in any case, buried along with the Bella Union and the Slop Chest and the Devil's Acre and old Chinatown beneath the rubble of the '06 quake and the city they erected on top of it; the current heirs to their underworld territory speak a dreary patois made up of sweepings from moving-picture title cards and cheap novels. In a little while, the last person who ever pattered the flash with a fly cull will be as dead as Barbary. I doubt the city fathers will dedicate a statue to any of them.

There was more to the conversation, but I didn't hear it. The door at the back of the room opened again and a man in a wrinkled suit came out, mopping his red face with a lawn handkerchief. He was either an unsuccessful drummer or the mayor. Quinn peered past him, nodded at someone inside, and looked at me over the tops of his spectacles.

Beecher and I rose and went in, nearly colliding with the impatient fellow in the morning coat, who had started forward from his position beside the hat rack when the secretary nodded. He stopped abruptly, checked at last by a graceful movement from Nero, and pulled at his sidewhiskers.

"Mr. Wheelock will see you next, Congressman," Quinn said as the door closed behind us.

14

"Oh, Lordy."

They were Beecher's first words upon being admitted to Wheelock's private apartment, and nine presidents later I haven't come up with any that serve as well.

After the businesslike reception room I'd expected to find an office, or failing that one of those fussy overstuffed parlors that varied only in minor details from townhouses on Fifth Avenue to ranches in Colorado, and were even mounted on wheels and coupled to trains going forty miles an hour between Dallas and the Black Hills of Dakota. There would be leather and brass and oak, possibly the head of some dead animal hung on the wall like an old master, and the smell of good cigars and whiskey. The lithographs of Prominent New York Homes in *Harper's Weekly* had stamped a sameness of interior furnishing and ornamentation across the most variegated continent on earth.

However, they hadn't crossed the threshold of Wheelock's cloister above the Bella Union Melodeon.

The walls were covered in blue silk, with peacocks and bridges and doves embroidered in silver and scarlet. Paper lanterns had replaced the gas jets in the corners, shedding warm amber light on the scatter of hand-loomed rugs, black lacquer boxes, golden Siamese dancers, rows of silk-bound books in a bamboo press, and the teakwood

table at which the master sat carving a grouse. A thread
of incense smoke coiled up from the lap of a plaster Buddha at his elbow, spreading sandalwood scent throughout
the room.

The chamber was twice the size of the reception area,
and yet the only Occidental items that had found their way
into it were a framed Certificate of Community Service
on one wall, issued to The Honorable D. W. Wheelock,
signed by members of the Committee of Vigilance for the
Protection of the Lives and Property of the Citizens and
Residents of the City of San Francisco, and the serge tunic and cap of a fire captain hanging from a peg. Cap'n
Dan himself wore a heavy silk dressing gown covered with
golden dragons, and a white scarf of the same material
around his neck.

The rest of him might have fallen off the wall of portraits at the Chicago Businessman's Association. His rectangular face was shaven clean and he had white hair fine
enough to strain sugar through, brushed back patiently
from a sharp widow's peak. There was the suggestion of
a beak about the nose, and a thin trap of mouth that looked
as if it spent most of its time shut tight while the chilly blue
eyes beneath their black brows (touched up, I suspected,
by the same gifted barber who scraped his pink chin) measured and dissected the speaker and weighed his bowels
on a set of postmortem scales. It was an Anglo-Saxon face
with a touch of the Nordic, a ruthlessly well-preserved
sixty. I'd never seen one more dangerous; and I'd made the
acquaintance of rapists, guerrillas, and multiple murderers
from Tombstone to Slaughter Springs.

When we entered, he laid aside his fork and silver-
handled carving knife, wiped his hands on a linen napkin,
and thrust his right across the table for me to take.

"Deputy Murdock. Two apologies. A matter of some
urgency kept you waiting longer than I'd intended."

"What's the other?" I'd encountered stronger grasps, but there was a bit of the show business in them. His was as natural as a panther stretching its limbs.

"For not rising. I have an infirmity which plunders the act of its meaning." He tipped his other hand toward the carved ivory stick that leaned against the table. It was the only reference he ever made to his club foot when I was present.

"I never could see the sense in it." I removed the sack of pennies from my coat pocket and dropped it in front of his plate. "Your man Tulip left this behind."

He smiled. His teeth were as white and even as Axel Hodge's, but it was my bet they fit him better at the end of the day. He looked at Beecher, who stood back out of arm's reach; a habit deeply ingrained, to spare both parties the embarrassment of an omitted handshake. "I don't know this other gentleman's name."

"Beecher."

"A noble one. I've read Mrs. Stowe's book and own a bound collection of the Reverend Beecher's sermons. Were you named for either of them, by any chance?"

"I was named for my father. I don't know where he got it. He was sold before I was born."

Wheelock was unabashed, or if he was otherwise, he didn't show it. "Please be seated. Have you gentlemen eaten?"

We said we had, although the sight of the grouse with its accompanying plates of green beans and sweet potatoes made poor stuff of the biscuits and gravy in my stomach. We drew up a pair of bamboo chairs and leaned our forearms on the table.

"Forgive me while I continue dining. I neglected to break my fast this morning and I'm under my physician's instructions to maintain a regular diet. Nervous stomachs are as common to my profession as gunshot wounds are to yours. You're both deputies?"

I said, "Only during regular business hours. After sundown, we're road agents."

"I heard something on that order, although I hardly expected you to confess to it. What's your home jurisdiction?"

"United States District Court, Territory of Montana."

"Harlan Blackthorne's bench. He's known even here, where we have no shortage of notorious characters. Is he as hemp-hungry as they say?"

"Only when he neglects to break his fast. He has a nervous stomach."

He showed irritation for the first time. It was probably intended. "I was hoping we could discuss this like gentlemen."

"There are no gentlemen here, Alderman. In Helena, we hang men like Tom Tulip. We hardly ever hire them."

"Well said. However, you cannot fail to have noticed that there is a great deal more difference between Helena and San Francisco than mere distance. When I was still a young man, before there was a Montana Territory, the ship's masters who docked here referred to the place as Port Hazard. They did not mean the treacherous conditions in the harbor. The gold strikes emptied their crews before they could even drop anchor. Once a mutineer, a man hasn't far to fall before he turns thief and killer, particularly after he learns that wealth is not so easy to come by as advertised."

"It's the same story where I come from."

"Only in the beginning." Wheelock forked a piece of bird into his mouth, chewed it thoroughly, and washed it down with water from a cut-glass goblet. "It's the natural order of things that a community is born in blood and pain, passes through an unruly adolescence, and stabilizes in maturity. Abilene and Dodge City have become as safe as houses, and Helena will follow them in time. San Francisco is an exception; the bad element simply will not leave. I blame the mild climate. You will remember that after God banished Adam and Eve from Paradise, the serpent remained.

"The brigands here have had thirty years to establish themselves," he went on. "They've survived fire and vigilantes and their own wicked company. It's been one continuous war for nearly as long as you've been alive, and you know what only four years of fighting did to the men of your generation, filling the frontier with daylight robbers and every other sort of pillaging scum. The sight of a blue helmet holds no terrors for these creatures. They have their own police force and their own system of justice, from which there is no appeal this side of Davy Jones's locker. Is it any wonder our decent citizens have been forced to adopt their methods in order to keep the peace?"

"The nearest Tulip ever got to a decent citizen was close enough to crack his skull and lift his poke."

"You malign him unnecessarily. He lives off his harlot wife, along with the small percentage I pay him to collect the tax from Nan Feeny and her fellow entrepreneurs. The proceeds go into the operating budget. It costs money to prevent anarchy."

"I didn't think the Hoodlums donated their time."

He smiled again, a strictly hydraulic operation. His face wasn't connected to the workings of his brain any more than an alligator's.

"You're not that much less infamous than your employer, Murdock. You've kept the printing presses in New York and Chicago busy recording your exploits. Even allowing for two parts exaggeration to one part truth, you're a prime example of the kind of officer that under other circumstances would decorate the lethal end of the gallows."

"The difference being that I never cracked a skull I thought belonged to an innocent man. It's a slim distinction, but it's what I've got and I'm hanging on to it."

"You're a fortunate young man. One wonders, when you let go, how hard you'll fall."

"I'm not a young man, Alderman. And you're not Abe Lincoln."

"Certainly not. I'm a Democrat."

Beecher had been exploring a flaw in the table's teakwood grain with a forefinger. He looked up. "When you two gentlemans is through scratching dirt, we can get to why we're here. I don't wonder you got so many people waiting outside. You blow more steam than Old Number Ten."

Wheelock, chewing, gave him a look so mild I knew there was murder behind it. Beecher was as good as a barometer for measuring pressure, even in calm weather. A colored man with opinions never failed to turn the tidiest hair.

The Man of the People finished his sweet potatoes and pushed away his plate. "Your friend has a point. You didn't return your plunder just to get into my good graces."

I found the second double eagle from the attack aboard the caboose and slid it across the table with my index finger. He left it where it was.

"That's hardly better. I've been offered bribes many times. The amount is usually more substantial."

"I didn't expect it to surprise you," I said. "It was minted right here in town, and you probably see a lot of them in this condition. By the time they get to Montana, they've usually changed hands a dozen times and banged around inside a herd of pockets alongside the coppers and cartwheels and ore samples and whatever else a man might carry with him from camp to camp. This one made it all the way to Gold Creek without a scratch. Can you explain that?"

"I won't try. I'm a politician, not a detective."

He seemed pleased with this assertion. There's no accounting for pride.

"It makes sense if the coin came straight there from San Francisco in the possession of someone who got it fresh from the mint. Short of a written command from a superior officer, I can't think of a thing that would travel with a man that far that fast. This coin is an order of execution."

"Indeed. Well, you'd know more about that sort of thing than I. Most of the murders here are committed in hot blood."

"Alderman, do you belong to the Sons of the Confederacy?"

"I have a sponsorship. I have one with the Grand Army of the Republic as well." He picked up his goblet and swirled the contents.

"Isn't that a conflict of interest?"

"No. I am not active. I belong to most of the fraternal orders. My constituents are gregarious. There are seven separate delegations among the tong alone, and several splinter societies inside each one."

"Do you have a sponsorship with the tong?"

"The Chinese don't vote. I would accept, however, if they were offered to Occidentals. It might lead to understanding, and prevent another war like the one we had in eighteen seventy-five."

I asked if he contributed to the Sons' treasury.

"No. That's what having a sponsorship means. If I were to start paying dues, I would be ruined in two years. The city pays me only six hundred per annum." He sipped from his twenty-dollar goblet.

"Chester Arthur's an active Freemason. He pays dues."

"Chester Arthur's a Republican."

"Back East they think you're involved somehow."

"I imagine a great deal is said of me back East, and that very little of it is true."

"Not that much is said. I never heard of you before last week."

"I'm not offended. I have no intention of seeking national office."

His burnished impassivity was getting the better of me. I wanted to peel it back the way Beecher had started to do. "I was told the Bella Union is the new rebels' headquarters."

"I understand they rent the theater once or twice a month, purely for socializing. However, you'll have to ask Sam Tetlow for details. He's the owner of the enterprise. I merely lease this floor."

"Where can I reach him?"

"I cannot answer that because I don't know. He's in seclusion, preparing for his defense. He's to be tried next month for murdering his partner, Billy Skeantlebury. They came to a difference of opinion, followed by an exchange of gunfire."

"Who's running the place while he's away?"

He sighed. "That is my privilege. I've assumed interim management at his request, in return for compensation in the amount of one dollar."

"Why didn't you say that before?"

"You would have asked me about Tetlow's arrangement with the Sons of the Confederacy, and you would not have believed me when I expressed ignorance. I'm only a custodian. I've no authority to make changes and I know nothing of any business conducted here before my tenure. That was the condition under which I consented to manage. A man in my position must be cautious."

"Not cautious enough to turn him down," I said.

He smiled his sterile smile. "Tetlow is a major contributor to the party. He may be acquitted. Stranger things have happened in Barbary."

"You might want to reconsider your arrangement. The San Francisco branch of the Sons of the Confederacy is implicated in more than two dozen murders. They tried to kill me twice, and each of the shooters had a shiny new gold piece in his kick. If this keeps up, they'll make me a rich man."

"Or a dead one."

"None of us is made of boilerplate," I said. "One of the men they killed was a United States senator. I doubt they'd hesitate to snap a cap on a city alderman."

"All the more reason to remain in the dark."

I sat back. "I don't suppose you could tell me who delivers the rent on the theater."

"You'll have to ask Quinn about that. He handles and records all the transactions."

"Can you call him in?"

He drew a thin platinum watch out of a pocket of his dressing gown. It was attached by four inches of plaited hair to a Chinese coin with a square hole in the center. "I would, but as you know, I am running late. You'll have to interview him outside."

"In front of half the Hoodlums in Frisco?"

"San Francisco," he corrected. "The native Spaniards insist upon it."

I rose. I'd broken myself against his wall. There wasn't a crack in it that I could see. Beecher got up, too, and we started out. Wheelock called my name. When I turned, he put a forefinger on the double eagle and scraped it my way.

"Just so there are no misunderstandings," he said. "A man in my position—"

"I heard." I went back and picked up the coin, tossed it

back and forth between my hands. "Who set the torch to Nan Feeny's place?"

His smooth brow creased. "That incident is still under investigation. The police suspect a man who calls himself Sid the Spunk. He was a frequent customer at the Red Rooster, but no one has seen him in almost two years."

"Did they drag the harbor?" Beecher asked.

"It's a big harbor, in a bigger bay. Every few years some civic genius proposes bridging it, which would claim the life of every Chinese laborer south of Sacramento Street. Perhaps that explains why the proposal keeps coming up."

We left. The reception room was as crowded as a theater lobby, with the impatient congressman fighting to maintain his position within view of the secretary. Under Nero's close scrutiny, we collected our hats and weapons and went out into the hall. The air was cooler there, away from all those anxious bodies.

Beecher said, "That man sure does use a lot of words just to tell you to go to hell."

"He told us more than that," I said. "He told us who runs the Sons of the Confederacy."

15

Axel Hodge elbowed Billy aside, poured Beecher and me a beer each, and set them down in front of us. This was remarkable enough in view of the fact that twelve hours earlier he'd begged Nan to let him kill us both, and more so when you considered the amount of engineering involved. He had to reach above his head to work the taps, then carry both glasses by their handles in his only hand to the top of his custom-built ladder without gripping the side rails, and he did it all without spilling a drop. He must have been a sight to see clambering up the rigging of a windjammer when he still had ten fingers.

"This one's on Pilgarlic, mates; that's 'Odge and no other, if you ain't fly. You're the first in here what's ogled the cove in his own crib to me knowledge. Was it all sparks and glisten? I've a finiff with Billy says he lives out-and-outer."

"I don't know about that," I said. "He's got the place done up like a Chinese whorehouse."

"Ha!" Billy stood in front of the back bar with his arms folded across his chest. The tattoo on his flabby right forearm was either an anchor or a mermaid.

Hodge turned hopeful eyes on Beecher, who confirmed the information with a nod. The little man's face fell. Then he hoisted it back up through sheer might.

"Well, there's 'orehouses and 'orehouses, even in chinks' alley, some as what the emperor himself wouldn't be peery to drop his galigaskin in. What's got over the devil's back goes under the devil's belly, I say. Cap'n Dan's flush of the balsam. Old Grim take me if he lives like a spung."

There was no reason I should have done Hodge a good turn, but I was too tired for the game. "He makes six hundred a year from the city and he was wearing more than that. Do what you like with it."

He hung half off his ladder and twirled his ball and chain at Billy. "Pony up, you mab's son of a lugger. You said he put on a parson's show."

"I never did. I said he always goes about in them fireman's britches like he hadn't a deuce." But he excavated a crumpled banknote from a pocket and tossed it onto the cracked marble bartop. Hodge swept it up and stuffed it down inside the neck of his jersey.

I asked where Nan was.

"In her doss. The old ewe don't stand the hours she used to. She said to knock her up when you fell in. She wants the hank on you and Cap'n Dan."

Pinholster had come in from wherever he lunched and taken up his post.

"It's not worth waking her up for," I said. "Just tell her the bill's paid through to October." I finished my beer and turned from the bar.

Beecher asked where we were going.

"*I'm* going to study the history of the four kings. Meet me back at the room in an hour."

"Yes, boss."

As I was drawing a chair out from under the gambler's table, Beecher banged down his glass, reclaimed his Le Mat from Billy, and left the saloon.

Pinholster belched into his fist and broke open a fresh

deck. "Your pardon. I got hold of a bad oyster, which in its turn has got hold of me. What's the matter with your friend?"

"Long hours, short pay. We can't all be tinhorns."

"*Artist* is the preferred term." He shuffled. The cards were a white blur. "How much would you like to lose today, and how fast?"

I said, "That depends on whether you can tell me where Wheelock's personal secretary spends his time when he isn't working."

He shook his head. "That's too close to the dragon's mouth. I own this concession by the honorable gentleman's sufferance. I own my life by it as well. Peaching on Tom Tulip's one thing; this place is rotten with Tulips. Quinn is Captain Dan's Beelzebub. Harm Buckingham, harm King Richard. Pluck as much as a hair off that fair head and Wheelock would burn down the Coast to find the men responsible. Then he'd pour coal oil on the wretches and make them burn longer. If you lived here as long as I have, you'd be afraid of fire too."

"You're talking as if you had a choice in the matter."

He belched again. He looked a little green, at that. "You're a good gambler," he said. "You should know the odds are always with the house."

"You spread them around when you told me where I could find Tulip. He's common coin like you said, not worth taking the trouble to find out who set me on him. It doesn't mean Wheelock won't send over a squad of Hoodlums if I save him that trouble."

"Is there no Hoyle in your profession?" He dealt himself a hand of whist, a game I hadn't seen since before the war. It wasn't a good hand, but you wouldn't know it by looking at his face.

"Hoyle's dead. So is Sid the Spunk, probably. He fell in the harbor after he set fire to the Slop Chest for Wheelock."

"It's a dangerous waterfront. Men have been known to slip on the wharves and stab themselves in the back."

I waited.

"A last request from the condemned." He gathered in his cards and shuffled again. "Will you play me in earnest, just this once? No stakes. I'd like to see if you can be beaten without any help from you."

I found Beecher stretched out fully clothed on the top berth, smoking a cigarette and blowing clouds at the ceiling six inches in front of his face. The smoke flattened against it, turned down in opposition to all the laws of nature, and tangled with the fog coiling in through the gaps in the siding. "How'd you do?" he asked.

"Lost three hands to two. I couldn't figure out how he was cheating."

"Maybe he wasn't."

"I wouldn't bet on it here."

"You did, though."

"We weren't playing for money." I took off my coat. "Rest is a good idea. We're working late again tonight."

"Doing what?"

I told him. He didn't say anything as I sat down on the bottom berth and pulled off my boots. Then:

"You need another man. I'm shipping east on the last train."

I studied the sole of my left boot. It needed a new heel. Cobblestones and hardpack were tough on shoe leather. I missed riding; and I hate horses.

"Doesn't the railroad take off brownie points or something for leaving a job unfinished?"

"It puts them on. Brownie points is bad. Pile up enough of 'em and they pull your tunic. No separation pay, no pension, just the door. Mr. J. J. Hill's a hard man, but he don't ask you to do work you didn't sign on for. If I wanted to be a highwayman, I'd of looked up Jesse James's brother Frank and asked if he was hiring. He pays better and you don't gots to sit around listening to a politician gas about operating budgets and such."

"Tonight isn't strictly a highway operation. Quinn's poke is safe."

"That ain't what I'm talking about."

"Then talk. You've got three hours before your train pulls out."

"That's the point. I gots to do all the explaining. You just bark orders and I'm supposed to say, 'Yas, suh,' and fall in behind. Seems to me a parcel of Yanks give up the ghost just to put a stop to that."

"They fought to pay for the privilege. Before that it came free. I thought you liked following orders. That's what parade is all about."

"I never took an order I didn't know the reason for."

That seemed fair enough. "We're after information. It happens you and I are in a line of work where the people who have it don't want to give it up. I can buy it from Pinholster, but I've got to answer to Judge Blackthorne for expenses. He's the man who barks orders at me."

He blew out a lungful of smoke. "Maybe so. I feel less like a nigger stowing white folks's possibles and changing their sheets."

I dropped the boot and stood up, folded my arms on the edge of his berth. In the gloom of the windowless room the scar on his cheek flared white when he drew on his cigarette.

I said, "I don't partner up often. Part of the reason is I move faster alone, and moving fast is why I'm still here to listen to you bellyache. The rest has to do with how many partners I've buried. Don't expect us to go home friends, if we ever see home. When I mustered out of the army, I brought my brother back to Montana in an ammunition crate. His grave was the last thing I ever shed tears over."

"Lots of folks lost folks in the war."

"I seem to keep losing them."

He finished his stub, crushed it out against the ceiling, peeled it, and let the shreds of paper and tobacco flutter over the edge of the berth to the floor. Old cavalry habits die harder than old cavalrymen.

"We've all of us buried our share. I dug a hole for my baby girl and cut her name into a hunk of granite. I wanted it to last longer than she done. Pine would of served."

"Is that why your wife's in Spokane and you're not?"

I wanted to take back the question right away. Violating your own rules leads to other bad habits, and it's the bad habits that kill you.

"That was her notion, not that I didn't see sense in it. Little Lucy had my mouth, and after she left us, her ma couldn't stand watching me pour whiskey into it." He touched his scar. They can start hurting again without warning. "Ask you something?"

"Why stop now?"

"Why'd you pick me?"

"I made a good pick. You saved my hide in Gold Creek."

"I was saving mine, too, don't forget. Them two Copperheads wasn't going to leave me standing to tell that pettifogging town marshal what I seen, even if they could figure out which of us was which in that caboose. And you didn't know I was any good at throwing chairs when you decided on me. Ain't you got no friends in Helena?"

"I just got through telling you I don't make friends."

He aimed his melancholy smile at the ceiling. "Now you sound just like Cap'n Dan. I keep asking why and you keep telling stories."

"Blackthorne asked me who I wanted to stand behind my back and your name came out. I think it's because of the way you handled yourself in that parlor car. I told you to go through a dead man's pockets and you set right to it. Some of those pockets were soaked through with blood."

"That just makes me a good nigger."

"That makes you one man in a hundred. In Murfreesboro I knew a sniper who shot twenty-nine rebels out from under their hats at three hundred yards with a Springfield rifle. He had a shooting stand set up just like a buffalo hunter, with an extra rifle and a man to keep him loaded. A thirteen-year-old Tennessee volunteer broke cover and bayoneted him through the liver before he could switch rifles. He had his own bayonet fixed and time to use it and he didn't lift his arms. He froze because he couldn't kill a man except in cold blood."

"You should of picked the thirteen-year-old."

"I bashed in his skull with the butt of my carbine. Wheelock would say I lacked vision."

"Well, I ain't proved myself yet. For all you know, I'm only good aboard trains."

Not having anything to say to that, I climbed into my berth. Three hours later, the whistle belonging to the last train east drifted in, sounding as lost as the foghorns in the bay. Beecher was snoring smoothly. I doubt I got fifteen minutes' sleep all told. I couldn't get rid of the feeling I'd opened my mouth and lost my luck: which was the only commodity worth hanging on to in Port Hazard.

PART THREE

The White Peacock

16

Quinn—whose Christian name was Wallace—roomed on a narrow side street off Montgomery, above a German restaurant. The way there led past a row of banks and brokerage houses built on interest rates that would have broken the back of a J. P. Morgan; Pinholster had referred to the muttonchopped dyspeptics who ran them as the boldest thieves in Barbary's history. The restaurant served its *Wienerschnitzel* and *Sauerbraten* in one of the prefabricated buildings that had sailed around the Horn in the middle fifties and been reassembled on site, an instant city. A flight of open-air stairs led from an alley in back to the secretary's quarters.

Before going around back, I peeped through a front window and located the beanpole seated at a corner table with a checked napkin tucked inside the V of his vest. He was slicing an immense sausage amid plates of mashed potatoes, baked beans, assorted relishes, and sauerkraut, with a wheel of cheese in the center of the table and a schooner of beer as big as a punch bowl at his elbow.

Beecher took his turn looking and straightened. "Man must have a tapeworm."

In the alley, the fog reached to the ground-floor windows. I stationed Beecher under the stairs and climbed to the room the gambler had identified as Quinn's. The door had a skeleton lock. I found a key that worked among the little collection I'd assembled over the years, let myself in, and relocked it behind me.

I didn't light any lamps, but a side window faced a corner gas fixture, and in any case there wasn't much to see: a single bed on an iron frame, a washstand, a small writing table laid with all the necessary paraphernalia, a chair set next to a lamp for reading, and a stack of newspapers and books on the floor beside it, including *Wealth of Nations,* Pitman's *Stenographic Shorthand,* and *The Adventures of Tom Sawyer,* a surprise. Stacked untidily under the bed was a number of cheaply printed pamphlets with pornographic illustrations, which wasn't. The room was a fair indication of the man who occupied it. I sat in the reading chair with the Deane-Adams in my lap and made myself comfortable.

It wasn't a long wait. After twenty minutes, the steps outside groaned and a key scraped inside the lock. I let him open the door and step inside before I called out.

"Quinn, this is Deputy Marshal Murdock. Stand where you are."

For a man who spent most of his time bent over a desk, he had sound reflexes. He jerked at the elk's-tooth fob dangling from a vest pocket and had an over-and-under derringer in his hand.

I cocked the five-shot. Quinn stiffened; not so much because of this as at the echoing click behind him. Beecher stood on the staircase landing with his Le Mat pointed at the secretary's back.

"We're not here to rob you or arrest you," I said. "We want to ask you some questions."

His spectacles made blank circles in the gaslight coming through the window. The narrow face behind them was a cypher. Wheelock hadn't chosen him for his penmanship. After a long moment, he returned the derringer to his pocket. "May I light a lamp?"

I said, "As long as a match is the only thing that comes
out of your pocket."

"I'm not a Hoodlum. One pistol has always proven sufficient." He produced a box from an inside breast pocket.
A moment later, warm yellow light glowed through the
glass hobnail globe on the writing table. Beecher came in
behind him and closed the door. At a nod from me he returned the pistol to his belt. I laid mine on my thigh and
rested my hand on top of it. "How was supper?"

"Adequate to sustain life. I'm not partial to German
food, but it's included in the price of the room." He seated
himself on the edge of the mattress, feet together, hands
folded in his lap.

"You sure can put it away," I said. "A man with a clear
conscience has a good appetite."

"I have a condition that requires frequent feeding."

"Told you," Beecher said.

"Please ask your questions. I'm sure my eating habits
are not what you came here to find out."

Beecher said, "He ain't such of a much when it comes
to being a good host. You want me to instruct him on the
finer points of etiquette?"

"Not yet." I smiled at Quinn. "Beecher's new to law enforcement. He's full of ideas about how to make it work
faster."

The secretary said nothing.

I said, "Your employer told us you're the one who collects the rent on the Bella Union theater from the Sons of
the Confederacy. He said you could tell us who pays it."

"I doubt he used those words. Private transactions are
matters of confidence. I could only discuss them under the
terms of a formal written directive, signed by a Judge."

"That's inconvenient. The Judge in this case is eight
hundred miles away."

"I'm afraid that isn't my concern."

Beecher tipped over the washstand. The pitcher and bowl shattered on the floor. Quinn started, but left his hands in his lap.

"Beecher was a buffalo soldier," I said. "Sometimes he takes it literally. What's your landlord's position on disturbances in the night?"

"Don't forget damages." A pair of muslin curtains framed the side window. Beecher took one in his fist and tore it off the rod with a violent jerk. Quinn winced, but kept silent.

I looked at Beecher and lifted a shoulder. He went to the writing table, pulled the stopper out of a square bottle of ink, and tilted it over the sheets of closely written foolscap spread out on top.

"Stop!" said Quinn. "You make a convincing point."

Beecher righted the bottle. A single drop had spotted the corner of one page.

"Letter home?" I asked.

Color stained Quinn's sallow cheeks. "I'm composing a novel. I don't intend to remain a secretary my entire life."

I nodded at Beecher. He resealed the bottle and returned it to its brass stand.

Quinn said, "The man's name is Flinders. Horatio Flinders. He was one of the first Forty-Niners to strike it rich, but he lost it all in the Panic."

"Copperhead?"

"There are rumors about his activities during the war. I don't think a case was ever made against him."

"The Bella Union can't come cheap. Whose money is he using?"

"I don't know."

I signaled to Beecher, who reached for the ink bottle.

"It's the truth! He pays in cash and I enter it to the Sons of the Confederacy. He's a foul-mouthed old tramp, filthy in his habits. One is hardly tempted to engage him in conversation."

"Where does he live?"

"I doubt he has a home. He sleeps in doorways."

"Not good enough."

Quinn kneaded his hands. "He's a slave to the pipe. He spends most of his time in an opium den on Sacramento Street. The White Peacock. It's a tong place, run by a man they call Fat John. I don't know any more than that."

"Chinatown?"

"Yes. You'll want to bring your man."

"He isn't my man," I said, before Beecher could open his mouth. "Give him your belly gun. We'll leave it outside."

He dangled it by its fob. "It isn't loaded. I'm not skilled with firearms."

Beecher took it and broke it open. He nodded.

I said, "You must be the only unarmed man in Barbary."

"There's one other. Mr. Wheelock."

Beecher returned the weapon. I stood and holstered the Deane-Adams. I asked Quinn where he was from.

"New Jersey. I came out here to apprentice in a law office. It burned down before I got here."

"What made you hire on with Captain Dan?"

"I thought it might lead to public office. I'm too good at what I do, evidently. If I quit, he won't write a reference, and he refuses to sack me."

"I'm indispensable myself. I haven't had a holiday since the last time I got shot."

"I hate it here. I hope to sell the rights to my novel for enough money to set myself up back home. Horace Greeley was a charlatan."

"What's the book about?"

He colored again. "It's a romance. It's about a charmaid who falls in love with a mining magnate."

"What are you calling it?"

"*Nancy's Knickers, or the Amorous Adventures of a Girl of the Serving Class.*"

I looked at him.

"It's a working title," he said.

We left. Out on the landing, I grinned at Beecher. "The ink bottle was a good idea. There's no quicker way to a secretary's heart."

"You be the renegade next time. If this gets back to Mr. Hill, he'll have me throwing tramps off freight cars." He started down.

17

The old-timers called them "Forty-Eighters."

There weren't many left to call them that, the first wave having either made its fortune and built marble mansions on Nob Hill or gone bust and drifted on, and those who were still stuck in shanty San Francisco were hard put to find anyone who would listen to what they had to say. Those who managed to attract an audience recalled aloud that the first three Chinese to land at California walked down the gangplank of a brig called the *Eagle* a scant five months after the first cry of gold rose at Sutter's Fort, well before the true horde of bearded western prospectors took to the hills with their picks and pans in '49.

What happened to those three adventurous celestials—two men and one woman—was unknown even to the old-timers, but officials counted ten thousand the next year, and by 1870, the census reported that the Chinese population of California had exceeded seventy thousand, with half that number settled in San Francisco. Dreams of wealth had forsaken them. They operated laundries—more than a thousand were going full steam during my visit—worked construction projects, performed domestic chores for well-to-do whites, made cigars, sewed in sweatshops, and peddled opium in an area three blocks wide and seven blocks long, known intermittently as Little China, Chinatown, and Chink's Alley. They were governed by a merchants' association called the Six Companies, which in return for paying their passage from the land of their ancestors claimed a percentage of their income from the jobs it obtained for them upon arrival. But a government was a poor thing without the means to enforce its rules of conduct; hence the tongs, about which more later.

In the beginning, the immigrants were herded into bungalows manufactured in China and assembled by the workers who had accompanied them. Tiny and crowded, they were by all accounts comfortable for the coolies who had known worse conditions back home; but they were gone, gone. Fire had devoured them, and the survivors and their descendants now lived in board-and-batten shacks, tumbledown lean-tos, and rat-infested cellars, the last entered by means of ladders and filled with poisonous smoke when flames raged, and plague when they didn't. These billets were rented, not owned, by their inhabitants, most were anonymous, and those that had names did not advertise with even so much as a sign with crudely painted Chinese characters. There was no reason for that, with hundreds more Chinese looking for lodging than there were lodgings, and still more every day. Such names as they had were given them by wags and journalists, and were far more colorful than the dreary reality inside: Devil's Kitchen, Ragpicker's Alley, the Dog Kennel, the Palace Hotel.

The streets were narrow and twisting and made of the same soup of mud and excrement, animal and human, that visited raw boomtowns everywhere, but which in this case had not changed in thirty years. Planks were provided here and there for crossing, but Beecher and I had barely stepped over the invisible line that separated Chinatown from Barbary proper when we saw an ancient woman, indescribably wrinkled, hoist her skirts and wade across

Dupont in the middle of the block, up to her knees in muck.

We made our way by moonlight and such illumination as spilled out through the cracks of shanties on either side; there were few windows and no gas lamps this side of Portsmouth Square. At corners, we took turns shinnying up posts and striking matches to read the signs. We got lost twice—several streets were unmarked, the posts fallen over or chopped down for kindling and never replaced— and we walked with pistols in hand. I'd felt more secure patrolling wide-open cowtowns on the wrong side of the deadline with a reward on my head, posted by the local association of Regulators.

In those places I was most vulnerable in the deserted sections. In Chinatown, the busy boardwalks in front of the laundries left me feeling open and unprotected. Even at that hour the better-lit streets were alive with pedestrians, male mostly, hurrying along in their plain tunics and pillbox hats, carrying baskets of sodden clothing or firewood and elaborately paying no attention to the only two Occidentals in sight. I'd put in my time among Indians and Mexicans and immigrant settlers and had sacrificed most of my ingrained opinions of people who didn't look like me or speak my language, but in that alien country buttoned into the middle of a sprawling American city, I was grateful for the extra pair of eyes I'd brought along. How Beecher felt, I couldn't tell, but he made no attempt at conversation and his face was so taut the scar stood out as if it were fresh.

As anticipated, the White Peacock was not as grand as its name. Like the crowded rooming houses that bordered it, it bore no sign, and like them, it didn't need to; its smell was apparent before the building came into sight. Opium had had its fashion in mining camps and ends-of-track I'd visited, and I recognized the odor, not unpleasant, of pills softening in the flame and of the prepared substance converting to smoke. It was like baked poppy seeds.

Beecher sniffed. "Don't need directions from here."

"You know the smell?"

"From the other side. It was the only place in Spokane where I dreamed about anything but little Lucy. I didn't take the habit, though. It felt bad, not feeling bad. You ever chase the dragon?"

"Once. I threw up."

The building itself might have been another rooming house except for the smell and a number of soporific Chinese sprawled inside the sheltered entrance, oblivious to the two Westerners who stepped over them to knock on the door. It had no windows, and the flat roof, which smelled of fresh tar, was low enough for a man to reach up and grasp the edge without straining.

I had the advantage of the Chinese who opened the door. He didn't know me, but I recognized him.

He looked from white face to black and back to white and made no sign of either familiarity or surprise.

"Chinee papah, mistuh man?" I said.

His expression went even flatter. He knew me then. He started to close the door, but I leaned my shoulder against it. I showed him the star.

"Horatio Flinders," I said. "He's a regular customer. Five minutes."

He shook his head. "No unnerstan."

I grinned. " 'Stubble your red rag, Jack Sprat!' "

He considered this direct quote. Then he smiled, and I wished he'd go back to deadpan. His teeth were a uniform shade of amber and filed to razor points. He flung the door wide.

We entered a low room, smelling of fust and the odor

already described, lit only by the small flame in an incense burner in the center of the floor. It was as dark as a cellar. As I stood waiting for my eyes to adjust, my right hand began to ache, and I realized I was squeezing the butt of my pistol in its holster hard enough to crack the gutta-percha grips. I relaxed my grasp, but only to restore circulation. I'd spent time in black alleys that felt more friendly.

The Chinese closed the door. The current of stirred air made the flame wobble and nearly go out. My hand began aching again. I was as afraid of the dark as any small boy.

Clothing rustled nearby. A moment later, sudden as lightning, a T-square of yellow light cracked the blackness at the opposite end of the room. A shadow fluttered inside it, then the light vanished. A door had opened, then closed, swallowing the Chinese and leaving us in greater darkness than we'd known.

"I'd rather be dragging a drunk through a day-coach than here," Beecher said.

In a little while I realized we weren't alone in the room. Customers lay like piles of clothes on wide upholstered benches—*divans,* they were called, lending the name to the dens they furnished, which then was shortened to *dives* by addicts whose tongues were too thickened by smoke to manage two syllables—and an old Chinese with a corn-silk beard and owlish turtle-shell spectacles sat cross-legged on a cushion on the floor, turning a bead of opium on the end of a long needle over the incense flame. Pipes, made of cheap bamboo, ornate jade, and everything that came between, lay about on the floor and on the divans where they'd slid from the smokers' hands. No one appeared to be paying us any attention, although I was sure the old Chinese was aware of us and every movement we made. He looked the part of a tong leader and I wondered if he was the proprietor Quinn had told us about.

The door opened again, and this time it didn't shut. The young Chinese stood in the opening. "F'an Chu'an say he see you."

I asked who F'an Chu'an might be. He showed his pointed teeth.

"Some white men call him Fat John."

"Horatio Flinders is the man we came to see. Does F'an Chu'an sound like Horatio Flinders?"

"He see you."

I looked at Beecher, who shrugged. We followed the man through the door.

It opened onto a flight of steep narrow steps leading into a shallow cellar, lighted by a paper lantern on a hook screwed into the sloping plank ceiling. The steps were blackened at the edges from an old fire and the stairwell smelled of char.

The cellar was indistinguishable from the ground floor, except for the absence of the old Chinese. In his place, a man half his age sat at an identical incense burner, stirring a thick brown syrup in a tiny crock with a needle. This was the raw opium, from which a dollop would be extracted and allowed to crystallize into a bead suitable for burning. More customers sprawled on divans and pallets, smoking, dreaming, and waiting for their next pipe. The atmosphere was thicker here, where decades of smoke had had nowhere to go but deep into the earthen walls and floor joists inches above our heads. A man had only to lick any surface to enter the astral plane.

We passed through another door and found ourselves in a room ten feet square, hung with faded tapestries. In them I recognized the same designs I'd seen on Daniel Webster Wheelock's silk walls, only much, much older, embroidered by hands long since gone to earthly corruption. Oriental rugs, nearly as ancient, covered the floor three deep, obscuring the chamber's subterranean nature;

it could have been a tearoom in any of the Chinese hospitality houses in the larger Western cities. In the center stood a small square table draped in black velvet, behind which a young Chinese stood pouring what looked like very strong tea—if it wasn't axle grease—into a tiny, handleless porcelain cup from a proportionately small pot. A gold-hilted sword in an ornate sheath studded with jewels, older than California, lay across the backs of a pair of ruby-colored china figures made to represent pug dogs, the table's only decoration. More paper lanterns, perched in niches hewn into portions of wall not covered by tapestries, shed light adequate to what looked like a delicate and possibly ceremonial decanting operation. It was enough to dazzle those of us who had just come in from the cave outside.

Our escort bowed and said something in Chinese to the man behind the table, who responded with one syllable. The other man bowed again and turned to face us.

"F'an Chu'an asks his visitors to seat themselves."

We hesitated. The man pouring tea was, if anything, younger than the man who had brought us, thirty at the oldest. Small and slender— "Fat John" was obviously as close as most Western tongues could come to pronouncing F'an Chu'an—he wore a yellow robe of plain silk, washed so many times I could make out the lean musculature of his arms and chest, and a black silk mandarin's cap with a jade button on top. His queue was black and glossy, carefully plaited, and hung nearly to his waist. His upper lip was cleft, a deformity of birth rather than the result of an injury sustained later in life. It affected his speech, so far as I could determine, not knowing the language, and reminded me of the infernal smile of a cat.

Finally we selected a pair of painted wooden stools from a collection of them scattered about and drew them up to the table. The two Chinese remained standing. The man behind the table finished filling the cup and started on another. He said something in a low, pleasant voice that suggested he was accustomed to speaking aloud without interruption. His impediment failed to embarrass him.

"F'an Chu'an apologizes for his inexcusable ignorance of English and asks me to translate. My name is Lee Yung Hay. He invites you to sample his disappointing tea."

I noticed that Lee Yung Hay had abandoned his pidgin dialect, which was not to be confused with his command of the local gutter slang. I said we'd be honored. I didn't add that since he'd already started pouring I wasn't in a position to decline. F'an Chu'an spoke again.

"You are the men called Mur Dok and Bee Chu'r. You waylaid the man called Tom Too Lip and gained an audience with Captain Dan Wee Lok. Both these things have impressed him."

I said, "Tell him I admire his intelligence system, as well as his hospitality. Wheelock took away our weapons."

The answer came almost before Lee Yung Hay finished translating. In response, the subordinate raised his right hand as if in greeting. It was holding a short-handled hatchet. He moved again and it was gone. I suspected he wore some kind of belt rig under his smock.

"F'an Chu'an is aware of the white man's reliance upon percussion weapons and that he would not presume to deprive you of their succor. He is grieved to add that I am capable of separating your hands from your wrists before you can cock your hammers."

I smiled. "Mine's a self-cocker."

"Thank you. I should be honored to begin with you."

F'an Chu'an finished filling a third cup and spoke.

"While you share his roof you are under the protection of the Suey Sing Tong. No harm shall come to you if you respect the customs of his house."

"We appreciate that. If he'll let us see Flinders, we'll be on our way and he can drink his tea in peace."

I heard Flinders's name in the translation and in the answer.

"You honor him with your association. The man Flin Dur is a guest as well and entitled to his protection also."

Beecher spoke up. "Fat John likes to hear himself talk, don't he?"

Lee Yung Hay interpreted this before I could break in. Our host smiled his cat's smile and set a cup in front of Beecher.

"F'an Chu'an apologizes for his disagreeable chatter. He is a man who enjoys conversation for its own sake."

I said, "Tell him it's a quality he shares with a number of Indian chiefs I've met. Good tea should be sipped slowly." I lifted my cup; apparently an unfamiliar custom, since the toast was not returned.

Our host was encouraged, however, and for the next twenty minutes entertained us with a history of the tong, a society that did not exist in China, but had been organized to protect immigrants from American oppression, and incidentally to ensure that the Six Companies were not forgotten by the laborers they'd brought over come payday. He did not explain why seven separate tong affiliations were necessary, nor why they occasionally went to war with one another, and no mention was made of the fees the expatriates were forced to pay to protect themselves and their property from the tong.

F'an Chu'an was a fugitive himself, having been compelled to abandon the study of medicine in Hong Kong when his father was unmasked as one of the chief conspirators in the Taiping Rebellion. While in hiding, the young student grew a queue, then took ship disguised as a common coolie. He'd sweated in a laundry on Dupont

Street for two years, at the end of which his education, native intelligence, and the combat lessons taught him by his rebel father had secured him a position with the Suey Sing Tong as a leader among the *boo how doy,* or fighting men. His cool head under fire spared his sect from humiliation in a pitched battle with the Kwong Dok Tong in 1875, when he was barely twenty, which ended in a bloody draw, and when the Suey Sing leader died several days later of injuries sustained in the fight, F'an Chu'an was elected to replace him. He'd spent the last eight years maintaining his position against challenges from below and without.

Beecher and I sipped tea and listened to the young gang leader enumerate his accomplishments in modest tones, translated with sneering bombast by Lee Yung Hay, for whom all other victories, including Yorktown and Waterloo, paled to insignificance. He was as hard to take as the tea, which was strong enough to bounce a cartwheel dollar off the surface. I broke in while he was trumpeting the Suey Sings' role in defending the Chinese population against bullying by Hoodlums, and the historic pact, supervised by Wheelock, that kept the Hoodlums in check in return for an agreement to confine the city's opium traffic to Chinatown.

"What can F'an Chu'an tell us of the Sons of the Confederacy?"

The subordinate twisted his lip, but put the question to his superior.

"Your civil war is of no interest to F'an Chu'an. China's most recent rebellion claimed fourteen years and twenty million lives."

"That isn't the question I asked."

"I did not finish. These fellows who cannot unshackle themselves from things gone are as jabbering women, to whom he turns an unhearing ear. As Confucious says,

'Things that are done, it is needless to speak about. Things that are past, it is needless to blame.' "

I'd had enough of Lee Yung Hay. "Does he feel that way about you peddling dope in Barbary?"

The whites of Lee Yung Hay's eyes showed. His upper lip curled back from his picket-shaped teeth, his arm jerked. Beecher and I both clawed at our revolvers, but the hatchet was out and sweeping in a horizontal circle toward me. Then something flashed and Lee Yung Hay's head tipped off his shoulders. A gout of blood made a rooster-tail in the air and splattered a tapestry. His headless trunk was falling, but the arm swinging the hatchet continued its arc, driven purely by reflex and momentum. My gun hand was in the blade's path. Something flashed again and the hatchet dropped to the floor, its handle still gripped in a hand that was no longer attached to its wrist.

F'an Chu'an stood holding the gold-hilted sword in both hands, his inferior's blood sliding down the vane and dripping off the point. He'd snaked it out of its jewel-studded sheath and swung it twice in less time than it takes to describe.

"I hnought tho," he said. His English was good for a man with a cleft lip.

18

It was a situation I'd been in before—three armed men facing off across a few tense feet of floor—but this one offered some unique features, including a grinning severed head bleeding into a valuable rug, a disconnected hand lying nearby, its fingers still tightly wrapped around the handle of a hatchet, and the body that belonged to the head and the hand sprawled between them on its back, one leg bending and straightening spasmodically as if it were trying to climb to its feet.

Oh, and a young Chinese with a visionary expression on his face, gripping a three-hundred-year-old sword.

I pictured the pensive look on Judge Blackthorne's face when I reported what had happened, heard his likely response:

Really, Deputy, the hand alone would have been sufficient. What is the nature of this obsession you have with melodrama?

At the moment, though, I was concentrating on F'an Chu'an. China's history—and what he had told Beecher and me of the tong—suggested that once one begins lopping off parts of the anatomy it's difficult to stop. I wasn't sure, once he resumed swinging, whether the two of us together could weight him down with enough lead to slow his hand before our heads joined Lee Yung Hay's on the floor of the White Peacock. He looked like a crazed butcher with the blade standing straight out from his body and a spray of blood staining his yellow robe.

The sound that brought him out of his trance might have been water dripping from the spout of a pump. The first gusher of blood that had struck the tapestry on the wall had saturated the venerable fabric, run down, and begun pattering off the bottom edge onto the floor.

His shoulders relaxed. He let go with one hand and lowered the sword until its point rested on the rug at his feet. We let our pistols fall to our sides, but we didn't put them away. He was still armed.

F'an Chu'an's vocabulary wasn't as broad as the dead man's and his pronunciation suffered because of his impediment, which may have explained why he kept his knowledge of English a secret from his followers. He groped for words, and a number of times we had to ask him to repeat a sentence we found unintelligible. He'd known for some time that a member of the Suey Sing Tong was selling opium outside Chinatown in violation of the agreement Wheelock had engineered between Barbary and the tongs, and had suspected that Lee Yung Hay was involved. All he'd lacked was proof, which the other man had provided by attacking me when I'd accused him. The sword was the only artifact he owned that had belonged to his father, who traced his ancestry back to a philosopher in the imperial court of Wan Li, and who had been arrested and executed by the current emperor for his part in the rebellion that had driven his son to emigrate to America; F'an Chu'an had smuggled in the sword inside a rolled rug containing the rest of his possessions, maintained the weapon in its original condition, and practiced daily the centuries-old warrior exercises for which it was intended. Lee Yung Hay's was the first human blood it had spilled since its first owner used it to commit suicide in 1579.

My responsibility as an officer of Blackthorne's court was to arrest him, and give testimony at the inquest. Chances were no charges would be brought against him, acting as he had in the defense of a deputy federal marshal. It seemed like a lot of trouble to go to just to get back to where we stood at that moment, so I did nothing. I admit that my decision was affected by the facts that he was the leader of an armed gang whose number I could only guess at, and that most of Chinatown and all of Barbary lay between us and the city jail. I watched him wipe the blade on the table's velvet cloth and put it back in its sheath and returned the Deane-Adams to leather. Beecher put away the Le Mat. His scar had lost some of its contrast, but he was the same man who had handed me a telegram across a fresh corpse on the train to Garrison. I imagine I was pale, too.

Our host bowed and apologized for the poor manners of the devil's son who now lay in pieces at our feet. He said he was in my debt for helping him to prevent another opium war. Then he excused himself, pulled aside a tapestry that masked an opening into another chamber behind the tearoom, and let it fall behind him. We were alone with what remained of Lee Yung Hay.

Beecher said, "Should we go?"

"Not without what we came for."

"What kind of place *is* this?"

"I don't know. Hell maybe."

The Chinese came back in wearing a different robe, this one faded green and if anything worn thinner than the one he'd had on before. Whatever the tongs spent their tribute money on, it wasn't their wardrobe.

We followed him into the cellar room where opium was prepared and consumed. He bent and whispered something to the man seated at the incense burner, who looked around through the gloom and shook his head. F'an Chu'an whispered again. The man was still for a moment; then he nodded. He got up and let himself into the room we'd just left. That made him the cleaning crew.

F'an Chu'an said Horatio Flinders was not in the cellar. He started toward the stairs. As he ascended, the hem of his robe made a serpentine hiss sliding off the heels of his slippers, which were made of fine paper with gilded dragons on the toes. Once again we fell in behind him.

The old man upstairs rose as his employer approached. He was tall for a Chinese, with the high brow and rounded shoulders of a scholar; the image of the Oriental ascetic that advertisers used to sell tarot cards and books of conjuring tricks. One of the eyes behind the huge, round spectacles was glistening white. He was half blind. When F'an Chu'an whispered, the old man bowed deeply from the waist and shuffled from divan to divan, bending over each one and examining the face of the man who lay upon it. Most of the faces were Chinese, but I thought I recognized one of the sailors I'd seen sprawled on Nan Feeny's front porch the day we'd arrived at the Slop Chest. High tide hadn't taken him very far.

I was thinking this when the old man returned. He bowed again and pointed to a divan in a corner that was almost enveloped in shadow.

Our host led the way. He stood aside as I bent over the man spreadeagled on his stomach. He stank of raw whiskey, rotten teeth, unwashed flesh, urine, and excrement. The overcoat he had on was rent up the back, darned all over with thread as old and brittle as self-respect, and filthy beyond description. It was of that color, neither brown nor green, common to the clothing given out at missions.

Horatio Flinders, one of the millionaires of '49.

I put a hand on his shoulder and shook him. His mouth dropped open with a wet smacking sound, informing me immediately of the decay that was going on inside, but apart from that, he didn't stir. I braved lice, grabbed a fistful of his dirty gray hair, and lifted his head. A thread of drool spilled out one corner of his mouth and made a glistening mercury pool on the divan.

"Slap him," Beecher said.

I slapped his cheek with my free hand. I didn't like the way his skin felt. Chances were I wouldn't have anyway.

I called for a match.

Beecher found one, struck a flame off the seat of his pants, and held it out. I took it and passed it back and forth in front of Flinders's eyes. I shook it out and lowered his head to the divan.

"Dead."

Beecher said, "One pipe too many."

F'an Chu'an grunted assent.

I set my jaw and made an examination. The body felt cool. A man could be dead a long time in a place like the White Peacock before anyone came to check on him. My hand touched something wet on his rib cage that was as familiar as it was unpleasant. I drew out my palm.

This time Beecher didn't wait to be asked. He struck a match and held it close.

"That's two in one night," he said. "I don't reckon the odds are high against it here."

I wanted to agree with him, even if it made my job harder. There is something inevitable and comforting about unthinking evil. It's like a natural disaster no one can do anything about. But the words stuck in my throat.

"Pinholster was right: Never bet against the house." I wiped the blood off on Flinders's coat.

19

oratio Octavius Flinders, it turned out, was one of
San Francisco's most beloved characters; the *Call*
said so in as many words in a black-bordered editorial
lamenting his loss. I saw no reason to question the statement. Newspapers are infallible in matters related to the
community.

Comparisons were made between the "vagabond forty-
niner" and the Emperor Norton, an addle-brained tramp
who'd strutted the streets of the city for twenty years,
claiming to be the ruler of America and dining on the cuff
in local restaurants, until he left this world in 1880. That
Flinders had slept in doorways, panhandled for opium
money, and only forgot the hunger that was eating him
from inside when he was dreaming black dreams didn't
make it into the editorial, possibly because it would have
confused the analogy. When his claim was paying off, he'd
tipped waiters twenty dollars, thrown champagne parties
at the Astor House that lasted three days, and sailed back
and forth across the bay aboard his custom-built steam-
powered yacht; that was the H. O. Flinders the *Call*
mourned. He sold more papers than the emaciated, vermin-
infested wretch the coroner's men dragged out of the White
Peacock, or the bitter rabble-rouser who advocated armed
insurrection against the United States government the day

Lincoln was inaugurated. Death and baptism will work miracles upon the soiled soul.

An inquest convened two days later found that the deceased had been stabbed through the heart by a person or persons unknown, armed with a blade that penetrated eight inches. I was in the gallery in the county courthouse, and I thought immediately of F'an Chu'an's ancient ceremonial sword. I also remembered the sword-cane carried by the Hoodlum who'd accosted Beecher and me on the train platform the day we arrived, and of the assorted knives we'd taken off Tom Tulip: Break one, confiscate the rest, it didn't matter. Replacements were everywhere. Everything that moved in Barbary and Chinatown could skewer or shoot or bludgeon at the drop of a handkerchief. Any experienced investigator would begin by eliminating those citizens who *didn't* arm themselves first thing after rising.

That was my opinion, in any case, but I wasn't asked. For some reason, the coroner's court Judge didn't call me to the stand, even though I was the one who'd discovered the corpse and was the senior officer on the scene.

The reason sat in the front row of the gallery, wearing the dress uniform, navy festooned with gold braid, of a captain in the San Francisco Fire Department.

Wheelock had entered shortly before the court came to order, leaning on his carved ivory stick and swinging his club foot in its specially built-up shoe in a practiced circle that nearly disguised his limp. He'd taken a seat directly in the Judge's line of sight and remained silent and motionless throughout, hands folded on top of the stick, while the party in gray dundrearies behind the bench shot him frequent glances during the coroner's testimony. No other witnesses were summoned. From gavel to gavel the proceedings took twenty minutes out of the county's time.

There was no uproar. Half the seats were vacant, and

most of those that weren't contained curious spectators drawn there by the editorial in the *Call*. That publication attended in the person of a scarecrow in frayed cuffs with an angry boil on the back of his neck, scribbling ferociously on folded sheets of newsprint with a stump of yellow pencil. Captain Dan put on his visored cap and limped out immediately upon adjournment. I tried to catch up with him, but got snared in a crowd in the hallway that was waiting to get into a more popular proceeding in criminal court. I apologized to a small, elderly gent in white handlebars for bumping into him; when he reached up to tip his bowler and tell me it was quite all right, I saw that he was handcuffed to an officer in uniform, who glowered and told me to move on. Afterward, I realized the polite little man was Charles E. Bolton, awaiting arraignment on a series of stagecoach robberies he'd committed single-handed under the name Black Bart. That made two prominent figures I'd almost knocked over during my visit to the City of the Golden Gate.

Wheelock had buttoned down the investigation into Flinders's murder, and for the time being, there was no approaching him about it. The pug who kept the peace at the Bella Union barred me from the stairwell to Captain Dan's quarters, and although Beecher suggested we try manhandling another Hoodlum, I was dead certain Wheelock wouldn't rise to that bait a second time. Truth to tell, I wasn't all that determined to question him. It was clear to me the old forty-niner had been killed to seal the identity of whoever was paying the rent on the use of the Bella Union theater for the Sons of the Confederacy to meet, and the honorable gentleman had tipped that secret by showing up at the courthouse and directing the inquest from his seat in the gallery.

"Ain't that all you need?" Beecher asked.

"Judge Blackthorne will want more."

"What do we do to get it?"

"We're doing it."

He grunted and drank his beer. We'd had this conversation before.

"This time the wait should be more entertaining." I folded the edition of the *Call* I'd had spread out on the ruined bar and showed him the cartoon on page three.

It was an old-fashioned rendering of leering Death, looming in his black robes like a dark cloud over ramshackle Barbary with his scythe raised in both skeletal fists high above his head. At the bottom of the panel lay a jumble of skulls, human rib cages, and other assorted bones, superscribed by numbers representing the murder toll to date, the numerals dripping black ink like the blood pattering off the tapestry in F'an Chu'an's tearoom. The artwork was realistic enough to rear nightmares in a generation of children.

"Looks like a ten-cent shocker," Beecher said. "There anything there folks don't know already?"

"Knowing isn't seeing." I read him the editorial that covered two columns beside the cartoon. It was headed THE CARNIVAL OF CRIME.

The Barbary Coast! That mysterious region so much talked of, so seldom visited! Of which so much is heard, but little seen! That sink of moral pollution, whose reefs are strewn with human wrecks, and into whose vortex is constantly drifting barks of moral life, while swiftly down the whirlpool of death go the sinking hulks of the murdered and the suicide! The Barbary Coast! The home of vice and harbor of destruction! The coast on which no gentle breezes blow, but where rages one wild sirocco of sin! In the daytime it is dull and unattractive, seeming but a cesspool of rottenness, the air impregnated with smells

more pungent than polite; but when night lets fall its
dusky curtain, the Coast brightens into life, and be-
comes the wild carnival of crime that has lain in
lethargy during the sunny hours of the day, and now
bursts forth with energy renewed by its siesta.

"*Sounds* like a ten-cent shocker. You reckon the places
around here paid for the advertisement?"

"There's more."

The article went on to rehash the details of Horatio
Flinders's untimely expiration—"the wreckage of the
once-gallant *Forty-Niner,* pulled from the stinking heap
of lost souls in the worst dungeon in Little China" and of
the court action that had disposed of the tragedy in less
time than required for the mayor to take tea with the governor, and called for "no less than the intervention of the
U.S. Army, or, failing that, determined action by decent
San Franciscans to eradicate this blight for once and all."

It was signed by Fremont Older, Editor-in-Chief; and
unlike the earlier dirge for Flinders it carried no black border. The effect was that of a robust gentleman of the old
school stripping off his pigskin gloves for a rough-and-
tumble behind the club.

Beecher finished his beer and signaled Billy for a refill.
" 'Eradicate this blight.' That mean what I think?"

"It happened before," I said.

"What'll that do to the Sons of the Confederacy, you
reckon?"

"Nothing, maybe. Everything if they forget to step out
of the way."

"What about Wheelock?"

"Wheelock's got no place to step. The only thing he has
going for him is there's no one else to keep Barbary from
blowing sky-high. If it blows anyway, he's just an alderman."

He smiled. "And a fire captain, too, don't forget. He sure does like to put on that uniform."

"A fire captain is only worth having as long as there's something to burn."

Wheelock had the Flinders investigation buttoned down so far as the legal and political system went in San Francisco, but he hadn't counted on Fremont Older. The editor-in-chief of the *Call* had started at the top of the journalistic pay scale as a forty-dollar-a-week compositor with the *Territorial Enterprise* in Virginia City, Nevada, lost that position during the 1873 Panic, and freelanced for grub-stake pay writing obituaries and editing agony columns throughout California before taking a steady job as a reporter with a paper in Redwood City for twelve dollars a week. That rose to eighteen when he fell into a part ownership. Upon taking the helm of the *Call*, he'd set up office in the same building that housed the United States Mint, where he'd spent much of his time coining purple phrases about conditions in shantytown, which for reasons best known to him he had chosen as the target of his personal mission for destruction. There were readers who insisted that Older was the man responsible for naming the region the Barbary Coast, after the den of depravity of that name in Africa, but that was more likely the inspiration of some anonymous sailor who had visited both places.

No matter. In that quarter, Older marked the sparrow's fall, whether it was the death of a coolie left to starve in an alley because he couldn't afford to pay the fees demanded by the Six Companies or the fate of the wandering daughter of a well-placed Philadelphia family kidnapped and sold into slavery on Pacific Street or the robbery and murder of a sailor in a house of pleasure in the neighborhood engagingly known as the Devil's Acre. He was there to report the facts when three young Chinese were hacked to death in a tong skirmish, and when there was nothing more scarlet to cover than a drunken derelict stumbling and falling under the wheels of a brewer's dray, he was there, too. On those rare occasions when a week passed quietly, he dressed an adventurous staff member in rags and sent him to live in a lodging house in Dead Man's Alley for three days, at the end of which he was expected to set down all the lurid details in type, and if he didn't have any, to make some up. I couldn't figure out why Older wasn't as successful as Joseph Pulitzer.

Whatever his complaint was with Barbary, he seemed to have found his handle with Flinders and had no intention of letting go. In the issue that followed "the carnival of crime," he surrendered his editorial slot to a long letter by someone who signed himself "Owen Goodhue, D.D., Maj., S.A. (ret'd)," offering to take Older up on his invitation and pledging the support, "spiritual and physical," of a Citizens' New Vigilance Committee, "with which I have the honor to consider myself a person of some small influence." The letter proposed that "one hundred substantial citizens of the City and County of San Francisco" be deputized by the sheriff's office, "with all due entitlement and authority to enter the area known as the Barbary Coast, not excluding Chinatown, and employ all means necessary to restore law and order." It added, in terms not too subtle for the more rudimentary subscribers, that if such deputization, entitlement, and authority were not forthcoming, it was the Christian duty of all respectable persons who agreed with the conclusions of the messrs. Older and Goodhue that civilization had broken down in the area referred to previously, "to seize, wrest, and arrogate the instruments of justice and force and visit punishment upon offenders, without regard to rank, gender, nationality, or property, public or private, at such time and on such a date as will be announced presently."

This compost heap of redundancy, tub-thumping rhetoric, and overripe declension took up a quarter of a page that might otherwise have been dedicated to enlightenment. It was answered the next day in the lead column on the front page by statements attributed to C. T. Warburton, Sheriff of San Francisco County, to the effect that the situation in Barbary was in hand and that he had no intention of cloaking "a collection of cranks and malcontents" in the authority of his office. Older made no comment, apart from a sly reference to the fact that Warburton was not facing re-election this year.

There was no hope from the military, either: A laconic item at the bottom of the second column reported that a wire sent to President Arthur asking for a declaration of martial law and dispatch of troops to San Francisco had received no response thus far.

I didn't see Wheelock's hand in any of this. Neither Warburton nor Arthur held jurisdiction inside the city limits, and both were old enough to remember the draft riots in New York City and the damages to life and property that resulted when civilians took up arms to no specific purpose. The sheriff may have witnessed the last time vigilantes set out to restore order in Barbary and made only chaos. In any case they could both claim that the affairs of their offices lay elsewhere.

On the following day appeared a full-page advertisement, with flags unfurling in the corners and a flaring eagle with arrows in its talons at the top, opposite the usual endorsements for Tutt's Pills, men's woolen drawers, improved harrows, St. Jacob's Oil, and the New Line of Fancy Goods obtainable at Clemson's Emporium on Market Street:

SUMMONED!
100 SUBSTANTIAL CITIZENS 100
To the Southeast Corner of Portsmouth Square
at 8:00 P.M.
on Friday, September 28th
Whence the Party will Proceed
Through the Area Known as the Barbary Coast
and Chinatown
to Arrest, Detain, and Discipline
Brothel-Keepers, Opium Peddlers, Pickpockets,
Assassins, Harlots, Procurers,
White Slavers, Pan-Handlers, Vagrants,
Burglars, Sneak Thieves, Confidence Men,
Burkes, Bludgeoners, Blacklegs,
Swindlers, Gamblers, Smugglers,
and Uncertified Celestials
100 SUBSTANTIAL CITIZENS 100
GATHER YE SONS OF FREEDOM

"I didn't see no niggers on the list." Beecher folded and returned the newspaper to me. "Reckon I'm safe. What's an 'uncertified celestial'?"

"Any Chinese without identification."

"Hell you say. When it's done there won't be a yellow face left 'twixt here and Seattle."

"I wonder who's this fellow Owen Goodhue."

We both looked toward Pinholster's table. The gambler had left for supper.

Billy the bartender spat on a glass and polished it with his bar rag. "Nan's the one to ask about Doctor Major Goodhue. She's had personal experience."

I asked what kind.

"Close as you can get with your duds on. She shot him once."

20

"That Billy would hang whiskers on a goat," Nan Feeny said. "I never shot Goodhue. The pepperbox misfired."

We were gathered in her quarters behind the saloon. Beecher and I were seated, he enjoying one of the late Commodore's well-preserved cigars. Our hostess wore a ditch in the floor between her bed and the decanter filled with peach brandy. She had on one of her long, high-collared dresses, topped off by the ribbon she tied around her neck to remind her how close she'd come to hanging for shooting a square citizen to death in that room. She'd have saved shoe leather if she didn't insist upon drinking from a tiny cordial glass like a woman of gentle breeding, but the trips back and forth didn't slow down her consumption. A miner would have been pressed hard to keep up with her with a tankard. All this vigilante talk had her more on edge than even the previous transaction with Wheelock's man Tom Tulip. Her speech had reverted to the broad accents of Boston and she kept abandoning the local vernacular for the variety practiced on the Eastern seaboard; which was a little easier to comprehend, if it didn't come at you like Confederate grapeshot.

Outside, Barbary continued unbowed. Eight or nine tintack pianos were clattering like steam pistons with not ten fingers of recognizable talent anywhere in evidence, the one-armed concertina player at the Pacific Club was homing in on "Jack o' Diamonds," a sailor's leather lungs let fly with a deep bass whoop, expressing either boundless joy or black anguish, a harlot or one of the sweet young *danseuses* at the Belle Union countered with a thin soprano shriek like crystal shattering. A shotgun barrel emptied with a deep round roar; a bartender punching a hole in the ceiling to break up a brawl, or in a customer to defend the cash-box, or maybe it was just a part-time rat-catcher paying for his drinks the easy way. The resident rodents were running as big as bobcats that season and paid more bounty than renegade Mexicans. If Owen Goodhue and his one hundred substantial citizens expected the advertisement in the *Call* to have a sobering effect on vice, they were in for disappointment. Somehow I thought the reverse would be true. They had hemp fever and would enjoy nothing better than to catch the pack in full howl.

"Why'd you try to shoot him in the first place?" I asked Nan. "And who is he?"

"The first answers the second. To look at the Sailor's Rest now, you'd not guess what it was at high tide, before Wheelock's slubbers put the spunk to it; glass all round, with curtained boxes for the fish to have their fancy and pretty waiter girls in short smickets and silk vampers hoof to hip. One night there's this row out front. I hooked my little barking-iron and legged it there and laid my lamps on that scrub parson Goodhue ducking one of my girls in the trough where they sluice the prads. Holding her under by the neck, he was, and her flapping her mawleys and trotters like a snaggled hen. I says, 'Here, what you think you're about, drownding that little molly?' He says, 'Tain't drownding her a-tall, harlot. I'm baptizing this child in the name of the Lord and the Salvation Army.'"

"White of him to put the Lord at the top of the bill," said Beecher.

She stabbed him with her eyes, gulped peach brandy, and lifted the decanter. Telling a story uninterrupted was one of the privileges of the mistress of the establishment.

" 'Baptizing be damned,' I says. 'Stand away or I'll let California climate through your bread-bag.'

"Well, he just showed me his tombstones and went on a-baptizing. The girl ain't fighting so hard by this time.

" 'Cock your toes up, then, you jack cove,' says I, 'and take your lump of lead.'

"Well, I shot the blighter; or would of, if the fog hadn't got to the powder. As it was, the cap snapped, and he heard it and left off his lay there and then. I pulled back the hammer again and he tucked tail and trotted, spitting Scripture over his shoulder and calling me whore and I don't know what else, except that there's none of it I ain't been called before, and by better scrubs than him."

"What about the girl?" I asked.

"She swallowed half the trough, but I got her on her back and pumped her out the way the Commodore showed me. Venus' Curse croaked her at the finish, up on Broadway after she left the Rest. Maybe it wasn't such a good turn I done her after all, though she was grateful enough at the time, and still more so not a month later, when Goodhue baptized another girl clear to Glory in a rain barrel in the alley back of the Fandango."

I asked if he'd stood trial. She laughed and shot brandy down her throat.

"Cove behind the bench was a Christian man; fined him twelve dollars for breaching the public peace and made him pay fifty to the girl's family for compensation. The Salvation Army took a rustier view of the whole transaction and told him to pad the hoof."

That explained the "Maj., S.A. (ret'd)." I'd wondered if he'd been any kind of real major. "Who does he work for now?"

"Owen Goodhue. He'd say God like as not, but with him they're one and the same." She set down her glass and bent over the packing crate she kept next to the barrel stove, filled with old numbers of the *Call* and other paper scraps suitable for lighting fires. After rummaging for a minute, she came up with a crumple of heavy stock, which she brought over to me.

It looked like a wanted circular, complete with a full-face photograph of an old road agent with broom whiskers chopped off square across his collar and a coarse wool coat buttoned to the neck like a military tunic. The base of his beard and the broad, flat brim of a campaign hat with dimples in the crown like the Canadian Mounties wore drew two parallel lines, with the fierce face framed between like a hermit's peering through a window. The eyes beneath their drawn brows were set close above an S-shaped nose, broken several times and never reset.

I didn't like the fact that I couldn't see his mouth through the coarse growth that covered the bottom half of his face. It reminded me of something I'd read in a book in Judge Blackthorne's personal library, now destroyed by fire, about creatures on the floor of the ocean that disguised themselves as heaps of moss in order to lure curious small fish into the hungry maws hidden beneath the tendrils.

Bold black capitals printed across the top of the sheet read:

LECTURE
AT THE EAST STREET MISSION
WEDNESDAY, APRIL 4th
7:30 P.M.

There followed the picture, captioned: "Owen Goodhue, D.D., Maj., S.A. (ret'd); Founder of the First Eden Infantry,

Army of the River Jordan." Beneath that, again in large capitals:

"WHEN GABRIEL BLOWS 'ASSEMBLY,' WILL YOU ANSWER?"

"Clever," Beecher said, when I'd read it aloud. "I always thought the army would be a lot more like hell."

A dense paragraph appeared under that heading, full of biblical quotations with chapters and verses. I noticed they were all from the Old Testament, always the most popular with the kind of devout party who liked to use words such as "seize," "wrest," "arrogate," and "punish."

I reread the caption. "D.D.," I said. "Is he a dentist?"

"Doctor of Divinity." Nan pursed her lips above her cordial. "If he got it from anyplace but the College of Queen Dick, I'm a sister of charity. His joskins hand out that scrip every couple of months all over Barbary. I wouldn't of took it this time except we had a cold snap and I was low on kindling."

"I'm glad it warmed up before you burned it. I always like to know what the devil looks like this visit."

"He ain't Old Nick, though he'd welcome the kick upstairs. Or downstairs, seeing as how it's the Pit we're talking about. He's just another black imp. The town's flush with 'em, and I ain't just referring to the picaroons round here. You'll find 'em in case lots on Nob Hill as like as down Murder Point."

She started to drink, then lowered the glass. "Don't think from that he ain't a cove to be ware hawk of. He was with the vigilantes what strung up Jim Casey and Charlie Cora at Fort Gunnybags in fifty-six."

"I don't suppose he stood trial for that either," I said.

"Nary a one of 'em did. The governor called in the U.S. Army, and dance at my death if the vigilantes didn't give them a proper caning and sent them slanching back to Sacramento. Goodhue was just a squeaker then. He's near thirty years meaner, and has got the Rapture to boot. He and his hundred substantial citizens'll go through Barbary like salt through a hired girl. This time I'm keeping my powder dry for when that Friday face of his shows up here three days from now."

"That pepperbox only fires six. Vigilantes travel in bigger packs than that. Why not just close up and leave town till it blows past?"

"I never thought of that. I'll take a parlor car to Chicago and crib up in a suite at the Palmer House." She drained her glass.

It was the tot that broke the camel's back. Her speech slurred and gradually became incoherent—even more so than when she was speaking the Barbary dialect—and when she tried to get up from the bed for another trip to the decanter she fell over on her face and began snoring into the mattress. Beecher helped me rearrange her into a position less likely to suffocate her. As we were leaving, she started talking in her sleep, blubbering endearments to the Commodore.

Wednesday morning's *Call* carried another full-page advertisement, bordered once again by flags and the ferocious eagle:

WARNING!

This was followed by the same list of miscreants that had appeared in the previous call to arms, beginning with brothel keepers and ending with uncertified celestials. This time a roster of specific names had been added:

"Little Dick" Dugan, Murderer;

Tom Tulip, Procurer;

Ole Anderson, Shylock;

"Hugger-Mugger" Charlie, Counterfeiter;

Fat John, Chinaman:

Axel Hodge, Procurer;

Nan Feeny, Harlot.

If Seen within the Limits of the City of San Francisco after 8:00 P.M. on Friday, September 28th, you will be Arrested and Detained for Trial by the Citizens' New Vigilance Committee, and if found Guilty of Presenting an Endangerment to the Civil and Moral Welfare of this Community, will be Dealt With in the same Manner as Those who in the Past have ignored this Warning; and if Acquitted, will be Escorted beyond the City Limits by such Means as will be explained directly the Verdict is Rendered; and should you attempt to Return, will be Dealt With as the Rest.

Arrangements to be Made by

100 SUBSTANTIAL CITIZENS 100
Of the City and County of San Francisco.

I'd gone out early after a night of little sleep and many bedbugs, and came back to show the page to Beecher, who paused in the midst of pulling on his boots to read it. He handed it back.

"Fat John's going to have a hard time beating that Chinaman charge," he said.

"He's no worse off than the rest. The only reason Good-hue didn't come out and say he'd lynch them all is Older wouldn't print it. What did Nan ever do to endanger the civil and moral welfare of the community?"

"Forget to check her powder before she shot at Good-hue."

I threw the paper into a corner. "Put on that other boot. We're going to the post office."

"Expecting a letter?"

"Sending a wire. Maybe Judge Blackthorne knows someone in Sacramento."

21

DEPUTY U S MARSHAL PAGE MURDOCK
SAILORS REST
SAN FRANCISCO

CANNOT INTERFERE CIVIL MATTER STOP BAR-
BARY WILL HAVE TO TAKE ITS BITTERS AS
BEFORE STOP IF YOU HAVE FORGOTTEN YOUR
ORIGINAL MISSION ADVISE AND I WILL REFRESH
YOUR MEMORY

H A BLACKTHORNE

I gave the boy who brought the telegram an extra quarter to make up for snapping at him for the delay. He explained he'd had to stop and ask several people where to
find a place called the Sailor's Rest before he found someone who could tell him it was the Slop Chest he was looking for. To save time on both ends I'd sent my long wire to
Helena without coding it, then had wasted a precious hour
by respecting Nan Feeny's sensibilities when I told Blackthorne where to send his reply.

I crumpled the flimsy and threw it into a spittoon. It was
full, and brackish water slopped out onto the floor.

"'ey!" Axel Hodge smacked the bar with his iron ball.
Billy was in back using the outhouse.

I told Hodge to go to hell.

His white porcelains flashed in his beard. "That top don't scare me, mate. I been to Brisbane."

"Why is it necessary to tell everyone you meet you're from Brisbane? It's obvious every time you open your mouth."

He stopped smiling. "It wasn't for Nan, you'd be togged out in a pine shirt."

I let him have that as a gift. He was on Goodhue's list.

I couldn't decide what irked me more: the Judge's refusal to bend federal regulations he'd already bent so many times they looked like pump handles, his little barb about forgetting the reason I'd come to San Francisco, or that annoying "H. A." at the end. In composing telegrams he generally signed himself "Blackthorne," nothing else. The showy use of initials warned me he might be considering another run for Congress.

I looked around the room, at the bottles on the shelves, refilled so many times with liquor inferior to their labels that the labels themselves were blurred and peeling at the edges; at the pickled eggs in the mammoth jar at the end of the bar, with pickled flies floating on top of the brine; at the glum sailors perched on the footrail and the even glummer creature slumped in her faded satin and wilted feathers at Pinholster's table, taking advantage of the gambler's absence to rest her feet in their broken high-topped shoes. I wouldn't have given a cartwheel dollar for the lot, but it had been home for two weeks, and in less than sixty hours a mob of angry townies stoked up on rotgut and Revelations was due to storm through with axes and truncheons and flaming pitch and reduce it to smoking rubble for the second time. It wouldn't rise again from its ashes, because the woman who had rebuilt it the first time would be strung by her neck from the nearest structure left standing.

Hodge had been right. Nan Feeny had spared Beecher

and me both from his portable cannonball after the business with Tom Tulip, and whatever good turn the vigilantes might perform for the Union by destroying Wheelock's base of power, and with it the Sons of the Confederacy, I had to stop them for her sake.

I slung my empty glass down the bar, hard enough to send it aloft when it hit the first dent if Hodge hadn't scooped it up on the fly with his one hand. I'd wanted to break something. I'd violated the only rule I ever bothered to keep, and I'd done it twice, making friends with my partner and a woman I barely knew.

Pinholster came in carrying a thick white mug of steaming coffee from the restaurant down the street where he took breakfast, shooed out the bedraggled boardwalk queen, who snatched up her reticule, snarled something at him that even he didn't seem to understand, and hobbled out into the street. For the first time since we'd met, he gave me an eager glance and shoved the chair opposite away from the table with his foot. I was curious enough to take it.

"I'm a condemned man," he said brightly, removing a fresh pack of cards from his inside breast pocket. "Did you see the paper this morning?"

"I didn't see your name on Goodhue's list."

"Yes, I was a bit disappointed. It's stellar company. Little Dick Dugan's done more to support the employees at the city mortuary than the last three fires combined. Ole Anderson's a bigger crook than Jay Gould, and Hugger-Mugger Charlie hung out so much bad paper the first month after he got his printing press up and running, you couldn't pass a good banknote anywhere in town. Even a trusting soul like Nan wouldn't take anything lighter than government silver. It's the more general list I'm talking about. Gamblers and blacklegs are the same thing and they both found a place. How about a quick game of three-card monte before Friday? That's the traditional hangman's day, you know. Leave it to Old River Jordan to come up with that. It saved him having to spell it out and getting his advertisement rejected." He broke the seal on the deck and shuffled.

"I can see why it would cheer you up."

"In this work, the ace of spades can be the next card you turn. If you hit a losing streak and it lasts long enough you can starve, or freeze to death sleeping in an alley. If, on the other hand, you buck the tiger too long, someone's bound to think you're shaving the odds and blow a hole through you on a busted flush. Stay in one place past your time and the city fathers think you're driving down property values and deal a wild card to the legal firm of Tar and Feather, which isn't nearly as funny as the cartoons in the *Call* make out. I've seen it; I know what boiling tar can do to a man's complexion, not to mention the effect of twenty pounds of goose feathers on the function of breathing.

"Oh, the silk hats will make noise afterward, arrest some of the buggers, and maybe send three or four of the loudest to San Quentin for a year; they can make it fifty, and you're just as dead when they come out as when they went in. Let's say you survive all that. The smoky saloons get to your lungs or one day the barkeep miscalculates the ratio of branchwater to wood alcohol and you drop dead in the middle of the biggest pot you ever had going. Just plain living kills you at the end of the day. Why *not* a rope? Cut it." He smacked down the deck.

I held up a palm. He shrugged and cut three cards off the top.

"Don't mistake me for Jesus," he said. "It's a good life and I don't intend to let go of it at Goodhue's price. The first wave of Substantial Citizens through the door of my room above the Golden Dawn Laundry will come away with a bellyful of buckshot for their eagerness. After that

I'll choose my targets. My little Colt derringer holds two. Maybe they'll even give me the chance to reload. That ought to put a hole in the One Hundred. Find the three of hearts." He laid the cards facedown side by side on the table, sat back, and lifted his mug.

I left them there. "Doesn't anybody run anymore?"

"That's an alternative I hadn't considered. I'll think about it while you're picking."

"The only reason Nan is on Goodhue's list is she stopped him from drowning one of her waiter girls. He'll have a hard time working that into his campaign for the public good."

"Granted, he went too far there. The State of California may even issue a bill of indictment before someone gets around to cutting her down. The good founder of the First Eden Infantry was among the conspirators named in the general arrest warrant after Casey and Cora were lynched at Fort Gunnybags. The charges lifted like morning fog. The cards are getting stale."

"What's the bet?"

"There isn't one. I'm just warming up the deck."

I watched him pulling at his shaggy moustache. "Where are you from?"

"I was born in Chicago and spent my life there, excluding my time in the navy. I'd flattered myself I'd lost the accent."

"You still lean a little heavy on your *R*'s. How long have you been here?"

"Six months."

I must have lost my poker face. He did, too; his eyes glittered like a greenhorn's over a king-high straight.

"How does a man who spends all his time at this table find out so much about Barbary in six months?"

"I listen. I watch. You know the process as well as I do. You can't talk all the time and concentrate on the game, and you can't win if you never raise your eyes from your hand. Three of hearts." He tapped the table.

"I don't feel like playing."

"Do me a favor. If you like, you can call it the pathetic request of a doomed fellow traveler."

"You're forgetting I can't be bluffed. You don't have any intention of letting Goodhue's men drag you out and string you up, with or without the shotgun and derringer."

"I wasn't referring to that. I have a lesion. Four doctors have told me I have a year left. Three, if I stay out of saloons. Which means I'll be gone with next year's leaves. Four of a kind beats a full house."

I studied his long, unshaven face for tells. Nothing there. "I'm still waiting for my answer," I said. "A man doesn't pick up as much as you in so short a time without asking a lot of questions of a lot of people. I've known gamblers to be many things, but curious isn't one. Who are you?"

"Pick a card. Please."

I grabbed one without looking at it and turned it over. It was the three of hearts. There was something underneath it. I turned over the other two. They were each the three of hearts, and each had concealed something. I looked at Pinholster.

He made an apologetic shrug. "I couldn't be sure you'd pick the right one."

I looked down again to see if anything had changed. Nothing had. Three pasteboard rectangles lay in a row on the table, much smaller than the playing cards he'd placed atop them. Each was engraved with the all-seeing eye of the Pinkerton National Detective Agency.

PART FOUR

The Vigilantes

22

"What's your real name?" I asked.

"Pinholster. Chicago discourages agents from using pseudonyms during undercover work. Answering to an invented name takes practice, and there's always the chance someone who knows you will see you and call out your name in public. As a matter of fact, I haven't told anyone a thing that wasn't true since I've been here. We're instructed not to unless absolutely necessary. If, for example, someone asks me if I work for Pinkerton, I'm permitted to dissemble."

We were speaking low and playing blackjack for the benefit of anyone watching. I said, "What about that lesion?"

"True as well, unfortunately. It's the reason I volunteered for this assignment. For obvious reasons, the local office didn't want to use one of its own operatives, and no less an authority than Oscar Wilde has declared that San Francisco has all the attractions of the next world. It seemed an excellent opportunity to find out what's in store for me."

"Who taught you to gamble?"

"My sainted father. He threw in his hand when a boiler blew up on the Ohio River near Evansville in eighteen sixty. Surviving passengers swore he was holding three aces with the likelihood of another bullet in the hole. The agency favors employing people from a variety of backgrounds. Who better to burrow his way into Barbary than a fellow who knows the history of the four kings?" He dealt himself twenty-one and scooped up the ante.

"What's the assignment?"

"A soap manufacturer in Exeter, England, died late last year, leaving an estate of seven hundred fifty thousand pounds, with a thousand set aside for an illegitimate son whom no one else in the family was aware existed. The young man was the product of a dalliance with a bookkeeper, who took ship to America with the infant twenty-seven years ago. The fare was a gift from the soap tycoon in return for the woman's discretion. The family cannot claim its inheritance until the bastard surfaces for his part, or until evidence of a good faith effort to locate him is submitted to Her Majesty's court.

"The New York office traced the mother to the charity ward of a hospital in Brooklyn, where she died of an indelicate disease in sixty-three. Circumstances had evidently obliged her to walk the Streets of Gold for victuals and lodging for her and her son. The child was placed in an orphanage, whose records were spotty, but agents managed to find a woman named Cruddup, who with her late husband had adopted the boy. She was uncooperative, but persistence and the bribe of a ton of coal—the interview took place in February—persuaded her to report that the boy, whose name was Seymour, had run away at age fourteen, after attempting to burn down the flat where the family lived. It was not his first attempt. Mr. Cruddup had been driven to flog him with his belt when he caught him pouring kerosene on a pile of clothes and old newspapers in the middle of the kitchen."

"Did she say what he looked like?"

"She said he was a 'funny-looking little monkey.' It wasn't helpful, and the inducement of another ton of coal did not succeed in prolonging the interview. I could have told them that. What possible use could one widow have for two tons of coal? One is sufficient to see the average household through an Eastern winter." He paused to rake in another pot; talking and concentrating on the cards seemed to present no difficulty.

He went on. "County records list a Seymour Cruddup, sixteen, in juvenile detention for nine months ending in sixty-six on two counts of arson, but none of the officials currently serving were there at the time, and there was no description on file. We have no description to date. He vanishes then, possibly committing additional conflagratory depredations under an assumed name, until Seymour Cruddup resurfaces on the employee manifest of the cargo ship *Bertha Day,* which left New York Harbor in eighty-one, rounded the Horn, and docked in San Francisco in January of last year."

"The ship's officers must have been able to give you a description."

"One would think that would be the case, but we shall never know. The *Bertha Day* went down somewhere in the Horse Latitudes during a storm last November with all aboard, including the officers who had served with her captain for two years. The rest of Cruddup's shipmates are scattered throughout both hemispheres."

"And so the trail ends there."

"So far as can be documented. However, I have a theory, which I've been working on, apart from the occasional inside straight, since March."

I let him take another hand while I waited. Figuring out what all this had to do with me helped kill time while Barbary was getting ready to blow itself apart.

"Criminals rarely change their lays," he said. "They're simple animals, and once they manage to work out a system that entertains and supports them, they tend to cleave to it unto death or the penitentiary. Fire appears to be young Mr. Cruddup's vehicle of choice, and an inflammable city like San Francisco is the ideal place in which to pedal it. The leap from there is not too great to the one man who can claim responsibility for most of the celebrated fires not attributable to chance."

"Sid the Spunk."

He nodded; the tutor abundantly pleased with his charge. "The young man has something of the poet in him. 'Spunk,' you cannot have failed to determine, is the popular argot for 'match' on the streets hereabouts, and 'Seymour the Spunk,' while equally alliterative, doesn't quite answer. With all these Sydney Ducks about, a fellow with origins in working-class England, reared by a cockney mother, would slide quite nicely in among the many transplanted Brits in this exotic place. Whether he christened himself or the monager was visited upon him by his admiring colleagues is beside the point. Admittedly, it's a long guess, but I'm convinced it's the right one. A good gambler plays the percentages; a great gambler proceeds upon instinct. As does a great detective. I'm a twenty-year man with Pinkerton. The old man is capricious, but he doesn't hold with deadwood."

"Congratulations. Why aren't you on your way back to Chicago? Sid the Spunk is dead."

"It's a point, and the conventional wisdom supports it. In the absence of a corpse, I'm not prepared to enter the conspiracy. Which brings me to why I'm taking your money. Blackjack again, old fellow. You must have angered the lords of chance today." He laid down two tens and an ace.

"I'll get it back when my luck changes."

"I shan't live that long. I hardly need explain that playing cards is a skill. You're good, but you haven't had my opportunity for practice. When I order breakfast, I am calculating the odds against having my eggs prepared precisely the way I request; and so the day goes, until I retire and dream of percentages. Just now, the law of averages supports Sid the Spunk's extinction, either on the night the Slop Chest burned down by his hand or shortly thereafter. Before that he was a legendary character in a place that does not want for them; a mysterious figure whom no one I've interviewed admits to having met face to face. An example is to be made through a destruction of property; the word reaches Sid; and the thing is done, after which the Spunk is doused and gone, to flare up again elsewhere when another example is required. The steep decline in the arson statistics directly the Slop Chest was put to the torch strongly suggests the Spunk was spent, possibly to prevent him from peaching to the authorities should he be apprehended later."

"It's a sound bet," I said. "I wouldn't take it up."

"You'd be wise not to. However, I'm persuaded to do so, by a piece of intelligence that recently came my way from the direction of Captain Dan's own firehouse."

He'd dealt me two cards, one up, one down. I left them.

"Since you're not a blind better, I'll assume the game is finished." He gathered it in, shuffled the deck, and placed it on his side of the table. "The alarm was delayed going into the firehouse. That was what was reported in the *Call*, and the veracity of a free press is above question. In any case, by the time the brigade reached the scene, the building was engulfed, and there was no help for it but to extinguish the blaze before it spread through the neighborhood. The volunteer I spoke to was not in the firehouse when the alarm came in, but came running toward the flames and smoke from the establishment across the street, where he had been taking his leisure with a woman of flexible reputation. I don't mind telling you I lost a substantial amount of money to the fellow in the course of winning his confidence, nor that it was the hardest work I've ever done, because he was an abomination with cards in his hands. You aren't the only man in this city who has cheated against himself, though I'll take an oath there aren't three."

"Play your card." I was losing patience with him, lesion or no.

"The young man swore he saw two men carrying a body away from the blazing building; which would signify nothing, except no casualties were reported in the fire, in the columns of the *Call* or anywhere else. I quite believed the fellow, for what would he gain from a lie? He already had most of my money."

"You think Sid died in the fire?"

"With the possible exceptions of a cannon loose aboard a ship at sea and the heart of a woman, nothing is less predictable nor more capricious than a fire in full blossom. Even an experienced arsonist, lingering to ensure the success of his enterprise, can find himself standing in the wrong place when a beam falls or a chimney collapses. Do I think Sid died in the fire? I have serious doubts. Why should anyone risk the victim's fate removing a corpse from the scene? Even money says he survived; or in any event that he did not expire on the site. He was injured, possibly fatally, but if so his condition was not so obvious his rescuers didn't think him worth saving. Was it Sid the Spunk? A steeper bet, perhaps, but not so steep I wouldn't hazard the odds. The man's very existence is a secret. Life is cheap in Barbary; one more struck down is unworthy of even a paragraph on the same page with the ships' arrivals. A life *saved* is a rarer thing altogether, and even a naysayer like Fremont Older could hardly be expected not to keep the details alive through three editions. Who but the man responsible for the fire could expect to remain invisible under the circumstances? Will you take the bet?"

I said, "I haven't seen your hole card."

"It's a common one hereabouts; but even a deuce can claim a pot if you know how to play it. My fire volunteer insisted the two men he saw carrying away the injured party were Chinese."

I don't know how long I sat there without moving or speaking. It was long enough I thought I might be attracting the attention of others, who would wonder why two men were sitting at a gaming table with a deck of cards sitting between them undisturbed. Pinholster thought so, too. He swept up the deck and began shuffling.

I anted, not bothering to look whether I was laying down a dollar chip or a twenty. "Your man could have misinterpreted what he saw. For all he knows, he was looking at two men carrying away a drunken friend."

"It's possible. It's probable." He dealt. "It's probable I don't have blackjack on this ten-spot. The hole card would have to be an ace, which is a chance of one in forty-six. What would you bet?"

I folded my hands on top of my cards. I hadn't even looked at what I had in the hole.

He turned his up. It was a seven.

"Too bad," he said, gathering in the chips. "However, cards are not life; and life in Barbary is not life anywhere else on earth. Sid the Spunk lives, and may even now be mastering the mystery of chopsticks in Chinatown."

"What if he does? That's good for you, but nothing to me. Why even bring it up?"

"It's nothing to me as the situation stands. I'm an undercover man, the hole card in this game, and as we've just seen, the hole does not always conceal the solution. I'm nailed to this table, whereas a face card such as yourself is free to act. I can't go haring into Little China, demanding answers and evidence. You can; you have, and the fact that you're here now proves you're the straight flush in this game."

"You don't have the bank to offer. Why should I sit in for you?"

"I can see you've never played bridge. No patience with partners." He fanned the cards out in a straight line, flicked one with a glossy nail, and flipped them all back the other way so that the suits showed. "You haven't seen my bank. I know where the Sons of the Confederacy are holding their next meeting."

"So does everyone in town. No one knows when."

He looked at me. His face didn't slip.

I sat back. "Oh."

He swept up the cards, reshuffled, and laid out two hands of bridge. "I'll teach you the basics. It's a civilized game, unknown in Barbary. Keep your cards high and your voice low."

23

The fog was rolling out to sea at midmorning, swept as by a broom made entirely of sunshine. An old man, his face burned red over several sandy layers of brown, paused in the midst of slitting open the silver belly of a fish to point with his serrated knife toward the end of the pier, where even as I looked the fog slid away from the figure standing with arms folded atop a piling. I went out there and stuck my hands in my pockets.

"Busy harbor," I said.

Beecher kept his eyes on the horizon, which was a spired scape of masts and complex rigging, overhung by smudges of black smoke from the stacks of the steamers, of which there were getting to be more than square-riggers. In a few years there wouldn't be a sail visible between Japan and the California coast.

"This ain't nothing," he said. "You ought to see Galveston when the cotton's in."

"I didn't know you got down that far."

He looked up at me from under the brim of his hat and smiled. The smile wasn't for me.

"I worked on a packet boat one whole summer. Left home in Louisiana at twelve and didn't look back. Looking forward, that's the spooky part."

"How'd you end up in Washington?"

"Plenty of sail and not much draw. The wind blowed

north after I mustered out of the Tenth. I was headed for Vancouver, but I dropped anchor when I met Belinda. That's when I went to work for Mr. J. J. Hill."

"Belinda, that's your wife?"

"Was last time I seen her. I can't answer as to now."

"Ever think about going back?"

"Only every day." He seemed to remember he had a cigarette smoldering between his fingers. He drew on it and snapped it out over the water. "How'd you find me?"

"Nan said you like to stroll down this way. I didn't know you two had gotten so close."

"Someone's got to smoke them cigars. They won't last forever."

A seagull landed on the next piling and began cleaning itself with its hooked beak. Beecher lit another cigarette and snapped the match at the bird, which flapped its wings but didn't take off. It resumed its search for lice.

"Bastards ain't afraid of man or fish," he said. "Feed on garbage and carcasses. I reckon they find their share here."

"Of what, garbage or carcasses?"

"Both. Any animal that won't run or fly from a man is just waiting its time till it can pick at his flesh. I seen 'em crawling like rats all over a dead Mexican in Galveston. Even a buzzard kills sometimes, just to keep its hand in. Not these bastards. They even stink like bad meat."

He straightened suddenly, drew the Le Mat, and fired a shotgun round at the gull. It exploded in a cloud of feathers and fell over the side of the pier.

My ears rang. "I see you've been taking practice. That why you come down here?"

"I come for the air." He plucked out the spent shell and replaced it with a loaded one from his coat pocket. His fingers shook a little. "Where there's sea air, there's gulls. You can take ship clear out into the middle of the ocean and there they are. Where do they roost?"

I changed the subject. I didn't think we were talking about seagulls anyway. "I just played a few hands with Pinholster."

"How much you lose this time?" He belted the pistol.

"I broke even."

I told him about Sid the Spunk and the next meeting of the Sons of the Confederacy. He refolded his arms on top of the piling.

"That's tomorrow night. They're carving it close with Owen Goodhue." He drew on the cigarette. "You reckon he's still in Chinatown?"

"Sid? He's that or dead, if he didn't quit town altogether. According to Pinholster there hasn't been a suspicious fire in Barbary since he put the match to the Slop Chest."

"Well, I doubt he left town. You heard what Wheelock said. They keep coming back."

"I wouldn't set much store by anything Captain Dan says."

"He's a politician through and through. You wonder why he bothers with the baby rebels."

"Barbary's a cesspool. All the scum in the country drains into it sooner or later. That's his power base. He'll do what he can to protect it."

"Reckon he'll send his Hoodlums after Goodhue?"

I shook my head. "Vigilantes aren't cattle, for all they look it when they're in full stampede. You can't turn them by just picking off the leaders. Some other fool with more sand than sense will step in and plug the hole. Same thing with gulls." I jerked my chin toward a piling farther down, where a fresh bird had just landed.

He glared at it. "What you fixing to do about Sid the Spunk?"

"Well, I'm not 'haring into Chinatown, demanding answers and evidence.' Pinholster's been reading dime novels. Luck's the only reason you and I didn't come out carrying our heads the first time. I came down here hoping you'd have an idea."

He pushed himself away from the piling and took out the pistol. I stepped back automatically, removing myself from the line of fire. He wasn't looking at the seagull, however. He was facing the opposite end of the pier.

I drew the Deane-Adams as I turned. Three Chinese were standing at the end, dressed identically in long dark coats, with slouch hats drawn down over their foreheads. When they saw our weapons, the two on the ends threw open their coats and raised a pair of shotguns with the barrels cut back almost as far as the forepieces. The hammers clicked sharply in the damp air.

"Steady." I almost whispered.

There wasn't another human in sight on one of the busiest waterfronts in the world. The windows of the brick warehouses looming behind the Chinese were blank and blind. Even the fisherman who had pointed Beecher out to me had slipped away, as quietly as the tide. The gull made a noise like a rusty shutter and flapped away.

Only the lower halves of the three Asiatic faces were visible beneath the shadows of their hat brims. The sharp checkbones, pointed chins, and straight mouths of the armed pair looked as much alike as Orientals were said to by Occidentals who never bothered to look twice. I was pretty sure they were brothers, maybe twins. The shotguns looked as if the recoil would shatter the fine bones in their slender wrists when the triggers were tripped. Of course it wouldn't. It hadn't all the other times, and the way the men held them said there had been plenty of those.

Beecher and I were standing at the end of the pier, with nothing behind us but the Pacific Ocean and nothing below us but undertow and the bones of others who had stood there before us. The only way off was through the three men standing on the landward end. I cocked the five-shot.

Beecher had already drawn back the hammer on his Confederate piece.

"The harmbor is a dangerous mplace."

The Chinese who spoke stood in the center, a step back from his companions. He was taller and thinner, and his speech was impaired by a deep cleft in his upper lip. In Western dress he looked more like a rangy alley cat than the pampered, well-brushed variety he had resembled inside his tearoom at the White Peacock. He stood with his hands at his sides.

I wet my lips. The moisture evaporated from them as soon as I finished. "Yes. Men have been known to slip and stab themselves to death."

F'an Chu'an—I still couldn't think of him as "Fat John," even in those clothes and this far outside Chinatown—reached up and pinched his upper lip between thumb and forefinger. I'd seen him do that before, to aid him in his English pronunciation.

"I'm told you seek the man called Sid the Spunk."

He made a slight motion with his other hand. The shotguns vanished beneath the long coats.

We lowered our revolvers. Beecher spat out his cigarette. It hissed when it struck the wet boards at our feet.

24

"We can talk in here," F'an Chu'an said. "I have an arrangement with the Six Companies."

We had walked from the pier to one of the brick-box warehouses that faced the harbor like a medieval redoubt, where he'd produced a ring of keys from a coat pocket, sprung a padlock, and let us in through a side door. Inside, sunlight fell in through high windows and lay dustily on rolls of material wrapped in brown burlap and stacked to the rafters thirty feet above our heads. The air was a haze of moth powder. From here, the bolts of silk, broadcloth, wool flannel, jute, and damask would be carried by wagon to dozens of basements where Chinese immigrants bent over needles and treadle sewing machines, making dresses and suits of clothes for catalogue merchants to sell to bookkeepers in New York, shopgirls in Chicago, and farm wives in Lincoln, Nebraska: more than a million dollars' of dry goods in that one building, and not a watchman in sight. That would have taken some arranging. There were birds' nests in the rafters, and probably a couple of dozen bats suspended beneath, waiting to unfold themselves at nightfall and thread their way outside through gaps no bigger around than a man's finger. Our footsteps rang on the broad floor planks running the length of the broad aisles that separated the stacks. F'an Chu'an's bodyguards had lowered the hammers on their shotguns and Beecher and I had put away our pistols.

"I apologize for the detestable presence of my escort," he said, pinching his lip. "Their protection is necessary whenever I venture beyond Sacramento Street."

Beecher said, "They look like knickknacks."

"They are my cousins, Shau Wing and Shau Chan. They have been with me since Hong Kong."

"Did you smuggle them in wrapped in a rug?" I asked.

He didn't answer. He might not have understood. I wouldn't have taken Pinholster's odds he hadn't.

"The Suey Sing Tong is one of the oldest in America," F'an Chu'an said. "It was organized in the gold fields in order to protect Chinese mine workers from resentful Westerners. It soon became necessary to protect them from other Chinese as well. The bandit tradition in the country of my birth extends back to before the first dynasty.

"From there our numbers spread to railroad camps, laundries, and cigar manufactories. The tong is young, but it is schooled in the ancient ways of combat. They include rules of behavior, which were regrettably ignored by the late Yee Yung Hay when his perfidy was exposed. Once again I ask your forgiveness." He bowed. The two Shaus bracing him remained as motionless as porcelain figures; Beecher had a good eye, as well as a gift for description.

I said, "Your father's sword took care of that. What became of the body, by the way? Being accessories after the fact, we ought to know."

"Your curiosity is perhaps reckless. Knowledge is often fatal here. There is a storm drain beneath the White Peacock, which leads to the bay. It was Shau Wing's idea to construct a shaft connecting to it, shortly after we opened for business. Waste disposal is a problem in Chinatown, but not at the White Peacock."

"If you'd used it to get rid of Horatio Flinders, today's situation might be different."

He bowed again. "With respect, Deputy Mur Dok, it was you who sent Deputy Bee Chu'r for the police."

"I know. Every now and then that star gets heavy in my pocket. Two unreported killings in one night and I wouldn't have been able to lift it."

"Yin and Yang."

That was one I didn't understand, but I let it float past. "How did you find out I'm looking for Sid the Spunk?"

"I have ears in many places."

I tried to remember who was in the saloon when I was talking with Pinholster. Most of them were strangers. You can lower your voice almost to a thought and still be overheard by an experienced eavesdropper.

I said, "I thought of you right off, when I heard a man who might have been Sid was carried away from the fire at the Slop Chest by two Chinese. How many people in Barbary know you studied medicine in Hong Kong?"

"There are few secrets here. Even death cannot conceal them utterly. It grieves me to report that Sid the Spunk is dead."

"You're not the first who's told me that. A lot of people seem to want to think he's a corpse. I wouldn't have expected a common Hoodlum to attract so much interest."

"I wish they were wrong. Everything possible was done to deliver him from his fate. I am a deplorable novice, and what skills I once had have withered through disuse. The injury was too great, and there was not time to put him in more competent hands."

Beecher spoke up. "The storm drain?"

F'an Chu'an affected to have noticed him for the first time. The class system that had produced the tong leader was older than ours by a thousand years.

"It was unfortunately the only recourse. The bay accepts without judging."

"I got to wonder how the ships make it in and out for all them bones."

"Who brought him to you?" I asked. "The Shaus?"

"They are never far from my side. I will not profane your ears with the names of the two wretches who came upon him and sought to win my favor by taking him to the White Peacock. They are filth beneath your feet."

He might have meant that literally.

"Why would they think you'd be happy to treat him? One Spunk more or less wouldn't make much difference here."

F'an Chu'an stopped pinching his lip. He was thinking. "What I say next must not leave this mbuild"—he pinched—"this building. Even the tong is only permitted to exist under certain conditions."

"Should I swear on my life?"

He might have smiled. It was hard to tell with his hand in front of his mouth. He said something in Chinese to the men at his side. One of them made a noise like a terrier barking and replied.

"Shau Chan says, 'The white devil is not without humor.' That is an unsatisfactory translation. I speak Mandarin, Szechuan, and Cantonese, but the delicate points of English are as a dragon."

I said his English was fine. It had improved since our last meeting. Judge Blackthorne had told me never to trust a man who pretended to be more ignorant than he was.

"I am a wicked man," he said. "I have slain innocent men, I have stolen bread from the starving, I have lain with women who were the property of other men. I poison my people for money. I offer no apologies for the path I have chosen. I submit, however, that I am not the tenth part of the nameless ogre who led the Hop Sing Tong since before I came. This beast of whom I speak lay with the virgin sister of Lem Tin, my most loyal lieutenant, and sold her into slavery, under whose torment she sickened and died. When Lem Tin went to him for vengeance, the ogre had his heart cut out of his living breast and sent to me wrapped with silk in a jade box. This was an intolerable insult.

"I requested a meeting with the leaders of all the tongs to protest the ogre's action and to call for his trial and punishment. I told them Lem Tin was my friend, closer to me than a brother, that he had been disgraced, and was within his rights under tong law to challenge the ogre. The other leaders conferred and reached the decision that the ogre behaved permissibly in the interest of preserving his life. I was asked to accept this conclusion and to offer the ogre my friendship. This I did, along with a pledge upon the bones of my father that I would not be the one to violate the accord. Fifteen minutes after it began, the meeting was adjourned, and the leaders went to the Rising Star Club to celebrate the peace they had made. The ogre was among them. I was not. That decision is the reason I stand before you this day."

The air in the warehouse felt clammy, in spite of the strong sunlight. I fought off a shudder. The men flanking F'an Chu'an would no doubt have interpreted it as a sign of weakness.

"There was a fire," F'an Chu'an said. "Most regrettable in this fragile place. It started, said the men who fought it, in the cellar, upon the ground floor, and atop the roof of the Rising Star Club, within minutes. The leaders of the Gee Kung and the Kwong Dock Tongs burned to death on their divans, unable to stir from their black dreams. Fong Jung of the Soo Yop escaped the flames, but the smoke destroyed his lungs and he returned to China to die in the land of his ancestors. The ogre who led the Hop Sings, Lem Tin's assassin and the defiler of his sister, was driven by the smoke and heat to leap from a window upon the second story. He shattered his spine and has not left his bed from that day to this.

"The gods are often indiscriminate. Three other leaders survived without injury. They joined the others' successors in accusing me of starting the fire. I was tried and would have been executed under tong law but for fifteen men of respect who came forward to swear that from the time I left the meeting until the alarm was raised, I could be seen casting lots in the White Peacock. I was exonerated."

At this point F'an Chu'an made a little bow, as if Beecher and I were the ones who'd acquitted him. The cat's smile was in place.

I said, "Did anyone happen to ask where Sid the Spunk was when the fire broke out?"

"His name was not mentioned during the proceedings. Chinatown is a country apart from greater San Francisco. He is not widely known within its boundaries. I remind you that we converse in confidence. It is not necessary to explain by what avenue we found each other. Perhaps you will think of him with charity when I say that he would not accept payment for his services. When I declared that I had no wish to chain myself in his debt, he said that the obligation was his, to one who had been close to him and who had been forced into degradation also. He would say nothing else beyond the fact that Lem Tin's sister was not unique in her experience. He would not abandon this position, and having come but recently from that infamous meeting, I lacked the strength of will to turn aside his offer. Do you wonder still why I did not hesitate to exhaust my poor skills on his behalf when he was brought to me later, broken and burned?"

I shook my head. "What about the bones of your father?"

"It is my belief they lay where they were buried."

I searched his face for amusement, or contempt, or some other sign that the words he spoke were connected to what he was thinking. I gave it up as a bad job. "Why risk leaving Chinatown to tell me, with your name on Owen Goodhue's list?"

"For that, you have Lee Yung Hay to thank. You cannot know the extent of the catastrophe had his activities in Barbary become known generally."

"I'd have thought saving our lives discharged that debt," I said.

"You force me to contradict you; a necessity I find most painful. My debt was increased by the act. In the country of my birth, to spare a man's life is to make that life one's own, with all the responsibilities that entails. When I learned of your interest in Sid the Spunk, I saw the opportunity to relieve myself of the burden. I could not guarantee your safety should your natural instincts lead you across Sacramento Street. That you did so once and survived was more fortunate than you know. I consider that you and I stand upon equal ground when I warn you that to venture again into Chinatown will be to resign yourself to merciless fate."

This time I said it. "The storm drain?"

"The bay accepts," he repeated, "without judging."

Beecher said, "I reckon we're even."

"That is my belief."

F'an Chu'an glanced from side to side. The Shaus stirred and the three of them headed toward the door. Beecher and I followed them out. F'an Chu'an fixed the padlock in place and left us without a word. Seconds later he and his companions disappeared around the corner of the warehouse. Later I wasn't sure I hadn't dreamed the whole thing.

25

On the last night but one for Barbary, Beecher and I set out with determination to get as drunk as we could and still find our way home to the Slop Chest.

Although the second part was problematic, the first was a dream easily obtainable anywhere within thirty blocks of our bug-infested berths. There were upwards of three thousand aboveboard drinking establishments in the City of San Francisco, most of them on the shady side of Nob Hill, and Nan Feeny estimated that an additional two thousand operated without licenses. These "blind tigers" sold home-brewed beer, whiskey cut with creek water—Beecher found part of a crawdad floating in his glass the first place we stopped—and turpentine laced with brown sugar to give it the color and approximate flavor of rye; the sightless beggars who tapped their way along the boardwalks and sat in doorways rattling the coins in their cups hadn't all lost their eyes at Shiloh, despite the signs around their necks identifying them as crippled veterans. An article in Fremont Older's *Call* placed the annual income from the local sale of intoxicants above ten million dollars, roughly three times what Congress shelled out to outfit the U.S. Army. Witnessed at first hand, it looked like more.

"I forget." Beecher looked up blearily from a glass recently evacuated of freshwater life. "Is this a dive, a bagnio, or a deadfall?"

I looked around. We were in the cellar of a warehouse stacked with barrels of sorghum, with greenwood tables and benches crowded to one side to make room for dancing. A glum-faced fiddler and a pianist with an eyepatch made a respectable job out of "Cotton-Eyed Joe" for the benefit of sailors, miners, and probable Hoodlums who were stepping on the toes of female employees of the establishment in short skirts and provocative blouses. I'd heard the blouses were a suggestion contributed by the police, who had raided the cellar a month or two earlier for parading the women around with nothing above the waist. I tried to remember where I'd been a month or two earlier and decided that wherever it was, it didn't compare.

"I think it's a dance hall," I said.

There was a brief interlude when one of a pair of customers who had each seized an arm of the same hostess smashed a bottle on the edge of the bar and threatened his rival with the jagged end. A bartender resolved the situation by slamming two feet of loaded billiard cue across the skull of the unarmed man, who then dropped out of the competition. The man with the broken bottle blinked, then discarded his weapon and dragged the young lady out onto the dance floor as the musicians struck up something lively.

"Reckon I'm drunker than I knew," Beecher said. "Looked to me like the barkeep hit the wrong man."

"He was closer. It came out the same either way."

"Everything's backwards here. I don't get out soon I'm going to start thinking this is the way the world works."

"It *is* the way the world works. You and I get paid to spin it the other way."

"Speak for yourself. I ain't seen so much as a nickel since we left Gold Creek."

I got out my poke, opened it under the table, and passed a few banknotes across his knees. "That's as much as I can spare. I wired Judge Blackthorne for expenses, but the hinges on his safe need oiling. You'd think it came out of his own pocket."

"It did, if he owns property."

"He owns twenty linen shirts, a dozen frock coats, and a bunch of books by a fellow named Blackstone. Whatever else he had burned with his chambers. It wasn't much. The grateful citizens of Helena gave him the house he lives in with his wife in return for defending civilization. I don't know how much the federals pay him, but he doesn't spend any of it. He's the property of the U.S. government, just like that monument they're building to George Washington."

"You feel that way, why don't you quit?"

"He's the best man I ever worked for."

"That's the way I feel about Mr. Hill; not that we ever met or that he wouldn't throw me downstairs if I showed up in his office." He gave me one of his rare grins with the cigarette he was lighting stuck between his teeth. Then he looked troubled. "Ain't one of us ought to stay sober? How we going to stand behind each other's back if we can't tell it from the front?"

"Take a look around. Shantytown's got a death sentence hanging over it. All the Hoodlums and cutthroats are too busy trying to have a good time while they still can to bother with two law dogs from out of town. I don't know about you, but I think we've earned a holiday."

"This got anything to do with Sid the Spunk being dead?"

"Don't be a jackass. Sid isn't dead."

Just then one of the dancing girls let out a stream of language that would have curled the edges of a slate roof and swung into a pirouette with nine inches of curved steel sticking out of her dainty fist. The brute she was dancing with saved his throat by stumbling and falling. As it was, the blade took off the top of his right ear. Bright blood arced out, ruining the costumes of two other dancers who were trying to get out of the way. The bouncer, a short, stocky albino with too much muscle bunched around his neck to accommodate a collar, sprang away from the wall, got hold of the woman's knife arm, twisted it behind her back, and hauled her off the floor with both satin-shod feet kicking. The bartender who had broken up the other fight threw a towel at the man on the floor, who jammed it against his lacerated ear. The other bartender, small and wiry in an apron that brushed his shoe tops, came out from behind the bar with a mop to clean up the carnage. Another brute built along the same lines as his friend helped the injured man to his feet and escorted him outside, the towel still held in place and staining bright maroon.

All this took place in about twenty seconds. The staff had rehearsed all the actions many times before, and even the two civilians had been through enough similar scrapes to take themselves out of the action without stopping to file a protest.

"Let's move on." I got up and slapped a dollar on the table to take care of the drinks. Beecher followed.

On the boardwalk in front of the dance hall, I put a hand on his arm. "Wait a minute."

The bleeding brute and his companion were standing in the middle of the street, sunk in mud to their insteps. The man holding the towel to the side of his head made a violent gesture with his free hand. They were shouting over each other's words. Other pedestrians, accustomed to such scenes, crossed the street on either side of the pair without pausing or even turning their heads. In Barbary, non-involvement wasn't just a policy; it was a law of survival.

The two men closed suddenly, as if embracing. They parted, and the man holding the bloody towel turned and came back toward the dance hall, leaving his friend standing in the street with his hands hanging empty at his sides. He looked after his departing companion, then shook his head, turned, and waded off through the mud toward the other side of the street.

I saw the squat-barreled pistol in the other man's hand as he mounted the boardwalk. I nudged Beecher and we parted to clear his path to the door. I let him pass, then drew the Deane-Adams, spun it butt-forward, and tapped him firmly on the back of the head with the backstrap. His knees bent, the short pistol clunked to the boardwalk, and I kicked it into the street, where the mud sucked it under in less than a second. It was out of sight before the man hit the ground.

"Slicker'n snot," said Beecher as we walked away. "I thought you was fixing to put a hole in him."

"It seemed drastic just for stepping on a girl's foot." I inspected the revolver for damage to the frame and stuck it back in its holster.

"How'd you know he'd come back heeled?"

"Wouldn't you, for an ear?"

Gunshots rattled a street or two over, traveling swiftly on the fog drifting in from the harbor.

Beecher said, "You're dead on about this place. Like a kid getting in his licks before someone boxes his ears."

"I saw it in Abilene, just before the city fathers voted to ban the cattle outfits from town. It's like a fever."

"You deputied Wild Bill?"

"It was after his time. Part of the hell being raised was mine. I was punching cows then. I hadn't got the call yet."

He shook his head. "We ain't the same, you and me. I'll have had my life's portion of hell after we leave here. From here on in, I'm polishing spittoons and liking it."

"Who for, J. J. Hill?"

"No, sir. For the first hotel or saloon I come to in Spokane that's hiring. Or some other town, if Belinda won't have me. I've had itchy feet since I left Louisiana. I want to see what it's like to stay put for forty or fifty years."

"You're a smart man. I wasn't too sure when you took me up on this offer."

"I didn't exactly have a choice."

"You could have left that chair standing where it was in that caboose."

He said nothing for several yards. I had the impression he was wishing he'd chosen differently.

When he spoke, however, it was to introduce a different subject. "You really think Sid the Spunk's alive?"

"Whenever someone goes out of his way to tell me something, my policy is it's a lie. F'an Chu'an owes Sid more than he owes me, and a debt to a dead man isn't worth paying. Also, a corpse doesn't need protecting."

"What about Pinholster? He lie, too?"

"No reason. His man saw what he said. Our Chinese friend is modest. He's a better doctor than he made out. He pulled Sid through, and he's either hiding him in Chinatown or covering up his tracks."

"Sid might of quit Frisco."

"Then there'd be no reason to convince us he's dead."

"We fixing to go on looking for him?"

"That's Pinholster's cradle. Let him rock it. Judge Blackthorne already thinks we're off chasing rabbits."

"Not tonight, though."

"Not tonight. Tonight we're getting drunk."

We entered a place called the Slaughterhouse, on the southern end of Battle Row. There, the patrons were gathered around a little platform built for musicians, where a red-bearded Irishman with leather lungs was auctioning off a drunken naked girl. Her ribs showed and she had tiny breasts, but there were no visible scars and the bidding was up to fifty dollars. Each new bid was louder than the one before.

Beecher leaned in close and shouted in my ear. "I thought this ended in sixty-three."

"I don't think it's a full sale," I shouted back. "Just an overnight rental."

The whiskey was a little better than turpentine, although it might have been useful in loosening rusty bolts. It burned furrows down our throats and boiled in our stomachs. A balloon opened in my head, making sounds echo and multiplying everything I looked at. The skinny girl went to a sailor for sixty-two-fifty and was replaced on the platform by three fat girls, or maybe it was just one, who was quickly stripped with some assistance on her part, and upon whom the bidding soared rapidly; the air outside was nippy and there's nothing like cuddling up to a heap of naked flesh on a cold night. A couple of sailors got into a fistfight over a fifty-cent raise, and part of the audience peeled away to form a circle around the brawlers. No attempt was made on the part of the establishment to separate them.

"Should we take a hand?" Beecher asked.

"I'll put a dollar on the little fellow."

I didn't see how the fight came out. Things and people were losing shape and time passed on a sliding scale. Two other customers argued over a spilled drink; one smashed the other in the mouth, and I thought I was only a witness until I woke up the next morning with my right hand swollen and throbbing and extracted a shard of broken tooth from the third knuckle. In order to examine the hand, I had to pull it out from under the naked woman who was lying on top of it, and half on top of me in my narrow berth at the Slop Chest. I extricated myself from the snoring creature, dressed, and wobbled out into the saloon, where Beecher grinned at me from the end of the bar.

"Sixty-five even," he said. "You beat out the nearest man by a dollar. You fixing to charge it to expenses?"

26

"Long live the emperor," Nan Feeny said. "Sluice your gob with this. It'll draw the sting from that rotten swig what they pour at the Slaughterhouse."

I watched her fill a glass with something orange and yellow from a canning jar. It glopped twice and she stirred it with a spoon until it assumed a uniform consistency as thick as sausage gravy.

"Should I ask what's in it?" I picked it up and sniffed at it. It had a familiar smell I remembered from childhood, mixed with something never before encountered. It wasn't entirely unpleasant.

"Buttermilk and grenadine, to start. I'm sworn to family secrecy as to the rest. My grandfather in Limerick died with a glass in his hand. Don't let it funk you," she said, when I set it down untasted. "He was shot by a vicar."

I picked it up again. "What's it do?"

"Well, it won't get rid of that baggage in your room. I ought to charge you extra rent."

"I packed her off with two dollars for her time. When was the last time something happened in the Sailor's Rest you didn't know about?"

She touched the ribbon at her throat, thinking. "Christmas Day, eighteen seventy-nine. I was down with the Grippe. Tip it down, and don't leave off till you can see me through the bottom. It won't work took in pieces."

I drank it in one long draught. It tasted the way marigolds smelled rotting. She saw on my face what was going on in my stomach and pointed at the spittoon in front of the footrail. I bent and scooped it up in both hands. It was a near enough thing even then. When I came up, wiping my mouth with the back of a hand, she was unstopping a bottle of ginger beer. "That should cut the copper."

I took two swigs. The metallic taste began to recede, and with it the pounding in my skull. My legs were still weak. I leaned on the bar for support.

"I'd of warned you away of the Slaughterhouse if you asked," she said. "The bilge they use to cut the squail's worse than the squail itself."

I'd wearied of the conversation, which I'd only half understood anyway.

"Where are Billy and Hodge? This is the first time I've seen you behind the bar." I was the only customer apart from a sailor losing steadily to Pinholster. Beecher, who recovered from the effects of strong spirits as quickly as he succumbed to them, had gone out in search of breakfast.

"It's Billy's morning out. He spends every rag he makes on a mollisher up on Telegraph Hill. Axel's down with a worse case than you, right along with the rest of Barbary. Come this time next week, they'll all be smacking the calfskin in Goodhue's congregation; them what ain't dancing at their death from the gas lamps."

"And where will you be?"

"Well, Goodhue's calfskin ain't mine, for all the words are the same. I ain't touched a drop of the peach since night before last, nor will I through tomorrow night, when I'll sit on the bed the Commodore bought, with my pepperbox close to hand and loads enough to see me through Gabriel's blast. I don't intend to sail to Hell unescorted."

"If that's Barbary's philosophy, Goodhue's Hundred are in for subtraction."

"A properly raptured Christian ain't so easy to kill as all that; ask Caesar. And a hundred has a way of becoming a thousand once they're kindled."

I couldn't argue with her arithmetic. I'd seen it put to the test in too many towns.

"What's Goodhue's draw? Bible slappers don't kick up much dust most places."

"Most places ain't Frisco. Every few years the swells get their crops full of Barbary and they don't look too hard at whoever steps up to the mark. After it's done they call in the army, hang the loudest, and dress for dinner. In the old country, we lit a candle. Here they light Barbary."

"Where does Goodhue hang his hat?"

She pursed her lips. She had something of the school matron in her. I remembered she'd been a governess in Boston before circumstances drove her West.

"He's got him a crib on Mission Street, courtesy of the God-fearing folk of San Francisco. It's a sin to own things if you can trade Paradise Everlasting for bed and board." She mopped the bartop, sweeping away marble splinters along with the spills. "I wouldn't aim for his heart, if that's where you're bound. The ball would pass through empty air and hit a soul worth saving on the other side as like as not."

"Don't believe what you read in the dime novels. I haven't shot anyone in weeks."

She stopped mopping. Her face went blank. "Steer clear of the Major Doctor. He's Black Spy in a collar."

"If he's human and speaks English, I've got nothing to lose by seeking him out."

"That's your second mistake. Your first is wanting to seek him out to begin with. He was a barrel-maker before he took to the cloth, and age ain't weakened him nor piety gentled his nature. He's throwed more than one poor sinner down the steps of the East Street Mission just for questioning his interpretation of the Word."

"I'll stay away from stairs."

"You'd profit higher staying away from Goodhue."

"Now I'm curious. I've never locked horns with the clergy."

"What's the percentage? I thought it was the Sons of the Confederacy you was after."

"I'm not forgetting that. I'm not forgetting I'm sworn to keep the peace, either."

"You got to have peace to keep it."

I smiled. I was feeling better by the minute, thanks to either the conversation or Nan Feeny's orange elixir. It put me in mind of the wisdom of a deputy marshal, dead these five years, who'd told me he couldn't understand people who never drank hard liquor, rising each morning knowing that's as good as they would feel all day long. He'd been stone-cold sober the day he was killed.

"Peace is just a time to reload."

She swept up the ginger beer bottle and clunked it into the ash can behind the bar. "I'll see they cut that into your stone," she said. "If I live through tomorrow night."

The sailor threw down his cards, scraped back his chair, and wove an unsteady pattern toward the bar. I slid into his place.

Pinholster, stacking his chips, shook his head. "If you ever decide to change professions, I don't recommend mine. When people win, they crow at you, and when they lose, they bring your parentage into question. You never see them at their best."

"I'm short of sympathy. You could have posed as a priest."

"Even worse. I'd have to listen to them complain about their losses in confession. I assume, since you've cleaned me out of both cash and intelligence, that you come with news."

"Sid the Spunk is dead."

He shuffled the deck. "May I inquire as to your source?"

"Let's just say I got it from the mysterious East."

"You surprise me. Celestials are renowned for their wisdom and their unwillingness to share it with the uncivilized West. Obfuscation is the one dialect common to all the provinces of China."

"Corroboration is a dangerous business in Chinatown. I'm expected to take a hatchet for the United States of America, not for Allan Pinkerton."

"It's Fat John, then?"

I said nothing. I'd forgotten how good he was at spotting tells.

He shrugged and set down the deck. "That's that, I suppose. My last assignment."

"Don't look so funereal. Now you can go back to Chicago before all hell busts loose."

"I'm haunted by the suspicion that Sid the Spunk will show up to see me off. I wouldn't care to go to my reward knowing I'd failed at the finish."

"Your reward may come as early as tomorrow night."

He scratched his ragged beard.

"I've never seen a lynching, though I've heard it described. I'd still take the rope over what's in store. Is it your conviction our yellow friend has told you the truth?"

I shook my head. "You didn't pay to see my hand."

"Nevertheless, I believe you've shown it to me." He

picked up the cards. "One last friendly game? Just to determine which of us is the better gambler."

"It wouldn't prove anything. You've got nothing to lose."

"I believe the condemned is entitled to a boon."

"How many last requests do you have coming?"

We played, however. The game ended in a draw.

Minutes later, standing on the boardwalk, I looked up at the slanted roof of the Slop Chest, my home away from the home I didn't have. A seagull, red-eyed and fat with carrion, was roosting on the peak of the stovepipe. That was an omen I scarcely needed on my way to see Owen Goodhue, founder of the First Eden Infantry, Army of the River Jordan.

27

Beecher caught up with me three blocks away from the Slop Chest. "What we doing today?"

I'd grown tired of the question.

"I'm headed to Mission Street. You can come along if you want. I don't need anyone to stand behind me this trip."

"I hear different, if it's Goodhue you're going to see. He broke a deacon's neck on East Street fighting over Jesus."

"I heard something along those lines. I don't intend to argue Scripture."

"Reckon I'll tag along. I ain't tried riding one of them cable cars."

"One streetcar's pretty much like all the rest."

"You shamed to be seen with me, boss?"

"Stop drawing lines in the dirt. This is a friendly visit. The reverend gentleman might not take kindly to two deputies dropping in."

"I'll wait outside."

"You're coming inside if you're coming with me. You're no good to me with a wall between."

"That's what I been saying."

The conductor, a sidewhiskered Scot with a short clay pipe screwed into the middle of his face, scowled at Beecher, but he took our money. We shared the car with some laborers traveling with their lunch buckets and a ladies' maid with a basket of knitting in her lap; the gentry were wedded to their private carriages and the conductor was adept at blocking access to the steps whenever someone of doubtful character tried to board. We alighted a block short of Mission and walked the rest of the way. Here the buildings were made of proper planed siding and brick, with flower boxes and well-tended gardens fenced off behind wrought iron. Five minutes from Barbary and we might have been separated from it by a thousand miles. The sight of a white man and a Negro walking together drew passing interest from the occasional pedestrian, no more. The Civil War and Emancipation were remote things to genteel San Francisco, like a revolution in Singapore. The male strollers wore brushed bowlers and silk tiles and swung ebony sticks with gold and silver tops. All the women were escorted. Policemen in leather helmets and blue serge congregated on street corners, twirling their sticks. We saw more officers in ten minutes than we'd seen in three weeks. The city had managed to pen up the bad element like Indians on a reservation. I saw then why respectable San Franciscans had little interest in closing down the whorehouses, deadfalls, and opium dens operating within walking distance of their townhouses and colonial palaces; they were protected by a trellis wall, and behaved as if it were made of iron. The place was a powder keg, but they were too busy walking their dogs and raising money to rescue someone else's wayward daughters to look down at the sparking fuse.

The address given to us by a policeman belonged to a modest two-story house with green shutters and a boot scraper shaped like a porcupine on the tiny front porch. I turned a handle that operated a jangling bell on the other side of the painted door.

"Yes?"

We took off our hats in front of an old woman in a floor-length dress with her gray hair in a bun. I inquired if this was the home of Mr. Goodhue.

"*Doctor* Goodhue," she corrected gently. "He is in his devotions at present."

I introduced myself and Beecher. "We're deputy federal marshals. We don't require much of his time."

She took in this information as if I'd told her we'd come to sweep the chimney and let us into a small front parlor containing some mohair furniture and what looked like a complete set of Bowdler's Gibbon next to *The Bible Lover's Illustrated Library* in a small-book press. "Please wait here."

She went out through a curtained doorway, leaving us alone with the smells of melted wax and walnut stain.

"Smells like church," Beecher whispered. It was a room designed for whispering.

I made a tour of the papered walls. Carved mahogany framed a series of Renaissance prints of the Annunciation, the Crucifixion, the Sermon on the Mount, and the usual Montgomery Ward's run of secular subjects: Cornwallis's surrender, the signing of the Declaration of Independence, fairies, a beefy tenor stuffed into Hamlet's tights. With a few variations, it was the same parlor visitors waited in fron New Hampshire to Seattle, a disappointment after what I'd been told by Nan Feeny. There wasn't a flaming sword or a scrap of brimstone in evidence. I began to wonder if anything she'd said was true, from Goodhue's participation in the violent uprising of '56 to the soiled dove she'd saved from drowning at his hands. Tall tales were a staple on the frontier and it looked as if Barbary was no exception.

"Dr. Goodhue asks that you join him in his cabinet."

We followed her down a short hallway with tall wainscoting, at the end of which she opened a door and stood aside to let us pass through. This room was scarcely larger than the parlor and unfinished. Plaster had squeezed out between the laths of the walls and frozen like meringue, the naked ceiling hung six inches above our heads, and the floor was made of unplaned pine, laid green so that the planks had warped and drawn apart; they bent beneath our weight, sprang back into shape when it was released, and invited drafts from the crawl space underneath. The addition of a rolltop desk, a wooden chair mounted on a swivel, and a low, plain table supporting a stack of books with burst and shredded bindings had done nothing to convince me we weren't standing in an unconverted lumber room. There was no window, just a copper lamp with a smudged glass chimney burning on the desk.

Our host sat on the swivel with his elbows on the desk and his head propped between his hands, studying a book that lay open and flat on the blotter. He was too big for the chair—nearly too big for the room—and at first glance resembled nothing so much as a tame ape perched on a child's chair for the entertainment of an audience. His shoulders strained the seams of a homespun shirt, his broadcloth trousers, held up by leather galluses, fell short of his ankles, and his feet were shod in farmer's brogans, either one of which was big enough to hang outside a cobbler's shop for advertising. At length he finished the paragraph he was reading, laid an attached ribbon between the pages to mark his place, closed the book, and rotated to face us with his hands on his thighs and his elbows turned out. The book was bound in green cloth, with the legend stamped in gold: *The Fairest Cargo, or The Christian Legions' Crusade Against the White Slave Trade in the New World,* by the Reverend Hobart Thorpe Forrestal. Just in case the point was missed, an illustration inlaid on the cover portrayed a female beauty with an hourglass figure and unfettered hair, clasping her hands to Heaven behind iron bars. No room in the clutter for trumpets and cherubim.

It all seemed like a theater set. I looked around, but couldn't tell for certain if he'd swept a copy of the *Police Gazette* into a drawer when he'd heard us coming. There is no showman like a minister, and no minister quite so authentic in appearance as one who is self-ordained.

"Welcome, gentlemen," rumbled Owen Goodhue. "I had scarcely hoped that our little campaign would draw the attention of Washington City."

His likeness on his flyers didn't do him justice. His head was the size of a medicine ball, with iron gray hair parted in the center and plastered into curls like a Roman emperor's ahead of his temples. Purple lesions traced the S-shaped path of his broken nose, and his close-set eyes burned deep in their sockets. The coarse beard began just below the ridge of his cheekbones and plummeted to its abrupt terminus across his collar, sliced off in a straight line as if with a dressmaker's shears. Here was yet another dangerous face to hang in my ever-expanding black gallery.

I said, "We haven't come that far, and we didn't hear about your crusade until we read the *Call*. However, it's what we're here to discuss."

"And which one are you, Deputy Murdock or Deputy Beecher?"

He had a powerful voice, shaped by the pulpit, and it required control to keep from shaking plaster loose from the laths. He might have trained it by shouting into the barrels he'd made, tuning it by the sound of the echo.

"Page Murdock. This is Edward Anderson Beecher. We represent the United States District Court of the Territory of Montana, presided over by Judge Harlan A. Blackthorne."

"I've heard of the man. Presbyterian, is he not?"

I said he was. "We're investigating an organization that calls itself the Sons of the Confederacy."

"A wicked lot. I supported Abolition in eighteen hundred and fifty-one, when it was far less popular than it became later. Are you familiar with the work of the Reverend Forrestal?" Without turning, he reached back and thumped the cover of *The Fairest Cargo* with a forefinger the size of a pinecone.

"I've neglected my reading these past few weeks, apart from the *Call*." I was trying to steer the conversation back to his pet crusade. He seemed to have a habit of following up each statement with a question that diverted the course.

"You would find it illuminating. The conventional wisdom is that the surrender of that godless man Lee put the period to slavery in these United States. Meanwhile, chaste young white women are being exchanged like currency in broad daylight on the streets of our greatest cities, and forced into degradation which to describe would bring a blush to the cheek of a base pagan. Are you aware of the threat posed by the nation's ice-cream parlors?"

Beecher laughed. Goodhue turned the full heat of his gaze upon him.

"You are amused, my Ethiopian friend; as well you may be, until I explain that most of these establishments are owned and operated by foreigners; Jews and papists, turned in the lathes of Mediterranean seaports where girls are auctioned off in public and conducted in chains to workhouses and brothels, never to be seen again by decent society. These scoundrels ply them with sweets and flattery, and when the tender creatures are sufficiently befogged, offer them employment—stressing that the work is undemanding and respectable—and by these lights lead them down the garden path toward the burning pit. One moment of feminine weakness, and someone's cherished daughter delivers herself to a lifetime of debauchery and an eternity of damnation. I would no sooner allow a child of mine to enter the polished whiteness of one of these emporia than I would escort her into a saloon. Ice cream, you say? The serpent's fruit, *I* say."

As he spoke, his volume rose, until the room shook with thunder. Just hearing it made me feel hoarse. I cleared my throat.

"I haven't seen any ice-cream parlors in Barbary."

"There is no reason why you should, since by the time this poor baggage arrives their purpose is done. Hell's broad avenue begins in New York and Boston and Chicago and ends in Portsmouth Square. Stare deeply into the eyes of the next harlot you see; disregard the painted features and tinted hair, the hollow cheeks and lying lips, and you will discern the frail, faded glimmer of the trusting girl who turned her back on church and home, never suspecting it was for the last time."

Beecher said, "You feel that way, you ought to set up shop in New York or Boston or Chicago. By the time they get here, they're gone for good."

"That is the crossroads at which the Reverend Forrestal and I part ways. He counsels eradicating this pernicious growth at the point where it blossoms, whereas I am in favor of burning it out at its root. Close an ice-cream parlor, incarcerate its proprietor, and two more will spring up in their place, so long as there is profit to be made. It is simple economics. Destroy the houses of sin, and with them the source of income, and there will be no need for the parlors. Smite the sinners, burn their tabernacles to the ground, baptize them in the blood of the lamb. Sacrifice the sheep that are lost along with those who led them astray, and spare those who may yet be folded back into the flock. In order to rebuild, one must first destroy."

The walls were still ringing when the door opened from the hallway. The gray-haired woman's face was stoic. "Owen, I have loaves in the oven."

His voice dropped six feet. "I'm sorry, my dear."

She drew the door shut. The exchange was the first indication I'd had that she was his wife and not just his housekeeper.

I said, "It's the destruction we've come to talk about. We want to ask you to postpone Judgment Day until we lay this Sons of the Confederacy business to rest."

"I am far more concerned with the daughters than I am with the Sons. I care not whether they prosper or perish."

"Some of the names on your list are no threat to anyone's daughter," I said.

"Infamous assassins, harlots, and thieves! Slay the hosts and the parasites will wither. These targets were not chosen arbitrarily. David declared war upon the Philistines, but he joined battle with Goliath, and thereby claimed victory with but a single stone. I wish you gentlemen well upon your mission, but your objectives are not mine."

"You won't reconsider?"

"I will not. Indeed, I cannot. Immortal souls are at risk."

I drew the Deane-Adams.

"That being the case, you're under arrest for obstruction of justice."

Beecher unbelted his Le Mat and cocked it.

Goodhue's brow darkened. The muscles bunched in his arms and thighs. He looked ready to pounce. Then he smirked in his beard. It wasn't a pretty sight, but I preferred it to Goodhue rampant on a field of hellfire. When he spoke, his tone was level.

"Are you so certain that placing a spiritual leader in a cage will postpone the event you fear, rather than accelerate it?"

I was still thinking about that when the door opened

again. Mrs. Goodhue took in the pistols without expression. "A man to see you. He wouldn't give his name."

The smoldering eyes remained on me. I returned the five-shot to its holster. Beecher lowered his hammer and put up the Confederate pistol.

"Ask him to wait in the parlor," Goodhue said.

The door closed.

I said, "Whorehouses are like ice-cream stores. There are two or three waiting to take the place of every one you burn to the ground."

"Work worthy of the effort is worthy of repeating. Always and again, until the mortal shells rise and the sorting begins. The price of salvation is patience and persistence."

"You're not the first man who tried to raise a private army for his own ends. They always come to grief at the finish."

"You've forgotten the late Mr. Lincoln. General Mc-Clellan was in favor of suing for peace. Lincoln answered him by inventing the draft. But for his interest in his own ends, the war would have ended three years earlier. History is written by the victors."

"He paid for it with his life," I said. "His and three hundred thousand others."

"I am prepared to answer to that account. Are you?"

"I swore an oath to that effect."

He smirked again. "I'm aware of the reading habits of my parishioners. I regret to say it is not confined to Holy Writ. Your exploits have not escaped the notice of the vulgar penny press, and I dare say they do not in all ways conform to the spirit of your oath. I judge not lest I be judged. My own methods are not always those of the Redeemer and His apostles, but I live in the modern world. Mark and Matthew could not have anticipated Barbary any more than the hedonistic Greeks could have foreseen

Sodom and Gomorrah. Although Samson found the jaw-bone of an ass sufficient for slaughtering infidels and idol-ators, I find that a powder charge is far more appropriate when transacting business with Daniel Webster Whee-lock's Hoodlums."

The atmosphere in that raw room was noxious. It might have been the lingering effects of last night or the smoky lamp on the desk, but there was hardly enough air to fill Owen Goodhue's lungs, let alone three sets at once. I wanted out of there, but I needed one more answer.

"I notice you didn't include Wheelock's name on your list."

"God has use for Satan, or He would have smote him centuries ago. In any case, Captain Dan is nothing with-out Barbary. He will shrivel and drift before the first clean draught that blows unhampered across the ruins."

"You keep talking about Barbary as if it's just a bunch of buildings," I said. "They have people in them."

"What is flesh? We leave it behind when we stand be-fore our Creator."

"Lying or hanging?"

"I do not propose to say. Joshua did not discuss his strat-egy before Jericho."

"But who will be left to write the Book of Owen?" I asked.

"I am a humble man. If in the outcome of this event my name should be erased from human memory, I hold the matter in no great regard. It is already written in the book of St. Peter. If I manage to spare even one young woman from the clutches of Demon Lust, I need not fear what is recorded beneath. Gentlemen." He rose, dwarfing the room further. He had to stoop to avoid colliding with the ceil-ing. It made you want to step back.

Beecher held his ground. "What's white slaving got to do with Horatio Flinders?"

Goodhue hoisted his shaggy brows. "Who?"

We left him. Entering the parlor on our way out, I stopped. Beecher bumped against me from behind.

Daniel Webster Wheelock used his ivory stick to push himself up from one of the upholstered chairs. He had on his fire captain's uniform, and he looked as surprised as I felt.

"Deputy."

"Alderman."

Mrs. Goodhue came in and led him out.

Nero, Wheelock's Negro bodyguard, stood smoking a cigar on the boardwalk in front of the house. He wore a tall gray hat and a full-skirted overcoat to match over checked trousers and gleaming Wellingtons. He lowered the hand holding the cigar and tipped his hat as we walked past.

PART FIVE

The Bonnie-Blue Flag

28

"That man Goodhue's crazier'n ten crazy men," Beecher said.

I nodded. "I can't figure out why he isn't famous."

"Well, he'll be plenty famous after tomorrow night."

We were sitting on a public bench at the top of Telegraph Hill, passing a bottle of Old Gideon back and forth; I'd made the mistake of swearing off liquor before making the acquaintance of the madman of Mission Street. The saloon-keeper in the stained-glass place where we'd stopped for a drink wouldn't serve us on the premises on account of Beecher, but he'd agreed to sell us the bottle when I showed him my star and asked when was the last time his gas line had been inspected.

The view was impressive, even for a native of the High Plains. It extended all the way down to the ships in the harbor and across the bay where houses were going up, so rapidly we could track their progress between swigs. Cable cars screeched down the slope and rattled back up, taking on and disgorging passengers on the fly. I saw my first omnibus. The place was busier than an antheap.

Both sides of San Francisco displayed themselves simultaneously, the stately homes on Nob Hill and the tumbledown shacks on Pacific Street; parasols blossoming to our left like desert blooms after a rain, pushcart peddlers crawling along like caterpillars to our right, hawking rags and cans of coal oil recovered from the dregs of lamps rescued from trash bins. We saw a liveried groom helping a lady in a bustle into a brougham and the assault and battery of an unsteady pedestrian, both at the same time. It was like looking through a stereoscope whose pictures had gotten mixed up back at the factory.

Beecher shared my thoughts. "What you reckon is holding this place together?"

"The same thing that keeps it apart. If it weren't for Barbary, the swells would have to pick fights with each other. Look what's happening on the frontier. We threw out the Indians and let in the lawyers and politicians."

"What makes you so smart?"

"I'm not smart. I'm just alive."

"You fought Indians?"

"I've fought Indians."

"And I know you shot it out with outlaws."

"Outlaws and lawmen."

"How old are you?"

"Forty-two."

"You're smart."

"Not smart enough to quit."

"Maybe you're smart enough to tell me what Cap'n Dan's doing paying a call on Goodhue."

"We'll ask Wheelock tonight at the Bella Union."

He drank, held the liquor in his mouth a moment, then swallowed. "I clean forgot about that meeting of the Sons of the Confederacy. You done any thinking as to how we're getting in?"

"I've been working on it. I still am. I don't figure that punch-simple bouncer from the saloon to set much of a challenge, but if Wheelock shows, he's bound to bring along that bodyguard of his. He knows us by sight, and Wheelock didn't strike me as the kind of politician who

keeps anyone on his payroll just because he looks well in
a stiff collar."

"Nero's colored. You leave him to me."

"Matching skin won't get you past him. I doubt he con-
cerns himself with brotherhood."

"It ain't getting past him I'm talking about. Some men
you just got to go through." He offered me the bottle.

I shook my head. It was already beginning to slosh. My
stomach was empty. I'd held my own against dog soldiers
and brute killers, but that morning I hadn't been stout
enough to face breakfast. "We can't risk shooting. The
noise would raise the South and it would be Bull Run all
over again."

He raised the bottle to his lips, then thought better of it
and thumped in the cork. "I ever tell you about the fight at
Buffalo Creek?"

"You scalped a young brave and stayed behind to burn
the lodges and shoot the ponies."

"No, the young brave was another fight, and I didn't tell
you how Buffalo Creek got won. We was climbing a hill
to attack the village. It was first light, and we was walking the horses with gunnysacks tied on their hooves so as
not to alert the sentries; cupping their snouts with one hand
so's they wouldn't blow when they smelled Indian ponies.
We was halfway up when a hunting party come over the
hill and spotted us.

"They was just as surprised as we was, and drawed rein
just to make certain they wasn't seeing spirits. They was
mounted, we was afoot, and if you tell me you ever seen
a good organized Arapaho charge you're a liar, on account
of you wouldn't be sitting here with hair under your hat. I
only heard about them myself, and hearing was enough to
satisfy my curiosity."

He grinned his sunrise grin. He was seeing something
other than the metropolis at our feet.

"We had this white lieutenant, Brigham was his name, only he sure wasn't no Mormon. When he broke wind, you thought it was the regimental band. I seen men who'd gut you with a bayonet turn green and spew up their rations when they caught the scent. Well, he got so scared he let one fly, loud enough to spook the horses, and you know something? That hunting party was so insulted they lost their manners and galloped down that hill all in a bunch, whooping like drunken cowboys, running right over each other, bumping lances and getting their bows all tangled. Meanwhile, Lieutenant Brigham remembered his training and got us into formation, front rank standing and firing, then kneeling to reload while the second rank stood and fired, and so on. We shot that hunting party to pieces and swung into leather and took out after the turntails and right on over the crest and down into the village. All on account of one man couldn't hold his beans."

He drew the cork, drank, and restopped the bottle.

"We called it the Battle of Brigham's Bowels."

I watched a wedding let out of a church on Stockton, men in morning coats and women in frilled capes spilling down the steps to see off the bride and groom in a phaeton tied all over with white ribbons.

"I don't remember reading about that one in *Harper's Weekly*," I said.

"Well, it wasn't Custer's Last Fight. The point is, you can train a man to overcome everything but his own bad temper. If them braves wasn't so concerned with their dignity, that village might still be standing." He stuck the bottle in a coat pocket. "You let me worry about Nero."

"You aren't going to break wind, are you?"

"That was just an example. I wouldn't never enter into a contest with Lieutenant Brigham. One time—"

"Save it for later. You don't want to use up all your best

stories at once." I stood and grasped the back of the bench
for balance. Old Gideon needed a four-course meal to tie
it down. "Let's get something to eat. We might not find
time for supper."

He got up. "What you in the mood for?"

"Anything but beans."

The Ancient rose from a blanket of fog that swathed the
gas lamps almost to their orange globes, pale and shim-
mering under a rustler's moon. It was as solid and yet as
otherworldly as the Sphinx, and it seemed to say, *I am
the Bella Union, I am Barbary. I was here before the Chinese, before the Sydney Ducks, and I will stand when all
the lesser establishments about me have burned or fallen
into splinters. Worship me with cheap champagne and expensive women.* We sidestepped a pool of steaming urine
at the base of the foundation and went inside. We were met
by the bouncer, none of whose scars had faded since the
last time. His head belonged on a hunched figure in trunks
and a tight jersey in a sporting print, not a thickening
body in a black frock coat and white shirtboard.

"Sorry, gents. The place is closed tonight for a private
party. Come back tomorrow."

We were alone in the foyer that opened into the saloon,
but I didn't know for how long. The auditorium door was
drifting shut behind the last body to pass through. I started
to turn away, then pivoted on my heel and hit the bouncer
square on the chin with all my weight behind my fist. I felt
the impact to my shoulder.

He took a step back, then lowered his head between his
shoulders and raised a pair of small, hard fists with ridges
across the knuckles where they'd broken and healed several times. He took a step forward. Beecher planted the

muzzle of his Le Mat against the bouncer's right temple and rolled back the hammer. The bouncer stiffened, then lowered his fists to his sides.

I held my star in front of his face. "We're here on federal business. Take a walk down to the harbor. Have a cigar. Have several. In San Quentin, they don't let you smoke in the cells."

"I don't use tobacco."

"Have a drink, then. Kill the bottle."

"I don't drink, either. I don't hold with most of the vices."

"Which ones do you hold with?" I kept my temper in check. I didn't know when someone might come in from the street or the theater. I didn't want to buffalo him. You can take only so many cracks to the skull, and the bumps and furrows showing through his close-cropped hair went the limit.

"I got a girl up at the Brass Check."

"Go see her. You've got to tend a romance if you want it to grow."

"I'll lose my job."

"There's plenty of work in San Quentin."

After a moment he nodded. Beecher withdrew the pistol and the bouncer walked past us and out the door. He didn't stop for a hat and coat.

"Thought you said he wouldn't set much challenge," Beecher said.

I shushed him, strode to the auditorium door, and cracked it. It opened into a carpeted alcove with stairs to the right and left, which I guessed led to the curtained boxes where the gentry plied Owen Goodhue's lost daughters with drink and pressed their affections in private. I hoped they'd be vacant that night. I drew the Deane-Adams and led the way upstairs. Voices buzzed in the orchestra. The place sounded like opening night for a revue from New York.

"Sir, I'm afraid you've lost your way."

I recognized the deep silken voice before I saw its owner. Wheelock's bodyguard stood in the center of the floral carpet that ran past the entrance to the boxes, his feet spread in patent-leather boots. Tonight he had on plum-colored plush, ruffled white linen, and black broadcloth, tailored to within a quarter-inch of his measurements. It made him look almost normal size until you realized that what appeared to be a ladies' pocket pistol in his right hand was a full-size Colt Peacemaker, with the barrel shortened to accommodate a concealed holster. It was steadied against his hip.

I said, "Nero, this isn't your affair. I represent the law."

I might as well have been throwing pebbles at a statue. The fact that I had a revolver in my hand as well meant no more to him than the color of my eyes. We'd neither of us miss the mark at that distance.

"Nero."

I twitched. Nero didn't. I hadn't realized Beecher wasn't behind me until he stepped around the corner behind the bodyguard and called his name. He held the Le Mat straight out from his shoulder with the muzzle aimed at the back of the big man's head. He'd climbed the other set of stairs and followed the carpeted walk all the way around the auditorium.

"That's Beecher," I said. "You met him the other day in your boss's reception room."

That bounced off him. He was a fixture. They'd built the Bella Union around him and he'd be the last thing to go come the next big fire. The Colt didn't move. Judge Blackthorne's deputies were trained in that situation to fire at their primary target, then if they were still standing, turn and try for the men behind them. In that moment I knew Nero had been taught the same thing. We were going to burn each other down, and God couldn't stop it. He'd turned His back on Barbary. My finger tightened on the trigger of the Deane-Adams.

"He won't remember," Beecher said. "We're all the same to him, a pat on the head and a scratch behind the ears. He'll wag his tail and lick the face of whoever comes around to see his master. Ain't that right, nigger-oh?"

He licked his lips. "Nero."

I couldn't fathom it. If Beecher had told me what he'd had in mind, I'd have refused to go along. You could see through it from a hundred yards, and the bodyguard wasn't a fool. But Beecher had known something I hadn't, something I never would. I relaxed my finger just a little.

"That ain't what I asked, you dumb coon. You must have cotton in your ears."

Nero didn't move. A vein I hadn't noticed before rose like a blister on his left temple. I saw it pulse.

"Let's us go," Beecher said to me. "This boy's got spittoons to empty out."

Nero twisted suddenly, bringing the Colt around with him. I made two long strides and swept the barrel of the five-shot across the bulge of his skull. His knees buckled. I reached past him, closing my hand over the Colt and jamming the base of my thumb between the hammer and the chamber. I sucked air when the hammer pinched flesh, but the cartridge didn't fire and I twisted the weapon out of his grip as he fell.

We gagged him with his cravat, used his belt and Beecher's to bind his arms and legs, and dragged him through a door into one of the boxes overlooking the auditorium. I told Beecher to watch him.

"What about you?"

"I came to see the show."

29

I t was my first time in the Bella Union's melodeon section, and if it weren't for what had brought me there,
I might have been entranced. Tombstone's celebrated
Birdcage and the candied theaters of St. Louis and Virginia City could boast of no features not in place in the
Ancient. The curtained boxes where customers could sip
brandy or sherry or Tennessee Thunder in comfort while
watching the show, or draw the curtains and enjoy a show
of their own with one of the *danseuses* from the saloon,
were stacked three high all around the orchestra, whose
seats were upholstered in green plush piped with gold
braid. Gas globes were stacked like eggs atop corner fixtures, and the stage glowed between mahogany columns
carved into towering shocks of wheat. Cabbage roses exploded on burgundy runners in the aisles. Laurels of gold
leaf encircled a coffered ceiling with a Greek Bacchanal
enshrined in stained glass in the center, lighted from above
so that the chubby nymphs' nipples and the blubbery
lips of the bloated male gods and demigods glittered like
rubies. It was as decadent as anything in that vicinity. A
Christian soldier like Owen Goodhue would shinny up
one of the wheat shocks to smash it bare-handed.

There was a particularly lecherous glint in the eye of
one deity, busy feeding pomegranate seeds from a cupped
palm to a hefty nude sprawled across his lap: a round hole

with yellow light glaring through. I was pretty sure it was a bullet hole, possibly a practice round fired by Samuel Tetlow, the Ancient's absentee owner, before he shot his partner.

The place dripped dissipation. Like most of its neighbors, it had burned several times during the tender years of the Gold Rush, and according to Pinholster it had reincarnated itself each time in a shape more lewd than the one before. There were old stains on the velvet seats and carpeting in the box I was in that I didn't think were made by spilled liquor, or even blood, and there was a smell of disinfectant that no cologne, no matter how liberally sprayed about, could disguise completely. Just being there made me feel like a dirty little boy, and I was on U.S. business. I could only imagine what it was like in the company of a young creature with soft flesh and hard eyes while ballet girls performed splits onstage.

A low groaning made me jump. It sounded as if whatever wounded animal had made it was in the box with me. I thought of checking on Beecher, who was in the next box, keeping an eye on Nero. Then came another groan, shorter and ending on a higher note. Someone was sawing at a cello.

Carefully I drew aside one of the swagged curtains and peered around it down onto the stage. The musician, a scrawny old fellow with white hair parted in the center and extravagant handlebars, squatted in evening dress on a low stool with the cello between his knees, searching for the scales with his bow. At last he found them, and as he neared the middle register, a violinist standing next to him joined in with what sounded like the first strains of "Turkey in the Straw," although it was more likely something by Bach or Vivaldi or some other wicked European whose music I couldn't hum no matter how recently I'd heard it. A third musician slid a chair across the stage, perched on its edge, and started tuning a guitar. He spent a lot of time between strums twisting the frets or whatever they were called, and each time when he tried it he seemed to find the same note. I have no ear for music.

A third of the seats in front of the stage were filled, with more visitors shuffling down the aisles. All were men. Some wore black swallowtails, others town suits and old overalls. A large number wore Confederate gray. The uniforms appeared tailored to fit, from far better material than the old shoddy, and were certainly in too good a condition to have gone through combat, or even hung in some cedar closet for eighteen years. There were chevrons and bars, some clusters, but no stars as yet. I had an idea the Sons of the Confederacy hadn't room for more than one general; or two, if Blackthorne and Marshal Spilsbury were right about the rift in the ranks.

The men in uniform were young, by and large; at the most, they looked to be in their late thirties, scarcely old enough to have exposed their regimentals to enemy fire. A few were barely out of their teens, with pimples on their foreheads and public first attempts at moustaches and imperials. Some of the officers wore sabers, and from the way they clanked against their heels when they walked, it seemed obvious they wouldn't know how to handle them when they were out of their scabbards either. If I were casting a play set at Gettysburg, I'd have called off the audition based on those who had responded.

I began to wonder if this was the same organization that had tried twice to kill me and had committed some two dozen murders for the cause of Southern liberty. But then I'd been all wrong about Owen Goodhue, on the evidence of his ordinary-looking parlor; caught up in the fire of his faith, he was a guerrilla, cut from the same vengeful cloth as Bloody Bill and Clay Allison. They don't always oblige you with horns and a forked tail.

Applause burst, making me jump yet again. The trio onstage had stopped tuning their instruments and hurled themselves into a lilting, pastoral ballad, no great success when it was first played in public, but which events had made something else of altogether. The older men in the audience recognized it first, started singing on the third note, and caught up with the melody by the fourth bar. By that time, the younger men had begun to join in:

O, I wish I was in the land of cotton;
Old times there are not forgotten.
Look away . . .

As the second chorus started, the instruments got louder, the tempo increased, and the deep purple velvet curtain glided silently upward, revealing at last the Confederate Stars and Bars, twelve feet by eight, strung by its corners from rigging suspended from the flies far above the stage. The flag was made of paper-thin silk that rippled in the air currents stirred by clapping hands. The applause rose volcanically, pulling the men in the audience to their feet and tearing cheers from two hundred pairs of lungs; for the theater was crowded now, without a vacant seat in sight. I felt my own heart lifting, and I'd fought the bloody rag for four years, burying close friends slain in its shadow.

That's how it's done. They snare you with bands and bright colors, and six months later you're sleeping with lice in a muddy hole, half-starved and scared half out of your mind.

The spell broke when a shrill cry rose above the cheering, high and thin and breaking at its peak, like a bull-whacker's whip. It froze my spine. I hadn't heard an authentic rebel yell since Petersburg, where Beauregard's men hung their naked backsides over the top of the redoubt and dared us to storm it. A wild boar shrieks like that when it knows it's beaten but won't die without taking some of the hounds along for company. I'd hoped I'd never hear it again. It was an even worse omen than the seagull roosting on Nan Feeny's roof.

I leaned out to see who was responsible for it, but I had to hold back to avoid being spotted, so I couldn't pick him out. The yell took me too far into the past to have belonged to someone who hadn't seared his lungs with cannon smoke, or slipped in blood and spilled entrails, fighting bayonet to bayonet with his enemy's sweat stinging his eyes. There was a real live big cat down there among the tin tigers. I had that feeling, like a falling sensation in a nightmare, that we would meet. Like attracts like.

When they finished playing, the musicians rose. Hands were still pounding, and I thought they'd take a bow, or follow up with "I'm a Good Old Rebel"; but they merely picked up their chairs and carried them and their instruments offstage. I credited them for maintaining perspective. A monkey with a tambourine would have gotten an ovation playing "Dixie" for that crowd.

The stage was empty for a minute, perhaps longer; long enough anyway for the spectators to reseat themselves, begin to fidget, and crack a nervous cough or two. Just about the time they would have started murmuring, a lone figure emerged from the wings, walked to the center, limping a little despite the aid of a stick, and turned to face the seats, holding the stick across his thighs like an officer's riding crop.

Polite applause started, then died. The audience seemed eager to clear space for the man's first words.

Daniel Webster Wheelock had traded his fire captain's uniform for the butternut tunic and military-striped trousers of a Confederate general. Knee-high riding boots engineered to draw attention from his club foot glistened like black satin and the tiny star on either side of his collar

clasp winked golden in the footlights. Modestly, he'd chosen a simple uniform design and had resisted promoting
himself higher than brigadier. Even in warrior dress he
was a politician to the core.

Another minute crawled past on its belly. Wheelock's
head turned slowly, as if to study each face in the orchestra. I withdrew deeper into the shadows, but he never
raised his eyes toward the boxes. His head stopped turning.

"Bull Run," he said.

Applause, nearly as loud as for the opening of "Dixie."

"Wilson's Creek."

A louder burst still, accompanied by a shrill whistle.

"Ball's Bluff!"

With the name of each Confederate victory, Wheelock's
voice rose, and with it the volume of approval from the
audience. Cedar Mountain, less well-known, drew an uneven response, strongest from among those old enough to
have read about it in the newspapers, been told about it by
veterans, and in one case at least, experienced it at first-
hand; that rebel howl managed to raise the hairs on my
neck once again. Fredericksburg met unanimous appreci-
ation, as did Chancellorsville and Cold Harbor, the last
unequivocal success for the Old Dominion; Wheelock's
listeners rose as one, feet thundering on the floorboards,
shaking Barbary's oldest continuing house of pleasure to
its foundation. A number of hats flew ceilingward and
drifted back down. I hadn't seen so many gray kepis in one
place since Lee's lost legions lined up to stack their long
guns and swear an oath to the Union.

On "Cold Harbor," Wheelock had raised his stick above
his head, striking a pose similar to Custer's with his saber
in a thousand lithographs, framed and hung behind the
bars of saloons from Concord to Cripple Creek. His face
was flushed, his gray eyes glittered. If I weren't sure he
prepared himself for these things in cold blood and abso-

lute sobriety, I'd have thought he'd helped himself to a pull from the bottle that had begun to make the rounds of the men sitting in the first two rows. Who needs whiskey when you can draw fire from the blood of a couple of hundred fellow fanatics?

When the swell subsided and everyone was back in his seat, Captain Dan lowered his stick to its former position. Now he spoke low, allowing the melodeon's acoustics to carry his words to the back.

"I have never owned a slave," he said. "I daresay none of these presents have. Some of us are too young ever to have seen a Negro in chains. Fort Sumter was not fired upon in order to secure the fetters of a misguided past, but to ensure States' Rights, that the fates of our farms and shops and hearths would not drift before the capricious current of Washington politics." (Applause.) "The two hundred fifty thousand who died in the field at Gettysburg, Chickamauga, and the Shenandoah Valley, among so many others, who succumbed to infection and fever in hospital tents at Mechanicsville and Pea Richmond, among so many others, did not give their lives to keep men in shackles, but to free them from tyranny." (Applause and shouting.) "For nearly twenty years, we have eaten the lies of our conquerors in place of bread, drunk the vinegar of their insults in place of water, and for this bitter sustenance we have been expected to pull our forelocks and give thanks. The time has come for us to rise from our knees and smite them to theirs; if not in ranks, as at Bull Run and Fredericksburg, then one by one, all across North America."

Once again the house was on its feet. The great flag rippled fiercely as in a storm. I wondered if the Ancient could withstand the foot-stamping; all it had had to face before was fire and vigilantes.

During this reception, Wheelock half turned and raised his stick, signaling toward the wings. The man who came out wearing the uniform of a sergeant and carrying a battered gray campaign hat looked familiar. He'd handed the hat to the alderman and struck a modest pose beside him, hands folded behind his back in parade rest, before I recognized Tom Tulip, the Hoodlum Beecher and I had robbed in order to arrange an audience with Captain Dan. I hoped he'd be given a chance to speak. I'd have paid admission to hear his cockney gibberish coming from a man fitted out as a volunteer with the 17th Mississippi.

I was even more curious about that hat. The brim was tattered, the crown stained through with grease or old sweat, the band was missing. It looked as if it had seen more combat than all the spectators combined. It was a long way from delicate, and carrying it upside down with the crown cupped in two hands as if it were some fragile vessel filled with rubies and sapphires, seemed unnecessary. Wheelock handled it the same way, clamping his stick under one arm so he could engage both hands and waiting for the noise to die down.

When it did and all were sitting, he continued in the same low tones as before. "I purchased this hat at no small expense from a dealer in curiosities in Richmond, Virginia, who had acquired it from a veteran who needed the money to support his family. The veteran picked it up from the ground where it had fallen when General James Elwell Brown Stuart was struck down at Yellow Tavern. This is Jeb Stuart's hat."

Awed silence greeted this intelligence, broken momentarily by a hushed murmur. Owen Goodhue might have gotten the same reaction from his congregation by displaying a splinter from the True Cross. Finally, applause crackled gently, so as not to disturb the spirit of the head that had worn the hat.

"I will ask Sergeant Tulip to place General Stuart's hat in the hands of the first gentleman to my right seated in the front row. Without looking inside, that gentleman will remove one of the coins I have placed in the crown and pass the hat to the gentleman to *his* right, who will do the same. The hat will continue to pass among you until it is empty. It will then be returned to Sergeant Tulip. I ask that you do not look at the coin you have drawn, nor show it to anyone else, until I instruct you to do so. Although I state this as a request, you will consider it an order from your commanding officer. Sergeant Tulip?"

Tulip accepted the hat from Wheelock and carried it into the wings. A moment later, he reappeared in the far left aisle and held out the hat, which was taken reverently by the man seated nearest him, who reached inside without lowering his head, rummaged about, and withdrew his closed fist. During the ten minutes it took for the hat to make the rounds, Wheelock entertained his listeners with an account of Jeb Stuart's activities during the war that stirred even me, ending with the general's own delirious refighting of all his old battles during his last moments and his one-sided conversation with his eldest daughter, who had died at the very moment he was deploying his troops on the Rappahannock.

"I offer this epitaph, spoken from the heart by General Lee upon learning of his old friend's death," the alderman concluded: " 'I can scarcely think of him without weeping.' "

Someone in the audience sobbed for the fate of a man who had died when he himself was too young to lift a rifle. Wheelock was a first-rate political hack, there was no doubt about that. He could wring tears from a doorknob.

When Tulip had finished his errand and returned the hat to its owner, Wheelock dismissed him to the wings. Wheelock cradled the hat in one arm, gripping his stick in his other hand, and called for more light. The gas globes in the corners must have been fed from a central pipe; they glowed more brightly, illuminating the orchestra as if the sun had rolled out from behind a cloud.

"Please oblige me by holding aloft the coins you selected so that I may see them."

Clothing rustled. The light found dull silver in most of the upraised hands; the hat had contained forty or fifty cartwheel dollars. However, even at that distance I could pick out the gold double eagles glittering among them. I counted eight.

30

"Will the gentlemen who drew the gold pieces join me?"

Some toes were stepped on and a couple of forage caps dislodged from a couple of heads, but the eight men found their way to the aisles and proceeded up the stairs that led to the wings and onto the stage. Most of them appeared to be in their twenties, self-conscious in their uniforms. One was nearly my age, wearing a corduroy coat rubbed shiny at the elbows over civilian trousers reinforced with leather and custom-made boots, the last worth more than everything else he had on put together. His sandy hair spilled to his collar and he wore a Custer moustache that concealed his mouth and most of his chin. There was something about his pigeon-toed walk, his backward-leaning posture, that suggested a lifetime in the saddle, and not necessarily with a lasso in his hand pursuing stray calves. I knew a guerrilla when I saw one; and I knew without having to think hard on the subject that here was the source of that bone-chilling rebel yell.

Wheelock made a show of examining each coin, as if looking for signs of counterfeiting, then returned it to its owner, leaning forward as he did so to whisper something. Some of the faces paled. In these cases, he stared at them until they nodded, then turned to the next man. When he was finished, he raised his voice to address the audience. The men with the double eagles stood strung out on either side of him like an unrehearsed chorus. A number of them were still shaken.

"I will not announce the names of the loyal members of the Sons of the Confederacy who stand before you," Wheelock said. "This is a precaution, and I trust an unnecessary one, as you have all sworn an oath of secrecy concerning what takes place beneath this roof, as well as to come to the assistance of a brother of the order under any and all circumstances. I remind those of you who know their names of the penalty of violating that pledge. We are at war, gentlemen. Make no mistake on that point."

A murmur thrummed through the orchestra. He raised his stick and it trailed off into silence.

"As each of these soldiers presented himself, I spoke a name in his ear. I did not speak the same name twice, and all will be known to the membership presently. Each man has committed the information to memory.

"At this time I ask Sergeant Tulip to return to the stage."

The Hoodlum came out from the wings with a hesitating step. He looked puzzled. This wasn't in the programme.

Skin prickled on my back. I wasn't sure why. My hand closed around the grip of the Deane-Adams in its holster. I hadn't willed it to.

Wheelock placed a hand on Tom Tulip's shoulder. "Sergeant, this meeting is about to adjourn. I ask you to lead the membership in singing 'The Bonnie Blue Flag.'"

Tulip appeared relieved and nervous at the same time. He probably hadn't sung in public since the last time he'd been drunk in a saloon, and from his unease it was clear he was as sober as a parson. However, he stepped forward, removed his cap, held it over his left breast, and raised his voice in an uncertain tenor:

> We are a band of brothers, and native to the soil,
> Fighting for the property we gained by honest toil;
> And when our rights was threatened, the cry rose near and far,
> 'urrah for the Bonnie Blue Flag that bears a single star!

When the song began, a few voices joined in from the audience, but the spirit didn't spread, and by the end of the second line Tulip was singing alone. He noticed it; his voice broke on "threatened." But he continued in a wavering tone. The first "hurrah" came out as a sob. He knew what was coming before I did.

> 'urrah! 'urrah! For Southern Rights, 'urrah!
> 'urrah—

The long-haired guerrilla stepped up behind him, hauled a Navy Colt from beneath his belt, and shot him through the head.

Tom Tulip's chin snapped down as if he were taking a bow, then jerked back up. He sank to his knees and fell on his face. The powder-flare had set his hair on fire, but it smoldered out quickly. Almost immediately the entire theater stank of sulfur and scorched hair and flesh.

The echo of the report rang through dead silence. Most of the faces onstage were pale now to the point of translucence. One of the younger men turned and vomited. A new stench joined the others.

The Deane-Adams was in my hand. I took a step back into the shadows of the box and drew a bead on Wheelock's chest. Then on the guerrilla's. I couldn't decide where to begin.

Wheelock was speaking again. I held off.

"Shed no tears for Sergeant Tulip. He was an opportunist, who joined the Sons merely to curry my favor and advance his own larcenous interests. However, that is not why he died.

"War is not won on the field of battle alone. The tragedy of Appomattox Courthouse taught us that, if it taught us nothing else. Diplomacy is a weapon as powerful as steel and shot. The Confederacy failed the first time because it had no allies in this hemisphere.

"This morning, I met with Owen Goodhue. You cannot fail to have heard the name. He has posted his vigilante manifesto throughout San Francisco, along with a list of the names of those whom he believes must die if the city is to live. To carry out this sentence of death, he was prepared to put the entire Barbary Coast to the torch, and to slay as many as attempt to stand between him and the condemned. Tom Tulip's name was near the top of that list."

I lowered the revolver. This was one political speech I wanted to hear to the end.

"The Reverend Goodhue has agreed to call off his crusade if the Sons of the Confederacy will carry out the sentence he has imposed. With Barbary at peace, we will be able to wage our war against the Union without interference from the vigilantes."

He passed his stick along the line of men standing beside him. All were rapt, except the guerrilla. He was busy replacing the charge he'd fired from the Navy.

"Each of these men has drawn a gold coin issued by the United States Mint here in San Francisco," Wheelock said. "It is symbolic of the enemy we have sworn to oppose, as well as the individual he has by his acceptance of the token agreed to destroy by his own hand. The names are as follows:

"'Little Dick' Dugan, murderer;

"Tom Tulip, procurer;

"Ole Anderson, shylock;

"'Hugger-Mugger' Charlie, counterfeiter;

"Fat John, Chinaman;

"Axel Hodge, procurer;

"Nan Feeny, harlot.

"One of these has fallen. The others must die by sunset tomorrow.

"You will, of course, have noted that there are seven names on this list, and that eight gold coins were drawn. I have added one more; a redundancy, I must confess, because his death was ordained two months ago, but he has thus far eluded his fate. He is in Barbary at present. His name is Page Murdock. He is a deputy United States marshal, and he is a dangerous man. The soldier who slays him will rise far in the ranks."

More murmurs. Under other circumstances I'd have felt the compliment.

"General, sir, I volunteer for that there duty."

The guerrilla had a Missouri accent, no surprise. He had Centralia and Lone Jack written all over his lean sunburned face.

"That won't be necessary, Lieutenant. You've discharged your responsibility. Your brothers have not yet tasted blood."

"I'll do it for one of them plug dollars. It wasn't Lieutenant when I rid with Arch Clements. I finished out a captain. I won't hide from my name, neither. It's Frank Hennessey, and I cracked a cap on my first bluebelly before most of these here children was borned."

"Your former rank is irrelevant. The order stands."

The way Hennessey rolled his pistol before he put it

away spoke pages about what he thought of Wheelock's order.

That made up my mind. I took aim on Hennessey's broad chest.

A hand closed around the revolver. I nearly tripped the trigger from shock.

Beecher's voice was harsh in my ear. "We'll be up to our chins in baby rebels."

"Did you see it?" I said.

"I seen it. I heard what came after, too. Now ain't the time. Let me work around to the other side. After you take your shot I'll pin 'em down while you hit the stairs."

"What about you?"

"I started out a brakeman. I've clumb up and down freight cars and hot boilers going seventy. I reckon I can find my way down a building standing still."

"Where's Nero?"

"He's out like the cat. I give him another tap just to make sure. Count to thirty."

"Twenty's all you get," I said. "My aim's better when I'm mad. And I don't intend to stop with that shaggy bush-whacker."

"I never thought you would." He slipped out of the box.

31

While counting to twenty, I set up my shooting stand. I tugged the Peacemaker I'd taken away from Nero out from under my belt, where the curved walnut grip had been digging a hole in the small of my back, inspected the chambers, and laid it on the polished mahogany of the box's railing. That made it handy in the unlikely event I managed to empty the five-shot before someone in the theater located the source of the reports and returned fire. I didn't expect to leave that box alive.

Shooting men isn't like shooting birds. With birds, you start with the one farthest away and work your way to the nearest, that being the sure target. With men, you pick out the most dangerous first, because you might not get another chance. Standing partially behind one of the side curtains, I lined up the Deane-Adams' sights on the third button of Frank Hennessey's shirt, drew back the hammer on the count of nineteen, and squeezed the trigger.

I didn't wait to see if I'd hit him. Trusting to the self-cocker, I swung the muzzle toward Wheelock and fired again. For a ward-heeler, he had fast reflexes; at the sound of the first shot, he'd flung away his stick and hurled himself toward the floor of the stage, and I couldn't tell if he was nicked or if the slug had missed him and gone through the Stars and Bars behind him. It seemed to me the flag snapped as if struck by a gust, but that could have been the wind of the bodies scrambling for cover.

Three shots barked on the other side of the auditorium. I ducked, but none of them came close to my box, and when I heard the wham of a shotgun blast I knew it was Beecher, giving me cover with his Le Mat from a box opposite. I saw the smoke there and knew it was time to leave.

I didn't. I had to know if I'd hit Hennessey.

The stage was a hive, Confederate Sons colliding with one another trying to get to the wings, slipping on blood, which may have been Tom Tulip's. They were bailing out of the seats as well, trampling their fellows and making a mess of their pledge to come to the aid of brothers in need. For Beecher, it was like shooting fish in a bucket.

I searched the stage—and drew a sleeve across my eyes to clear them of smoke. I thought I'd seen Tom Tulip rise from the floor. He was still there afterward, in a cautious crouch. I couldn't fathom that. A head shot at close range leaves no room for uncertainty. Then I saw him sliding backward on his heels, spotted a corduroy sleeve across his chest under his rag-doll arms, and I knew it was Hennessey using Tulip's corpse for cover as he tried for a vantage point. At that instant, smoke puffed over Tulip's right shoulder and a fistful of splinters jumped up from the railing a foot to my right. The guerrilla had spotted me.

I sank down on one knee, steadied my arm in a downward slant across the railing, and fired at Tulip's throat. It offered the least amount of resistance to a bullet intended to pierce his body and hit what was behind it. The Confederate flag jerked. I was hitting high and to the right. I'd messed up the sights when I struck Nero's skull with the barrel instead of the butt. I made the mental adjustment and tried again. Just as I fired, one of the Sons who had drawn a double eagle crossed in front of Hennessey. The Son threw up his hands, ran out from under his body, and fell on his back. I caught a flash of corduroy slipping around the edge of the flag and punched a hole through one of the stars.

Wheelock had spotted me, too. He was standing again, near the front of the stage, shouting something and pointing his stick toward my box. This time I overcompensated, shot low, and shattered a footlight. Fire licked out and found something it liked; a decorative curtain tied back to frame the stage caught. Flames raced up it, across the tassels hanging down in a straight line across the top of the stage, and lapped at the gilded wood of the proscenium. The alderman put the stick to its intended use and hobbled offstage on the double. I tried for him a third time. The hammer snapped on an empty cartridge.

A bullet pierced the side curtain just above my hat and slammed into the plaster near the door of the box. Hennessey, firing from cover, or someone else who had seen Wheelock pointing, had joined the fight. It was time to make my exit.

I leathered the five-shot, scooped up Nero's Peacemaker, tore open the door, and threw myself across the carpeted passage, flattening my back against the wall on the other side and looking both ways with the Colt raised. I was alone. I ran for the stairs.

Two men in gray were coming up from the ground floor. The one in front had a pistol in his hand. A slug from Nero's .44 struck him like a fist and he fell backward, taking his partner with him. I clattered down, leapt across the tangle they made on the floor at the foot of the stairs, snapped a shot into a crowd of Sons barreling my way toward the exit, and ran out through the foyer. It was filling with smoke. Somewhere on the edge of hearing, a fire bell clanged; that would be Captain Dan's own company, on its way to prevent Barbary from burning down yet again.

"Here's where I make good on that Yankee gold."

That harsh Missouri twang cut through the smoke like water gushing from a hose. The guerrilla's rangy figure stood across the open door to the street with feet spread and his Navy Colt thrust out at shoulder height, the muzzle six feet from my face.

I jerked the Peacemaker's trigger. Both shots roared simultaneously, and I knew we were both dead.

Then the doorway was clear. Frank Hennessey lay on his face on the floor of the Bella Union with a dark stain spreading like crow's wings between his shoulder blades.

Beecher stood on the boardwalk, smoke uncoiling from the Le Mat's top barrel. His left arm hung limp and covered with blood.

"First white man I ever shot," he said. "They'd lynch me for it in Louisiana."

Then he collapsed.

I knelt over him, found a weak pulse in his neck. The volunteers vaulting down from the firewagon, shining in their oilskin capes and leather helmets, were too busy uncoiling hose and hoisting their axes to help. I shouted to them that there was a man bound and unconscious in one of the boxes upstairs.

"Who the hell done that?" one of them asked. But he was in too much of a hurry to wait for the answer.

Beecher was still conscious. He said he'd shattered his arm when he lost his grip while climbing down the outside of the building and fell ten feet. A shard of polished bone gleamed white where it stuck out of the skin above his elbow. "I think the building hit a downgrade." He grinned weakly.

"Save it for a pretty nurse." I tied my neckerchief around his upper arm and used the barrel of the Colt to twist it tight.

"That ain't proper. Shove over. I seen it done."

Something hard bumped my shoulder. It was an iron ball attached to a chain. Axel Hodge bent over Beecher, undid the tourniquet one-handed, tied a different kind of knot—it looked nautical—and twisted the barrel until the bleeding slowed. Flames were shooting through the Ancient's roof, flickering off his bowler and bearded face.

I said, "He needs a doctor."

"They're all drunks and hoppies hereabouts. He needs the Chinaman."

"What Chinaman?"

"Fat John, who the hell else? Who you think saved me own arm?"

It was my first time in the room behind F'an Chu'an's tearoom in the White Peacock. It contained a cot where I assumed the tong leader slept, some good lamps with glass shades that shed clean light from oil not obtainable from the local pushcart peddlers, a Persian rug ancient by standards unknown in California, and polished teakwood shelves lined with bottles and jars labeled in Chinese characters. It smelled like an apothecary shop. Shau Wing and Shau Chan, the knickknack cousins, helped us lay Beecher on the cot and fetched items from the shelves. F'an Chu'an snapped orders at them in Chinese. He cut off Beecher's sleeve with steel scissors, removed shreds of cloth from the wound with forceps, and poured chloroform into a clean handkerchief, which he spread over his patient's face. When Beecher was breathing evenly, he removed the handkerchief, opened a morocco-leather case, and spread it open on his workbench, revealing a glittering collection of saws, scalpels, and bone chisels. I was feeling faint already, from the fumes and exhaustion, and as the Shaus stepped forward to hold Beecher down by his shoulders in case he woke up in the middle of the operation, I removed myself to the tearoom. That was when I realized Axel Hodge had left. I would not see him again for a very long time.

At the end of an hour, the leader of the Suey Sing Tong joined me. He had removed his apron and put on his green robe. His face was drawn. He was too tired to reach up and pinch his lip when he spoke, and I had to ask him to repeat himself in order to understand what he was telling me. He'd had to remove the arm. Beecher was sleeping, but he'd lost a lot of blood and his recovery was in the hands of the gods. I offered to pay him, as his earlier debt had been discharged. He declined, explaining that there were others to whom he was still obliged. That meant nothing, but then I might not have heard him right. That cleft lip was one more barrier between us.

The night was overcast, but Barbary's jagged edges stood out starkly against the glow of the Bella Union in flames. Fire bells clanged, residents in varying stages of undress bustled about hauling baskets and wheelbarrows piled with clocks, clothing, and other personal possessions, in case the flames spread to their homes the way they had so many times before. I was too tired to care if the place burned down around me. I wobbled back to the Slop Chest and threw myself into my berth. I didn't bother to take off even my boots, but I'd reloaded the Deane-Adams and I lay with it on my chest and my hand on top of it, ready for any of Wheelock's Hoodlums and Confederates who came looking for me. I'd left Nero's Peacemaker in Chinatown.

I awoke well after sunup and went into the saloon without stopping to change clothes or splash water on my face. I was anxious to learn if Beecher had survived the night, but I needed a drink more than news.

The room was deserted except for Pinholster, who was busy playing a game of two-handed Patience against himself. He appeared to be winning. I plunked myself down across from him.

"You look as if you just crawled out from under a charred beam." He laid a six of hearts on a seven of clubs.

"I did. Where is everyone?"

"Billy's helping put out the fire. I'll wager you were unaware he's a volunteer with Wheelock's brigade. The town is filled with such ironies. I haven't seen Hodge since yesterday."

"I saw him last night. Any news about Wheelock?"

"He seems to have vanished. It's unlike him not to make a show of himself on these occasions, directing the pumping crews and working the winch; man of the people, so long as he doesn't expose himself to actual danger. Unlike him, I say, but not surprising. One hears rumors."

That was an opening, and a pretty obvious one for as good a gambler as he was, but I didn't walk through it. "Fire under control?"

"They contained it to the Ancient. I understand it's a dead loss. They'll rebuild it, of course. I heard they pulled a body out."

"Wheelock's bodyguard?"

"No, a stranger. They say he was shot. Another local mystery, like Sid the Spunk's disappearance." He looked up from the card he'd just laid down.

"You forgot that one's solved. So the number of mysteries stays the same."

"I think there are some more. However, it's not up to me to investigate any of them. I'm to Chicago on the noon train. They can spread my ashes on Lake Michigan."

"I thought you intended to stay through tonight."

"There is no tonight. Tonight is canceled. You didn't hear?"

I was tired of hearing him ask questions he knew the answers to. I was just plain tired, but this morning I was more tired of Pinholster than anyone, even Daniel Webster Wheelock. He was too quit of life to make good company.

He went through his deck, looking for the black deuce he needed to win the game. "This morning's edition of the *Call* will be late, I'm afraid. They had to remake the front page twice: first to report the fire, then to carry the tragic news of Owen Goodhue's death."

I felt the same prickling I'd felt when Tom Tulip stepped forward to sing his own dirge.

"Nan Feeny went out first thing this morning," Pinholster said. "One more in a string of broken precedents. It was too early for the cable car, so she must have walked all the way to Mission Street. Mrs. Goodhue, who didn't know her, but who was accustomed to women of her type coming to the reverend gentleman for absolution, let her in.

"There are several versions of what happened next. The least dramatic, and therefore the most believable, is Nan emptied that pepperbox of hers into Goodhue's back while he was kneeling in his cabinet, praying for his crusade's success. She was still there when the widow showed in the police. They have her up at the jail. Ah! There it is."

He turned up the deuce of spades and played it. "Not the ace, but life isn't poetry."

32

The Barbary Coast is no more. The 1906 earthquake managed to do what a half-century of good intentions and sporadic fires could not. A determined rebuilding campaign, followed by journalistic pressure of the Fremont Older type, repressive ordinances, and a beefed-up police presence erected a new city directly on top of the old; one in which there was no place for opium dens, bordellos, and gambling hells in number. It took an act of God to turn the serpents out of Eden once and for all.

I wasn't there to see it. When Edward Anderson Beecher was well enough to travel, I shook his remaining hand at the San Francisco depot, slipped an envelope into his coat pocket containing the money Judge Blackthorne had wired to cover his wages, mileage, and a bonus in partial compensation for the loss of his arm in the service of the United States, and handed him his ticket to Spokane. I was taking a different train to Helena, scheduled to pull out fifteen minutes behind his.

"I reckon I'll have to stay put now," he said. "Can't lug around no steamer trunks with one wing."

"Ask a blacksmith if he can fit you with a ball and chain."

He understood this for the apology it was. "I slipped, boss. You didn't push me."

"It didn't stop you from saving my skin for the second time."

He smiled that thin lost smile. What it lacked in candlepower compared to his full grin, it made up for in sincerity.

"Well, it's pale, but it seemed worth saving both times."

I never heard from him after that. Neither of us had promised to write. We'd been through too much to lie at the end. I like to think that he found his wife and that they took up where they left off; but I'm a sentimental old man who always wants what's best for his friends, having outlived most of them and not having had too many to begin with.

Judge Blackthorne wasn't sentimental. He'd read the report I'd sent, and had only one question for me when I delivered the rest in Helena:

"Are you satisfied with your performance in this affair?"

"I performed it."

He didn't remind me that my orders were to widen the rift between the violent and nonviolent wings of the Sons of the Confederacy so that U.S. authorities could nullify their power in criminal and civil court, and that I'd disobeyed them by taking on Wheelock's killers directly. To do so would have been an embarrassment, because when deputy federal marshals boarded Captain Dan's train just below the Canadian border and placed him under arrest on more than thirty counts of conspiracy, the entire organization fell apart; Sons from all over the Western states and territories came forward to turn United States' evidence against the killers and those who had directed them. I don't flatter myself that in forcing Wheelock to abandon the security of his position in San Francisco I averted a second Civil War. I just prevented a few more murders and put a dangerous lunatic behind bars.

Not actual bars. Wheelock had still drawn enough water with his former associates to raise ten percent of his million-dollar bail and shot himself in his hotel room in Sacramento the day after he was arraigned. He left a note saying he'd planned to elect himself president in 1884 with the Southern vote. Eight senators and fifteen congressmen from the states that had formerly belonged to the Confederacy issued statements to the press that day, insisting that they'd sooner have backed a Republican.

Nan Feeny stood trial for the murder of Owen Goodhue, was found guilty, and sentenced to hang. Throughout the appeals process and several stays, I pictured her pacing her cell, touching often the ribbon she wore at her throat to remind her how close she'd come to hanging the last time she'd shot and killed a square citizen. (Perhaps not; I picture her as easily untying and discarding it during the long walk from the Slop Chest to Mission Street with the pepperbox pistol growing heavy in her reticule.) Judge Blackthorne wrote a letter to Sacramento at my urging, asking for a commutation to life. Whether it was because of this, or in response to a march on the state capitol building by a ragged band of peg-legged harlots, three-fingered pickpockets, and sundry other shades from Barbary—broken up by some head-smashing on the part of city police, reported in the local papers and carried by wire across the continent—the governor of California granted the request. Nan served ten years in a women's workhouse, then after her release for model behavior opened a restaurant in San Francisco, representing investors who knew how to profit by her notoriety, if not the quality of the bill of fare. The restaurant was the only building on its block not demolished by the big shake; she converted it into a hospital and nursed dozens of the maimed and homeless. When she died in 1916, the supervisors of San Francisco County voted to place a plaque in her honor on the wall of the bank that was built on the site of the restaurant after it was torn down. I'm told it's still there, but I haven't been back to see it.

After San Francisco, I asked Judge Blackthorne for a month's holiday. He let me have three days, at the end of which I was expected to board a train for Oregon; but that's a story for another volume of these memoirs I won't live to finish.

I don't get out much these days. Gout, ancient injuries, and the effects of an intemperate life have banded together to keep me in this furnished bungalow in a dust trap called Culver City, where Famous Players-Lasky pays my rent. In return, I'm supposed to provide expert advice on scenarios for photoplays intended to dramatize life on the old frontier. The producers hardly ever send me anything, however, and I suspect they're trading charity for the privilege of drawing on whatever faded luster my name retains by including it on the title cards. They're fools for their own advertising and think just having it there makes the stories authentic. They're not, the ones I've seen, anyway; not by a rifle shot, but the truth won't play and I'm an old hypocrite, correcting dates and place names and telling myself I'm earning my billet.

A few months ago, someone knocked on my door. I was expecting a courier with a new scenario and stayed put in my chair, calling out that the door was unlocked.

"An old U.S. cove like yourself ought to know better than that," said my visitor. "There's jigger-dubbers all about this padding ken."

The sun was behind him. I couldn't see his face, but he had on a long coat like you seldom see in Southern California, with one sleeve hanging empty. It happened I'd been thinking about Barbary just that morning, and I thought at first it was Beecher, come at last to pay a call on an old comrade. Then I saw the stunted legs sticking out the bottom of the coat and knew him for an old enemy.

"You'd think after forty years you'd learned English," I said.

Axel Hodge wobbled in and closed the door behind him. He was hatless and bald, and his beard had turned white as ash, but his grin hadn't changed. He'd be on his third or fourth set of porcelains by now.

"I was just tipping you the office," he said. "I ain't spoke but a piece of the lingo for years. It never did signify outside Frisco, and now not even there. I meant what I said about locking that door. This town's boiling with border trash."

I slid the Deane-Adams out from under the copy of the *Los Angeles Times* I had spread open on my lap and laid it on the lamp table.

He grunted. "That old barker still bite?"

"Only people get old. What happened to the ball and chain?"

"It got too heavy to pack around. I don't miss it. I was running out of things to bash. Old Nan sure served me hell every time I smacked that bar of hers." He stopped grinning. "You heard she died."

"Years ago. News travels a lot faster now."

"I know. Prohibition agents got radio-telephones." He drew a tall bottle out of his coat pocket and set it on the floor. "A little present from Glasgow, by way of Tijuana. I own the distributorship from here to San Diego."

I said, "I thought you'd be living off your inheritance."

He spread his coattails, tugged at the knees of his trousers, and sat on the foot of my unmade bed. His ankles were no bigger around than striplings. He'd been stumping about on those shriveled sticks for close to sixty years.

"The Hodges never did have two coppers to rub together. I told you my granddad was a convict."

"Your granddad was the father of a soap manufacturer, who named you in his will. You don't have to lie to me, Seymour. Sid the Stump isn't wanted anywhere now."

He showed his teeth. "Too bad it weren't that way when I could collect. Seymour couldn't put in a claim without digging up Sid, and Sid couldn't be dug up without stagging the tappers. When'd you smoke me out?"

"That last night, when you helped me with Beecher. You said Fat John saved your arm. You forgot you'd told me you lost your hand aboard a ship from Australia. I had my suspicions before that; you talked too much about Brisbane. It was as if you were trying to convince yourself you weren't Seymour Cruddup from Exeter. You're the one who overheard Pinholster asking me about Sid and told F'an Chu'an. And you knew that last night you'd made a slip. That's why you left town."

"I felt bad about that. I never told Nan good-bye."

The conversation threatened to become maudlin. I asked him if he knew who killed the old forty-niner in the White Peacock.

"Flinders? I always thought he was Wheelock's."

"Captain Dan wouldn't be caught dead in an opium den, or doing his own killing. I figure it was Tom Tulip. He did it on his own, to please Wheelock. He wasn't pleased. It brought in Goodhue, and in order to hold him off, the Sons of the Confederacy had to alter their plans to include Goodhue's list of scapegoats. That's why Tulip was the first to go."

"Poor ponce."

"Why'd you do it?" I asked.

He wrinkled his bald head. "You just said it was Tom."

"I don't mean that. Why'd you help Beecher? Before that you tried to talk Nan into letting you kill us both."

He nodded.

"I thought about that. Still do, time to time. I figure I owed God an arm."

"What's that mean?"

"There was a fire, and a man with his arm gone and him set to follow. Fat John didn't have to help me in that same spot. I didn't have to help the colored bloke. But he done, and I done. Fat John'd find a better way to say it, wherever he wound up. Under six tons of Chink's Alley would be my guess." He scratched his stump. "You ever hear from him?"

"F'an Chu'an?"

"Beecher."

"Not a word."

"Maybe he struck it rich up North and won't truck with our like."

"You're a sentimental old man."

"Well, stow that under your shaper. I got to keep up me own south of the border."

We talked a bit more about Barbary and then he left. We didn't have anything in common beyond that. He didn't ask why I hadn't told Pinholster that Sid the Spunk was alive; I wouldn't have had an answer that would satisfy him any more than his had satisfied me. It might have been enough for Sid, who had offered his arson skills to F'an Chu'an free of charge for the memory of a mother forced into the streets of Brooklyn. I wasn't sure it would be enough for Axel Hodge the bootlegger.

A week or two later I read a small piece in the *Times* about a rumrunner named Hodge, slain by U.S. Prohibition agents during a gun battle on the Mexican border. The agents said they'd returned fire when Hodge opened up on them with a submachine gun. Submachine guns require two hands to operate. Some things about crime and politics don't change, earthquake or no.

I took a drink of his *postizo* Scotch to his memory. For all I knew, we were the last two people on earth who'd remembered the Slop Chest, the White Peacock, the Bella Union, and all those who passed through their doors. The rest are as dead as Pinholster, whose lesion must have done for him long ago.

There was no follow-up to the story, and the entire account took up just two inches on an inside page near what we used to call the telegraph column, with its news of Washington, miners' strikes, and beer-hall revolutions in Munich. Another column on the same page announced the monthly meetings of the local chapters of the various fraternal orders. It listed the Sons of the Confederacy along with the Elks, the Freemasons, the Rotary Club, and the Knights of Columbus. The current members are doddering veterans and younger men who wish they'd been born early enough to fight for States' Rights. They've never heard of Daniel Webster Wheelock, and I'm not about to educate them. His bones and Barbary's can rot together.

A Guttersnipe Glossary

During the nineteenth century, the English language developed more rapidly than during the thousand years that preceded it; and most of that development took place in the gutters of London, New York City, Sydney, Australia, and San Francisco's Barbary Coast. The special vocabulary of the career criminal had its origins in the cockney rhyming slang of the East End ("twist and twirl" = girl; "whistle and flute" = suit) and spread throughout the Western Hemisphere when the police cracked down and those who spoke it fled by sail and steam to safer venues, bringing with them the tools of their unlawful trade.

While most dialects evolve by accident, the terms and phrases that baffled Page Murdock and Edward Anderson Beecher upon their arrival in San Francisco were coined deliberately, in order to avoid arrest. Employing this code, a pair of "tobbies" (street toughs) could plan to "stifle a stagger" (murder an informer) within a police officer's hearing without alerting that authority to the fact that a homicide was being discussed; assuming, that is, that the policeman was not a "fly cop" (an officer who knows the score). This subterfuge would be borrowed by killers for hire during our own gangster era, when U.S. racket busters scratched their heads over conversations on wiretap recordings about "putting out a contract for a hit."

Thieves' cant has changed. Much of the terminology common to Spitalfields, Hell's Kitchen, Murder Point, and Sydney Harbor is as incomprehensible to us today as it was intended to be to the swells and squares outside Barbary. But much of it remains, sprinkling spice on the American vernacular, crossing all class barriers, and piercing even the walls of the White House. If the reader has doubts, perhaps he'll reconsider the next time he "fobs off a shady deal on some oaf." It's also more than likely that just moments ago he replied to a question in the affirmative, using the once-trendily misspelled phrase "oll kerrect"; although he probably referred to it by its initials.

For details about the fascinating hell that was shanty San Francisco, as well as his introduction to the idiom, this writer is indebted to Herbert Asbury's *The Barbary Coast* (New York, Alfred A. Knopf, 1933), still the standard work on its subject after seventy years. However, a Rosetta Stone was required to unlock the secret of what in blazes half the characters were talking about, and this was found in two sources: *A Dictionary of the Underworld* (New York, Bonanza Books, 1961), first published by Eric Partridge in 1949 and updated in a new edition twelve years later; and *The Secret Language of Crime: The Rogue's Lexicon* (Springfield, Ill., Templegate Publishers, 1997), compiled in 1859 by George W. Matsell, a former chief of police of New York City. From "Abraham" (to pose or sham) to "Zulu" (a vehicle employed to transport an immigrant's personal effects), these invaluable references provide a history of the evolution of the crooks' code from 1560 through the Great Depression.

Unfortunately, the entries are not cross-referenced, and the process of writing dialogue, normally a breezy affair for this writer, slowed to tortoise pace while he searched for the proper crude term for "throat" and stumbled, at weary length, upon "gutter-lane." Perhaps in later editions the editors will take pity on their readers and bring out the equivalent of an English-to-sewer-rat dictionary.

Although efforts were made to use this special slang in a rhythm and context that would guide understanding (except during the conversation between the two Hoodlums in chapter thirteen, which was presented as nearly impenetrable for demonstration and comic effect), some readers may still be at sea. (This is in no way a condescending remark; it means they are square citizens, who wouldn't be caught dead cracking a ken or munging a duce.) For them, the following terms and definitions may be of use.

ARTICLES . . . Clothing

BARKING-IRONS . . . Handguns

BEAK . . . A Judge or magistrate

BENISON . . . Blessing

BLACK OINTMENT . . . Raw meat

BLACK-SPY . . . Satan

BLOW . . . To inform upon someone

BLUNT . . . Money

BOB MY PAL . . . Ladyfriend (Gal)

BOOLY-DOGS . . . Police officers

BREAK A LEG . . . To bear a child out of wedlock

BUFE . . . A dog

BULLY . . . A lump of lead, handy for bludgeoning

CALFSKIN . . . The Bible. ("Smack the calfskin"—Kiss the Bible and swear)

CALLAHAN . . . A billyclub

CAP . . . To join in

CHANT . . . One's name

CLY . . . A pocket; also, to pocket

COLE . . . Money

CONIAKERS . . . Counterfeiters

CONK . . . One's nose

COVE . . . A man

CRABS . . . Feet

CRANKY . . . Insane

CRIMP . . . A recruiter for a sailors' boardinghouse

CRUSHER . . . A policeman

CUES . . . Points in a game of chance

CULL . . . A man

CUT ONE'S EYES . . . Become suspicious

DADDLES . . . Hands

DANCE AT MY DEATH . . . May I hang

DARBIES . . . Manacles

DAWB . . . A bribe; also, to bribe

DEAD GAME . . . Certain

DONEGAN . . . A privy; also, it can't be helped

DOSS . . . A bed

DUFFER . . . A man posing as a sailor

DUSTY . . . Dangerous

EARTH-BATH . . . Burial

EASE . . . To rob or kill

EMPEROR . . . A drunk

ETERNITY-BOX . . . A coffin

FACER . . . A glass filled so full that one must bring
one's face to the glass instead of the other way around

FAMS . . . Hands

FINIFF . . . Five dollars

FISH . . . A sailor

FLAPPERS . . . Hands

FLASH . . . Knowing; to speak knowingly ("Patter the
flash")

FLIMP . . . To wrestle

FLUSH . . . Rich

FLY . . . Wise

FRIDAY FACE . . . A glum visage, Friday being the
traditional day of hanging

FUNK . . . To frighten

GABS . . . Talk

GAGE . . . Money; a pot

GRIM . . . Death

HANDLE . . . One's nose

HEDGE . . . To bet on both sides; to side with God and Satan at once

HICKSAM . . . A fool

HOIST A HUFF . . . To rob violently

JACK . . . A small coin

JACK COVE . . . A worthless, miserable fellow

JACK SPRAT . . . A small man

JADE . . . Hard time in prison

JOLLY . . . One's head; also, a sham

JOSKIN . . . A country bumpkin

KICK . . . A pocket

KNOCK-ME-DOWN . . . Strong drink

KNOLLY . . . One's head ("Knowledge-box")

LAMPS . . . Eyes

LAY . . . One's particular scheme; M.O.

LOPE . . . Run away

LURCH . . . Get rid of

MADAM RHAN . . . A faithless or immoral woman

MAWLEYS . . . Hands

MOLLISHER . . . A woman, usually a harlot ("Molly"; "Moll")

MONAGER . . . One's name or alias

MUMMER . . . One's mouth

NEB . . . One's face

NIP . . . To rob

NODDLE . . . A fool

NUB . . . One's neck

NUG . . . Dear one

OAK . . . Strong; dependable

OFFICE . . . A signal ("Tip the office")

OLD SHOE . . . Good luck

ON THE SHARP . . . Smart and not easily cheated

PACKET . . . A lie

PADDING KEN . . . A rooming house

PAD THE HOOF . . . Walk or run away

PANNAM . . . Bread

PANTER . . . One's heart

PEACH . . . To inform

PECK . . . Food

PEERY . . . Suspicious

PEGO . . . A sailor

PERSUADER . . . A weapon; a spur

PHARSE . . . The eighth part

PLUMMY (or **PLUMBY**) . . . All right

POLISH IRON . . . Go to prison ("Polish iron bars with one's eyebrows")

PONCE . . . A kept man

PONY . . . Money; to post one's money

PRAD . . . A horse

PRIM . . . A handsome woman

PUPPY . . . Blind

PUT . . . A clownish fool

PUT UP TO ONE'S ARMPITS . . . Cheat one of his possessions

QUEEN DICK . . . Never ("The reign of Queen Dick"; a nonperson)

QUEER . . . Counterfeit money

RABBIT . . . A rough, rowdy fellow

RAMMER . . . One's arm

RED RAG . . . One's tongue

RHINO FAT . . . Rich as Midas

RUB . . . Run

RUSTY . . . Bad-tempered

SCOLD'S-CURE . . . Death

SCRAG . . . Hang

SCRUB . . . A cruel man

SEA-CRAB . . . A sailor

SCOT . . . A young bull

SCOUR . . . Run away

SCREAVES . . . Bank notes

SERVE OUT . . . To thrash someone

SHAPER . . . A hat

SHINERAGS . . . Nothing

SHOP . . . Prison

SINK . . . To cheat

SKEP . . . A money cache

SKIPPER . . . A barn

SKYCER . . . A worthless parasite

SLAG . . . A chain (also, "Slang")

SLANG . . . To chain something (also, a chain)

SLINGTAIL . . . A chicken

SLUICE ONE'S GOB . . . To drink ("Wet your whistle")

SMICKET . . . A woman's skirt

SMOKY . . . Suspicious

SNAGGLE . . . To wring the neck of a chicken or other fowl

SPEEL . . . Run away

SPLIT OUT . . . To end one's association

SPOONEY . . . Gullible

SPUD . . . Worthless coin

SQUAIL . . . A drink

STAG . . . To inform upon

STIFF . . . A letter

STRETCH . . . One year

STOW ONE'S WID . . . Be silent

STUBBLE . . . Hold ("Stubble your red rag" = "Hold your tongue")

STUN ONE OUT OF HIS REGULARS . . . To cheat one of his rights

SWABLER . . . A filthy fellow

SWIG . . . A drink

TAPPER . . . A police officer

THIMBLE . . . A watch

TICKRUM . . . A license

TOBBING . . . Waylaying by striking one on the head

TOMMY . . . Bread

TOP . . . To cheat

TOP-CHEAT . . . A hat

TOPPER . . . A blow on the head

TOP-ROPES . . . High living

TRINKETS . . . Burglar tools; weapons

U.S. COVE . . . A man in the employ of the United States

VAMPERS . . . Stockings

WARE HAWK . . . Beware

WHIFFLE . . . To cry out in pain

WHISKER . . . An elaborate lie

YACK . . . A watch

The following is a rough translation of the conversation Page Murdock overheard between two Hoodlums in Daniel Webster Wheelock's reception room (pages 331–32):

"I'll be hanged if it isn't old Pox. I heard you were in prison."

"No, Freddie, that was a lie. Some sharpers impersonating police officers tried to cheat me out of my goods, but I saw it was a swindle and ran home."

"You always were a smart fellow."

"Well, I'm not blind. How's your girl?"

"I haven't seen her in a year. We broke up."

"The devil you say. I thought you were all right."

"As did I. She informed on me to the police. Cheated me out of my rights, she did, and I gave her a good thrashing."

"I'd have bet my shirt she was honest."

"You'd be a fool if you did. I tell you, she's as bad as they come."

"You must have felt yourself a clown."

"Shut your mouth, Pox. You wouldn't know a no-good woman if she picked your pocket right under your nose."

"Don't take offense, you young bull. If she betrayed you, why aren't you in prison?"

"I had good luck. I was facing a long sentence sure as death, but Captain Dan bribed the Judge and arranged for a not-guilty verdict."

"Do you swear to that?"

"Look at my hands. Am I in manacles?"

"What does Captain Dan have in mind?"

"That's why I'm here. If he wants me to hit people on the head and rob them, I'm his man."

"He can get anyone for that. He'll want more for his money."

"The old fox keeps his plans to himself, that's for sure."

"I agree with you there, Freddie, my friend. Throw me over for five dollars if I don't."

Read on for a preview of the latest
Page Murdock Mystery

CAPE
HELL

· LOREN D. ESTLEMAN ·

Available now from Tom Doherty Associates

A FORGE HARDCOVER

1

Halfway back to civilization, Lefty Dugan began to smell.

It was my own fault, partly; I'd stopped on the north bank of the Milk River like some tenderheel fresh out of Boston instead of crossing and pitching camp on the other side. I was worn down to my ankles, and the sorry buckskin I was riding sprouted roots on the spot and refused to swim. The pack horse was game enough; either that, or it was too old to care if it was lugging a dead man or a month's worth of Arbuckle's. But it couldn't carry two, especially when one was as limp as a sack of stove-bolts and just as heavy. I was getting on myself and in no mood to argue, so I unpacked my bedroll.

A gully-washer square out of Genesis soaked my slicker clear through and swelled the river overnight. I rode three days upstream before I found a place to ford, by which time even the plucky pack horse was breathing through its mouth. In Chinook I hired a buckboard and put in to the mercantile for salt to pack the carcass, but the pirate who owned the store mistook me for Vanderbilt, and then the Swede who ran the livery refused to refund the deposit I'd made on the wagon. So I buried Lefty in the shadow of the Bearpaws and rode away from five hundred cartwheel dollars on a mount I should have shot and left to feed what the locals call Montana swallows: magpies, buzzards, and carrion crows.

The thing was, I'd liked Lefty. We'd ridden together for Ford Harper before herding cattle lost its charm, and he was always good for the latest joke from the bawdy houses in St. Louis; back then he wasn't Lefty, just plain Tom. Then he took a part-time job in the off-season blasting a tunnel through the Bitterroots for the Northern Pacific, and incidentally two fingers off his right hand.

Drunk, he was a different man. He'd had a bellyful of Old Rocking Chair when he stuck up a mail train outside Butte and was still on the same extended drunk when he drew down on me not six miles away from the spot. I aimed low, but the fool fell on his face and took the slug through the top of his skull.

Making friends has seldom worked to my advantage. They always seem to wind up on the other side of my best interests.

It was a filthy shame. Judge Blackthorne had a rule against letting his deputies claim rewards—something about keeping the body count inside respectable limits—but made an exception in some cases in return for past loyalty and present reliability, and I was one. It served me right for not allowing for Lefty's unsteady condition when I tried for his kneecap instead of his hat rack. The money was the same, vertical or horizontal.

To cut my losses, I lopped off his mutilated right hand so I could at least claim the pittance the U.S. Marshal's office paid for delivering fugitives from federal justice. I packed it in my last half-pound of bacon, making do for breakfast with a scrawny prairie hen I shot east of Sulphur Springs. I picked gristle out of my teeth for fifty miles.

The money from Washington would almost cover what I'd spent to feed that bag of hay I was using for transportation. After I sold it back to the rancher I'd bought it from just outside Helena, I was a nickel to the good. I rode the pack horse in town until it rolled over and died. I wished I'd known the beast when it was a two-year-old, and that's as much good as I've ever had to say about anything with four legs that didn't bark and fetch birds.

I spent the nickel and a lot more in Chicago Joe's Saloon, picked a fight with the faro dealer—won that one—and another with the city marshal—lost that one—and would have slept out my time in peace if the Judge himself hadn't come down personally to spring me.

"You'd better still be alive," he greeted me from the other side of the bars. "This establishment doesn't give refunds for bailing out damaged goods."

I pushed back my hat to take him in. He had on his judicial robes, but the sober official black only heightened his resemblance to Lucifer in a children's book illustration. I think he tacked the tearsheet up beside his shaving mirror so he could get the chin-whiskers just right. His dentures were in place. They'd been carved from the keyboard of a piano abandoned along the Oregon Trail, and he wore the uncomfortable things only when required by the dignity of the office. It was unlike him to go anywhere straight from session without stopping to change, especially the hoosegow. I was in for either a promotion or the sack.

"How's Ed?" I asked. The city marshal's name was Edgar Whitsunday, but only part of his first name ever made it off the door of his office. He'd been named after a dead poet, but being illiterate he sloughed off the accusation whenever it arose. He was a Pentecostal, and amused his acquaintances with his imperfect memorization of Scripture as drilled into him by a spinster aunt: I think my favorite was "I am the excrement of the Lord."

"He's two teeth short of a full house," Blackthorne said. "I told his dentist to bill Grover Cleveland."

"That's extravagant. What did you do with the rest of the piano?"

He scowled. The Judge had a sense of his own humor, but no one else's. "You realize I could declare court in session right here and find you in contempt."

"And what, put me in jail?" I looked at my swollen right hand. "At least I used my fists. Ed took the top off my head with the butt of his ten-gauge."

"You should be grateful he didn't use the other end." He sighed down to his belt buckle; it was fashioned from a medal of valor. Just what he'd done to earn it, I never knew. Even scraping forty years off his hide I couldn't picture him scaling a stockade or leading a charge up any but Capitol Hill. Probably he'd helped deliver the Democratic vote in Baltimore. "You cost me more trouble than half the men who ride for me. A wise man would let you rot."

"You make rotting sound bad." I slid my hat back down over my eyes. "Find somewhere else to distribute your largesse. This ticky cot is the closest thing I've had to a hotel bed since I rode out after Lefty."

"You can't refuse bail. Marshal Whitsunday needs this cell. The Montana Stock-Growers Association is in town, and you know as well as I those carpetbaggers will drink the place dry and shoot it to pieces."

"Good. I was getting lonesome."

"Shake a leg, Deputy. You're needed."

That made me sit up and push back my hat. He wouldn't admit needing a drink of water in the desert.

He said, "I'm short-handed. Jack Sweeney, your immediate superior, went over my head to Washington and commandeered all my best men to bring the rest of Sitting Bull's band back from Canada to face justice for Custer."

"They gave that bloody dandy justice at the Little Big Horn nine years ago. What's the rush?"

"Sweeney's contract runs out in September, and there's

a Democrat in the White House." He held up a key ring the size of Tom Thumb's head and stuck one in the lock. "Go back to your hotel, clean up, and report to my chambers at six sharp."

"Since when do you adjourn before dark?"

"I swung the gavel on the Bohannen Brothers at four. You've got forty-five minutes to clean up and shave. You look like the Wild Man of Borneo and smell like a pile of uncured hides."

"How'd you convict the Bohannens without my testimony? I brought them in."

"They tried to break jail and killed the captain of the guard. That bought them fifty feet of good North Carolina hemp without your help."

"Bill Greene's dead?"

"I'm sorry. I didn't know you were close."

"He owed me ten dollars on the Fitzgerald fight. I don't guess he mentioned me in his will."

His big silver watch popped open and snapped shut. "Forty-four minutes. If I catch so much as a whiff of stallion sweat in my chambers, I'll fine you twenty-five dollars for contempt of court."

"Collect it from the stallion."

"That's twenty-five dollars you owe the United States."

I swung my feet to the floor, stood, wrestled for balance, and found it with my fists around the bars. "What's so urgent? Did we declare war on Mexico again?"

He looked as grim as ever he had during damning evidence. "What have you heard?"

BRAZEN

A NEW VALENTINO MYSTERY

FROM THE AWARD-WINNING AUTHOR

LOREN D. ESTLEMAN

When actresses are murdered and their bodies staged to reenact the deaths of
Hollywood's blond bombshells, the police call on film archivist and sometime film
detective Valentino. With his encyclopedic knowledge of Hollywood, Valentino
must help catch a serial killer of doomed blondes before he can strike again.